TO

Together they stood, back to back, the Shoshone and the Irishman, prepared to meet the enemy's rush. The yelling of blood oaths, the grunts of pain as the Sioux and Cheyenne lunged forward toward the two who stood over the bodies. Running with a fury into the fire the rest of the allies poured into their enemies across the narrowing distance along the slope.

First came three of the Lakota who made it through the dusty haze to reach the bodies before they fell to the bullets that could not miss. Then the rush of a handful as the Irishman and Shoshone levered cartridges through their overheated weapons again and again and again. And finally more than ten appeared like apparitions out of the dust, vaulting over the bodies of their fallen to rush the lonely pair.

Weapons empty now, both defenders swung their rifles savagely, like two long and slender scythes reaping those stalks of wheat rushing before the giant blades.

Swinging and singing as they cut through the dust and gunsmoke, chopping viciously through the curses and war songs and shrieks of pain and grunts of terror as bones were broken and skulls cracked and bullets struck bare flesh and sinew.

And brave men went down in blood, thinking of loved ones back home.

As brave men always will.

BOOKS BY TERRY C. JOHNSTON

Carry the Wind
BorderLords
One-Eyed Dream

Cry of the Hawk
Winter Rain

SON OF THE PLAINS NOVELS

Long Winter Gone
Seize the Sky
Whisper of the Wolf

THE PLAINSMEN NOVELS

Sioux Dawn
Red Cloud's Revenge
The Stalkers
Black Sun
Devil's Backbone
Shadow Riders
Dying Thunder
Blood Song
Reap the Whirlwind

REAP THE WHIRLWIND

The Battle of the Rosebud
June 1876

Terry C. Johnston

BANTAM BOOKS
New York • London • Toronto • Sydney • Auckland

REAP THE WHIRLWIND
A Bantam Book / February 1994

ISBN 0-553-29974-3

Published simultaneously in the United States and Canada

Bantam Books are published by Bantam Books, a division of Bantam Doubleday Dell Publishing Group, Inc. Its trademark, consisting of the words "Bantam Books" and the portrayal of a rooster, is Registered in U.S. Patent and Trademark Office and in other countries. Marca Registrada. Bantam Books, 1540 Broadway, New York, New York 10036.

PRINTED IN THE UNITED STATES OF AMERICA

OPM 0 9 8 7 6 5 4 3 2 1

FOR NEIL MANGUM

of the National Park Service—
author, historian, friend—
the one who, more than anyone else,
helped me put this story together
and made three battles
make sense as one

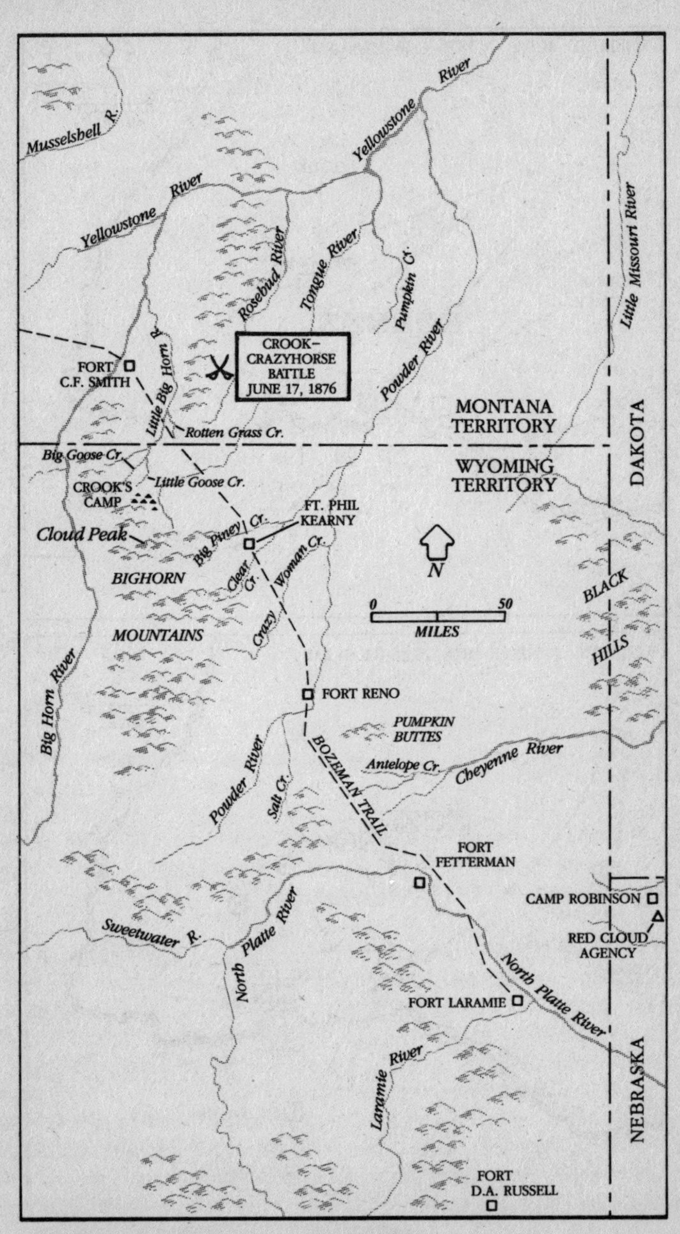
Musselshell R.
Yellowstone River
Yellowstone River
Rosebud River
Tongue River
Pumpkin Cr.
Powder River
Little Missouri River
Little Big Horn R.
FORT C.F. SMITH
CROOK–CRAZYHORSE BATTLE JUNE 17, 1876
Rotten Grass Cr.
MONTANA TERRITORY
WYOMING TERRITORY
DAKOTA
Big Goose Cr.
Little Goose Cr.
CROOK'S CAMP
Cloud Peak
Big Piney Cr.
FT. PHIL KEARNY
Clear Cr.
Crazy Woman Cr.
BIGHORN MOUNTAINS
N
0 50
MILES
BLACK HILLS
Big Horn River
FORT RENO
PUMPKIN BUTTES
Antelope Cr.
Cheyenne River
Powder River
Salt Cr.
BOZEMAN TRAIL
FORT FETTERMAN
CAMP ROBINSON
RED CLOUD AGENCY
Sweetwater R.
North Platte River
North Platte River
FORT LARAMIE
Laramie River
NEBRASKA
FORT D.A. RUSSELL

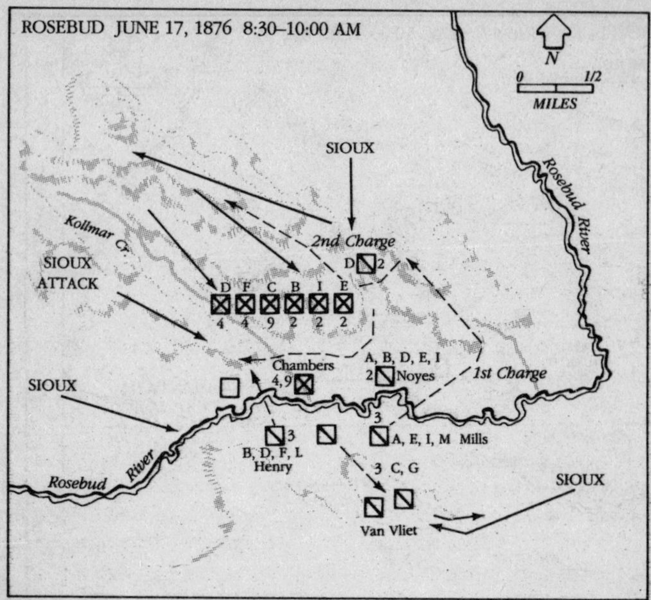

ROSEBUD JUNE 17, 1876 8:30–10:00 AM
N
0 1/2
MILES
SIOUX
Rosebud River
Kollmar Cr.
2nd Charge
D 2
SIOUX
ATTACK
D F C B I E
4 4 9 2 2 2
A, B, D, E, I
2 Noyes
Chambers
4,9
1st Charge
SIOUX
3
3
A, E, I, M Mills
B, D, F, L
Henry
3 C, G
Rosebud River
SIOUX
Van Vliet

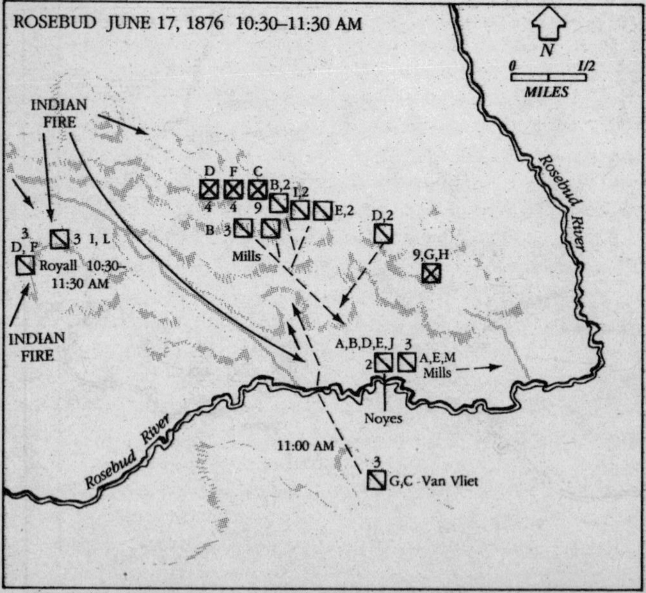

ROSEBUD JUNE 17, 1876 10:30–11:30 AM
N
0 1/2
MILES
INDIAN
FIRE
Rosebud River
D F C
4 4 9
B,2
I,2
E,2
D,2
B 3
Mills
3
D, F
3 I, L
Royall 10:30-
11:30 AM
9,G,H
INDIAN
FIRE
A,B,D,E,J 3
2 A,E,M
Mills
Noyes
Rosebud River
11:00 AM
3
G,C Van Vliet

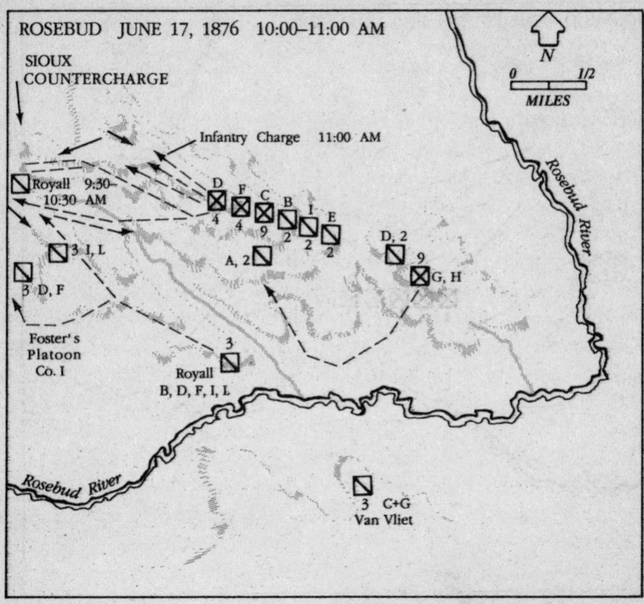

ROSEBUD JUNE 17, 1876 10:00–11:00 AM

N
0 1/2
MILES

SIOUX
COUNTERCHARGE

Infantry Charge 11:00 AM

Royall 9:30–
10:30 AM

D F C B I E
4 4 9 2 2 2

A, 2

D, 2
9
G, H

3 I, L

3 D, F

Foster's
Platoon
Co. I

3
Royall
B, D, F, I, L

Rosebud River

Rosebud River

3 C+G
Van Vliet

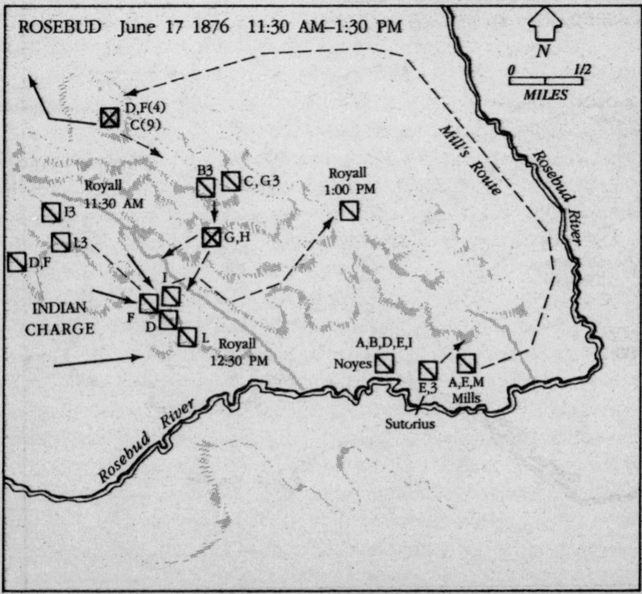

ROSEBUD June 17 1876 11:30 AM–1:30 PM

N
0 1/2
MILES

D,F(4)
C(9)

Mill's Route

Rosebud River

B3
C, G3

Royall
1:00 PM

Royall
11:30 AM

I3

I.3

G,H

D,F

INDIAN
CHARGE

I
F
D
L

Royall
12:30 PM

A,B,D,E,I
Noyes

E,3
Sutorius

A,E,M
Mills

Rosebud River

In the barracks, the men knew too. Some took [Crook's pending summer campaign to the Rosebud] with the veteran's professional calm; such firebrands as the fighting Irish were jubilant. Full-dress uniforms and the new spiked helmets, along with sabers, were packed and stored; field uniforms donned. Blankets were rolled and tents and stoves, sure to be dropped in the first forced march, were stowed in wagons. In contrast with the general exhilaration was the patent disgust of officers ordered to remain in garrison. They could only wait for news from the front and scan the casualty lists. They would, they knew, pause in grief over the name of a brother officer killed in action but shortly be irresistibly drawn to thumb through the pages of the *Army Register* murmuring: "Poor fellow, I'm sorry he's gone. Now how many files does that give me?"

There would be a spate of promotions in this bloody year of 1876.

—Fairfax Downey
Indian-Fighting Army

The Battle of the Rosebud . . . represents an atypical encounter on the Western frontier because large masses of troops rarely clashed with extensive Indian forces.

—Neil Mangum
Battle of the Rosebud: Prelude to the Little Bighorn

I believe if it had not been for the Crows, the Sioux would have killed off half of our command before the soldiers were in a position to meet the attack.

—Frank Grouard
Frank Grouard, Army Scout

The Battle of the Rosebud represents a strategic victory for the Sioux and Cheyenne against the U.S. military troops staged at the zenith of the Sioux War of

1876–1877. . . . The Indian victory at the Rosebud was a prelude to and directly led to a still greater triumph eight days later on June 25, 1876, when Lt. Col. George A. Custer and his immediate command were wiped out to a man by these same warriors who had opposed Crook on the Rosebud.

J. W. Vaughn
With Crook at the Rosebud

Old soldiers who had served in the Civil War commented later that this was as desperate a struggle as any they had experienced in the great war.

—Fred H. Werner
Before the Little Big Horn

The [Battle of the] Rosebud was lost not because of poor tactics or negligence on the part of any of the participants, but because of the overwhelming superiority of manpower and firepower on the side of the Indians. They outnumbered the soldiers three to one and were armed with the latest model repeating rifles. For one of the few times in the history of Indian warfare the whites were confronted with a really superior force, which, though composed of "savages," used a system of tactics, dividing the troops and attempting to destroy them in sections. This same condition obtained once more, eight days later [on the Little Bighorn].

—Martin F. Schmitt, editor
General George Crook, His Autobiography

One point that has been made by practically all the historians—the Indians were very short of guns and ammunition. War clubs, bows and arrows, and lances were used by most of the warriors in this battle. Most of the cartridge cases and slugs that I found [on the Rosebud Battlefield site] were those used by the soldiers.

—Fred H. Werner
Before the Little Big Horn

In [Crook's] retreat [to Goose Creek after the Battle of the Rosebud], rather than the casualties, lay the full measure of the defeat, for it neutralized him at the most critical juncture of the [Great Sioux Campaign of 1876].

—Robert M. Utley
Frontier Regulars

. . . It seems reasonable to say that the Battle of the Little Bighorn would not have been fought or would have ended quite differently had Crook's campaign been successful or had he taken what appears at this late date to have been reasonable action, by sending information about the fight to the military forces under [General Alfred] Terry.

—J. A. Leermakers
"The Battle of the Rosebud"
Great Western Indian Fights

By stopping General Crook, the Indians also gained renewed confidence in their ability to cope with the white soldiers. Just one week later, these same Indians met Custer on the Little Big Horn River and recorded a victory that shook our nation to its very foundation.

—Fred H. Werner
Before the Little Big Horn

If General Crook is to serve further against the Indians it should be in a subordinate capacity.

—Editorial
The New York *Herald*
Thursday, July 6, 1876

The Indians reached the zenith of their power at the Rosebud and the Little Big Horn. After expending their supply of ammunition in these battles, they were strictly on the defensive and did not dare to meet the soldiers in open combat.

—J. W. Vaughn
With Crook at the Rosebud

Sheridan and Crook, Gibbon and Terry and Custer were numbered among the most renowned generals of the Civil War, their reputation won on many a hard-fought field. Yet they totally failed to corner the Sioux, who inflicted two severe defeats upon the converging armies, and in the end [those Indians] succumbed only to superior resources and to paucity of food and other supplies.

—Milo Milton Quaife, Editor
War-Path and Bivouac, by John F. Finerty

. . . [The Indians] were patriots fighting for the possession of their native land. Bravely they fought and well . . . and with what brilliant success they battled, until they were run down, worn out, scattered, killed or captured.

—Cyrus Townsend Brady
Indian Fights and Fighters

Prologue

Late April 1876

Him?

Going to be a father?

Why, it had been the better part of three weeks already and still Seamus Donegan was having a bit of a real donnybrook of it with some of the innermost parts of himself—those places where he kept buried the sentimental shreds of family: his memories of a beloved mother; his remembrances of that playful leprechaun of an uncle Liam O'Roarke; and finally his thoughts back on the solidness of Uncle Ian, a man firmly and undeniably rooted in the soil of that Oregon country* like his crops, raising family and stock.

Raising children? Sure, and it was a fact that if ever there was a man born to be a father, Ian was truly that man. Dependable he was, rock solid and responsible—that one of the O'Roarke boys. Seamus could almost see him still, standing there with the moist dirt of that farm country splattered on the man's boots, forever caked beneath Ian's nails, forever darkening every wrinkle and crack and crevice worn into the farmer's hands. Such permanent tat-

---

* THE PLAINSMEN Series, vol. 5, *Devil's Backbone*

tooing bothered Ian not, Seamus knew. For Ian possessed the earthy, heady scent of that land buried deep within his nostrils—like the musky perfume of a willing woman stretching herself below him, beckoning, reaching out to pull him to her bosom, to bury him in her moist richness.

But for this big, square-jawed Irishman who stood some three fingers over six feet, it was almost too frightening: him, to settle down with one woman, with a child coming . . . in one place? Begora! Faith, but did such a trembling thought as that give a man like him real pause. More pause than he had felt when facing down the barrels or staring back at the howling maw of Cheyenne Dog Soldiers.* But pass up Samantha Pike he could not. To live without the smell of her rising to him, the way her fingers licked traces of fire along his skin, and how the very feel of her had crept well below his hide. His passion for her was something he could not deny.

Truly, it hadn't been until somewhere on that trail north from the Panhandle country of Texas that Seamus had finally admitted that marrying a fertile woman like Sam would one day mean the coming of children. Still, the reality of hearing the news of it come from those lips, finding himself speechless as she gently drew his head down to her swelling belly, told to listen to his child growing deep within her. It was there that he first stroked that rounding tummy of the full-bodied Samantha Donegan—not as if caressing a woman he was about to mount and mate, but instead as if it were truly the face of his own child he could feel beneath the callused fingers of a man more comfortable in the company of other horsemen and their animals on the distant prairie.

Since that first night listening intently to the unknown, Seamus had returned again and again to lay his ear against that smooth, taut skin just below the generous curves of Sam's flowering breasts. Watching his wife, studying her changing shape, straining to hear something each time she did and murmuring to their child deep in the womb, Seamus had come to believe in the reality that this child

* THE PLAINSMEN Series, vol. 3, *The Stalkers*

was every bit as tangible and real as the hand he could hold before his face. Though he would have to wait to clumsily hold that wee one in arms unaccustomed to cradling babes, Seamus believed and truly accepted that he was already a father.

So he had taken to him a wife, vowing before friends and Goda'mighty Himself to settle down with that one woman until death did them part this earthly plane. And now in these last few weeks Seamus had come to experience the terror of those newfound emotions of fatherhood. Paternity still scared the bejasus out of this man of bone and sinew and whipcord muscle. But with each new day he was coming to terms with his misgivings, even his outright fears after these precious hours they spent walking down to the rain-swollen river below the log-and-stone buildings of Fort Laramie, those long nights alone with Sam, holding her budding body against him as she fell to sleep.

No, it wasn't the fact of cleaving to a woman, nor even the reality of the child coming that still gave the Irishman pause. It was this thing of settling down. What Ian had done so easily, nephew Seamus struggled with most. It was there with putting down roots that the heart of Liam O'Roarke in Donegan grew faint.

Seamus was having himself a struggle with something he could not see, something he could not test his muscles against, some *thing* he could not bring into the buckhorn and blade sights down that worn, blued barrel of his trail-weary seventeen-shot 1866 Henry repeater. As much as he hated to, Seamus had finally come to admit he was again wrestling with some *thing* in himself. This dread of settling down. Taking a wife along with him as he moved from one river valley on over the verdant crests to the next swell of hill and prairie sky was one thing. Trudging along with a babe, a child, a youngster . . . was something entirely different.

To have to put down roots now?

Why, it shook Seamus to his marrow.

His was a struggle to grapple with the true meaning of the news Samantha gave him upon his return from Fort Fetterman. Upon his escape out of the frozen wilderness of the Tongue and the Powder rivers.

In the end it had been enough just to emerge whole in mind and body from that winter wasteland—the power of Crook's cavalry squandered by Colonel Joseph J. Reynolds in his aborted attack on a sleepy Powder River village every military man in the entire Department had chosen to believe was the camp of none other than the feared war chief Crazy Horse.*

It had been a campaign that made Seamus wonder on this life of wandering, this profession of leading the soldiers against the hostile warrior bands, this trail of blood and war he had chosen as far back as sixty-one when first he became a horse soldier for Lincoln's Union Army. Those early weeks and months of the great war had been much like the first days of Crook's Powder River Expedition: rich in zeal and rife in the promise to end the conflict early—exactly as the army had believed that one swift strike against the wild northern bands would drive them all back to the reservations and peace would descend like a long-awaited benediction upon the frontier. The Northern Pacific Railroad would push west, the Black Hills would at last revert back to the white man, and settlers would pour in to bring Christian industry and virtue to the wilderness. Such was the thing of hopes, of fond dreams.

What else but tragedy does a man call it when his dreams are shattered? What less than tragedy itself?

Following the disastrous war against Red Cloud's Bad Faces in 1866–67,† the army abandoned its three northernmost posts along the Bozeman Road into Montana Territory and ceded to the wild tribes all rights to the Black Hills as well as their beloved hunting grounds along the Tongue, the Powder, and the Rosebud.

But two years ago gold had been discovered among those streams and pine-draped hills the Lakota called their Paha Sapa—the white man's precious yellow rocks found dangerously near the sacred Bear Butte where the Northern Cheyenne for generations had come to seek the wisdom taught their grandfathers in vision quests. Crazed prospec-

---

* THE PLAINSMEN Series, vol. 8, *Blood Song*

† THE PLAINSMEN Series, vols. 1 and 2, *Sioux Dawn* and *Red Cloud's Revenge*

tors who would rather take the chance of being scalped than live poor flooded into the Hills where the gulches of the Spearfish and Deadwood and Rapid creeks bustled with the profane placer camps like Deadwood City itself, each new tent and clapboard settlement filled with gamblers and the gaudy, painted women, gold camps overflowing in whiskey and blood, camps deafening with the sound of pistols fired in anger and avarice. Gold dust was the currency, whiskey the lifeblood. Quartz and placer claims were worshiped as most precious above all. And life was cheap.

This was a fever the government would not be able to deny.

That discovery meant that the populist administration of Sam Grant found itself perched precariously on the sharp horns of an uncomfortable dilemma: to take the Hills away from the Indians, which action would break the law of the land; or, find some way to force the wild tribes themselves to break the treaty they had been living under since 1868.

In midwinter when the Bureau of Indian Affairs sent runners out from the agencies to inform the warrior bands that they had to be in to the reservations and accounted for, only a select handful of government and military leaders knew the true course already plotted for events yet to come. Secret plans were laid in Washington City that when the hostile bands did not uproot themselves and plod obediently back to the agencies in the dead of winter's worst, the Indian Bureau would then turn over the disposition of those refractory bands to the War Department. William Tecumseh Sherman and Philip H. Sheridan would then have the war for which they had been waiting a decade, the war they knew would end the struggle on the Plains for all time. Their armies would drive the hostile bands back to the reservations, where the warriors would become farmers and God-fearing wards of the government at long last.

While any who would not go back in peace would be exterminated.

With the 31 January deadline come and gone, the obedient Indian Bureau informed the War Department that the hostiles were now in the army's lap. Sherman and Sheridan set about putting the cogs of their Sioux Campaign in motion, whereby they would snare the villages between three prongs, three armies, any one of which was surely strong enough to crush the few warriors the Indian agents claimed were off the reservation for that winter. But back in February, General Alfred Terry's army was winter-locked at Fort Lincoln, and Lieutenant Colonel George Armstrong Custer was to become a political prisoner held hostage back in President Grant's Washington City, while Colonel John Gibbon's troops were struggling to move out of Forts Ellis and Shaw in a Montana Territory racked with the snow and subzero cold of a hundred-year winter come to visit its fury on the northern plains.

This left Phil Sheridan with one and only one army capable of moving against the hostiles, capable of probing and penetrating the last great hunting ground of the wild tribes. As Sheridan's hammer, General George C. Crook hurriedly forged the spearhead of his assault from the Second and Third cavalries and pushed them north from Fort Fetterman that first day of March, pointing their noses toward the land of the Tongue and the Powder, dead on into the brutal, icy torture of an arctic winter visited once in a lifetime on the high plains. Theirs would be the lance the army would use to prod the hostiles loose, to push the hostiles back to the agencies, to deliver the death-strike straight to the heart of those wild tribes. Once and for all time.

It was a chance few military men would ever be given to accomplish alone—this war to end all wars. This expedition right into the heart of that last great hunting ground. This campaign so filled with the promise of glory and honor.

On the Powder River, Seamus and Crook's half-breed scouts found the village the army was hoping to corner. While the general ordered Colonel Joseph J. Reynolds to make an all-night march and pitch into the hostile camp, Crook promised to rendezvous later with the attacking battalions upstream. But some of Reynolds's companies cowered out of the fight beneath the shelter of a protective mesa while other troopers unsaddled and boiled coffee, eating hard-bread while their fellow soldiers found themselves pinned down under a hot and deadly fire from angry warriors flushed from their lodges and now dug in along the bluffs above the village they had just abandoned with their families moments before.

After putting everything in the camp to the torch, even burning the meat that would have filled the bellies of his army and destroying the buffalo robes and blankets that would keep his troopers from freezing, Reynolds pulled back his companies in such a precipitous retreat that he even abandoned the bodies of his dead. That withdrawal from the field was but the beginning of the second battle of Powder River: officer against officer, soldier against soldier.

Up at Fort Fetterman, down at Fort Douglas near Cheyenne City, and even here at Laramie, the morale sank among those troopers who had marched with the Second or Third cavalries on that cold day in hell attacking that hostile village on the Powder. There was renewed grumbling in the barracks and stables, in the company messes and on the sun-warmed parades—renewed talk of desertion.

"I'd sooner go over the hill than fight for a goddamned officer what'd leave his dead behind for them bloody savages to get their hands on!" claimed more than a scattering of those horse soldiers who had been under fire on the Powder River Campaign.

While only one civilian newsman had accompanied the expedition, once Crook's troops returned to Fetterman, the press made hay of the campaign's failure to accomplish its professed goal of dislodging the hostiles from "gold country." Major Thaddeus Stanton of Crook's Omaha headquarters, officially along to the Powder as chief of scouts as well as acting as a correspondent for the New York *Tribune*, blamed in print the actions of Reynolds and Captain Alexander Moore during the battle. The Omaha *Daily Herald* echoed the same sentiments when it proclaimed the "Imbecility of Gen. Reynolds and Flagrant Cowardice of Capt. Alexander Moore of the Third Cavalry." Even the Cheyenne *Daily Leader* proudly declared in a banner headline to its many eager readers that incompetent cavalry officers had led to the ruin of "The Brave General's Well-Laid Plans."

Furious at finding himself with anything less than complete victory over the hostiles, upon his return to Fetterman, Crook chose to prefer charges against Reynolds and two more officers who had served in the attacking column, before the general quickly fled back to his Omaha headquarters with his adjutant, Lieutenant John Bourke.

With the regiment's colonel now under arrest and unable to lead the Third Cavalry into Crook's forthcoming summer campaign, Lieutenant Colonel William B. Royall was now given command to prepare his troops for their march north. As good a soldier as ever rode a horse on the Plains, Royall did as he was ordered—but not without a deep and long-smoldering resentment for what he saw as not only an attack on his regimental commander, Joseph J. Reynolds, but as nothing short of a slur against the good name of the Third Cavalry itself.

As the posts across southern Wyoming Territory began to reoutfit and resupply for the coming summer campaign, word was in these last days of April that Royall was already anxiously chomping at the bit to be given free rein to pitch right into the hostile Sioux and Cheyenne with his horse soldiers so that he might wipe clean the sullied reputation of his regiment.

Lieutenant Colonel William B. Royall was soon to learn that harshest of lessons taught in Plains warfare: be careful of what you ask for, because you just might get it.

The troopers who would again ride north into the land of the Sioux and Cheyenne were soon to get everything that Royall had wished for.

Chapter 1

Moon of Shedding Ponies
Pehingnunipi Wi

At long, long last the winter moons had gone. The Moon of Terrible Cold. On its heels the Moon of Hard Times. So for now the surrounding hills no longer lay beneath a blanket of white. Warmed by the sun, kissed with the gentle rains of the season and nourished by a hard and long winter's runoff, this great hunting land of his Hunkpatila was blooming once more.

In the high places just below the snowcapped peaks the Mother's breast lay thick with tiny flowers of a hundred hues. Buds unfurled into a leafy green to drape every tree along the creeks and rivers with a rustling warmth that foretold of summer's coming. The gently rolling, virgin slopes lay smothered in the fragrant blossoms of buffalo pea and sego lily, dragonhead and purple fleabane. It was truly a time of spiritual renewal for his people.

But Crazy Horse knew the soldiers would return. It was only a matter of time.

So for now the people traveled once more accompanied by the rhythmic circle of the seasons just as the Lakota had for generations without number. And for the present, Crazy Horse reminded the young warriors to keep their weapons in readiness. In these warming days they could watch their ponies grow sleek and fat on the new grass that stretched across the hills clear to the spring sky as far as the eye could see, then farther still.

The Hunkpatila had only to wait, Crazy Horse told them. The *wasichu* would be back.

Perhaps not this moon. More likely come Wipazuka Waste Wi, the Moon of Ripening Berries.

If Crazy Horse understood anything about the pony soldiers, it was that he shared in common one undeniable trait with the white warrior chiefs: neither they, nor he, would give up as long as there was strength left in muscle, a drop of blood left unspilled in this last great struggle between their peoples.

Those soldiers who had charged into the sleepy, unsuspecting Shahiyena camp of Two Moon would return one day soon. And as sure as he was of anything, Crazy Horse knew his people would be ready when that day dawned on this land of the Tongue and Rosebud and Greasy Grass. This time the Shahiyena and seven fires of the Lakota nation would be ready for the *wasichu.*

This time there would be no running. This time the warriors would do more than merely cover the retreat of their villages.

This time—Crazy Horse swore before the grand council fires—this time the red horsemen of the northern plains would exact a great reckoning, for once and for all days.

This he knew, for Crazy Horse had long ago accepted that he had been chosen. He was a mystic.

For three hard, hungry winters now, winters of empty bellies and snow blindness, winters of poor hunting and crying children, this slim warrior chief had experienced visions that presaged the coming summer's great battles. Dreams that reminded him that the days of glory were not over. Dreams of bloody clashes with the white man, instilling the Hunkpatila war chief with hope for this approaching time of glory and honor.

It had been a long, long and treacherous path coming to this spring moon.

First the messengers had arrived from his old friend, Red Cloud.

"Come in," the old Oglalla chief had asked the Hunkpatila people gathered around Crazy Horse last winter. "Come in to the agency and let your people eat. The soldiers will be coming for those who do not."

At first he had just shaken his head, saddened that so great a war chief as Red Cloud, champion of the early days against the soldier forts, had now become an old woman cowed by his trips east to the land of the white man's Grandfather. Red Cloud was no longer a warrior chief to the Oglalla. Now instead, the once-great leader was a tired old man content to suck on his *kukuse*, the white man's pig meat, rather than feasting on buffalo and elk and the sweet antelope of these greening hills.

"The snow is too deep," Crazy Horse had told the messengers. "And our ponies are too poor with this long and terrible cold."

"There are others who are coming in," Red Cloud's messengers told the Hunkpatila. "They are fighting the snow rather than fighting the soldiers. Despite the cold, they are pushing their ponies south."

The Horse had nodded, staring at the dancing flames in that lodge, listening to the feral howling of the wind outside like some gaunt-bellied, lank-legged wolf prowling the outskirts of his village.

And in the end Crazy Horse had told those messengers, "It matters not to me that others choose to take that trail south back to the white man's agencies. As for the Hunkpatila, you tell Red Cloud—my old friend of the days when we fought the Battle of the Hundred in the Hand,* the days when we attacked soldiers hiding behind the barricades near the Pine Fort† —tell my tired old friend that this is still *my* country. Tell him that no one—not the white man, and not Red Cloud himself—will ever tell the Hunkpatila where to go and how to live."

"The soldiers will come. Red Cloud wished only to warn you."

"Tell Red Cloud I have been warned," Crazy Horse replied. "The soldiers will know where to find me. I will not run this time. They will know where to find me."

---

* Fetterman Massacre, THE PLAINSMEN Series, vol. 1, *Sioux Dawn*

† Wagonbox Fight, THE PLAINSMEN Series, vol. 2, *Red Cloud's Revenge*

And the soldiers did come.

It wasn't that Crazy Horse had ever doubted Red Cloud's warning. Nor had he ever doubted that the white man's army would march north into this last great hunting ground of the Lakota and Shahiyena. It surprised him only when the soldiers attacked a small village of those who were struggling against the great cold and deep, icy snow to force their way back to the agency at White Rock. Shameful, that attack was. To charge into a village of those who were attempting to return so that their children and old ones would be warmed by the soldiers' thin gray blankets, so that the sick ones would have some of the moldy flour and the white man's pig meat to put in their hungry bellies.

It still hurt Crazy Horse to think back on that parting from his old friend He Dog, who was taking his family and eleven lodges south to join Two Moon and Old Bear on their trail back to the White Rock Agency. Like a tearing of flesh from flesh after all that tragedy had visited upon the lodge of Crazy Horse in recent winters: friends slaughtered in war against the many enemies of the Lakota; a brother killed in battle; a daughter cut down in her youth by a white man's disease that struck the weakest among them.

It was such an evil thing, this white man's disease—slashing at a man when he had no way to fight back. Such a season of blackness it was become, a season of despair.

Even with his wife, Black Shawl, here with him ever since—he had been so alone. So very alone.

And then He Dog chose to leave.

Crazy Horse vowed he would find a way to strike back, to avenge himself on the enemies that had visited so much grief upon his lodge.

This he swore would be a summer of blood. He swore he would stand ankle deep in *wasichu* blood, cover himself with the gore and reek with the spoils of battle. This was to be the summer of his dream.

Everything happened just as it had been foretold, exactly as he had seen it in his troubled sleep: winter's leaving on the heels of those messengers as the prairie became boggy with the melting snow. Then as suddenly as winter's cold breath had disappeared, it returned—this time with a vengeance in the Moon of Snow Blindness, colder than all but the oldest of old men could remember it had ever been. But by then his Hunkpatila were safely camped on a creek near the Little Powder. All of his people, except the lodges moving south with He Dog.

If the soldiers did not catch them on the trail to the reservation, the killing winter might easily claim them all.

Crazy Horse had worried. Not a quiet moment passed, not a day's short path of the sun across the sky, when the war chief did not brood on those eleven lodges pushing through the great cold and the deep snow toward the White Rock Agency.

Then a runner from a village camped close to the soldier forts appeared among them, saying that the soldiers were claiming they had destroyed the camp of Crazy Horse. The warriors and women, the children and old men around that messenger had laughed at his declaration. But the Horse had not laughed. True, his camp had not been destroyed.

Yet that meant the soldiers had exacted a savage blow on some village. Crazy Horse prayed there would be survivors.

All too suddenly that cold, leaden afternoon as the gun-barrel gray clouds hung so low a man could almost reach out and touch them, they heard a shout from one of the sentries posted on the hills overlooking their camp along the Little Powder.

"People coming! People coming on foot from the south!"

Young men and boys ran up the icy, crusty slopes among the snow-draped cedar and stunted pine to see for themselves.

Crazy Horse did not need to look. He already knew.

Turning to the women of his camp, he had ordered them to stir life back into their sleeping fires, to dig out all extra food and clothing, blankets and robes, to bring forth their bags of roots and herbs they would need for the fingers and noses, ears and toes, bitten savagely by the cold, for the wounds caused by soldier bullets.

Only when preparations were under way had he climbed that hill himself and looked down into the next valley to see the broken line of survivors straggling through the deep, icy snow that cut their naked, unprotected legs. Tears had come to the eyes of Crazy Horse as he looked upon the Shahiyena of Two Moon and Old Bear, upon He Dog's own Hunkpatila. Most struggled through the snowdrifts on foot. A few warriors rode in front, breaking trail, cutting through the deep snow with their heaving, struggling ponies. More warriors rode the mares and colts along the flanks of that sad, weary, frozen procession—young men bristling with their weapons, ever watchful as they brought their families back north to the protection of the Crazy Horse people.

But try as he might, often wiping the tears from his eyes, the Horse could not see the one he sought most among those warriors. His heart feared the worst. Such cold it brought to his chest, like a lump of river ice beneath his ribs.

With a wave of his arm, the war chief had ordered his young men to fetch up their own ponies, to ride through the hills toward the weak and old, the small and sick, to carry them into the village. He stood there as the Shahiyena moved past the great war chief in silence, most with shreds of frozen, threadbare blanket wrapped around their feet, stooped under the charred burden of what they had rescued from the blackened lodges burned by the soldiers of Three Stars.

His eyes searched each of those passing slowly by, face by face by face. Looking for the one he sought.

When he looked down on the tracks made by those who hobbled slowly past the place where he stood, there were far too many footprints spotted with blood from their brutal three nights straggling north to reach his village.

As the first of Two Moon's and Old Bear's clans approached the outer ring of brown lodges, the voices of his own people began to ring out:

"Shahiyena—come eat in my lodge!"

"Shahiyena! Come, make yourselves warm in my blankets and robes!"

"Come, Shahiyena, all that I have I offer to you!"

Such a reception had sent a thick ball of sentiment high into his throat—to see how his people opened up their hearts to these who had been driven into the cold and snow by the soldiers of Three Stars Crook.

"Crazy Horse."

Without turning, he had known that voice the moment it called out his name there in the midst of the noisy celebration of those Shahiyena and Hunkpatila once more among warmth and security.

Slowly he had eventually turned, his eyes misting. "He Dog," he had whispered.

At long last Crazy Horse beheld the face he had feared he would never again see.

That night, and for three more, the warriors of He Dog and Little Wolf told of the battle on the Powder River, argued on what now to do. But there was no longer any talk of returning to the agencies. Never again would they try the white man's way.

The *wasichu* called the Indian in to the agencies, at the same time it sent out the white soldiers against them.

What was the price of a slab of the white man's greasy *kukuse?* What was the price of one of those thin, threadbare blankets, or a bag of moldy flour, or a few head of some skinny beef that never came when it was promised?

Was that price the blood of their women and children on the snow?

"If so, then this is a price we will never pay!" He Dog had shouted, his voice reverberating from the firelit lodgepoles.

"It seems the soldiers wish to make war on the Shahiyena," one of the old Lakota had argued. Others nodded or grunted their agreement. "The soldiers attacked a Shahiyena camp. We know of no Miniconjou, no Sans Arc, no Blackfoot or Hunkpapa village attacked by soldiers. I think we should give the Shahiyena what we can: food, clothing, blankets, and lodges. Then let them go on their way."

"Yes," another voice assented. "The soldiers must be looking for the Shahiyena."

So it had made the heart of Crazy Horse soar when He Dog had stood suddenly, glowering at all the small-hearted among them.

"I for one will not send the Shahiyena on their way!"

he had bellowed over their heads. "I for one will stand beside the warriors of the Shahiyena and fight the white man. When he sends his soldiers against any band wintering in these hunting grounds, he sends his soldiers against us all!"

There had come a great commotion of muttering and argument.

But then Crazy Horse had stood, to take his place alongside He Dog. To stand and be counted among the resistance.

"The Shahiyena came this far north only to hunt for meat and to visit us," the Horse said, wanting to whip them with his words just the way a man would lash a pony with his rawhide quirt. "They are like cousins. Let any man among you tell me these Shahiyena are not like our own family."

No one had dared speak. The war chief's words had begun to shame them, to sting as they landed about that war council.

And in the end, that ring of warriors, old and young, had decided to march north to the Chalk Buttes where the Hunkpapa of Sitting Bull camped. These Hunkpapa numbered more than any of the other seven lodge fires of the Lakota nation. Surely the Hunkpatila should visit with the Hunkpapa and seek the wisdom of the great medicine man on so weighty a subject as forming an alliance with the Shahiyena.

"We will go north to counsel with Sitting Bull," they decided.

"And remember," Crazy Horse had told them with a smile on his face, "remember what Sitting Bull told our families and relations still on the reservations before last winter."

The heads had nodded, and there had been much murmuring among that war council.

"He told them all to come join him," the Horse continued. "Told them to come north because there would be good fighting, plenty of coups to be earned and guns to be taken from the soldiers we would defeat in battle. Plenty of big American horses. Come north, he told everyone. Come north for one last, big fight!"

The lodge had rocked with cheering and celebration as they remembered the words of the great Hunkpapa medicine man who had issued his call for the many bands to gather about him for the coming season of fighting and warfare and blood.

Then Crazy Horse had hushed them, and when the lodge had quieted once more, he continued.

"I for one am glad that Three Stars did not wait until the Season of Fat Horses to make war on any of us. I am glad that he struck early. Glad I am, for now we have the chance to see who is for giving in to the white man, and who is for fighting the soldiers. No more can any of you walk a thin line—you must plant your feet on one side or the other. The decision seems as clear to me as the waters rushing down from the mountain snowfields come spring runoff. There are but two paths to choose. Each of you must select the path your feet will take."

"What path does Crazy Horse walk now?" He Dog had asked, his eyes misting with respect and courage as they gazed upon his Hunkpatila war chief.

"The path I have always taken," he had responded in that hushed assembly. "Since the white man wants war . . . we will give him a fight he will never forget."

Chapter 2

Mid-May
1876

"*I'll be wanting you to wash your pecker off with something, dearie.*"

For a fleeting moment John Finerty studied the faded rose blushing the cheeks of the painted whore standing in what was left of the dim, late-afternoon light sneaking through a smoky windowpane into the narrow crib where the older woman plied her trade of earthly pleasures here on the high plains. He gazed longingly at those big, fleshy breasts spilling like pale, rounded melons from the top of her faded bustiere, their flattened nipples a deep, purplish hue in the growing shadows.

"That what you expect of me, is it now? To wash myself off before you'll jump in this bed to go a dance with me?" He looked down at the swelling flesh he held absently in his hand.

She stepped over to him with a scrap of rag she had wrung out in the cracked china bowl splattered with faded tulips that sat sublimely upon a pine box where the woman stored her working clothes: bloomers and camisoles, stockings and an extra garter hung on a crooked nail.

"You'll want me to wash you off, you will," she told him huskily. "Once I get started, you'll wonder why no other whore ever washed your sweet pecker before they humped you."

Pushing Finerty's hand aside, she took a firm hold of his penis, giggling when it jumped and swelled beneath her deft touch. Then she began to stroke it as gently as she could with the scrap of coarse cloth. Cool as the damp rag was, Finerty sensed heat rising in his cock, feeling it seep into his groin, creeping into his inner core—he groaned and lay back atop the musty comforter, his legs dangling off the side of her narrow rope-and-tick bed.

"You do much more of that, my love," he told the chippie, "I won't last long enough to get it inside you."

Obediently she stopped her washing, bent over him, and kissed the swollen head of his penis. "No worry now, dearie. I know tricks that can make a man last a long night through if I've a mind to. Don't you go fretting none—sweet Ellie here is going to make sure when you fire your cannon off that you're firing it where it will do us both some good."

And with that she straightened and flung the rag back toward the china bowl, where it splashed the murky water onto the pine box and some of her underthings, dislodging the garter hung on the crooked nail. Squirming quickly out of her bloomers, she came to stand between his legs, half-naked.

Finerty's eyes widened, finding himself staring at the dark triangle of curly, matted hair that stood out like a stark delta against her alabaster skin.

Letting him rake his eyes over her, the whore stood there wearing those tall stockings held up with faded, torn garters, as well as the bustiere she had laced around her ribs, the whalebone stays climbing in a strain of delight from her navel to support those fleshy melons that jiggled as she kneed her way onto the bed, looming over him like two pale, winking moons. Taking his flesh in one hand, the whore guided him center. At long last she eased down on the full length of him.

Groaning a bit louder now, Finerty closed his eyes and thrust his hips up at the woman, seeking to plant himself even deeper.

"Here, dearie—put your hands to work on these," she

whispered, hot-breathed, at his ear, then took both his hands and brought them to cup her breasts. "I likes a man who licks and sucks on my breasts while he's diddling me with his hot pecker."

"Anything—" he muttered, knowing he wasn't going to last much longer, couldn't possibly last. "Anything you want."

Then she was nuzzling his neck, chewing the long strap of muscle with those browned teeth of hers, biting all the way up to his ear. Finerty was enjoying this more than he could ever remember enjoying a poke before.

He swallowed hard. "How . . . how long you got with me today?"

"How long you want with me, dearie?"

"Again," he replied low and husky, urgently. "Least one more time."

"You close to shooting, ain'cha?"

"Re . . . real close," he got the words out, struggling to talk while concentrating on tightening himself off so he would not climax at just that moment.

Then she had a hand behind her, reaching between his legs, wrapping some fingers about his scrotum, pulling on it gently, holding it, squeezed like that, long and sure—so sure that Finerty suddenly believed that he could actually relax a bit.

"We can take all night if you want to, love," she purred at his ear, over his face, licking his eyelids, her breath heavily scented with the bitters she preferred to drink while they had been out front nuzzling at a smoky table near the bar.

Finerty, on the other hand, had taken his whiskey straight since they had no rye in this wilderness.

"Young, handsome lad like yourself," she went on at his ear, nibbling and licking and whispering, "why—it could damn well take all night with my new, randy friend from . . . where'd you say you was from again, dearie?"

"Chi—Chicago," John answered, thrusting himself up at her. He sensed her shudder for a moment, and for the second time since he had come back here to this chippie's cramped crib at the back of the Hog Ranch, Finerty believed he would really enjoy this one he had picked.

By the time he had found his way across from the fort, she and another were all he had to choose from while the rest were occupied. Business was good now, good and busy, what with the infantry and cavalry units coming in across the past few days, soldiers and packers and wagon teamsters. They all had to be serviced. So he had looked over the two, then motioned her over to his table, peering at the deep, shadowy crevice of cleavage she hung before him, not much left to the imagination by that threadbare dressing gown she had tied about her. There was but a glimpse of the bustiere. And that had excited him all the more.

He should enjoy her, enjoy this, enjoy the sweating, grunting, heaving beast with two backs after all. He had all of the Irishman's heart for the ladies—any lady, in fact, if his brief history of his coming to manhood and the few years hence was any testimony. And John Finerty surely had all the Hibernian's fondness for getting himself into scrapes, be they scrapes due to his love of rye whiskey, or troubles come of the love for a woman. Still, it had been much too long since he had fit his pecker inside the anatomy of some warm wench. Hell, he hadn't been planted inside any wench at all since departing that city of big shoulders by the lake.

Truth of the matter was, it had simply taken him too damned long getting west from Chicago to this godforsaken wilderness post the army called Fort Fetterman.

"You're the young man Clint Snowden recommended for this trip to the Plains?" asked the tall, white-haired handsome man of some sixty years.

John Finerty scraped his hat from his head and nodded. "Yes. I am, Mr. Storey."

"Come in, and sit," Wilbur Storey replied, motioning to an empty chair beside his big desk here in the expansive office several stories up from the rainy streets of Chicago that morning in late April. The old man with expressive, granitelike wrinkles chiseled in a pair of rivulets down his cheeks stroked that white beard and smiled genuinely as he went around the desk to take a seat himself.

Finerty marveled that the old man was so tall. Not a bit of stoop. Damned well over the hill, and he still looked spry enough to arm-wrestle with any of the boys down at the loading dock. And bloody handsome too, despite the march of years that told on Storey's face.

"How soon can you be ready?" Storey said, striking right to the point without formalities.

John had heard of just this characteristic about his new employer. Also heard that Storey was a native of Vermont and an ardent, lifelong Democrat who had opposed Abraham Lincoln every step of the way in the President's prosecution of the Civil War.

"I suppose I can be ready whenever you decide for me to be, sir," the Irishman answered.

"You'll need your outfit first," Storey replied perfunctorily as he pulled a pad to the center of the desk and carefully extracted a pencil from a marble holder, where more than a dozen swirled like the radiating petals of a yellow daisy. He licked the point and began writing. "Better to get some of what you need here—perhaps all, come to think on it. Things get pretty pricey out there in the west, I'll bet you."

"Yes, sir," John replied. Then cursed himself for the stupid, childlike sound of it here in the office of the owner of the Chicago *Times*. Still, Storey did not look up from his work over the pad, nor did the man's face register any ridicule despite Finerty's burning embarrassment.

"You're going with Crook's column, you know that, don't you?"

When John did not answer, struck dumb with surprise at the question, Storey eventually looked up.

"General George Crook is his name. A real goddamned hero of the Apache campaigns. A good man to boot." Storey went back to scratching across his pad. "A good man, George Crook is."

"Sir?" It sounded a little weak and squeaky. Not at all like Finerty's voice.

"Yes?"

"I . . . I had believed I was going to march with Custer, Mr. Storey."

"Now, why would you think that?"

"Mr. Snowden, my . . . your city editor—"

"Snowden doesn't have a goddamned thing to do with

assigning war correspondents, Mr. Finerty." He pointed the pencil between the reporter's eyes. "That's my job. Always has been. Long as I own this paper, it always will be my job."

"Yes, sir. Very good. It's just that . . . I've met . . . weren't you told that I know General Custer?"

Storey snorted. "I doubt there's a half-decent reporter working this side of the Missouri River that George Armstrong Custer hasn't met, Mr. Finerty. Glory hound that he is. Be that as it may, far as I know, for the time being your friend Custer is still cooling his heels down in Washington." He snorted a little chuckle. "Much as I hated him as a general, Sam Grant's made himself an interesting caricature as President. Seems, Mr. Finerty, that Sam Grant is exacting his pound of flesh out of Custer for a blunder Custer made with those Congressional bribery hearings."

It was like the air had gone out of him, slammed to the earth, like falling from a horse on the gallop. Finerty had so hoped to march with the famed lieutenant colonel of the gallant Seventh Cavalry, planned on being in on the kill when Custer's regiment caught up with the hostiles of Sitting Bull and Crazy Horse. Now his hopes for writing that story of a lifetime were dashed on the rocks of Wilbur Storey's respect for this other soldier named George Crook.

"Seems there's a fella who works for the small press out in Bismarck, across the river from Custer's duty station," Storey explained. "He's the one I heard is marching with the Dakota column."

"Bismarck?" Finerty said, the first syllable a bit squeaky. Pushing a finger down inside his collar grown suddenly tight and damp, he asked, "Custer's not going to fight the Sioux this summer, sir?"

Storey wagged his head, then shrugged. "Maybe so. Maybe not. Just telling you the last thing I heard out of Washington. General Terry's the one heading up the Dakota column. And that comes direct from Sheridan's headquarters here in town."

Finerty swallowed, wishing now he had refilled the small hip flask he was never without. But he had drained it to the last drop on the way here simply to fortify himself for this visit to Storey's office. Goda'mighty—but it would taste damned good about now. His mouth had gone dry with disappointment—not getting to ride with Custer's regiment into the conquered villages.

And the smooth fire of that rye tracing down the length of his throat just might help calm some of his discomfort at the sudden change in plans, giving him its comfort and serenity as it hit his belly, all warm and rosy where he had neglected to eat breakfast. Time enough for that later.

"Mr. Storey, I suppose I'll be going with General Crook then, sir."

The publisher smiled at his young correspondent. "I'm sorry to see you're disappointed. But you must realize that General Terry commands over Custer anyway. And besides"—he waved a veiny hand in the air as if dismissing Finerty's concerns—"Crook knows more about the Indians than either of them. It's Crook who's likely to do the hard work of things—again. Leave Custer to opt for the cheers from the parade grandstands and the swooning of the ladies. But a man like George Crook—now there's a solid soldier who gets the job done."

Finerty was beginning to sweat beneath his high, starched collar. "I'm sure you're aware of General Custer's Civil War record—"

"Custer's a brave man. I'll give you that. None braver, in fact," Storey replied. "But Custer's been out there for eight years already and has not succeeded in bringing those damnable Sioux to a decisive engagement."

"But this General Crook did well in the Apache campaign?"

"Exactly. Bill Sherman knew what he was doing when he transferred Crook north to the plains, Mr. Finerty."

"Yes, sir." There it was again, that soft, mushy sound of it—words that rang with nothing more prissy than bootlicking the boss.

The publisher ripped the page from his tablet and folded it lengthwise. "No matter this discussion of Custer and Terry's column. Your part in this affair is settled, Mr. Finerty. If you're working for me, you are going with Crook. He was, you'll recall, the first into the field after the deadline for those hostiles came and went."

"But the papers said all Crook accomplished was to scatter the wild tribes."

Storey flared. "That was that bumbling idiot Reynolds! Senile old hen! Make no mistake about this, Finerty—Crook will be the first into the field this summer. The first again. And mark my word that his column will be the one to strike the Sioux first. And hardest. Here now."

Finerty took the paper from the veiny hand. "Yes, Mr. Storey?"

"Take it to Mr. Patterson down in warrants. He'll see that you get what funds you may need to outfit you. Any other expenses you and he may feel you'll require. Report back to me only when you're ready to depart by rail for Cheyenne City."

From the moment he had stepped out of Wilbur Storey's office, it hadn't taken long for the young reporter to put together the clothing others advised him he would need for the high plains: rugged britches and cotton shirts, a sturdy coat and a wide-brimmed pinch hat, a gum poncho and those tall boots he would need for those days and weeks, maybe months in the saddle chasing the elusive warriors who always ran away rather than fight. John had wondered if his ass was truly ready for what he was going to demand of it as he purchased blankets and a canvas bed wrapper, a small mess kit and toilet articles. That, and all the pads and pencils his city editor threw at him.

"You write down everything, Finerty," Snowden instructed him. "Write down everything anyone says or does. Later on you'll have the luxury of taking the time to decide what to use and what to forget."

"Everything. Yes, Mr. Snowden," he had answered, and then went down to the street, turned north to the corner, and pushed into the closest pub near the *Times*'s offices.

Three days later when he was nearing departure, Finerty paid a call on General Philip H. Sheridan, presenting his card at the headquarters of the commander of the Division of the Missouri.

"There—that should do you, Mr. Finerty," Sheridan said a half hour later as he handed the reporter a signed letter of introduction. "I've addressed that to General Crook. As a matter of fact, my signature on that will serve you well with any officer you should encounter on your way to Fetterman."

Finerty rose, slipping the letter into an inside pocket. "Thank you for seeing me on such short notice, General."

"Mr. Storey and I go back a ways," Sheridan replied.

"Thank you too for your help, sir."

"If I may," Sheridan replied. "A word of advice. Perhaps a word of caution."

"Caution?" Finerty asked, then he grinned, sensing an inside joke. "You're going to warn me to watch out for my hair with all those scalping knives around, General."

A quick smile crossed Sheridan's face, but faded as quickly. "No. This has to do with General Crook. You will find him a hard campaigner."

"I'm ready for the march, sir. Whatever Crook's soldiers can take, I can handle."

This time Sheridan chuckled, seeming to measure the reporter a bit more closely. "Perhaps you can. Very well. Then I won't feel obligated to say any more."

"A hard campaigner, this General Crook."

"Yes. He spares himself no deprivation, Mr. Finerty. He wants the enemy bad enough, he will spare no deprivation to bring the quarry to bay."

"For the first time, General—I think I just might enjoy this chase going after Sitting Bull's savages."

"Then have at them, Mr. Finerty," Sheridan replied with a full grin, extending his hand.

"I will, sir. Believe me, if General Crook can find them for me, I will have a go at the red bastards myself!"

John Finerty departed Chicago a little before dawn on that Saturday morning, two days later, in the darkness of 6 May with Wilbur Storey's words reverberating in his thoughts.

"You are now a war correspondent for the *Times*. You're working for me, Mr. Finerty. You are to spare no expense in getting your story, and by all means use the wires as freely as you deem necessary. Whenever practicable. No matter what it costs—just get me the full, unvarnished story from Crook's forthcoming march. I want you there at his side when the old braided beard goes in for the kill."

"Yes, sir," he had answered on that platform, a gust of lake wind blowing his coat collar against the side of his face as he shook hands with Clint Snowden and Wilbur Storey. "I swear to you I'll be front and center when the general rides in for the kill."

Chapter 3

Mid-May 1876

Ever since that Tuesday morning, the ninth of May, when he had boarded the train that inched west from Omaha in the company of George C. Crook, John Bourke knew he was not going to enjoy campaigning with the general's other aide.

Azor H. Nickerson was simply everything that Bourke was not: mean-spirited, carping as a New England spinster, a nagging shrew of an officer who derived more pleasure in the security of four walls around him, happier to bed down when clean sheets were to be found beneath his weary head. From the moment Crook informed Nickerson that he was going to accompany the general this time out, Captain Nickerson began his wheedling and niggling, his whining cant raised with most every detail of their pending trip west into the land of the Sioux and Cheyenne.

Unable to help himself, Bourke chuckled about that again, remembering how Nickerson's face went white, almost apoplectic with consternation, perhaps some downright fear, to learn that he was going to have to suffer the privations, the toil, the outright danger Bourke himself had endured during the Powder River Campaign that had fizzled to an inconclusive finale only that previous March.

It wasn't that Nickerson was a coward. No man could

ever accuse him of that—what with his record serving the Eighth Ohio Volunteers with commendable bravery during the Battle of Antietam, as well as his extended frontier service with the Twenty-third Infantry. It was just that the captain had put in his time as a stoic and long-suffering soldier and believed he had therefore earned his position in Crook's Omaha headquarters by judiciously climbing one ladder rung at a time. So it was that he lost no opportunity telling any and all that he deserved to be treated better than to be ordered back into the field. Once more against the goddamned Indians, no less!

As much as he was an accomplished horseman, Azor Nickerson had come to hate being in the saddle. Maybe it was something to do with age, Bourke thought. Old bones and old butts don't sit well for hours in a McClellan.

Yet Bourke had to hand it to the older Nickerson. At least the captain was savvy enough to understand he was wasn't plopping down into the same set of circumstances he had encountered when commissioned into the Twenty-third Infantry back to sixty-eight. Now the tribes were much better armed than right after the Civil War, and they even appeared to be acting in some crude congress with one another, and above all else it seemed that with the passing of winter an unusually large migration from the agencies into the unceded territory had left the reservations practically empty this spring. Why, even as late as 27 April, the army had received intelligence that the young warriors at Standing Rock were buying weapons and ammunition, mounting up and heading west in weighty numbers. West to join what the army called the wild tribes. The winter roamers.

That same date saw another report telegraphed to Crook from Captain W. H. Jordan of the Ninth Infantry. As commander of Camp Robinson located at Red Cloud Agency, Jordan requested relief for the agency's Indians, who were starving after a terribly long and hard winter, their third in a row. If they did not receive their long-overdue beef ration soon, the captain warned, he predicted they would be compelled to jump the reservation and join the free-roaming hostiles where they would unleash their raids on white ranches and settlements.

On more than one occasion this past few weeks Bourke had watched Crook's face as the general studied the reports. And more than once the lieutenant found himself realizing that Crook was giving that intelligence nothing more than passing consideration.

"With all the doomsayers," Crook often said, "there's one agent among the many who denies that his Indians are in a bad way of it."

On 5 May James S. Hastings contradicted Captain Jordan's assertions and informed his superiors at the Indian Bureau that his wards at the Red Cloud Agency "had never been more peaceful."

"It's not the number of warriors we'll encounter at all, John," Crook had told him repeatedly. "You remember what they tried to tell us before we marched to Powder River last March?"

"But what Reynolds ran into wasn't anywhere near the number of warriors we are supposed to encounter off the reservations this summer, General."

"Exactly my point, John. The problem we'll have this summer will not be the number of warriors. That's always been a matter of conjecture and even some outright rumor. Instead, it will be the tactical problem we've always had with Indians: the red sons of bitches just won't stand and fight."

"Always running—to fight another day," John replied.

"And if the warriors are fleeing the reservations this spring because they intend to gather in great numbers for some hunt they have planned . . . why, mark my words, those bands won't stay together for more than a few days of hunting at the most. Out there, on the Tongue and Powder and the Rosebud—there's not enough goddamned game and grass to support a massive village like that for very long at all."

"They have to break up again," Bourke echoed.

"Exactly," Crook confirmed. "We'll once more be forced to defeat them in detail, piecemeal. Band by band. If I can ever get them to stop and fight at all."

While the general feared only that the enemy would flee before his column, spring had renewed the frontier, bringing new grass to the plains. As the winter snows retreated, that road the miners took north into the Black Hills was reopened—making the blood course hot in the veins of the young Lakota. As the weather mellowed along that route to the gold camps, reports of the inevitable clashes began to drift into headquarters at Omaha.

Things were heating up to the point that even John M. Thayer, governor of Wyoming Territory, petitioned Crook for relief for civilians harassed and murdered, set upon and robbed by the lawless warriors roaming beyond the boundaries of their assigned reservations. When Crook did nothing beyond ordering Captain James Egan's K Company of the Second Cavalry to patrol the Black Hills Road, Thayer hurried to the White House personally, begging for troops to protect the civilians. Grant smiled benignly and informed the governor he had been promised by both Sherman and Sheridan that with summer the coming expedition would remedy the "Indian problem" for all time.

Of late Crook had wind of the complaints but took them in stride as he threw himself into preparations for the campaign. For some unexplained reason early on, he chose to rehire only three of the original thirty-two quartermaster's scouts he had used on the march to Powder River. Perhaps bristling under the criticism leveled at him from various nonmilitary quarters, the general became convinced using civilians in such a capacity was a mistake. Instead he determined to repeat his success in Arizona Territory. It was there he had hired Apache auxiliaries to stalk Apache hostiles for his troops.

"You're going to hire Sioux to hunt down Sioux, General?" Bourke had asked on that train ride west from Omaha to Cheyenne.

"Damn right I am. This is one soldier who believes in Indian allies," Crook growled, pulling the stub of the unlit cigar from his mouth. "Remember, John, what we proved to the doubting Nellies down there: nothing so demoralizes our enemy as having his brother warriors defecting to fight on the side of the army."

Three days after leaving Omaha, Crook's entourage reached Cheyenne and proceeded immediately to the outskirts of town to Fort D. A. Russell, where the general was again embroiled in the quarrels and politics of the Third Cavalry. Emotions were strung taut as a cat-gut fiddle string, morale sunk as low as a latrine pit, here where dissension still reigned following Colonel Reynolds's disaster on Powder River. Delays in the courts-martial ordered by Crook had left two of the regiment's top officers hanging in limbo. So it was a chilly reception Lieutenant Colonel William B. Royall of the Third Cavalry, acting in the absence of Colonel Joseph Reynolds, provided for the general's staff. Crook did what he could in that roughened way of his for which John Bourke had a warm affection, the general trying his best to ease the ruffled feathers of the officers who, like Royall, had taken great offense at the insult Crook's charges brought to the regiment as a whole.

"Tell me, John," Crook began thoughtfully early the morning after their arrival as he and Bourke were preparing to ride out from Fort Russell with their escort for Camp Robinson, "does it seem Colonel Royall is chafing at having to serve under an expedition commander who brought both a superior and a subordinate officer up on charges?"

Bourke patted the neck of the mount he would ride south toward the Red Cloud Agency. "I suppose he's got his grounds to be a bit icy with you, General."

"Does he now?"

"Yes, sir. Speaking frankly?"

"Of course, John. I've always wanted you to speak your mind."

"I can't say as I blame him. Thinking of a man in his position. Now in charge of the Third—a regiment officered with fighting men the likes of Anson Mills and Guy Henry who you can always count on to do their job and then some, men who have unquestioned careers of gallantry and bravery before the enemy—to have these sorts of charges leveled against two of their highest officers must make them believe the whole world considers them to be poor soldiers at best, cowards at the worst."

Crook's eyes narrowed, two deep furrows carved between the bushy blondish brows. "Beginning to sound like you've changed your mind on what you saw Reynolds and

Moore do or not do at that hostile village on St. Patrick's Day, John."*

"No, sir," he answered quickly. "They were both wrong and I'll never change my mind on that. I was there to see it with my own eyes. It's just: I know how the fighting men must feel. So I feel for them. No man out here, asked to do what the army has asked of these soldiers, wants to have his fighting ability ever questioned, much less his courage."

Crook rose to the saddle, and the lieutenant in charge of escort detail ordered his soldiers to mount as one. Nearby, Robert Strahorn, correspondent for Denver's Rocky Mountain *News*, settled atop his saddle.

Pulling the brim of his slouch hat down to shade his eyes, the general spoke quietly to his young aide. "It's precisely because of those fine soldiers in the Third Cavalry that I brought their superior up on charges, John. You let the rest of them know that. You let those soldiers know that George Crook did it for them—so that the world will know that the Third is a fighting outfit. To know that the ranks of the Third Cavalry are filled with brave soldiers not afraid to take on the likes of Sitting Bull and Crazy Horse. It's just some of their officers who have smudged their fine reputation. You tell them that, John."

He watched Crook wheel his horse sharply and give heels as the escort sergeant quickly ordered his detail to move out. It was left up to Bourke to bring up the rear, his belly cold and unsettled that the general had taken offense. How he chastised himself across those first few miles heading southeast, on into the afternoon and that evening as well. He hadn't said what he had meant to say, and now felt miserable for the unintentional insult.

Yes, he decided, vowing again not to make this mistake in the future. John Bourke promised himself he would tell the men of the Third Cavalry that George Crook had brought Reynolds and Moore up on charges for one reason and one reason only: to protect the courageous fighting reputation of their beloved regiment.

• • •

---

* THE PLAINSMEN Series, vol. 8, *Blood Song*

Things had gone to hell with the army in Wyoming Territory.

Since their return from the fight on Powder River, men in the Second and Third Cavalry had been deserting, slipping off the post, disappearing into the crush of civilians flooding toward the Black Hills. It was next to impossible for anyone to catch a deserter if a man truly wanted to disappear. He could sell his uniform, his rig, and even trade his weapons for a grubstake outfit that would get him to Deadwood Creek or one of the many streams feeding the Belle Fourche.

But there wasn't a soul could look at Seamus Donegan with suspicion. Weren't many men who looked less "army" than the tall Irishman. He had allowed Samantha to trim the full beard he had cultivated during the winter campaign to the Powder River to a neat Vandyke below his shaggy mustache. That was all she wanted to take the scissors to—adoring the long, wavy hair that hung well past his shoulders like a bushy shawl. Down in the Panhandle country of Texas he had first begun to grow it, at Sam's gentle nudging, then came to like it himself as he moved in the company of the hide men, those buffalo hunters of the Staked Plain who took great pride in their distinctive and singular appearance. The buffalo men stood out in any crowd.

So no one was ever going to mistake Seamus Donegan for a soldier.

"Here, Seamus—listen to your son."

He remembered her words now as he reined up below the bluff where Fort Fetterman sprawled beneath the sunny May skies. How Samantha had taken his hand and laid it upon her belly for what they both knew was to be another long absence. Perhaps so long that the great swell of life within her would be born by the time he returned: the infant son she had promised him. A son they had created together.

From the pleasure they had taken in one another's bodies, they had created this pure wonder of new life. A son!

"Say farewell to him too," she had whispered into his ear back at Laramie. "There are two of us you part from today. From now on you have family."

He couldn't remember holding her any tighter than he had yesterday morning at dawn in the long shadows of officers' quarters near the parade. How she had shuddered with the spring cold, perhaps trembling in remembrance of how he had held her, caressed her, coupled with her so fiercely in those predawn moments that still gave a blush to her cheeks.

"I've never made love to a pregnant woman before," he had told Samantha.

"Well, I've never allowed a man who was a father such liberties with me, Seamus Donegan," she had replied, wearing that special grin that cast an angelic light across her face. It was all she wore as she lay with him amid the tangle of sheets and comforter on the small bed in that tiny attic room above the quarters peopled by officers' families.

"Even though you have no promise of work, you still believe you must go?" Samantha had asked him as he held her there beside the big piebald gelding he had saddled, ready for the hundred-mile ride to the northwest.

"There'll be work," he had whispered into her hair. "Always plenty of work when the army marches off to make war. Don't worry—I'll find something to do to feed my family."

He recalled how she had choked down a sob before answering. "Family. I suppose we are already, aren't we now, Seamus? No longer are we just Seamus and Sam. No more are we only a couple. From now on—we'll be family."

He had held her out at arm's length, studying her red-rimmed, moist eyes, gazing at the way the salty tears had brightened the blush of her full lips. Even now as he peered over the prairie below Fetterman, blooming with the white of regimental tents, Seamus remembered how looking at her that last time had excited him again, though they had torn themselves from one another's bare flesh only minutes before he had saddled and prepared to go.

"I'll find something." He repeated now the words he had used to promise her. "Don't you worry—I'll find something to do when Crook marches north again."

If not scouting with Grouard, Big Bat, and Reshaw, then he would see if the wagon master could use a strong man willing to learn to handle the teams. Willing to do what it would take to feed his family.

As he urged the gelding up the dusty, rutted trail toward the top of the bluff overlooking the North Platte, Seamus gazed across the river at the Hog Ranch: three adobe, wattle, and clapboard shanties squatted not far from the mouth of LaPrele Creek. A saloon and dance hall in one, a small hotel with canvas walls in another, and a sizable restaurant in the last of the buildings, all owned by Kid Slaymaker, who had made the Hog Ranch famous for hundreds and hundreds of miles around. It was the first good place east of Fort Bridger in Wyoming Territory, south of Fort Ellis in Montana Territory, and the last place north of Laramie where a man could count on finding those things most dear to a plainsman's heart.

"A good stove, strong whiskey, and sweet-smelling women what're willing to pleasure a man! That's what's waiting for us at the Hog Ranch."

Seamus smiled now, the words spoken by one of Thomas Moore's packers brought to mind as he looked down at the small herd of horses tied up outside the shanties, at all the milling foot traffic moving to and from and around the bustling establishment.

Men going off to war, he thought to himself. Perhaps never to return. What's wrong with a man having himself a real hurroo, getting blind drunk and climbing atop a chippie or two back in those dank, smelly cribs before Crook's column pulls out?

It's for sure the Hog Ranch would be sorely missing the trade of the Second and Third cavalries when the general gave the order to march.

Seamus prayed he would be pulling out with the rest.

Thinking on that little family he had left behind at Laramie.

Chapter 4

Moon of First Eggs

Most of all, Wooden Leg missed the tobacco.

Only recently had he learned to smoke, joining the other young men, the older warriors and aged counselors, when they talked and enjoyed their pipes. And he truly liked the tobacco.

Sugar and coffee were in pretty short supply too. There was far too little of this and that, most of it of no real consequence to the great encampment of Lakota and Shahiyena that was spread down the east bank of the Tongue River like a gathering of crescents, each of the swelling camp circles opening their horns to the east, toward the awakening sun as the earth warmed, the grass raised its head from the renewed prairie, and the pale-pink buds bloomed on the wild roses along the creek bottoms.

With all that they lacked, that great village did not suffer a shortage of powder and bullets. With every band of warriors who rode into camp from the reservations came more guns, more ammunition, and more horsemen should the soldiers again try to attack a village of women and children.

This time it would be different! was the oft-repeated rallying cry. This time they would not wait for the pony soldiers to attack their camps. Now they planned on confronting the soldiers, man for man, gun for gun—to stop the white man's army, turn it around, and drive it out of this last great hunting ground. And those soldiers the warrior bands could not cower and drive off, the Lakota and Shahiyena would slaughter.

Their blood would nourish these hillsides that provided food for the antelope and elk, deer and buffalo that in turn provided meat and hides, clothing and shelter for this growing camp of wandering peoples, all come to gather around the mystical shaman called Sitting Bull. In every camp were the proud war chiefs who kept their scouts riding out every day, watching to the south for the soldiers, roaming to the north along the Elk River* for more of the white man's army. Revered and acclaimed war chiefs like Crazy Horse, White Bull, Little Wolf, Iron Star, Low Dog, and Crow King.

Surely, the soldiers would have to be crazy, touched by the moon to come looking for a fight with this encampment.

But then—Wooden Leg knew the white man had never been known for having good sense, for doing the smart thing.

For now Wooden Leg and many of the other young Shahiyena warriors would watch over the great pony herds. Most of the mares were dropping foals in the new grasses that nourished their winter-gaunt animals. The people celebrated and danced, feasted and coupled. There were weddings and births. And there were deaths as the old ones went to walk the long Star Road to Seyan, where they would join their ancestors.

Even the old ones could die at peace, content, perhaps even happy in their final days at having seen so great an encampment that swelled in size nearly every day. No man then living had ever witnessed so grand an event as this gathering. Surely it would bring joy to an old man's heart to cast his tired, rheumy eyes on the ever-widening camp circles—at long last to know that when he took his last

---

* Yellowstone River

breath, his people had truly reached the zenith of their power.

There likely was never to be another summer like this.

"*Hopo!* Wooden Leg!" a friend called out from the lodge circle, waving as the young warrior rode slowly past. Chief Comes in Sight said, "You go to the herd?"

"My ponies, I'll take them down to water."

"I'll join you. Perhaps even bring my sister, Buffalo Calf Road Woman, and her friends, yes?"

"Yes!" Wooden answered, his voice low, but the grin on his face nonetheless speaking with a great volume of joy.

Now reaching young manhood this spring, Wooden Leg sensed his heart swell again as he rode through the camp of Northern Cheyenne on his way to the herds grazing along the benchlands of the Tongue. The pretty girls looked at him from behind their dark eyelashes, and he again felt his loins stir with the wonder of life. How he marveled on the mysteries that brought a man and woman together. How would he know what to do when the time came? Would the time ever come? How soon? Would it be this summer?

Oh, how Wooden Leg wanted it to be this summer!

Two moons had waxed, then waned, since the soldiers had attacked the camp of Two Moon and Old Bear on the Powder. A long, cold, agonizing march north to find the Hunkpatila of Crazy Horse. Then three long days of talks before it was decided to press on with the Oglalla for Chalk Buttes. North and east of the Powder River, every day they plodded through mud that froze each night, marching to the camp of Sitting Bull, where his Hunkpapa fed and housed those who had been stripped of everything by the white man's army.

"These Shahiyena have been made very poor by the soldiers!" cried an elderly camp herald riding slowly among the lodges. "Everyone who can give a blanket, can give a robe—everyone with a lodge or meat to spare—come give your gifts to our guests!"

The Hunkpapa were wealthy in all that the wandering tribes would ever need. For generations they had avoided the white man, seeking to stay as far away from the soldiers as they could. But now, sadly, the Hunkpapa people believed they were being forced toward a great confrontation with the *wasichu.* He was building his railroad, pointing it like a lance at their last, great hunting ground. He was attempting to buy back the sacred Paha Sapa.* His soldiers allowed the white miners to invade the land the grandfather's government had granted them at the end of Red Cloud's war.

With all this, was it not understandable that the young men should want to ride out to find the soldiers, instead of waiting? Waiting?

But for the time being, the Shahiyena and Hunkpatila of Crazy Horse would wander with the Hunkpapa of Sitting Bull, taking pains to stay out of the path of the white man and his soldiers as they crisscrossed the Lakota hunting ground. For the time being, the Hunkpapa would share all that they had with those who had lost everything to the soldiers on the Powder River.

A young girl of perhaps ten winters had dragged a heavy buffalo robe through the village and dropped it at Wooden Leg's feet. Such a sour ball of fierce pride had clogged his throat that the young warrior had been unable to do more than nod his head in expressing his thanks. Yet there in his heart, Wooden Leg vowed on his life that he would give the gift of his body to protect his people in the coming fight with the soldiers.

Everyone knew the big fight was coming.

A few suns later Wooden Leg rode with a small hunting party that discovered a lone white man dressed in shabby clothing that appeared to have belonged to a Lakota. He had looked hungry and in need of a good meal. When asked what he was doing dressed in Lakota leggings and war shirt, the white man said he had belonged to a band of soldiers but had decided he did not want to fight Indians. He had run away from the soldiers and found the body of a dead warrior. Not wanting to be discovered in Indian country wearing a soldier's uniform, the man explained, he had stolen the leggings and shirt from the body.

Still, he had kept his soldier pistol and cartridge belt. It

* The Black Hills

was that pistol one of Wooden Leg's companions coveted. But the others disagreed, saying that they shouldn't kill the white man, and were turning to ride away when the lone Shahiyena shot the white man. In going over the body, they found a leather parcel lashed to the dead man's belt. In it they discovered some charred chunks of horse meat that had been cooked over an open fire.

Wooden Leg felt sorry for the white man who had wanted to be an Indian. Hungry and on foot alone in a strange land. Forced to eat stringy horse meat. It would have been one thing to kill one of the soldiers who had driven the Shahiyena from their village on Powder River, putting women and children and old ones afoot in the middle of winter. But it was an entirely different matter to kill a solitary, starving white man who so wanted to be friends with that band of young warriors.

From that campsite the three lodge circles had moved slowly north to headwaters of Sheep Creek, where the Sans Arc joined them about the time the new grass began to poke its head above the prairie. Within seven more suns the slopes of the hills had turned as green as most could remember them ever having been. Here a number of Santees and more Cheyenne from the agencies wandered in to join the great encampment at the mouth of Mizpah Creek on the Powder River. West to the bottomlands, where Pumpkin Creek dumped itself into the Tongue River, the Shahiyena led the camp circles, followed by the Hunkpatila of Crazy Horse. Behind them camped the Miniconjou. Bringing up the rear was the Hunkpapa camp of Sitting Bull. The combined tribal councils knew they would have to move their camps frequently as their numbers grew: sufficient grazing would have to be found for the immense pony herds; game would be driven quickly from the countryside by so large a village; the bands needed not only to follow the buffalo herds, but as well they sought the nomadic herds of antelope for meat and soft hides.

In the early days of this Moon of First Eggs far-ranging scouts had first spotted a soldier column marching out of the west along the Elk River. For three days the wolves kept an eye on the soldiers plodding east. Then some half a hundred warriors made their first raid on the white men, discovering that it was the troops of the Limping Soldier.*

Unhurried and unpursued by the army, the great village moved its encampment up the Tongue River three days later. It was during this time that the Blackfeet Lakota joined the main procession. They camped closest to Sitting Bull's circle, as did the Santee, or Waist, Lakota, who had few ponies—only big dogs to help them pull their few belongings. As the sun rose and fell in succession, a few Assiniboine lodges, and a handful of Burnt Thigh lodges, all came in to join the summer's hunt. Each night the great village grew more festive in its continuing celebration of life, of the hunt, of living the old ways.

In leading the entire march, the Shahiyena kept scouts out in the van, the Oglalla and Miniconjou maintaining scouts on the flanks, while the Hunkpapa saw to it there were scouts watching their backtrail. At their camp at the mouth of Ash Creek after three more sunrises, another large band of Shahiyena under chief Lame White Man arrived. One more move took the great gathering still farther up the Tongue. It was from that camp that Wooden Leg had joined the others in a second and even more daring raid on the Limping Soldier's troops.†

And just today the whole valley buzzed with the news that their huge encampment had been spotted by a scouting party sent out from the soldiers who were being supplied by the smoking houses that walked on the waters of the Elk River to the north. Most of the young men from the gathered bands wanted to set out immediately, to again strike the soldier column—this time in great numbers. Wooden Leg, like most of the others in whose veins flowed blood hot for making war on the enemy, was sorely disappointed when the old men and chiefs decided it best for the great encampment to avoid the white men.

"Raiding the soldiers to steal their American horses, making war on the soldier camp—all of this only wastes the energy of our warriors," the old ones decided.

Another added, "Our young men must put their energy

---

* Colonel John Gibbon, 3 May 1876

† Colonel John Gibbon, 13 May 1876

into hunting for meat and the hides we need for shelter and clothing."

"For now we will avoid the soldiers," concluded another.

So it was that the people continued to celebrate and sing, to dance and feast on the bounty of the hunt provided by the Everywhere Spirit of the Shahiyena, the Great Mystery of the Lakota bands.

For this young warrior who had daringly rescued nearly half of the village herd during the heat of battle on the Powder River, for this young Shahiyena who had been blooded in that fight with the soldiers in the brutal cold of the Sore-Eye Moon . . . the time to make war would come again. The fight of every warrior's dreams would be at hand. Patience, the old ones counseled. That fight is promised you: the young warriors who protect our nations.

But for now they would wait.

The young men could only clean their guns, sharpen their knives, fletch more arrows, and watch their war ponies grow strong and sleek on the new grass.

One day soon the fight would come.

"**D**amn their savage souls!" George Crook roared as he stomped into the small quarters given over to him at Camp Robinson at the Red Cloud Agency.

John Bourke quickly slammed the rough-hewn door shut on its wrought-iron hinges and threw the bolt into its hasp. He watched the general seethe, pacing the length of the tiny room in three strides. "We can still count on the Shoshone and Crow tribes, General. Don't forget them."

Hammering a fist into his open palm, Crook replied, "I bloody well can't forget them now, John! I've got to wire Fort Ellis up in Montana Territory—asking them to enlist some Crow auxiliaries for us. See that the commander over at Camp Brown is sent my wire as well: get him to sign on a hundred or more of the Shoshone. Those warriors are my last hope. They're our salvation now that these goddamned Sioux refuse to provide me any scouts. In the morning I'll telegraph ahead to have those steadfast allies sent down to meet me on the road north. By God, I vow to fight Indians with Indians—however I can!"

Late the day before, Crook's party had arrived at the agency, accompanied by Frank Grouard and Louie Reshaw. That evening they had conferred with Captain William H. Jordan of the Ninth Infantry, commander of Camp Robinson, setting plans to meet with some of the minor chiefs in the morning despite what the agency's assistant clerk had already done to dissuade the tribal leaders from having anything to do with the visiting soldiers. After breakfast Crook did have an audience with some of the Sioux subchiefs in preparation for that evening's major council with Red Cloud and Agent James S. Hastings, along with some of the other headmen from the various bands.

During that first informal meeting, Sitting Bull of the South and Rocky Bear agreed that even if no other chief in the tribe assisted Three Stars, they would still gather as many young warriors as they could to send along on the army's campaign to drive the hostile Sioux back to the agencies. An elated Crook and Bourke had whiled away the rest of the afternoon, initially assured of success.

But by the time the formal evening conference began, it soon became clear that the local agent had worked some magic on his chiefs: Blue Horse, Little Wound, American Horse, Three Bears, and Old Man Afraid of His Horses.

With the stoic Hastings present for this major council, and while Grouard translated, Crook had proposed to hire as many of the old chief's young warriors as wanted to go along.

"I will pay your scouts a good wage, feed them, and supply them with the weapons they will need when we hunt down the winter roamers," Crook had explained.

Red Cloud and the other chiefs listened, each man of them clothed in what had become known as "agency dress": loose wool trousers of dark-blue cloth, likely some surplus from the Civil War, moccasins covered with beads, and around every shoulder a dark-blue blanket transversed by a wide band of rosetted quillwork from which hung scalp locks or tinkling tin cones fashioned at the ends of narrow thongs. Shells from the distant ocean and large African beads hung from their necks, brass rings hung from their ears or coiled about their wrists.

In the end Bourke watched the lines of worry score

more and more deeply into their grave copper faces as Three Stars Crook attempted to sell the chiefs on his plan of using reservation Sioux to hunt down their hostile brethren.

It wasn't long before Bourke had finally realized this was nothing more than a futile trip and wasted breath. Red Cloud had been brief, his terse reply translated to Crook.

"The chiefs won't ask none of their warriors to go with you, General," Grouard finally admitted to Crook and his officers. "They say they ain't fighting no more. Not fighting against soldiers. And sure as hell ain't fighting against Lakota . . . the Sioux."

Crook's mouth had gone thin and pale before he asked evenly of Grouard, "They say why they won't join us in this fight?"

The dark-skinned half-breed's eyes had flicked to old Red Cloud, then back to Crook before he answered, "They say they won't be party to the white man's army coming in here to cheat the Sioux again."

"Cheat the Sioux?" Crook demanded, a little too loudly.

"They won't help you go out to steal the Black Hills."

The general had glared at the agent, who sat nearer the Indian side of the cramped office awash in saffron lamplight that evening.

"This your doing, Hastings?" Crook snapped.

Bourke had to admit he even found himself loathing the agent, what with that smug look of victory smeared on his face.

"General Crook, you must understand I'm less than enthusiastic about anything you might suggest for my wards."

"Why is that, Mr. Hastings?"

He cleared his throat, smoothing his palms down the length of his thighs before he spoke. "Your official report of action on the Powder River enumerated quite a list of goods confiscated from the enemy's lodges."

"Most of it ammunition my soldiers destroyed."

"In your official report, which made its way not only across all the circles in Washington City, but into the press as well—you stated that ammunition came from my Red Cloud Agency."

"It was so marked, clearly," Bourke broke in, feeling the heat of anger burn his neck. "I saw much of it for myself. Bullets and powder that killed my fellow soldiers."

Hastings wasted no time in looking at the lieutenant. Instead he kept his eyes on Crook. "I told you that you could meet with these chiefs when you asked for permission."

"But you've gone on record with them advising Red Cloud and the rest that they shouldn't accompany the expedition?" Bourke asked.

"Exactly."

All the while, Grouard had been leaning to the side, his head near Red Cloud as he busily translated the heated words between the soldiers and the agent. At that moment Red Cloud held his eagle-wing fan out, a signal that brought silence from the white men.

Standing, the chief had stated, "Three Stars will understand that the Lakota—and especially the Hunkpatila Lakota who are known as the Crazy Horse people—have many warriors. Sitting Bull's Hunkpapa have many, many more. There are many guns, many ponies in those camps you are seeking. Each warrior is brave and ready to fight for their hunting ground, for the country given them in treaty, to fight for their families."

Taking a step closer to Crook, Red Cloud continued, "Those warriors you seek are not afraid of Three Stars, not afraid of all the soldiers you can take against them. On the Powder, the Tongue, the Rosebud, and the Greasy Grass—every lodge will send its warriors against your soldiers. Every lodge cries out to you and the rest of the Great Father's dogs: 'Let the soldiers come!' "

Now back in their cramped quarters following that disastrous council with the chiefs, Bourke wagged his head. "I think I'm more angry with Hastings, General."

Crook nodded. "As am I."

"I can almost understand Red Cloud's position."

"Yes. It's not the old chief I really blame," Crook growled.

"But—what fails me is why Hastings won't support his

government on this. Why he won't bring his influence to bear and get us some scouts for the job now at hand."

"The real shame of it isn't that now I have to enlist the Bannocks and Shoshone, and some of the Crow to make this campaign work. The pity is that for every Sioux I could hire to fight *alongside* my soldiers—it would have meant one less Sioux fighting *against* my soldiers."

"With you in charge of the fighting this time out, General," Bourke cheered, "we can still whip whatever the hostiles can put in the field against us."

Crook turned away, toward the tiny desk near the small Sibley stove squatting in the corner of the smoky room. "Perhaps it is all for the best in the long run, John," sighed the general as he sank to a chair with a creak. "I'm beginning to think these Lakota of Red Cloud and Spotted Tail couldn't hold up anyway."

"Hold up, General?"

Crook shook his head emphatically, staring at a spot on the floor. "I don't think they have the fiber, the grit, the Apaches do. Now, those Apache—there was a worthy enemy, John."

"Begging the general's pardon," Bourke replied, "but the enemy I met face-to-face on the Powder River was every bit as worthy a foe as those Apache we chased through the mountains down in Arizona."

Crook smiled faintly, then it was gone like a clap of summer thunder. "Perhaps these Sioux are a worthy foe, John. But—by God—they have yet to prove it to me."

Chapter 5

Late May
1876

"*Hey, you, there—fella! C'mon over here an' gimme a* hand!"

She turned slowly, squaring her shoulders as she had learned to do over the years of traveling in the company of roughened, trail-worn men.

"Me?" she asked, her voice growling octaves lower than normal.

"Yeah, you. You got anything against work, fella?" the tall, homely teamster called out.

Another one appeared, about as tall, but much more stout. Now he, she decided, he was almost handsome enough for her.

"That's right," the newcomer said, heaving a pile of harness onto the ground before him. "In this outfit we all work together, or you don't go north with Crook. Pull your weight, or clear out."

"No man's ever had to pull my weight for me," she told them both as she strode their way, eating ground in long strides that made the mule ears on her tall boots slap their stovepipe tops. "And from the looks of things here, you boys need some help with that goddamned double-tree."

"That's more like it," the skinny one said, smiling to reveal two missing teeth.

She decided it gave him a look that reminded her of the idiot she had seen years before at one of the tent shows back in northern Missouri when she was a young girl. The way that poor idiot-man's eyes had stared out at the all the others staring in at him with wonder and pity and awe and downright disgust. She even recalled that silly, drooling look to the idiot's mouth.

"You'll do well to throw in with the rest every chance you can," the bigger of the two teamsters grunted as he hefted up the tree, waiting for the others to back the teams into harness. "That way, they'll accept you as one of the boys."

"Thankee," she replied in that practiced grumble of hers. "I'll remember that. Ain't got nothing against being one of the boys."

Just like I'd have nothing against bedding down with a few of these boys from time to time, she thought—if I could drop my britches and have me some fun without getting caught for being a gal.

Martha Jane Cannary was a stout thing, born to run wild with her two younger brothers and their male friends. Just weeks ago on the first of May, she had passed her twenty-fourth birthday, an occasion for real celebration. In the company of males hurrying south from Deadwood after hearing that Crook was putting together a wagon train bound for the Injun country, Martha Jane had celebrated all the way in due and practiced form. In the back of a wagon she proceeded to paint her tonsils with a larruping good dose of bluegill and got gloriously drunk, wrassling with the best of the lot, then threw up and passed out.

Coming to with her head banging against the sidewall of a springless wagon on that rutted road heading south to the horizon where lay Laramie, and beyond that the end of the rainbow—Fort Fetterman itself—Janey's head hurt with that heavy sogginess so different from the light airiness she usually felt when well into the cups. She was dead broke too. The last sutler back at Deadwood had taken what he felt he was due for the damages she had caused in the ruckus raised at his trading post, then ordered the rest of the drunk's companions to promptly pack the shrill troublemaker right on out of there.

There was a time or two out here in recent years when she was almost to the point where she felt like owning up to being a woman with some man she met one place or t'other. As much as she tried to hide it, bury it, swallow it up with huge draughts of raw and raunchy living—Martha Jane still sensed that she would be forever troubled by that generous, giving, kindly hearted and womanly soul deep within her. Nonetheless, she kept her secret to herself for the most part, and carried on in this wild land every bit like those men most suited for it. Martha Jane Cannary had always been a wild-eyed, auburn-haired, fiery-tempered thing. Right from jump and scat.

The first thirteen years of her life Martha Jane had spent growing up in the hardwood hills outside Princeton, Missouri. She had loved adventure in the out-of-doors, learning to ride and handle stock at an early age. It was a talent that would hold her in good stead for the rest of her life. And something that had taught her much about the behavior expected of horsemen as well.

With their squeaky wagon, a two-horse team, three milk cows, and a brace of yellow Missouri hounds, in eighteen and sixty-five the Cannary family had joined the many hundreds of gold-seekers pressing west along the great Platte River Road, pushing over South Pass, then turning north to Virginia City by a route that skirted the worst of Indian country. Slow as he might have been, Bob Cannary was quick enough to realize he wasn't going to keep his wife Charlotte anchored to the land for the rest of her life. A woman of her nature desperately needed something more: fancy clothes and liquor, as well as music and dancing and horse races, and laughter above all. The finer things of a life he just might be able to provide if he staked himself out a good claim among the gold diggings in the Rocky Mountains.

Right from the start Martha Jane had not been one to join the other teenaged girls who each long day lagged behind with their mamas near the wagons along their route west. Instead, Martha Jane took her gun and joined her father and the rest of the men of the party in hunting to fill supper kettles. At every town and fort, post and way stop along their journey, the young girl heard the talk come from the lips of those painted women who were so outnumbered on the frontier—talk that confirmed the truth in the old saw that at each trailhead, every end-of-line camp where men laid rails, every mining claim and soldier outpost, a woman could make her fortune simply for having a woman's body.

Strange talk to Martha Jane's way of thinking. For her it was still far more fun being a boy, what with the travails of lowering wagons by rope over sharp ledges, crossing streams, and always being wary of bogs and quicksands that soon gave the girl an education in handling four- and six-hitched teams. Thirty-foot bullwhips cracking above the backs of snorting oxen and heaving horses, husky young men sweating beside their animals and turning the air blue with the profane glory of their profession.

Lord, but it was this raw life of the male on the frontier that still appealed to the girl! Barely in her teens by the time the emigrant party reached the diggings at Alder Gulch, young Martha Jane Cannary was already considered an astounding shot and a fearless rider, two remarkable feats for a woman of any age on the frontier.

What a grand place that bedlam of gold country had been! Row upon row of high mountain peaks had spilled twenty-some-thousand miners into a narrow river valley where practically every foot of the narrow meadows was covered by tent canvas or board shanty, where tarred torches smoked and yellow lanterns swung on the winds in front of precarious, hill-perched saloons, where dance halls and gambling houses both blared the same sour, off-key music of drunken laughter and too-loud talk, the shrieks of pain or pleasure or both at the same damned time. Where fistfights settled precious little in the mucky, bloody streets. Where long, wide blades flashed when two men laid claim to the same sluice, the same whore, or ill-happed to sing the battle song for the wrong side from that Civil War still raw in every man's heart. Alder Gulch—where guns were drawn quickly and men died cheap.

Alone now, Martha Jane heaved against the draft horse and got it and the other three moving away from the Fort Fetterman loading dock. Lord, but there was enough work for every man putting an army into the field. Then she laughed right out loud. Enough work for every man? There was even enough work for her!

With a loud and unmistakable squish, the far lead horse shat and dropped its fragrant apples onto the rain-damped ground where the pile steamed until flattened under the hooves of the animal coming along behind it. The earthy odor struck Martha's nostrils as something familiar and good, even wholesome, not anything like the smells she remembered emanating from those mining camps. Stale whiskey breath and rotting teeth, tobacco stains on shirts not washed since the last rain, rotting sluice timbers and fresh-turned earth dug for new privy holes, rank meat and bones left for the wolves and coyotes that would slink down from the hills once the shadows grew long enough of every evening. The stench of punk sticks kept lit in every doorway, the sweetish fragrance of opium pipes the Chinese laborers preferred to the puke-bellied whiskey, the thick and oily perfumes the whores used hopelessly to cover up the forwardness of their sweat-slickened bodies.

She had watched her mother finally all but abandon her family, going off to pursue what a middle-aged woman could of that good life Alder Gulch offered. But right from the start Charlotte Cannary was unable to compete with the younger, firm-breasted, flat-bellied working girls. Besides that, Charlotte was simply too hot-tempered and quick-tongued to make her fortune flat on her back. Her dreams ended one night after Martha Jane had gone back to her father's shanty to care for the younger ones. All there was the next morning were whispers of the argument, the rising voices, the threats and oaths over this man or that old insult, and finally the gunfire exchanged between the two whores.

Martha Jane had helped her pa wrap his unfaithful wife in a greasy blanket, helped dig the hole and bury her mama on the slope of a nearby hill near the end of that cruel winter of 1866. Come spring, Bob took his family away from Blackfoot, Montana Territory, and moved south to Salt Lake City. But a short year later he too died, leaving his three teenaged children to fend for themselves in the land of the Mormons.

With nary a shred of reluctance that following spring,

Martha shuffled off for Wyoming Territory to find work for the army at Fort Bridger and Fort Steele in 1868. After a season hauling supplies over South Pass from Cheyenne City, she found employment with the construction gangs of the Union Pacific working out of Piedmont. And ran smack into Allegheny Dick—the frontier's most noted card shark besides being the most handsomest man-type of creature that ever walked the earth. Without complaint, Janey allowed the pasteboard shuffler to take her heart in ransom—but suffered a cruel dash of love's bitter gall when one gray morning after many weeks of using her soft, scented, moistened woman's equipment to the best of her ability to trap and hold a man, she awoke to find Allegheny Dick gone. And gone for good.

A woman scorned, Martha Jane once more donned teamster's clothing, a masquerade that allowed her to move about in the rough company of these men on the edge of this frontier. Besides, she told herself: the more layers of clothes, the better—all the better to hide her wounded, mourning heart.

Time is said to heal all things, she had heard. By the time another winter had come and gone, Janey knew some scar tissue lay weathering on the surface of her heart. A heart destined to be broken once more with the advent of spring, the warming of the prairie, and the blooming of wildflowers that carpeted the high prairie.

Throwing caution to the wind, Martha Jane once more left her masquerade long enough to don hoop dresses, brush her hair, and rouge her cheeks—all so she could give herself fully to a handsome and lonely soldier, a Lieutenant Somers—and promptly got herself with child.

To tell her lover of the coming event would have been a joy—only to find a few days later the gay blade of an officer was off to a new duty station, having requested the change of scenery himself. Only in his leaving did he finally fess up to the fact that he was already very much married.

Once more mending her broken heart and with her newborn babe turned over to an upright family, Martha Jane again donned men's clothing and plunged back into the world of males on the rough frontier. Not a strange thing to do, to remember it now as she unloaded freight for Crook's army. Not strange at all, for she was only carrying on what she had learned at no less than her own mother's knee—this lunging, gasping chase after life's rawest excesses.

Her pa, Bob Cannary, a young and innocent farm boy on a visit to Cincinnati, had become entranced with a young woman's beauty and forwardness when he visited a "bawdy house" for the first, and last, time in his life. That very day he proposed to Charlotte, making the pretty one his wife just so that he could take her back to the farm with hopes of reforming the girl who had come north to escape a dismal existence in Kentucky. From there the couple moved across the Mississippi to Iowa and started raising crops and milk cows and kids.

Charlotte Cannary's eldest child, Martha Jane, whelped on Missouri Methodist lawn socials, was not about to make herself another "good woman" in a long, long line of pioneer women who adhered to the virtue found in wearing themselves out with bone-wearying housework, long-suffering the chills, fevers, and tick-sicks of the frontier, the interminable childbearing and toddler-raising that destroyed a woman's youth and made her a stooped and wrinkled hag in a handful of years after her twentieth birthday.

While her pa was best known as a listless man who likely wouldn't amount to much of anything, Martha Jane had learned much more the ways of life from her own mother in those years on the family farm at the Collins Church settlement. Mother Cannary was a copper-haired, bright-eyed woman who smoked, drank, flirted brazenly, and publicly cursed when it damned well suited her. Charlotte's bold ways suited her daughter just fine. Especially when Martha Jane was but a girl of eight or nine dashing about on dappled ponies, prancing like a gray squirrel through the virgin hardwood forests, chewing leaf tobacco and swearing with the best her male playmates could claim to know. Those had been days when no parent restrained the young, gangly girl from raiding the sugar bin or plunging naked into the swimming hole when the mood struck her. Very fitting indeed that Charlotte's only daughter came to be known as the county's wildcat.

What fitting training that had been, she so often thought in the years since Charlotte's sudden death in Montana Territory: to be the daughter of a woman who was not about to raise her daughter like every other girl. Given free rein to hunt and ride, free to acquaint yourself with other hill folk in how to swaller down an occasional hooker of raw lightning without so much as a shudder quaking through your skinny frame. Mother Charlotte, God only knew, had come home drunk enough nights to Bob's disapproving glare and her children's muffled laughter as she let go with a long string of colorful, harum-scarum bawdy talk, interspersed with mountain stomps that shook the timbers of the cabin floor.

"Grab it up, fella!" Martha Jane growled to the man working beside her at the tailgate of the freight wagon.

He squinted, sizing her, then took hold of the long wooden case of Springfield carbines. Together they heaved it out of the wagon, onto the loading dock, and wheeled in the mud and horse dung to grab the next.

It had been in the west that Martha Jane had found her true and ideal man: the showy but taciturn, curly-maned frontiersman who could perform the greatest feats of riding and marksmanship, spout lore of animals and Injuns alike, knew the passes and rivers and mountain peaks, the sort of man who lived life without apology, gulping whiskey and women down in the same breath.

While mother Charlotte had given birth to her daughter, and while the Missouri forests and the five-month trip west to the Rocky Mountains had whelped Martha Jane Cannary, it was without a doubt the hellish, roaring camps lining Alder Gulch that had made her Calamity Jane.

"Better you watch out for your hide, Grabber."

Frank Grouard only rolled his eyes to the side to see who had come up behind his shoulder with the whispered warning. It was Baptiste Pourier. Better known out here in this country as Big Bat.

The bodies and shadows swirled past Grouard and the music throbbed that chill evening at the reservation. Red Cloud and American Horse had called for a dance to be held. The fires were leaping toward the sky, there was singing and courting and occasionally a young buck would leap out front and count his coups—vowing to count even more on the white soldiers this summer.

"You don't think I should dance, Bat?"

"Dance if it suits you, Grabber. But if you do, trust that I'll watch your backside for you."

"Reshaw ain't stupid enough to try anything here."

The half-breed Pourier wagged his head, still whispering, his eyes watchful as the Sioux celebrants throbbed and spun and cavorted past. "It ain't just Louie. He's got a lot of family here. Likely they'll make quick work of you."

Grouard snorted. "No, they won't."

"How you so goddamned sure," Bat demanded.

" 'Cause I got you to watch while I find me a squaw to dance with."

Frank heard Pourier chuckling as he pushed into the whirling maze of dancers, ablaze and resplendent in beads and blankets, in feathers and all their finery for this dance called by the tribal chiefs to take the minds of all off the lure and beckoning from the leaders in the north country. So these agency Indians would not dwell on the seductive siren call of Sitting Bull and Crazy Horse, offering the sweet appeal of the free, roaming life on the high prairie.

Earlier that evening Red Cloud and his headmen had left Agent Hastings's office in a huff, and an angry Crook and his soldiers stomped off into the darkness, leaving Frank and Bat alone with the agent and that smirk of Hastings's.

"I hear the drums," Pourier had suggested.

"Suppose we ought to see what's going on," Frank had replied, knowing that this was Louie Reshaw's ground.

After Reynolds's attack on the Powder River village failed and Crook returned his column to Fort Fetterman, the general disbanded his cadre of scouts, save for the three who would await the outfitting of the spring campaign. Grouard was to stay close, assigned to Fort Fetterman. Pourier was dispatched to cool his heels down at Fort Laramie. And Crook sent Reshaw as far away as he could from Frank Grouard—all the way down here to Red Cloud Agency to wait out the coming of spring.

But here they were, thrust together again. Bad blood

and all, tempers smoldering after the disastrous winter march into the Powder River county.

When Crook headed out from Omaha, he telegraphed ahead to have Grouard meet him in Cheyenne after coming through Laramie to pick up Pourier. The pair would accompany the general on his questionable mission to enlist Sioux scouts and auxiliaries.

"They gonna try to get close enough to me to use a knife?" Frank whispered as he slid back beside Pourier, winded and sweating from the exuberant dance.

Bat shook his head. "No. Plan is to shoot you when you leave here."

He smiled, his dark eyes flashing. "Then I got time. I'm going to dance some more."

"Keep your eye on me, Grabber. I'll let you know, I see anything shaking loose."

He wasn't on the floor very long before he caught sight of Bat bobbing his head toward a group of four half-breeds hugged up against a near wall. As Frank turned back to the young woman to excuse himself from her, he found she had melted into the crowd. Just about the time a woman shrieked and a man grunted.

Grouard wheeled to find Big Bat had seized a man's arm, shoving it into the air, a pistol trembling at the end of it. With his fists Pourier hammered the half-breed back into the stunned crowd, then whirled on the other three. He caught one by the collar as Frank leapt upon the other two, riding them clear to the floor.

It was only seconds before Hastings was in the middle of things, along with Bob Strahorn, the newsman out of Denver. They were pulling the young half-breeds out from under the pummeling Pourier and Grouard were handing out.

By the time the government man ordered the two army scouts out of the agency buildings, the dance was all but broken up. Frank stooped to retrieve his hat, nodding toward the door where Strahorn stood grinning.

"Ready?" Grouard asked Pourier.

"Lead on," Bat replied.

Strahorn slapped Grouard on the shoulder as the

scouts came to the open doorway. Lamplight backdropped them, inky darkness lay ahead.

The newsman said, "You boys just won't leave fighting to the army, will y—"

A percussion cap flashed, streaking the blackness beyond the doorway with a spurt of flame inches from Frank's eyes. He was blinded for a moment by the flare, ducking backward against the two men at his shoulders. Someone shoved him roughly to the side as the air filled with oaths and running feet. There were two shots fired as Grouard's eyes finally adjusted to the darkness and he could again see. His pistols already filled his hands.

Strahorn crouched beside him there at the wall. Inside the room Hastings was cursing the army scouts for causing this trouble, for bringing their quarrel with Louie Reshaw to Red Cloud Agency. Out of the darkness loomed Pourier, his pistol hung at the end of his long arm, a wisp of smoke still curling from its muzzle into the cool night breeze.

"Party's over, Mr. Agent," Big Bat snarled.

Hastings came to the doorway, glaring. "You kill anyone, you son of a bitch?"

Pourier shrugged, looking at Grouard. "Don't know. Maybe not. They're lucky tonight, Mr. Agent. Me and Frank, we'll finish 'em next time."

Hastings's voice rose an octave. "You hit anyone?"

Pourier smiled. "Just said I didn't kill no one. Found something that looked and tasted like blood along the wall of that near building." He turned to Grouard. "Think I winged one of the bastards for you, Frank."

"That's good enough. We'll call it even for now."

Pourier asked, "You not hurt?"

"Only my pride. When I saw that cap flash, I ducked instead of drawing."

"Likely it saved your life," Pourier replied. "They might've gotten off a second shot at you."

"And had a good cap under the hammer that second time," Strahorn replied.

Frank looked up at the reporter from the Rocky Mountain *News* who had accompanied Reynolds's column to the enemy village on the Powder last March, a newsman who had even charged down on the enemy with Teddy Egan's K

Company of Second Cavalry. The young, handsome Strahorn was not altogether a city fella who didn't know the ways of hard men and firearms.

"Likely you're right, newspaperman," Frank said quietly, his eyes flashing like dark flints at the agent he detested, although he had known the government man less than a day.

"C'mon. Let's get some sleep, Frank," Pourier suggested. "Crook wants to be on the road back to Laramie by sunup."

"Yeah," Strahorn agreed. "The general's got himself a war he wants to fight."

"And got his enemy to catch," Grouard said, pulling his slouch hat down on his shoulder-length hair. "Like Crook, I know all about enemies."

Chapter 6

Late May 1876

"*By the stars—of course, I remember you!*" Thomas Moore declared as he held out his hand to the tall Irishman before him.

They shook. "Was hoping you would," Seamus replied to the man who had been in charge of George Crook's mule trains since the days of the first Apache campaigns down in Arizona.

"Hell yes, Donegan! You was all Cap'n Mills and Teddy Egan talked about for some time after we jined back up with you fellas couple days following your fight on the Powder."

Seamus had begun to feel a bit sheepish, standing there as some of the other packers wandered up, drawn to the conversation between the long-maned plainsman and their grizzled boss.

"If that don't beat all!"

Donegan turned at the exclamation, finding the gray head of Richard Closter shoving his way through the ring of packers.

"Uncle Dick!" Seamus called out, lapping his arms around the old mule skinner, clapping him on the back with the hand not clutching the Henry repeater the Irishman had carried ever since his first ride onto the plains of the far west.*

Then he held the old man out at arm's length, admiring the packer's face well-chiseled by wind and tracked with all the miles he had followed the cantankerous animals that were his life. Faint brown streaks tattooed his white beard, as well as darkening the blue blouse beneath it.

Seamus inquired, "How's Johnny Bourke?"

Closter's head bobbed and he smiled even bigger, one that seemed to fill the whole bottom half of his face. "The boy's just fine. Just fine! Maybe you don't remember, but Johnny's going to put me in that book he's writing. Why, if I ain't told you about it, c'mon now and I'll buy you a drink down to the Hog Ranch."

"Hog Ranch, eh?"

With a devilish glint, Closter winked. "I'll tell you all about it—and then we'll give the girls a tussle or two, just 'cause we're riding out for Injun country again."

With a chuckle Donegan patted the packer on the shoulder. "I know all about how Johnny's going to make you as famous as General Crook, Uncle Dick. Bourke told me on that last campaign. You did too. More'n once."

Closter nodded his head, scratching his cheek absently. "Maybeso I did. Lots of long nights at the fire. Cold son of a bitch, Seamus. That was a march to make its mark on a man."

"I figure I put on ten rings last winter myself, Dick."

"So," Closter said, "what you figure on doing this time out? Going to scout again with Grouard and the rest?"

Moore eased back up by the two, wagging his head. "Don't figger he will, Dick. General's made it plain he ain't hiring no more'n three for this march."

"That's right," Donegan agreed. "And I ain't one of 'em."

Closter squinted one eye into the sun, looking up at the tall Irishman. "I'll bet my next drunk that every one them three are half-breeds."

---

* THE PLAINSMEN Series, vol. 1, *Sioux Dawn*

"You're right," Moore answered, then turned to Donegan. "So why you come back to Fetterman when I hear you got a wife down to Laramie?"

"Need work."

Moore instantly beamed. "Work? Why I got all the work you can handle."

"Him?" Closter snapped sourly, rocking back on his heels and appraising the Irishman. "This soft-handed young sprout? Him—a mule skinner? Shit, Tom—that'll be the day!"

"With a recommendation like that from one of my oldest and best hands," Moore exclaimed, "you're hired, Donegan!"

"Whoa! Hold on," Seamus replied, not really sure he could believe it would be this easy finding work, pay, and a way to feed his family, if only for a few more months till the babe was born. At least until this goddamned war was over and he could take Samantha north to the diggings around Helena up there in Montana Territory. Samantha and . . . their son.

"What—you too good to work for a living, Irishman?" Closter growled, backing a step, plopping his two hands on his hips and giving Seamus a critical, appraising once-over. "Told you he was soft-handed, Tom. Likely the youngster's soft-headed too. These mules of ours going to prove smarter'n this mush-brained potato-sucker!"

"Got something against Irishmen, do you?" Moore asked.

"Present company excluded, Cap'n," Closter apologized with a slight bow.

Then Moore's face went serious. "You want the work, don't you, Seamus?"

Donegan grinned. "I *need* the work more than want it. Even damned grateful for it. It's just . . . I didn't figure I would get hired—"

"Wouldn't get hired?" Moore replied. "Why, we knew you was coming for more'n a week, Seamus."

"Knew? How'd you—"

"Crook wired up from Laramie. Got there just after you left to ride up here. Spoke with your wife, the way it sounded."

"Leastways," Closter broke in, "Crook found out you were headed to Fetterman hoping to find something in the way of work. The general wired up here to Moore—have Tom hire you on."

Seamus turned to the chief packer. "General wired you about me?"

Moore shook his head. "Crook didn't wire me. He wired Colonel Royall—told him to let me know you was coming, and that I was to hire you on, no matter what."

"Seems Crook wants you join us this march north," Closter agreed.

Donegan wagged his head, sorting out the dangling pieces of it. "Royall?" he asked, feeling a nagging pull of something from memory. "This colonel's name couldn't be William, is it?"

Moore shrugged. "I think it is."

Donegan declared matter of factly, "Can't be the same Major William B. Royall what was with the Fifth Cavalry back to Nebraska."

"That's him!" Dick Closter cheered. "One and the same, Seamus. Only he's a lieutenant colonel now."

"I'll be god-bloody-damned!"

"So you see, you was hired before you ever got here," Moore stated. "Crook wanted you along even though he wasn't hiring you to scout for him. And when he informed the colonel to make sure I hired this Seamus Donegan, Royall come to tell me he remembered an Irishman by the same name what scouted for him down when the Fifth Cavalry went in and crushed Tall Bull's Dog Soldiers at Summit Springs."*

"Royall told us all about you and Bill Cody his own self, scouting for him on that campaign," Closter added.

Seamus asked, "What you hear of Cody these days?"

"Only what Royall told me when he was remembering back to them days with Carr's regiment."

"Sixty-nine, it was," Seamus said.

"The colonel says Cody's got himself a good business now," Moore said.

---

* THE PLAINSMEN Series, vol. 4, *Black Sun*

"Safer'n being a scout in these goddamned Injun campaigns," Closter growled.

"What sort of business? I remember he used to work teamster for one of the plains outfits."

"Seamus! You mean to tell me you ain't heard of Buffalo Bill's Wild West Shows?" Moore asked, his eyes widening.

Donegan shrugged. "S'pose I haven't. Only thing I know was this Irishman rode with Bill Cody the first time he got called Buffalo Bill."

"Don't say?" Closter commented with no little admiration.

"So what's this Wild West Show of his?" Seamus asked.

"Riding, rope tricks, fancy shooting," Moore explained.

"Cody would be good at all that," Seamus agreed. "Knew he'd make something of himself one day."

"Royall heard Cody even stages how he led the Fifth into that Cheyenne village at Summit Springs and saved them women the savages held prisoner."

The smile drained from Donegan's face. "We only saved one of 'em, fellas. Tall Bull put a hatchet in the back of the other gal's head."

"But the story goes that Cody kill't Tall Bull at the end of that battle," Moore said.

"Cody did. Although Lute North and his brother been claiming otherwise ever since."

"But you got the other gal out with her life," Closter added.

"That's right," Donegan replied, suddenly prodded to think on a certain woman left behind at Laramie, brooding with a hope that she would never share the fate of Susanna Alderdice, who lay in an unmarked, trampled grave beneath the sands beside Summit Springs in Colorado Territory. Captured at the hands of savage warriors sweeping down on the Kansas settlements, long-suffering prisoner to unspeakable acts . . . just as Cheyenne and Sioux, Kiowa and Comanche women suffered at the hands of white men and soldiers. Where would it stop? And when?

"Goddamn these Injin wars," he muttered, turning

away to peer into the distance as he struggled to regain some composure.

"You taking the job, Seamus?" Closter asked, grabbing Donegan's arm.

He visibly shook the dark mantle of it from his shoulders, his long hair settling like a shawl over the collar of his canvas mackinaw. Then presented his hand to Moore. "Yeah. I'm taking the job. And thank you, Tom."

"You'd do well to be thanking Colonel Royall too, Seamus."

"I will. Believe me—I'll thank him when I can find him. Didn't know the Fifth Cavalry was going along on this march."

Moore's brow furrowed. "The Fifth ain't got a damned thing to do with this march."

"But . . . Royall?"

"He's been assigned to the Third for some time, and its for certain Royall's in charge of the Third now—what with Reynolds and Alexander Moore both under arrest and brought up on charges for pulling that boner up on the Powder."

"Where's your outfit, Seamus?" Closter asked.

"Yonder there by the quartermaster's stables," Donegan replied. "Where's camp?"

Moore and Closter looked at one another in amazement as most of the other packers in that circle laughed loudly.

Moore slapped a hand on Donegan's shoulder. "You mean you ain't an idea where me and my boys put a few hundred head of mules? Why, just give a listen."

Donegan cocked his head, grinned, and nodded. "I hear 'em now."

"Ah, the sweet sound of a mule brigade!" Closter cheered.

Donegan replied, "Noisy bastards—ain't they?"

"Welcome to working for once in your life, Seamus!" the old man said. "No more easy living as a scout for you, you soft-handed, mush-brained, potato-sucking mick Irishman!"

• • •

"The hostiles know we're coming, General," John Bourke said in George Crook's office at Fort Fetterman that third week of May.

"It doesn't make a bloody damn to me if they know now, or when I get this outfit finally on the march. I'll find them. By God, I'll find them, John."

"I can understand you feeling personally about this, sir."

Crook whirled, worry etched on his fair-skinned, sunburnt features. "Wouldn't you, Lieutenant? Knowing those Sioux bastards planned to assassinate you? Wouldn't that make it something personal?"

"But they didn't get the job done, and now you can return the favor—in a manner of speaking."

"They did kill that mail courier, John!"

"Yes, sir. A sad thing too."

"And likely committed that murder as they rode north to raid some other ranches and steal more cattle or a horse here and there."

"Or worse yet, they went on north after killing the courier, heading for the camps of Sitting Bull and Crazy Horse."

He watched as Crook returned to glaring at the tumble of maps skewed across the small table in this cramped office the general had turned into his war room. It was here that the Big Horn Expedition was being whipped into form.

They had pulled away from Hastings's Red Cloud Agency at first light, four A.M., on the morning of 16 May, riding north and west back toward Laramie through a valley where ran what the Sioux called the White Earth River. An impressive contingent of strength including Crook's own small escort of a dozen men, with newsman Robert Strahorn, as well as the general's three scouts for the coming campaign—Frank Grouard, Baptiste Pourier, and a sullen and chastised Louie Reshaw, who by and large kept to himself at the end of the column. But as events would soon prove, it was fortuitous that Crook's escort had been reinforced by a strong detail accompanying Paymaster Thaddeus H. Stanton, who had just completed his regular pay trip to the agency, as well as escort accompanying the inspector general for Crook's Department of the Platte, Major Marshall I. Ludington, who was that morning returning from his own review of troop strength among the far-flung outposts along the departmental border. To this force of sixty-five men was also added the strength of at least a dozen cattlemen who had a vested and personal interest in convincing Crook that he should clamp down hard on the Sioux, who had been making a steady practice of raiding their stock on ranches surrounding the lower Sioux agencies.

That well-armed force hadn't been on the trail long when Big Bat had come riding up from the tail of the long column that cool spring morning.

"General. Take a look there." Pourier had pointed southeast to the horizon as Crook twisted in the saddle.

"What you make of it?" asked the general, his eyes flicking quickly to Grouard.

Bourke made a note that Grouard was for the moment watching Reshaw, more intent on his fellow scout's reaction to the sighting than he was in studying the column of smoke in the distance.

"Signals. Telling someone we're coming," Pourier replied.

"You expect trouble?" Crook asked.

Pourier shrugged.

Crook turned to Grouard. "How about you, Frank? We have anything to worry about?"

The chief of scouts finally tore his eyes off Reshaw, their lids shading his contempt, anger, and undisguised suspicion of the other half-breed. "No, General. I figure we're too strong for them to try something."

"Then, let's press on," Crook said, resettling in the saddle.

"But," Grouard interrupted the general as he raised an arm to signal the resumption of their march, "those Lakota likely figured you was riding out of the agency with only the few soldiers we rode in with. Not all these men. Ain't that right, Reshaw?"

"What you mean by that, Grouard?" Reshaw snapped, his hand flying to the butt of the pistol in the gunbelt he had buckled on the outside of his coat.

"Hold it right there, Reshaw!" Crook's words hammered the sudden, stunned stillness of the spring morning. "What in the hell are you talking about, Grouard?"

"I figure Reshaw knows something about those Lakota making smoke-talk to someone up the trail. Maybe up around the headwaters of the White Earth. That the right place for a ambush, Louie?"

"You're crazy, you half-breed nigger!" Reshaw spat.

Grouard smiled that cold, mirthless smile of his. "Louie's your man at the agency, General. He oughtta know what's going on with them figuring to jump you."

"I ain't there no more," Reshaw growled.

"Likely you know what they're planning," Grouard said quietly, coldly. "Or you ain't as good a scout as the general figured you was."

"I'm good—even better'n—you'll ever be, nigger!"

"Hold on here," Crook snapped, wagging a hand. "So you don't think we ought to take another route north, Frank?"

Grouard finally shook his head. "No. They won't attack us."

"They want me that bad?" Crook inquired, some of it finally appearing to sink in.

"Maybe you—yes," Grouard answered. "On the other hand, maybe me."

"You?" Bourke asked. "Why they want to kill you? Just for leading us to Crazy Horse's village last March?"

Grouard shrugged. "Maybe not just for that. Maybe 'cause Louie's got friends and relations down there at Red Cloud. And Louie's got real bad blood for me."

"Reshaw, you stay back with Colonel Stanton's men for the rest of our ride to Laramie."

The half-breed nodded, reining his horse around and loping off without another word.

"Bat, you ride with Colonel Ludington's group now—right behind Stanton and Reshaw. I want to know immediately if Reshaw does anything the slightest bit suspicious."

"All right." Pourier pulled his own pony out of column and urged it back down the trail on Reshaw's heels.

"So, Frank. You feel better now?"

"I'll feel better we get back to Fetterman and go hunt for Crazy Horse again."

"You still have a score to settle with him, do you?" Bourke asked.

"Crazy Horse. Him and a warrior named He Dog."

Later on, just before noon, Grouard had suggested a rest near the springs at the head of White Earth Creek. There the men loosened the cinches on their saddles and spread out in the shade of what few trees there were, eating a lunch of hard-bread and jerky pulled from their haversacks after watering the stock. As the soldiers and civilians were preparing to remount, a solitary figure rumbled down the trail from Laramie toward them, coming out of the north.

"Charles Clark, General," the civilian introduced himself after stepping down from his small wagon.

"You've got the mail contract, I take it?" Crook inquired.

"I do. On my way to Red Cloud now," he replied, throwing a thumb back to indicate a pair of small canvas bags.

"Any mail for me in there?" Crook asked.

Clark smiled. "No, sir. Not that I know of. Figure you always get your news on the wire—don't you, General?"

Crook grinned too, holding out his hand to shake the civilian's. "Yes. And not a fragment of it has been good of late, Mr. Clark. Good luck to you."

"Good luck to you on your expedition north, General. Here's hoping your campaign can quiet things down and bring all the Injuns back to the reservation for once and for all."

After the civilian had slid into the seat of his wagon and snapped leather down on the backs of his two-horse hitch, Crook ordered his column into the saddle, resuming their march.

Upon reaching Fort Laramie, the general received a terse telegram from Division Headquarters in Chicago:

Dakota Column embarked from Lincoln on 16th. At last report winter roamers believed on Little Missouri or tributaries. Best

intelligence puts hostiles at 1500 lodges.
Urge you to put off as *soon as possible*.
Strike them hard.
Lieutenant General Philip H. Sheridan

As well, it wasn't until they had settled in again at Laramie that Crook received a wire from James Hastings informing him that Charles Clark had been late in arriving at the reservation, so the agent had sent out a party to search the road to Laramie. Halfway to the spring at the head of White Earth Creek they found the civilian's mutilated body, the charred remains of his overturned wagon, and the litter of mail caught in the stunted grass and sage, like flecks of icy snow left behind after a spring storm.

"The sons of bitches couldn't get me," Crook had growled at Bourke, wagging his head and stroking one of the two braids fashioned from his reddish beard. "So in their blood lust they had to kill someone."

"But now you'll have your chance to give them a bellyful of war, General."

Crook's steely eyes leveled on his aide-de-camp. "The Sioux will remember me after this campaign. By God, John —I swear those red bastards will remember me."

Chapter 7

21 May 1876

"*You figger these grass dummies of ours gonna fool them* Sioux out there?"

Frank Grouard studied the worry scoring the soldier's face. "This better work. Or my goose is cooked same as yours."

The half-breed scout gazed at the nine other soldiers gathered at the creekbank. Fifty yards away the roaring fire they had made spewed fireflies into the spring night with tiny explosions. There was questioning, even doubt, in the eyes of some of those troopers, downright fear in the eyes of most. They were putting their lives in his hands at that moment. What with a Lakota war party of unknown strength lurking somewhere out there in the darkness, likely crawling ever closer to their camp at that very moment, Crook's chief of scouts had had little choice but to disobey the general's orders. Nothing else to do but take a different route on this reconnaissance to the Powder River crossing of the Montana Road.

That very morning Crook had called him into his cluttered office at Fort Fetterman, where officers came and went on one mission or another, as well as the repeated visits of Tom Moore, the civilian put in charge of the general's mule train first made famous during the army's

Apache campaign down in Arizona Territory. When the army reassigned Crook to take over the Department of the Platte, the general brought his head packer north to Omaha with him. Last March both veterans of Cochise's war in the southwest had been initiated into the cruel brutality of winter on the northern Plains. After rejoining Reynolds on the Powder River, Crook had promised Frank Grouard that he was going to take his cavalry back to the hunting ground of the Sioux and Cheyenne to finish the job he had started.

And botched.

Now the warrior bands were gathering in strength and numbers heretofore unheard of on the plains. But that sort of thing made no matter to Crook, Frank understood.

"All that concerns me is that I get in my licks before Gibbon and Terry show up," Crook had told Grouard earlier that morning while dispatching the half-breed north to scout the Powder River Crossing. "After Reynolds botched his attack—I'm going to see that the Second and Third get this chance to wipe the stain from their reputations."

Crook ordered Frank to lead Sergeant John A. Carr, A Company, Second U.S. Cavalry, and a squad of nine handpicked men north along the route of the campaign's impending march.

"The Powder will be running high, won't it, Grouard?" Crook had asked.

"Yes. Just like the Platte out there," and he threw a thumb out the open door. "Fast and wild—what with the runoff, General."

"Find us the best crossing you can. For horse and mule. Remember I want to get these wagons over too. Drag them as far north as I can to establish a resupply base for my cavalry to work from."

"A good crossing. All right, I'll find you one."

"When can you be back?" Crook asked. "I want to get under way as soon as I can."

"You wanna push north behind me a day or so?"

Crook had shaken his head. "No, Frank. There's still much to do. When will I see you again?"

He calculated, staring at the moccasins on his feet. "A

week at the most—depending on how long it takes for us to find a good crossing."

"The twenty-eighth. Good. Then we can count on pushing north with this column on the twenty-ninth."

Loading their saddles, weapons, and other supplies into the ferry boat shortly before noon, Grouard and Carr's soldiers had stripped before swimming their horses and the two pack mules across the rain-swollen Platte. On the north bank they waited for the ferry to make its treacherous ride, straining and creaking both pulleys and cable to their limits as the high, raging waters shoved and battered the flat-bottomed craft lashed to the taut, humming cable overhead.

A half dozen miles north of the crossing, Frank had discovered they were being watched from the nearby hills. Likely scouts from the hostile villages were keeping a close eye on the army's preparations at Fetterman and would now dog Grouard's line of march to the Powder River country.

By the middle of the afternoon he had decided the bigger part of his assignment was getting this detail back to Fetterman alive. The farther north they pushed, the deeper into hostile territory they would plunge. Just past three o'clock, Grouard suggested an early camp some fifty yards past their crossing of a high-flowing creek.

"Why you want to call a halt so early?" Carr had asked as his horse stood shaking itself after the crossing.

Frank had shrugged. "Got water here. Good grass for the horses. Besides, Sergeant—we got plenty of cover for what we got to do after dark."

"What you got for us to do after dark, Grouard?"

"Make it look like we're all still plopped down in camp—while we slip out, one at a time."

The sergeant's eyes had narrowed, and he had motioned Grouard off to the side of the road so they could talk out of earshot of the rest of the detail. "We got trouble?"

"Big trouble."

Carr straightened. "All right. What you need us to do?"

"Get the horses unsaddled," Frank began. "After dark we'll hide saddles and blankets down there by the river in that timber. Back in the willows where it's hid real good. For now, you drag up as much deadfall as you can for a fire. *Big* fire, Sergeant. Then get the horses picketed in that patch of grass down by the bank."

"Out of sight?"

"Right."

As dark had slithered into the valley with crooked fingers of lengthening shadows, Grouard issued more orders.

"Sergeant, I want you alone to go down into the timber and take all our rations from the packs on those two mules. Divide it between every saddle."

"All of it?"

"Every bit of rations you can split up between every last man of us. We'll need it."

Carr shook his head. "Injuns out there ready to lift our hair, and you ain't leading us back to Fetterman?"

Grouard watched a few of the others amble up, likely drawn to the sound of their sergeant's anxious voice.

"No," he answered. "We aren't going back. General ordered us to find a crossing at the Platte."

"Just how in hell you think—"

"You do what I tell you to do with the rations and the rest of it—by the time these Lakota scouts find out we've pushed on, and they cross our trail, we'll be hours ahead of 'em."

Carr had taken a deep breath, then nodded as he looked around the firelit circle at his platoon. "All right. So we make a night ride of it north. Then what?"

"Why—we just do everything to keep hold on to our hair best we can, Sergeant."

With a big supper in their bellies and that glorious bonfire roaring in the middle of their camp, Grouard told the soldiers to prepare their beds with blankets and plenty of the new grass they could tear up down in the timber by the bank. With rocks and that grass they were to make their eleven blankets look as much as possible like soldiers sleeping near those leaping flames.

Then he himself went down to the good grass by the creek and cut the two pack mules loose so they could wander away as they grazed through the night. With a pair of extra army blouses, Carr had fashioned two dummies, which he sat on either side of the fire at the edge of the light by the time Grouard returned from the creek.

When twilight had seeped into the black of prairie night, Grouard had Carr's soldiers mill back and forth around the fire as if nothing were untoward. Then, one by one, the half-breed had the sergeant's men slip out of the firelight and into the thick willows and timber by the creekbank, where they saddled up and waited until Frank was the last to clear the camp.

Harshly, he whispered his orders, "Tell your men to walk their mounts into the stream, quiet as they can. Single file. Show 'em how to pinch off the horse's nostrils. Keep a hand on the nose until I tell you we're clear."

"What the hell for?" Carr had demanded in a harsh whisper.

"Them horses of yours gonna smell Injun ponies—maybe even the stink of the grease on that Injun hair. They'll let out a whicker or whinny . . . and our asses will fall out of the frying pan and into the fire, Sergeant. Now—do you understand what I've told you to do?"

"Understood."

He watched Carr slip back through the nine soldiers and whisper among them, showing the youngsters how to clamp off the hard cartilage bridge behind a horse's moist nostrils. When the sergeant returned and nodded, Frank led them off the bank and into the cold water. He turned right, moving slowly upstream, heading west. In the opposite direction they had been marching.

It would take that sort of thing, and a long night's circuitous march, to make it through the net the Lakota wolves had likely thrown up around that soldier camp the eleven were abandoning back there.

That, and one hell of a lot of luck to reach the Powder and back to Fetterman with their hair.

Oh, go to the stable,
All you who are able.
And give your poor horses
Some hay and some corn.

For if you don't do it,
The captain will know it.
And you'll catch the devil
As sure as you're born!

Seamus sang the words to "Stable Call" as the bugler blared the notes while the Irishman headed past the last of the quartermaster's corrals and began his descent into the valley of the North Platte, down from the bluff where Fort Fetterman was perched above the mouth of LaPrele Creek. As one of the frontier's larger army posts, Fetterman was home to three infantry companies and four troops of cavalry, along with more than a hundred civilian employees. But for the moment, down in the valley where Donegan gazed, there stood a forest of row upon row of white dog tents, endless crescents of wagons, a sizable herd of beef along with a thousand pack mules, in addition to more than a thousand cavalry mounts—all of it awaiting the beginning of General George Crook's "Big Horn and Yellowstone Expedition."

"Yes, indeed: we're going to push this column all the way to the Yellowstone River this time out," John Bourke had explained to him earlier that day.

"To join up with Gibbon and Terry, I hear," John Finerty had replied. He and fellow newsman, Bob Strahorn, had joined Seamus at the fort that morning after breakfast.

"That's right," Bourke said. "Gibbon's been ordered to hold the hostiles at the river. Terry's keeping them from running east. So we'll be beating them north ahead of us. We'll crush them between us at the Yellowstone—if not before."

"*If* Crook can get his hands on them before Gibbon and Terry come on the scene," Seamus commented.

"Don't you figure the general deserves to have the first crack at Crazy Horse?" Bourke inquired.

The Irishman nodded. "I believe the Second and Third Cavalry are owed first crack at the hostiles, Johnny—for what they endured last winter."

"Damn right, they are," Bob Strahorn echoed. "For what we all endured."

"There's some who aren't marching again, Johnny," Donegan said. "One face in particular I find missing."

"Teddy Egan?"

"No—you've told me his company is protecting the Black Hills Road," the Irishman explained. "I've been asking about for Ben Clark."

"Clark didn't stay on with the General," Bourke explained.

"He going to stay here at Fetterman, then?"

The lieutenant had an inexplicable look on his face as he flicked his eyes about that group and finally back to Donegan's. "Clark left the service of the army right after we come back from the Powder River, Seamus."

He shrugged a shoulder, saying, "Yeah. Everybody got mustered out until this summer campaign."

Bourke finally replied. "No. I mean he left for good. He was pretty upset about what Reynolds didn't do to protect his men, upset about what Reynolds did to that camp."

"Why? Ben Clark's been an army scout for years, John," Seamus said. "Why did he quit over the army burning that Crazy Horse village?"

"Because Clark says it wasn't Crazy Horse's village."

"Frank Grouard claims it was!" Strahorn said. "That half-breed says he saw some of Crazy Horse's ponies in the herd."

Bourke turned back to the Irishman. "Clark steadfastly says that was a Cheyenne village."

"Cheyenne?"

With a nod the lieutenant continued. "A bunch of Cheyenne heading south to go in to the reservations."

"Just like the goddamned government officials wanted 'em to in the first place!" Seamus growled. "And we jumped 'em on the way?"

"Whoa!" Bourke said. "There isn't a shred of proof that was a Cheyenne village, Seamus."

"There's something real wrong here." Donegan moaned. "Grouard is supposed to know the Sioux like no one else. But when it comes to Cheyenne, I'll trust Ben Clark all the way."

"He's a squaw man, isn't he?" Strahorn inquired.

"Yes," Seamus answered. "Do you know where he's gone off to, John?"

"Said to some folks that he was heading south to the Territories. Go back to his wife's family down there on the reservation."

"He'll miss out on all the fun we're going to have," John Finerty replied.

"Maybe he's the smartest one of us all—getting the hell out of here and going back to be with family," Seamus cautioned. "I'm reminded of what my dear mither taught me when I was learning the ways of God and man at her sainted knee back in County Kilkenny."

Finerty placed a hand over his heart and snatched his hat from his head in the bright May sunshine. "May God Himself always smile on that sainted green isle!"

"Another bleeming patlander, longing for the soil of Eire!" Seamus roared.

Finerty stuffed his hat on his head and dropped his arms over Bourke's and Strahorn's shoulders. "The four of us—Irishmen all! May we be the first to strike the blow against Crazy Horse and that demented medicine man, Sitting Bull!"

"As I was trying to tell you Irishmen," Donegan continued, "something I learned at my mither's knee long, long ago—"

With glee Finerty interrupted, "When he was such a wee one!"

"—and what I learned from her is something a man should pay heed to as he goes marching off to make war on the Sioux and Cheyenne in their own bloody hunting ground."

"Where else would you have us find the bloody savages, Seamus?" Finerty inquired. "Chicago, by God?"

Donegan ignored the chuckles of Strahorn and Bourke. "Mark my words, boys. Mark my mither's own words if not on my account: 'What you have sown on the wind—so will you reap on the whirlwind.' "

On 22 May three companies of the Ninth Infantry had marched north from Fort Laramie, bound for Fetterman, which was situated on the North Platte not far from the point where the Bozeman Road headed north to Montana

Territory and the Mormon Trail pushed on west toward Fort Caspar and South Pass. The next day the main horse column of the Third Cavalry out of Fort D. A. Russell near Cheyenne City had crossed the swollen Platte at Fort Laramie using the new iron bridge after enduring a cold soaking in crossing the Chugwater. By crossing downriver the horse soldiers could go into camp opposite the fort without having to make another crossing of the raging Platte upon reaching Fetterman two days later.

"Just look at how they're beating a path to the Hog Ranch down there!" Strahorn marveled.

The four of them stopped, gazing down the slope at all the throbbing activity swirling around Kid Slaymaker's saloon and whorehouse.

"Here," Bourke began, pulling a folded paper from his pocket. "I wrote this yesterday evening about the place: 'Each of these establishments was equipped with a rum mill of the worst kind and each contained from three to half a dozen Cyprian virgins whose lamps were always burning brightly in expectancy of the coming bridegroom and who lured to destruction the soldiers of the garrison. In all my experience I have never seen a lower, more beastly set of people of both sexes.' "

"Why, Johnny!" Finerty replied. "I'm one of the virgins' best customers!"

"No, you're not!" Strahorn growled, slugging Finerty on the shoulder. "*I* am!"

Crook's expedition was quickly taking shape in the valley below the fort. Besides the three companies of the Ninth, two companies of the Fourth Infantry had been ordered up, all five under the command of Crook's West Point classmate, Major Alexander Chambers of the Fourth, in whose hands was placed the responsibility for protecting the supply depot Crook was planning on establishing in hostile territory.

Without question the spearhead of the expedition would be fifteen companies of cavalry under the command of Lieutenant Colonel William B. Royall of the Third. Under him would operate Colonel Andrew W. Evans, commanding ten companies of the Third Cavalry, which had marched east to Medicine Bow Station via the Union Pacific Railroad, north from there on muddy and impassable roads to reach Fetterman, as well as Captain Henry E. Noyes, commanding five companies of the Second Cavalry. Less than a month before Noyes had undergone court-martial at Fort D. A. Russell, charged with neglect of duty before the enemy during the battle of Powder River. In that trial, during which the captain did not deny that he had allowed his men to unsaddle their horses and boil coffee while other companies were conducting their fight for the village and awaiting reinforcements, Noyes nonetheless repeatedly maintained that it was never a battle in his estimation, nothing more than "a little skirmish." After finding Noyes guilty as charged, the court determined that he should be reprimanded by the department commander, Crook himself, then returned to duty. Just in time to prepare his troops for a second march on the Sioux and Cheyenne strongholds.

Fifty-one command and staff officers were now in place, most of whom were seasoned Civil War veterans, given charge of 1,002 soldiers who would again press into that last great hunting ground of the wild tribes.

In the camp bounded on three sides by a bend in LaPrele Creek also sat Tom Moore's 250-mule train and 81 packers, as well as some 106 wagons brought up from Camp Carlin by 116 teamsters, who would soon push their six-mule teams north under the command of wagon chief Charles Russell. Their freshly greased axles would groan under the weight of three hundred thousand pounds of grain for the stock, as well as thousands of pounds of ammunition, along with the standard army fare: pork, beans, coffee, and sugar. Not all the rations were going north in the wagons; some would plod along the Bozeman Road on the hoof—twelve hundred head of commissary beef, which at present competed for pasturage with the mules and cavalry mounts.

From sunup to twilight the ferrymen struggled to muscle every pound of weapons and rations, forage and blankets, beef and bullets across the Platte, constantly repairing the leaking ferry or the worn cable each time it snapped—man and equipment strained to the breaking point without letup by a river running as high and fast as a millrace. Just that morning one of Russell's teamsters, a man named Dill, had fallen off the ferry when the cable snapped, sending the ferry keelhauling into the foaming current. Dill was swept downstream before any man could act, and his battered body was later found caught among some snags a half-dozen miles below Fetterman.

"Don't go getting morose on us now, Seamus!" Strahorn chided the Irishman. "We was to bloody hell and back together last March!"

"Bob's right," Bourke agreed. "This will be a lark compared to that Powder River campaign. Why, every officer staying behind down at Russell and Laramie is telling us, 'Oh, you will have a holiday trip this summer. So different from last winter's campaign, you know!' "

"Absolutely!" Finerty cheered.

"What the divil would you know about our march on Powder River?" demanded Seamus.

"Nothing," Finerty replied sheepishly. "But I do know I come at just the right time to enjoy nice warm days and pleasant, cool nights this time into Indian country."

"Just remember this ain't going to be no bleeming picnic march, boyo!"

"I'll remember you said that when General Crook's got the savage bastards on the run back to their agencies!" Finerty cheered as they all watched a company of infantry march by in close order, rifles at their shoulders, bayonets glittering in the spring sunlight.

Each soldier would be marching north well armed with the Springfield model 1873. A single-shot rifle that fired a .45-caliber bullet, the cavalry model chambered a fifty-grain cartridge and had an effective range of some six hundred yards, while the longer-barreled infantry model, affectionately called the "Long Tom," chambered a bigger seventy-grain cartridge and could kill out to a thousand yards. In addition the horse soldiers also carried the standard-issue single-action '73 model Colt's revolver in .45 caliber.

"And what of these other two columns we'll rendezvous with when we reach the Yellowstone?" Seamus inquired.

"Gibbon and Terry?" Bourke asked, incredulity crossing his face. "Forget about them! We'll be the column to defeat Crazy Horse simply because Crook's the only one who is showing any conviction to get into the field. Last news we had was that Gibbon's inching east along the Yellowstone, feeling his way along like a cautious ol' biddy, almost afraid to come in contact with the hostiles. And word is that Terry's just departed Fort Lincoln with Custer in tow—with plans to join up with Gibbon before he even tries hunting for the Sioux."

"Don't you ever think Terry's got Custer in tow," Donegan said.

Finerty snorted and replied, "Bet you're right: I figure Custer's likely got his superiors whipped into line by now!"

"No recent news of either column?" Strahorn asked.

Bourke shook his head. "That is going to be the major handicap Crook must now face: he's simply not able to communicate with the other two columns, what with the hostiles between us."

"But I've heard the major obstacle will be the hostiles themselves," Finerty intoned. "Seems all three columns are worried about getting the wild tribes to stand and fight. So Crook's got to be concerned that he won't catch the villages long enough to defeat them or drive them back to their reservations."

"The general wants them bad," Bourke reminded his friends. "He's angry enough to spit horseshoe nails over the fizzle on Powder River. And now he's already received a warning from Crazy Horse through some friendlies."

"That's the stuff of headlines, John!" Strahorn growled. "The general is warned by Crazy Horse—and you don't tell us so we can get a column or two of print on the front page out of it before we push off?"

Seamus went serious as the newsmen chuckled. He asked, "What's Crazy Horse warning?"

Bourke answered, "He's sent word to Crook—telling the soldier chief not to cross the Tongue."

"Why not warn the general not to cross the Powder?" asked Strahorn in jest. "Or better yet—warn Crook not to cross the goddamned Platte out there! Save us all a long march driving the bastards back to their agencies!"

Finerty slapped Strahorn on the back. "And we could just stay right here near the Hog Ranch!"

"Seamus, why do you think Crazy Horse warned Crook about the Tongue?" Bourke asked, ignoring the exuberant newsman.

Donegan shrugged slightly, gazing at the far horizon. "I figure it can only mean we'll find the hostile villages north of the Tongue. We go across—from there on out, we'll be deep in it."

Chapter 8

22–26 May 1876

"*You can't be serious!*" *growled Sergeant John Carr.*

Frank Grouard glanced over the faces of the others. Nine young soldiers. Likely none of them ever had to stand up to a charge by a Lakota war party. If he played this next hand dealt him with some savvy, Frank hoped they never would have to face such a daunting task.

"I got my orders. And you got the same," the half-breed replied. "We were sent to the Powder to find a place for Crook to cross his soldiers."

Carr's face was brightening to a rose as his widening eyes bounced over his men. He sputtered, "Let's just get our asses back to Fetterman while we still have our hair."

Grouard thought on it a moment, the breeze nuzzling the hair down in his eyes as he took off his wide-brimmed hat. The wind would likely come up now that dawn was fast approaching. And the sun always rose early this time of the year. They had stopped to wind the horses they had punished throughout that long night escaping from the Cheyenne River crossing where they had heard the war party shooting at the blanket-wrapped dummies as they rode into the dark.

Here they halted, stopping only when Frank figured they had enough of a lead on the Lakota warriors to give his scouting party the luxury of climbing out of the saddle for those precious few minutes. Frank knew he had little time to do what he needed to do: to find the enemy before the Lakota found them.

Grouard sighed and turned away from Carr, stuffing a moccasin into the off-hand stirrup and rising to the saddle. He adjusted the reins in his left palm. "All right, Sergeant. You win."

"That sounds more like it, Grouard," Carr cheered, turning to his soldiers. "Boys, let's get mounted up for home."

"Go on back if you're going to," Grouard continued, bringing his mount alongside Carr's. "I'm pushing on to the Powder."

"You . . . you mean we'll go back without you?"

He nodded. "Just tell the general that I went on without the escort he decided to send with me. Besides, he oughtta remember I told him I didn't need no soldiers with me in the first place."

"Wait! Wait a minute here," Carr called out, clipped and anxious, reaching for Grouard's bridle to stay the half-breed. "We can't go back if you don't!"

"I ain't going back, Sergeant. General pays me for doing a job. I'm gonna give the man his money's worth."

Carr was wagging his head in exasperation. "Even we get ourselves killed?"

"Maybe so," Grouard replied. "But I figured 'cause you was soldiers—fighting Injuns, getting chased and shot at, was all part of your job."

"All right—all right." Carr snarled, wheeling on his confused detail. "Single file, men. Keep it quiet in the ranks. We're following this black-assed half-breed son of a bitch to the Powder River. And maybe even into hell if he ain't careful."

Grouard let it pass as he heeled his mount into motion. He'd been forced to rub up against folks who didn't care for his color or his breeding nearly all his life. This wasn't the first time Frank had been asked to ride with stupid soldiers. He just prayed it wouldn't be the last.

"What you got in you? Nigger blood?" Louie Reshaw

had asked him last winter when they were signing up to scout for Crook's march to the Powder.

"I'll kill him," Grouard had said quietly to the chief of scouts, Ben Clark. "You tell him he ever talks about nigger blood to my face, behind my back—I'll kill him and take his scalp straight to his father."

Frank's own father had been black-skinned, an escaped slave with a flair for talk and knack for weapons in the early part of the century. A fur trapper in those first days in the far west. One of the handful of dark-skinned ones who came west as freedmen—men like James P. Beckworth and Edward Rose. His mother was a Gros Ventre captured as a child and raised among the Shoshone, where the coffee-skinned trapper eventually made her his wife. As beaver began to sink in value, he took his family south toward the land of Brigham Young's Saints. It wasn't long before Frank took a different trail from his family, and set about inventing his own family tree—enough of a tall tale to convince an upstanding Mormon family to take him in as a helpless orphan.

After educating him with the finest of books and the strictest of their spiritual teachings, the Pratts tearfully let Grouard go when it came time for the fifteen-year-old to make his own way in the world. He hauled freight north into the gold camps of Idaho and Montana territories—a fitting occupation for a youngster already six feet tall and weighing over two hundred pounds. Not only could he handle animals and a gun with equal skill, but he could read and write as well.

It wasn't until six years later, however—in January of 1870—that Frank's adventure of a lifetime began.

He was carrying contract mail from Fort Hawley to Fort Peck up Montana way that hellishly cold winter, forced to point his nose into the brutal wind, when he was knocked from his horse—finding himself face-to-face with a small war party. What tribe they were, he had no way of knowing right then. But what they wanted wasn't near so hard to figure out. They had taken his rifle and pistol, and they were leading his horse away. They began yanking on his big, heavy buffalo coat. That was the last straw. He'd die out here in the blizzard without that coat of his. So if they killed him for fighting to keep it—it didn't seem to make that much difference.

As a brash warrior was lowering his rifle muzzle to press it against Grouard's chest, another warrior rode up in a swirl of snow to knock Frank's attacker aside. After a stiff argument, then due deliberation between all thirteen of the war party, Frank's rescuer strode up and handed Frank the reins to his horse, motioning for the prisoner to follow the war party.

All the time they were riding to the Milk River, Frank had had no idea just how important his captor was among his people. All he knew was the Lakota's name was Sitting Bull.

For those next two years he traveled the high plains with the Hunkpapa, learning everything it took to become a Lakota warrior, learning the language, sign, and customs. Sitting Bull even bestowed a special name on his adopted son: "Grabber," as the Hunkpapa chief recalled how Grouard had looked when they first met—like a huge bear in that buffalo-hide coat, reaching out to embrace its victim.

Little more than a year later, Frank's idyll with the Hunkpapa was destined to take an evil turn when Grouard agreed to help the soldiers and civilian trader at Fort Peck put an end to the illegal trading going on between the warrior bands and the Red River Metis, who slipped south across the Canadian border with their contraband of weapons and whiskey.

When Sitting Bull learned of Grouard's duplicity, the chief grew angry enough to kill the one who had betrayed his Hunkpapa. Grouard saved his hide only by seeking the safety of the great medicine man's mother before moving on, this time going to live with Crazy Horse's Hunkpatila just before the Long Hair's Seventh Cavalry was protecting a party of surveyors along the Elk River* in 1873. With Crazy Horse and his brother Little Hawk, Grouard roamed and hunted, raided for ponies and courted women. Then Frank fell desperately in love with He Dog's sister.

* Yellowstone River

It was at times like these, heading back into that great hunting ground he had roamed with the Lakota for six winters, that Grouard again felt that cold, empty hole ache inside him. Forced again to remember that woman—the feel and smell and taste of her skin as she grew damp each time they mated. Here again to remember the hate-filled eyes of her brother, the warrior friend of Crazy Horse . . . the one called He Dog.

In the end Grouard chose to leave the Lakota rather than face the coming showdown with his brother-in-law. Telling everyone he was going on a hunt by himself, Frank slipped away to the south, where he had shown up at the White Rock Reservation—the place the white man called the Red Cloud Agency. It hadn't been long before word of this Frank Grouard and what he knew spread; last February, General George Crook had called the half-breed in for a talk.

"How long were you with the Sioux, Frank?"

"Six winters, this one, General."

"Well—now, why don't you tell me just why in the goddamned blazes you ended up leaving the blanket and coming back among civilized folk."

"You're suspicious of me?"

"No. Never was suspicious of a man I can look in the eye and he can look right back at me when I asked him a troubling question."

Frank had never taken his eyes off Crook's as he began to tell the general why he left the Hunkpatila. About a woman and her crazed brother named He Dog. To tell Crook that he would do anything to guide the general's soldiers north to hunt down the warrior band of Crazy Horse.

Moving out of that copse of trees now with Carr and his platoon behind him just before daybreak, Grouard figured he had pushed them far enough west to trust in reining north once more. They rode out at a lope against the rising sun, ten soldiers following the half-breed scout who was angling back toward the east in a great arc. Heading for the Powder River.

He had a job to do for the general. Even more—Frank had something he had to do for himself. At the Reynolds's fight on the Powder River in the Sore-Eye Moon he had called out to Crazy Horse and He Dog, challenging them to come forth from the captured village and fight him like warriors. They had not appeared. So now it was once more up to The Grabber to lead the soldiers back into Lakota country. Back to the land of the Hunkpatila. Where he prayed he would at least be granted his chance to put his hands around the throat of the woman's brother—He Dog.

Yes, Frank vowed. He would take untold chances to reach the Powder River crossing once more. To find a way for Crook's soldiers to get across and plunge into that last hunting ground where the wild tribes roamed. He would do all that he had to do just so he could once more come face-to-face with the Hunkpatila warrior who had vowed to take his life.

By the time the rising sun caused the prairie light to balloon around them, Grouard led the ten soldiers across some rocky ground where their big American horses would not make tracks on the rain-softened earth, guided them down into a narrow, dry ravine, and ordered Carr to wait.

"Where you going now?" the sergeant demanded.

"I'll be back. Soon."

To the side of a hill, just below the crest, Frank crawled on his belly and peered between the new grass, damp and heady with the richness of the new season. After a long time he saw them. The Lakota scouts had run across the iron-shod hoofprints where he had led the soldiers out of the creekbed. In the distance he could see them moving along slowly, watching the trail the eleven had left behind in making their escape.

He hoped this rocky ground the soldiers had just crossed would be enough to throw the war party off. And prayed the iron horseshoes had not scraped the rocks, leaving behind the telltale scar of a white man's passing.

He held them in that ravine for the rest of the day, the weary soldiers at the ready should their trail be discovered. Twilight brought a cool breeze that nuzzled its way down the low places, past the soldiers who were dozing, unable to fight sleep any longer. Frank kept himself awake thinking on the woman, wondering about her—had she remarried?

What of the child she said she carried in her belly just before he left? His child? He might well be a father by now.

And he wondered if he would ever get a chance to even the score with He Dog and Crazy Horse's Hunkpatila.

When slap dark gripped the prairie, Grouard nudged them all awake and wordlessly motioned them to their mounts. With only a signal, the half-breed reined about and led them up onto the rolling, vaulted tableland cut with the turkey-track coulees and dry washes that stood out like veins across the silver landscape rolling horizon to horizon below the muted starshine. Near sunrise he had brought them to the head of the Dry Fork of the Powder.*

"How close are we to that goddamned crossing Crook wants you to scout?" whispered Sergeant Carr.

"A day's ride. Maybe less."

"So we'll ride out come nightfall and reach it tomorrow morning. Decide on a crossing, then get our tails high behind and back to Fetterman," Carr declared.

Frank wagged his head. "Can't wait till sundown, Sergeant. I gotta take the chance riding through the day."

Carr swallowed, but this time he gulped down his anger. Thin-lipped he said, "Why, in the devil's name, do you want to ride right out there in daylight when there's those red bastards dogging our backtrail?"

"General asked me to keep a eye out for the Crow he wired to come join him."

"Crow?" Carr squeaked. "The goddamned Crow?"

He nodded. "Crook says he expects they'll be coming to join the soldier column—and he wants me to find them."

"What the hell for?"

"Tell 'em the general is on his way. To sit tight. To say Crook will be here shortly to whip the enemies of the Crow."

Carr started chuckling softly. "If that don't beat all! Not only are you going to ride out there in the middle of the day to find a river crossing while we've got redskins ready

---

* Present-day Salt Fork, or Salt Creek, of the Powder River

to lift our hair riding down our ass . . . but you're gonna go looking for some other goddamned Injuns to boot!"

Evenly, almost dispassionately, Grouard answered, "That's about the size of it, Sergeant. You coming with me when these horses had a chance to rest?"

Carr chuckled softly again. "What choices I got, Grouard? To turn around and ride right back into the teeth of those bastards been following us? Or ride on with you, hoping to stay ahead of one war party while we go looking for another war party to join up with?"

"Glad you get the picture, Sergeant," Grouard said. "Truth is, I'm glad to have you and your men along for the ride."

After an hour of grazing the horses and watering them at a scummy pool of rain seep, the half-breed ordered the soldiers back into the saddle. Through that morning and into the early afternoon he kept the troopers hugging the bottoms and ravines for the most part while he himself rode on ahead, scouting the country for as safe a route as he could find. Doing everything he could think of so that Carr's detail would not be spied against the horizon by an enemy that refused to let up, refused to stop for rest, refused to abandon their hunger for soldier blood.

After less than fifteen miles of that arduous ride through the broken countryside, Grouard reined up at the brow of a bluff, hanging back in the shadows as he peered down upon the vast expanse of country tumbling away to the Powder River crossing. He could almost see the river. Almost.

And down there too he caught a glimpse of the first dust rising behind a ridge off to his left.

Quickly glancing behind him, he spotted the soldiers still coming on, down in the coulee and still some distance behind him.

Turning back north, Frank realized the Lakota had figured out where the soldiers might be heading, so had hurried on ahead to cut off the white men at a good place for an ambush. In that country sloping down to the Powder, there would be any one of a handful of beautiful places the enemy could use to lay their trap. And once the soldiers would ride into the snare, there was no coming out alive.

Grouard urged his mount out of the shadows at a hand gallop, feeling the animal spring into life as it was finally given its head and a chance to run. Reaching those hills directly above the Powder River crossing, he dismounted and bellied up to the crest, looking down on the Lakota war party as it prepared its trap for the soldiers. The trail Carr's men were taking would lead them right down the forks of a creek heading to the Powder. As the soldiers rode toward the snare, the Lakota dispersed along either side of the trail so they would capture the white men in a deadly cross fire.

He turned to look behind the hills to the south and saw the faint smudge of dust against the afternoon sky. He had to act soon—and give up ever reaching the Powder River.

Knowing there was little sense in staying completely silent any longer, Grouard sprinted to his horse, wheeled about, and rode back to meet Carr, signaling for the soldiers to halt.

"Turn 'em back, Sergeant," he said tersely.

The soldier craned his neck and asked, "Them red bastards up there at the river?"

"Laying in the shadows, waiting for you."

"Where to now, Grouard?"

"Fetterman."

"Fetterman?" Carr shrieked. "Goddammit, man, that's—"

"A hell of a long way. Now get these men riding."

"And you?"

"I'll be along shortly, after I take care of something first. Now, get moving and don't spare the spur if you have to."

"Grouard—if we live through this, I'll buy you a drink of whiskey," Carr growled with a grudging smile. "If we don't live through it—you'll see me in hell!"

"You'll owe me a whole bottle, Sergeant. Now get going—I'll see you back at Fetterman."

He watched the soldiers disappear once more into the coulees, then spur the horses up onto the flat, rolling, broken prairieland, their ten mounts kicking up a cascade of dust shimmering like spun gold in the afternoon light. Frank sawed the reins about, let the animal out, and stopped only when he had reached the top of the hill overlooking the Lakota's ambush.

Unmoving, Grouard sat there until he was sure the enemy had spotted him silhouetted against the skyline. He sat there a while longer, kept rising in the stirrups and looking behind him as if he were awaiting the soldiers who would come up to the crossing with him. When he felt he had given enough time for the proper effect, the half-breed waved enthusiastically, then signaled expansively to the imaginary platoon to come on. Slowly he left the crest of the slope as if he were going to meet the soldiers and lead them to their destruction.

Once out of sight, however, Frank hammered his moccasins into the flanks of his big American horse. If forced to, he would push Carr's soldiers and their mounts all afternoon and into the night. It wouldn't take very long for those Lakota to realize the soldiers weren't coming—and then they would be following with a vengeance. Blood in their eyes, screeching and ready to put an end to this long chase.

He would just have to keep the soldiers going as long as their mounts held up. And not try to think about how goddamned far it really was back to Fort Fetterman.

Inch by inch he let the horse have more of the rein, let it have its head as it tore up and over and down and around that broken ground, heading south toward LaPrele Creek and Crook's army.

Tearing flat out, with the soldiers racing for their lives in the middistance ahead of him.

Turning to glance over his shoulder, he saw them. Specks at first, dark as beetles bobbing against the murky haze of the horizon. But they were coming. A whole shitteree of them too.

Flat out they were all racing now—red and white, and a half-breed too.

The soldiers would likely lose their scalps if they lost this long run back to Fetterman. But the Lakota would likely try to take Frank alive—saving him for some delicious, exquisite torture at the hands of Sitting Bull, Crazy Horse, and He Dog.

Grouard had made enemies, many enemies among those Lakota who were coming behind at a ferocious, screaming tear, whipping their grass-fed, long-winded little ponies hot on the heels of the soldiers.

Once again the half-breed was running for his life.

Chapter 9

29 May 1876

"*Those sons a bitches didn't give up the chase until they* were within rifle shot of the soldier tents down on the bottoms," Frank Grouard had told Seamus as he slid from the saddle at the top of the bluff where Fort Fetterman stood. To a young soldier he gratefully handed over the reins to his lathered army mount.

"Came close to getting your hair?"

"My scalp's tingled a time or two before, Seamus," the half-breed continued. "But I ain't never been in as close a scrape as that."

"Breathing down your neck, was they?" Donegan asked with a grin, trying to cheer up the half-breed.

With a nod Grouard replied, "All the way from the Powder River."

"That's a long race of it if ever there was one, my friend! Glad to see you made it back whole . . . and with your hair still locked on!"

For what must have been the first time in many hours, Grouard finally grinned. "If there'd been a pool to bet on the winner of that race, Seamus—by God, this time I would've bet on the Injuns myself!"

It was well after dark that Friday, 26 May, when there arose a commotion down among the teamsters' and packers' camps. Voices boomed along the river, men hollered, then echoed with some weary cheering and laughter as the half-breed led the ten soldiers back to the safety of the army's great gathering on the north bank of the Platte River. Leaving Sergeant Carr and his detail behind, Grouard roused the ferrymen back into service and crossed the river to climb the plateau to the fort itself.

There he finally dismounted, received a hale and hearty welcome from some friends, and then in the company of the Irishman strolled over to have an audience with Crook. While the general wasn't entirely happy not knowing for certain what sort of a crossing he would have at the Powder near old Fort Reno, Crook was nonetheless expressive in his happiness to have his chief of scouts back in one piece.

Slapping Grouard on the back and winking at Donegan, the general declared, "It won't matter much in a few days, anyway. I'm ready to start moving this army across the Platte."

"We should be away on the twenty-ninth after all!" John Bourke added.

Crook nodded agreeably. "We get the cattle herd and the rest of our ammunition across—we'll march for Crazy Horse country, Grouard. That ought to take some of the sting out of that horse race of yours."

The half-breed glanced over at Donegan before answering. "It will, General. It sure as hell will. I'm going to do everything I can to catch Crazy Horse again for you."

By late the afternoon of the twenty-seventh, the personal effects of the officers had been recrated, stenciled, and piled aboard the ferry, on their way back across to the south bank of the Platte, there to be stored in the quartermaster's warehouse at Fort Fetterman for the duration of Crook's Bighorn and Yellowstone Expedition. Orders were given up and down the chain of command that every last pound of gear not absolutely necessary to the campaign was to be left behind. The infantry suffered the most, ordered to give up the warmth of an extra blanket these cold spring nights on the high plains. Grumbling at the unfairness of the order, the foot sloggers complained that the horse soldiers would continue to sleep beneath the warmth of the standard issue of one blanket, in addition to the thick saddle blanket as well as an extra blanket most of the veterans folded under their saddles.

Still, cavalry sergeants were assigned to search every trooper's equipment carefully, pulling out things like currycombs and brushes, among more of a man's more personal articles. Time would come, the horse soldiers were reminded, that they would need to pack along extra ammunition, extra rations, an extra fore and rear shoe for their mounts—in every way to live "off the hoof" this time out chasing the Sioux and Cheyenne.

Those who had served under General George Crook before needed no reminding.

From first light until well past twilight each evening, the ferrymen toiled to move ammunition and grain, rations and cattle across the Platte. Time and again the cable snapped, requiring hours of delay in repairing the hausers. Even a new cable hauled up from Laramie was not immune to breaking under the severe strain this campaign was putting it to. And Captain Charles Meinhold of the Third Cavalry, in attempting to swim the horses of his B Company across the swirling river, had problems urging the mounts off the south bank and into the water. As a hundred head of the horses wheeled about and tore away from the riverbank, their handlers were left standing in panic behind them. While some were eventually recovered by Meinhold's men, a good number never were rounded back up.

"No matter, I'll still be happy to quit this post at long last," John Finerty told Seamus on the evening of the twenty-eighth as the multiple camps settled down into their last night before marching out for enemy territory.

"You've been working those girls over to the Hog Ranch pretty hard, John," said Donegan. "Even for a ever-loving Irishman!"

They laughed together there at the fire; then Finerty sighed as several of them gazed back up the far bluff at the fort buildings in the fading light at dusk. He finally said, "Fetterman is now all but abandoned. It's a truly hateful post—in summer pure hell, I hear. And in winter no less than the icy slopes of Spitzbergen itself! The whole army dreads being quartered here, fellas."

"Alas, all have to take their turn," Bob Strahorn commiserated.

"Then it's one more reason for me never to join up, bucko!" Finerty cheered, slapping Donegan on the shoulder as he pulled out his German silver flask. "A drink to our bidding Fetterman a fond farewell."

"Yes!" Strahorn echoed. "Here's to bidding the Hog Ranch a fond farewell!"

"Good show, Robert!" Finerty called to his fellow correspondent. "And on to Indian country!"

"Indian country indeed," Donegan added, a little less enthusiastically.

Early on the following morning, Monday, 29 May, George Crook ordered that fine-looking Prussian Captain Meinhold with two companies of the Third Cavalry to march ahead to reconnoiter the road north. As well, Captain Frederick Van Vliet had already been sent ahead with his own Company C, joined by First Lieutenant Emmet Crawford's G Company, both of the Third Cavalry, each man outfitted with eight days' rations and with orders to keep a watch out for the Crow and Shoshone allies the general was expecting to rendezvous with him somewhere in the vicinity of old Fort Reno.

At long last, shortly after noon that Monday, George Crook gave the orders for Chambers's five companies of infantry to lead out, taking the van of what was generally believed to be the most efficient, battle-ready fighting force ever put into the field against the Indians of the northern plains.

In addition to a pint canteen, over his right shoulder each infantryman carried the blanket he had rolled up inside a gum poncho, then lashed together at the ends. On his back as well was the haversack where a foot soldier kept his issue of rations and mess utensils. Around each waist hung a canvas or leather belt, its loops clutching the cartridges for the Long Tom Springfield rifle each man carried at port during the march. The soldiers would soon break in their leather bootees, generally called "Jefferson boots," all dyed black but quickly covered with the fine, talc-like dust of the trail, the soles sturdily fastened with small brass screws. Some wore the standard issue, wide-brimmed black slouch hat, while others preferred civilian-style headgear and even some straw hats purchased from the post sutler. A few sported the '72 model kepi with its narrow leather visor, most generally worn only in garrison while on fatigue detail.

Less than a mile north of the Platte along the road to Montana stood Kid Slaymaker's Hog Ranch. A half-dozen weary, bleary-eyed working girls emerged into the dazzling spring light to wave handkerchiefs and blow kisses at the passing foot soldiers as they trudged along, raising small clouds of dust.

Next came Seamus Donegan in the company of Tom Moore's pack train—all 81 men and 250 mules. Behind them rumbled Charlie Russell's 116 teamsters riding in 106 canvas-topped, six-mule wagons. At the rear, eating the dust of all this first short day of march, came Crook's cavalry. They had been ordered to break camp later than the infantry and had jealously watched the footsloggers pass them by at noon. The horse soldiers were the last to turn out, climb to the saddle, and wave fare-thee-well to Slaymaker's girls. No matter that the chippies were all a little too old, perhaps a little too fleshy, and for sure a little too crude to secure themselves employment anywhere but here on the utter edge of Indian territory. They had more than worked for their wages in the past few weeks as the expedition gathered in the shadow of the fort, and well earned this vacation now that George Crook was taking his army north.

That long black line snaked away from this last outpost of the frontier army, a column covering more than four miles from van to rear guard. Dust billowed up, made iridescent in the streams of sunlight that May afternoon, sunlight that caught the gleam of carbine and rifle, bridle and spur. Wheels creaked and the overladen beds and axles groaned. Moore's mule train protested feebly as Donegan and the rest of the packers urged the balky animals up the Montana Road, the mules bellowing loud heeraws to signify they found no happiness in putting to the trail at long last.

Back in Chicago at his headquarters that same afternoon, Lieutenant General Philip Sheridan, commanding the Division of the Missouri, received the telegraphic message from Crook that the expedition was embarking for Indian territory. The general again cautioned Sheridan that his concentration of troops for the campaign had left the settlements with little protection against any marauding raiders.

The fiery Irish banty rooster, hero of the Shenandoah campaign that ultimately brought an end to the Civil War, now danced a bit of a jig before his brother, who had carried the flimsy into the commandant's office.

"Be damned—I've finally got all three of my columns pushing into the field, Michael!" Sheridan gloated. "Now I can whip those sons-a-bitches into subjection and exterminate all the rest who won't go in!"

Sheridan wheeled and pulled a fresh sheet of foolscap to the center of his writing pad and with a flourish dipped a pen with a metal quill into the inkwell, preparing a telegram he would transmit back to Crook:

> Have already anticipated movement of Indians from agencies and have made application to General Sherman to be permitted to control Indians at all agencies, so that none can go out and no hostiles or families come in, except on unconditional surrender. What say you to my running up the majority of the 5th Cavalry to Red Cloud's and Spotted Tail's reservations?

"Get that on the wires to Fetterman right now. I'll see if I can catch George before he gets away."

"Yes, General," Michael Sheridan replied, turning to the door.

"I just had a splendid idea," Sheridan exclaimed joyfully. "I'm going to write Bill Sherman about all this glorious news now too!"

> . . . As no very accurate information can be obtained as to the location of the hostile Indians, and as there would be no telling how long they would stay at any one place, if it was known, I

> have given no instructions to Generals Crook or Terry, preferring that they should do the best they can under the circumstances and under what they may develop, as I think it would be unwise to make any combinations in such country as they will have to operate in. As hostile Indians in any great numbers cannot keep the field as a body for a week, or at most ten days, I therefore consider—and so do Terry and Crook—that each column will be able to take care of itself and of chastising the Indians should it have the opportunity.
>
> . . . I hope that good results may be obtained by the troops in the field, but am not at all sanguine, unless what I have above suggested be carried out. We might just as well settle the Sioux question now; it will be better for all concerned.

How wrong the coming events would soon prove the little general to be.

A twelve-mile march beneath the afternoon sun had Frank Grouard bringing Crook's command to a barren flat bottomland at the Sage Creek crossing, where the soldiers went into camp and started their greasewood fires for supper. The beef herd came up beneath a thick cloud of dust and was allowed to graze on the opposite side of the bivouac so that it would not mix with Moore's mule train. Just after the evening mess, a mail courier arrived from Fetterman, and Crook ordered these last letters handed out among the men while he read Sheridan's telegram.

Frank Grouard watched the tall Irishman take his envelope, smell it as if it might prove to be a flower, then slip away into the darkness to return to the packers' camp. As the men read their letters to themselves or shared them with their companions, that first camp grew eerily quiet. Tomorrow they would be marching in earnest—like the point of Crook's lance being laid against the heart of Indian country. But for now the lowing of the cattle on one side of the bivouac and an occasional bray from the other served to lull the soldiers into restful slumber—a sleep that was, for the time being, untroubled by anything resembling nightmares of painted, screeching savages.

Before sunrise the morning of the thirtieth, Crook had Bourke fetch up Captains Charles Meinhold and Peter D. Vroom of the Third Cavalry for a brief meeting at headquarters. The general's half-breed chief of scouts was already there at the fire by the time Bourke returned.

Over coffee Crook instructed, "Meinhold will be in charge of this reconnaissance. Captain Vroom will be second in command. I'm sending Frank here as your guide. I want you to work north, west of our line of march—rejoining us at old Fort Reno."

"Are we to scout for hostiles, General?" Meinhold asked.

"No, Captain. We're all but dead certain the hostile villages are to the north and east."

A veteran of the Apache wars in New Mexico ever since 1868, Vroom beamed as if he knew the answer to Crook's puzzle. "If we're not to scout for hostiles, then may I assume that our duty is to reach Reno and locate a suitable crossing for the command?"

Again Crook shook his head. "I've already got Van Vliet's detail up there. I don't need your battalion to find a crossing for me when he's already at the Powder."

"Just what is it you've got Grouard taking us to do?" Meinhold inquired.

"The Shoshone, Captain," Crook replied. "They are coming east from Camp Brown. That's due west of us now. They have my instructions to meet us at Reno, so I'm expecting them to show up on this road any day now. So as you march north, you will keep your eye out for the Shoshone auxiliaries promised me by their chief, Washakie."

"How many days do you want us on detached service, sir?" Vroom asked.

"Ration your battalion for four days, gentlemen," Crook answered. "Should you meet with the enemy, return to the main column immediately after your engagement. If nothing untoward occurs, then I will not see you until we rendezvous with you and the Shoshone at the Reno crossing on the Powder."

Chapter 10

30 May–2 June 1876

"*You gotta tie that son of a bitch tighter, Irishman,*" growled Tom Moore as he slid a thin sliver of plug tobacco he had just cut into the side of his cheek.

"I can do no better," Seamus Donegan snapped too quickly in reply, disgusted at his failure, furious at the mule, and angry most of all that here he was on this first morning of the campaign—having actually to work rather than riding off to scout and track the enemy.

"You'd damn well better keep trying till you get it right," Moore answered as he strode off, showing his wide back to the Irishman.

Donegan took a step after the head packer, sputtering, "Just a bleeming minute—"

"Here, lemme give you a hand," Richard Closter offered as he shouldered up to cut Donegan off.

"He always like that?" Seamus asked. "Back there at Fetterman when he hired me on—seemed he was a nice fella."

Closter looped the loose end of the rope back through itself to begin forming the second diamond and ran it down into the sawbuck frame.

"When he's on the trail—he's a different man," the old packer answered.

"Not sure I like that a'tall."

He turned back to watch Closter pulling on the loose end of the rope after lashing a perfect diamond over the canvas-wrapped load. Without a warning the packer suddenly kicked the animal squarely in the belly with his dusty boot toe. As the mule blew and brayed in protest, Closter yanked up all the more savagely, tightening the hitch more than Donegan thought possible.

"You ever had problems with a loose saddle cinch, Seamus?"

"I have."

"Then you'll realize why you've got to do the same with these gaddurned mules."

"You've got the son of a bitch nearly cut in half now—them ropes is so tight!"

Closter shook the load heartily, then patted it and turned to Donegan with a smile. "You see'd how it was done on this'un. Now go to work on that'un over there, Irishman."

He watched the white-bearded packer stride off across the ground covered with stunted bunchgrass, scraggly sage, and some varieties of small, cruel cactus. The noses of some of the animals bristled with the flax-colored spines this morning, showing where they had grazed a bit too close to the hearty desert plants.

All around him it was commotion in the first light of that thirtieth day of May as the column prepared to march away from their Sage Creek campsite. The cattle were being wrangled onto the trail by civilian herders as the pack mules continued their chorus of protests. Between the two herds, the infantry was ordered into line for morning inspection before they promptly moved out. Minutes later the cavalry put its hooves on the trail followed by wagon wheels stirring dust into spinning sheets of gold-tinted flecks above that road north to Montana Territory.

Cursing in a blue streak that rose to the heavens above the 250 mules, the eloquent packers lashed their animals into a crude and rudimentary line as they beat and whipped, cajoled and shoved to get the mules moving. All was pandemonium, with the eighty-some packers dashing here and there among the animals and one another, yelling, screeching their oaths, bringing their rawhide quirts and long, black, shimmering bull-snake whips down on the stubborn backs.

Of a sudden a half-dozen mules lurched into motion, hurrying off so quickly, it caught the lead packers by surprise. And with those first few animals finally moving, the rest brayed their last heer-awww and followed suit. The entire herd would likely remain quiet the rest of the day now that they had gotten their protests out of their systems and been put to the task.

Strange animals, these—thought Seamus Donegan. Perhaps a lot like a soldier: give him a chance to complain and get it off his chest, then he'll bloody well march himself down to his raw shanks for an officer.

That evening after a twenty-mile march, Baptiste Pourier selected a campsite on the South Fork of the Cheyenne River, a poor excuse for a stream. It struck the Irishman as nothing more than a collection of muddy sinks and gyp-laced pools lined by thriving cottonwoods and a thick tangle of undergrowth along its banks. At the blackened circle where a huge fire had been built, Bat told Donegan he figured this for the place Grouard had Sergeant Carr's men feed their bonfire and stuff their blankets to resemble dummies. Not one of the bullet-riddled blankets remained, only rocks and tufts of grass scattered about the site by the angry scouting party.

After the packs were removed from the mules and the animals set out to roll and graze in contentment on the poor grass, Seamus returned to the creek and knelt to drink. With that first sip he found the water laced with so many minerals that he dared not drink any more than what he could cup in the first handful. It was here on Crook's winter march north that the Indians had attacked and killed the young herder, Jim Wright, and spooked the herd to stampede. As the cattle loped south that cold winter night, Crook had expressed real satisfaction, glad that from that point on his campaign would not be encumbered with the slow-moving commissary on hoof.

The night passed without an encore visit from the hostiles here beside the South Fork, so the next morning Crook's command resumed its march along the Bozeman

Road. It was quickly becoming a broken, brutal country, and would be for many, many days to come.

Twenty more hot, dusty miles and the column reached the North Fork of the Wind River as the wind mysteriously came about, now blowing out of the north. A plainsman's nose knew the difference, and knew what the gods had in store for this high country where winter was always long and fickle in going. The soldiers could only pull on their standard-issue wool overcoats, turn up the collars, and plod ever northward into the face of the capricious weather. While Crook had ordered the tent stoves left behind at Fetterman, at least for now they had their tents to offer some small solace and shelter. So with little wood to be found, water totally unfit for drinking, even for brewing coffee, and that howling edge of the wind foretelling of snow, the entire Big Horn and Yellowstone Expedition turned morose and sullen.

That evening a courier from Captain Meinhold's battalion came in to report to Crook that a soldier had accidentally shot himself. Crook dispatched the expedition medical director, Surgeon Albert Hartsuff, and an ambulance to bring in the campaign's first casualty. Late that night they wheeled Private Francis Tierney into camp, suffering greatly from the jolting ride. A member of Meinhold's B Company on reconnaissance miles to the north, he had shot himself in the thigh earlier that same evening at their bivouac on Seventeen Mile Creek, a dry fork of the Powder itself.

"Poor fella was setting to chopping some wood for the mess fire and unbuckled his revolver belt. Tossed it to the ground," John Bourke explained to Seamus late that night when the aide-de-camp came round for some coffee and talk with the night owls. "Pistol likely landed butt first, firing right beside him. Bullet went in his leg," and the lieutenant pointed with a finger well up on the thigh. "About here. Hartsuff says the bullet never came out. But the path it took went on up into his belly. Likely lodged in the man's kidney."

Seamus winced. "Ain't no coming back from a wound like that, Johnny."

Bourke clucked. "Just a matter of time."

"Crook going to send him back to Fetterman?" Seamus asked, offering more coffee from the big, blackened pot steaming over Richard Closter's mess fire.

Bourke shook his head. "General told the surgeon he couldn't spare a detachment to take the man back to Fetterman at this time. Not when we're just setting out on our march north. Besides, the fella's bound to die anyway. Nothing anyone can do to save his life now. So Crook wants him kept as comfortable as possible with some laudanum in one of Russell's wagons."

"And the poor sojur will ride north to Injin country with us, eh?"

"The looks of it, Seamus."

Another slashing gust of wind made Donegan wonder where spring had gone. Here it was, time for summer, and winter was circling back to hammer the plains with one last chilling visit. Truly, March had passed into April on this land, bringing an end to a long, brutal winter, ushering in a spring late in coming. As the seasons turned, the snow had finally disappeared, eventually soaking into the skimpy crust of soil unable since time immemorial to clutch much moisture to its parched breast. Yet like beacons of perennial hope, the buds of the wildflowers and prairie roses had begun to emerge even as Crook set forth from Fetterman.

But with this second day of the march, winter had returned to the northern plains for one last, exuberant gasp of bone-numbing cold.

The coming of dawn that first day of June brought with it a snowstorm careening down from the glaciers on the high slopes of the Big Horn Mountains. Whereas the day before the soldiers had sweated through their long march, now they rolled out, shivering as the slashing gusts of wind drove the icy spring blizzard into their faces. As the sun rose, a pale pewter glob behind the snow clouds, Surgeon Hartsuff's thermometer registered zero degrees. The hurricane-force gale made it feel inhuman.

Hurriedly moving about camp and their morning chores to prepare for the day's march, soldiers and civilians fought the wind and shivering hands to light their fires. Water brought up from the creek in kettles and coffeepots began to slick within a matter of minutes. And there was a lot of talk from those who remembered Crook's march to the Powder River.

"Damn well didn't know Crook's two half-breed guides steered us in the wrong direction, Seamus!" shouted John Finerty, motioning his fellow Irishman over with a steaming cup of coffee. "Look like they've gone and taken us all the way to Alaska Territory!"

"Welcome to Injun Country, Mr. Correspondent!" Donegan replied, taking the steaming tin.

"It's damned well snowing here as hard as it does in Chicago. And there isn't even a lake nearby!"

No matter the wet, pelting snow given wing on cruel gusts of wind, Crook had the column up and moving out by five A.M. By midday the freak spring storm broke, the skies brightened as the clouds began to part, and some streaks of sunlight burst through the gray ceiling, lifting nearly every man's spirits. That day the expedition passed three large Indian encampments, evidenced by the tipi rings and blackened circles of fire pits, as well as the refuse of bones and scraps of abandoned hides.

"Recent sign. Likely these were some of the bands moving off the reservations, heading north for the spring hunt," Donegan told Closter.

"Not that Crazy Horse bunch?"

He shook his head. "They'll be farther north. Don't figure they'd come this far south now. Not with soldiers preparing to march up to make war on 'em."

"Sure it ain't the camps for them war parties been sending smoke signals about us?"

Donegan waved an arm across the extent of the campsite. "This is too damned big for a war party. Besides, warriors on the scout don't bring along lodges. They'll sleep under the stars—or if the weather turns bad like it did yesterday, they'll fort up under some blankets or hides they can spread over some willows down by a creek."

"My, my—where'd you go and learn all that about these red devils?" Closter inquired.

"Been out here going on a decade, Uncle Dick. First year I met no less than Jim Bridger himself. But a man has to learn a lot all on his own if he figures to keep his hair in Injin country."

That afternoon Captain Azor H. Nickerson, one of Crook's aides-de-camp, raised his field glasses and intently peered into the west for a few minutes. When he eventually took the glasses from his face, the captain tore off to inform the general of what he believed to be a party of Indians massing off the left flank of their line of march. Like wild prairie fire the rumor roared down the length of the entire column. Nearly every man shielded his eyes as he trudged along in formation, straining to make out the far-off enemy. Yet at so great a distance, the unaided eye could discern nothing more than some rapid movement of those faraway objects.

"Dick, you better remind some of the others not to dawdle," Seamus advised Closter. "Get 'em to hang closer to the column."

The old packer turned off to scurry among the other eighty packers, shouting his command.

Just as the order to close up ranks was coming back from headquarters at the front of the march, Seamus watched Captain Guy V. Henry's D Company of the Third Cavalry rein oblique left and form up in column of fours, moving away at a fast trot to reconnoiter.

"Close up! Close up!" a pair of sergeants shouted, echoing one another as they galloped past, one on each side of the trail.

"You figure there's gonna be a fight of it?" Closter asked Donegan.

"Don't know for sure, Uncle Dick. But one thing is certain—those warriors would be the dumbest creatures I ever fought if they figure on attacking this column all by themselves."

"I don't figure them red bastards for having much sense, anyway," Closter grumbled under his breath.

He watched Henry's company loping toward the distant objects that appeared to be coming on without letup. Then the order came down the line of march for the column to halt. Beneath the afternoon sun it appeared to the Irishman as if the unknown riders wore cavalry blue. From time to time sun glinted from reflective objects carried by the oncoming party.

And just when a clash was expected between the hostile

war party and Captain Henry's company, the whole lot of them stopped on a nearby prominence, stood for a few moments, then re-formed and turned back for the column as one.

"A goddamned fuss about nothing!" Closter grumbled later when word was passed down that the "war party" had turned out to be the Meinhold and Vroom reconnaissance, returning from their scout to the Powder River and Old Fort Reno.

Word had the officers and Grouard reporting that they had found no new trail made to the fort site, nor had they seen any sign of Indians—either friendlies, or the hostiles who had been dogging the line of march.

For the time being Crook said nothing, successfully hiding his great disappointment. Seamus figured that either the Shoshone had been delayed in coming to join up with the column, or worse: the Snakes from Camp Brown weren't coming at all.

On top of that, all day long the entire command had seen more and more smoke signals rising in the chill air from hills to the north and east. When there was sun, an occasional mirror was flashed from the nearby ridges and bluffs.

After another twenty-one-mile march along the trail that traced a bare backbone of high ground above the ravines and gulches, the column was ordered to bivouac on the Dry Fork of the Powder. What little firewood they could find was located down in the brakes, where the men hacked at what few scrub junipers and greasewood grew there. Still, the grass was improving each day, given more time and moisture. The horses grew stronger, being readied for their moment with destiny and the hostile warrior bands of the north.

"They're talking about us, ain't they?" Dick Closter had asked as he came up to Donegan's mess fire after their march that day.

"Who's talking about us?"

"Them smoke signals."

Donegan replied, "Sending word north that the soldiers are coming."

"Won't do 'em no good," Closter growled, then spat a

stream of tobacco juice to the side of the fire pit, where it sizzled and steamed on a rock. "Crook'll find 'em—then these soldier boys can pitch into 'em real fancy. Makes no matter them gaddurned smoke signals and mirrors."

Donegan had to agree. The advance warning would likely matter little. If anything counted in fighting Indians, it was in keeping the enemy set in one place long enough to bring the warriors to battle. With a decade of Injun fighting already under his belt, the Irishman knew the real test would be getting the Indians to stand and fight long enough to make a battle of it. Usually they engaged the soldiers only as long as it took to get their families out of camp—then they would disappear like woodsmoke on a strong gust of wind.

If Crook could only get Sitting Bull and Crazy Horse to stop their running, to turn around and engage his cavalry—then the tide of events on the northern plains would thereafter run a far different course. Just get the red bastards to stand and fight.

"Where are these heathens been lighting those signal fires?" Closter asked later as their own mess fires were dying to a red glow in their pits.

"Don't you worry," Tom Moore said before anyone else could comment. "If those Sioux want to show themselves, we'll hear it when and where we least expect it. Right, Seamus?"

"Why, yes," he answered, surprised that Moore had asked his opinion after the scolding he had gotten over a poorly tied diamond hitch.

"Last trip they serenaded us damned near every evening after we got north of the Platte," Moore continued. "Not the same this time, is it now, fellas?"

"I remember how one night Johnny Bourke near got so scar't that he about shat his pants!" Closter roared.

"What's the story to that?" Donegan asked.

"Johnny was going over some maps in his tent the night we camped on the Crazy Woman last March," Closter explained. "You remember that place, Seamus?"

"Indeed I do, old man. Go on."

"A few of his fellow officers come in and said he was a damned fool for having that candle of his lit, what with the way the Injuns'd been firing into camp every night. But the lieutenant just laughed and was telling them that since they'd gone a few nights with no halloo from the drabbed redskins, he didn't think the warriors'd be back when—of a sudden—all hell breaks loose! Bullets spitting into camp—and one of 'em, don't you know, goes right through that tent and snuffs Johnny's map candle right out!"

"Sweet Mither of Christ!" Seamus exclaimed. "I'll bet John was a believer after that!"

Closter was near tears in laughter as he replied, "Johnny told me he'd never try again to cipher on the character of Injuns."

"A wise decision for any man contemplating living long enough to have grandchildren," Donegan added.

The second of June greeted the column with a raw, blustery cold in the wake of the passing storm. With coffee and hardtack down for the morning march, Crook moved the column out, their noses pointing north by west, where they began to catch glimpses of the magnificent Big Horn range, mantled in pristine white shawls clear down to the foothills. Off to the east, any man with field glasses could make out the dark concentration of the Black Hills, where hordes of miners dug and drank, gambled and rioted in the shadows of those sacred places where the Sioux and Cheyenne came to pray. And finally, just to the east of north, Seamus could begin to discern the hulking plateaus of Pumpkin Buttes that would run north almost all the way to old Fort Reno itself.

That noon during the midday rest with Donegan and Finerty, Robert Strahorn quickly penned his observations of the general as Crook passed by the knot of correspondents gathered in a circle to light their pipes and share comments on the march.

> The general rode at the head of the column, his long blonde side-whiskers wrapped in twine after the manner of an Indian scalp-lock. . . . He is a strange man. Singularly quiet and reticent, he is thought cold and perhaps heartless by many. Certainly his face indicates ambition, determination, and a crafty—almost fox-like—shrewdness.

> . . . One who knows him well said, "He's just like an Indian. He can live on acorns and slippery elm bark,"—and I believe it.

On their march that Friday afternoon Crook's column passed by some hastily dug rifle pits. Investigation by the scouts showed the pits had been used by a party of miners passing through the country of late. In one pit the scouts discovered a board with a message carved in it. Another board showed that fire-pit charcoal had been used to scrawl a notice to passersby, stating that Captain St. John and Captain Langston had their combined civilian parties, numbering some sixty-five men, here on the twenty-seventh of May while on their way out of the gold fields in Montana and making for the Whitewood mining district of the Black Hills.

One of the newsworthy messages read:

> DRY FORK OF THE POWDER RIVER, May 27, 1876
>
> Captain St. John's party of Montana miners, sixty-five strong, leave here this morning for Whitewood. No Indian trouble yet.
>
> (s) Daniels, Silliman, Clark, Barret, Morrill, Woods, Merrill, Buchanan, Wyman, Busse, Snyder, A. Daley, E. Jackson, J. Daley

While another and more humorous inscription declared:

> DRY FORK OF THE POWDER RIVER
> May 27, 1876—
>
> Tony Pastor's opera troupe of emigrants from Montana, on their way east, camped here. Don't know how far it is to where they can get water, so have filled nose-bags and gum boots, and ride on singing, "There's Room Enough in Paradise."

Chapter 11

2 June 1876

"Listen to this, ladies!" Martha Luhn squealed, waving the sheets of letter paper she had just unfolded and begun to read.

Interrupted in her own hurry, Samantha Donegan looked up from tearing at the seal holding her envelope closed. On that wrinkled envelope, in her husband's hand, were written the words:

Samantha Donegan
in care of
Post Commander's Officers Quarters
Fort Laramie
Wyoming Territory, U.S.A.

"What's he say?" begged another of the army wives gathered in the post commander's small parlor, where they had been called this morning to receive the mail posted down from Fort Fetterman, the last post they could expect to receive from their husbands for some time. How long, not one of those long-suffering soldier wives could answer for Samantha.

"Gerhard says he got the bread!" Mrs. Luhn gushed,

holding the letter against her breast for a moment as she caught her breath in the excitement. "I can't believe it got there without getting eaten by someone! Here, let me read you this first part, ladies. Oh, my! Gerhard says the general ate supper with his F Company their last night at Fetterman before marching off to Indian country. Here he writes, 'General Crook dined with us and praised your rye bread very highly.' "

While some of the others went on to chat back and forth among themselves, sharing this tidbit of news with that latest rumor from Fetterman, Samantha eased herself down into one of the ladder-back rockers and let her eyes again rush over Seamus's scrawl on the much-handled envelope. Like someone yearning to tear into that letter, yet feeling reluctance for the experience to be over all too quickly, she finally succumbed and pried open the sheaf of pages.

My dearest heart,

We set off tomorrow. Again to Indian country. This time I will not be in the van with the scouts. Crook hires only three this campaign. All three are good. Two are friends of mine.

Instead, I will work for my wages. And truly work. My job is to convince some nasty, single-minded animals that they should carry the burdens I have lashed to their backs all the way to the villages of Sitting Bull and Crazy Horse, then back home again.

Home again to you, Samantha. And our child.

To wait until autumn for the event. Ah, but I will. I must, for God Himself heeds not man's desires, but commands all in His own time. It will be here before we know it. Do not fear for I will be at your side. Nothing will keep me from being at your side at the moment of birth, Sam.

Word is that we should capture the enemy villages without delay. There are two other columns in the field this spring. Not like the winter's march when Crook and Reynolds was the only army marching. Now we are assured of capturing the hostiles between us, driving them back to their agencies and marching back home before the leaves begin to turn there on the cottonwoods beside the river where we have walked on so many afternoons.

I hate the idea of marching north with this army as a packer, not able to have the freedom to ride and roam. But I am assured in one thing, and you can find solace in this too, that I will not be on the front of any fighting. The packers are not hired mercenaries. Crook has ordered some Crow down from Montana, as well as some Shoshone coming over from Camp Brown on the Wind River Agency. Our job is only to see that the general's soldiers get to the battlefield with their ammunition and rations, and back to Fetterman again.

With my job done I can return to Laramie for you. And once more we can ride north to the gold diggings in Montana. Where the muscles of my back won't have to pack mules, but will wrench our fortune from the rocks and soil of that rich land. That done, I can finally dress you in the velvet and lace and silk you so deserve. Our fortune made, I can build you the house where we both want to live out the rest of our days, raising all the children we have talked of, until we are both gray and lined with years. Ah, to dream of those days yet to come, Sam. Thinking on our grandchildren coming to visit us on those special holidays.

Is it so strange for me to think about my grandchildren already? When I have only just come to accept that I am going to be a father?

Why, I'll make a d——d good father, and a d——d good grandfather! Of that there is no doubt in my mind.

Nor in my heart where you rest now. If only you could rest on my shoulder, in my arms. Here, with me on the edge of this Indian country. Where I could once more lay my head against that growing belly of yours, and hear the faint thumping, the recognition in that young life that his father was indeed near.

If only I could hold you, Sam. Remember I am there with you in the days and weeks to come, until I can return to you and this land will at last be at peace. I am with you, remember during the longest nights and all those days to come. I am with you, my heart traveling to you over the miles and the hours until I can hold you as tightly as I hold this paper now, the paper you will touch and hold to your breast in only a matter of days, a matter of a few sunrises.

I am with you, my dearest heart. And soon, very soon, I will once more hold you in my arms, and feel your lips softly, sweetly, laid on mine, murmuring my name.

Your loving and faithful husband,
Seamus

She looked up, blinking, her eyes brimming, to gaze around at the faces of those other women who had come west with their husbands, come to the edge of this wilderness with the men they loved. She had that in common with these new friends. With them she felt such abiding kinship at this moment. With them she shared the unfairness that life dealt the wife of an army officer: the frequent and most untimely changes of duty station; the hard lot of a wife forced to camp in the open on the march between stations; the politics of rank and command and the impolitic scramble for private quarters; the shortage of servants on the frontier; the dull sameness of army rations; the low pay and the drudgery of life with a husband away on campaign; as well as the harsh limitations on properly educating the sons and daughters of those officers assigned the farthest-flung outposts of the Republic.

As she peered through the smoky window to the parade beyond, the sun glittered off the patches of snow left behind by the recent storm. She wondered how he had fared, if he had stayed warm and dry as the spring blizzard blew down on Crook's army. She looked back at Martha Luhn, wishing now she had baked something for Seamus too, and sent it north to Fetterman for him to eat before setting off for Indian country. Something for her husband to taste, if he could not right then taste her mouth.

But then, she wasn't yet used to this life of being married to a man called to protect the frontier. A man called to tear himself away from his wife.

Sam peered down at the letter, rereading those few precious words he had written in his ungainly scrawl, trying to imagine feeling his lips laid softly, sweetly against hers. It made her yearn so, made the ache grow and gnaw within her. Filling her eyes with those tears so many in that room shared at that very moment.

So, as lonely as she was, as dark and interminable as these nights seemed, as long and endless as the days to come would be, Sam decided she was not alone. She carried his child within her, growing bigger and stronger with every day.

She would go on and do what Seamus had asked of her. To wait for his return. To wait for his arms. To wait for his first eager, hungry kiss.

To wait.

Martha Jane Cannary had fixed on the mule-packer, that big tall one with the long, wavy hair and the gray eyes who looked like a man who knew his way around a woman as much as he knew his way around animals and weapons and Injun fighting.

He had the mark of a man Martha Jane wanted to paw her.

Wagon master Russell said the packer was known as the Irishman. He didn't know no more about him.

But then, Martha Jane knew she'd find out. When she fixed her sights on any man, she always found out everything she could. Especially how big his equipment was.

She was a teamster now. In full disguise, strutting and cursing, chewing and spitting with the best of them hired by Charlie Russell to lace the backs of those six-mule hitches with solid rawhide and curl the air with profane invective. Calamity Jane, in the company of better than a thousand men! All alone on this road to old Fort Reno and

Injun territory—and not a one of 'em knew she had breasts yearning for fondling, not a one knew of that moist place between her legs where she wanted that Irishman to diddle her good, back in the bushes where no others would know her secret.

Back in bushes beside Powder River, where she would let that big Irishman in on her secret.

How she wanted to have him breathing hot and wet at her ear as he humped her good, on top of her or behind, pawing at her breasts freed from what little restriction there was beneath the loose-fitting calico shirt, her pants down at her ankles just like his would be as the one called the Irishman hammered her like a blacksmith seating hot iron upon his anvil.

It usually happened this way in recent years out here on the frontier. She would fix on one particular frontiersman whom she found a beautiful specimen of western manhood and desire his intimacy for a week or more while on the trail. Then, again, there had been times when Janey had encouraged a handful or more rawhiders and bull-whackers of chance meeting, and with a loud screech of delight take them all on with equal ferocity after throwing lots for who would climb atop her first, second and on and on in ribald order until every last one of them was spent and she no longer hungry. Yes, indeed—there were spells when she just could not get enough of men, Martha Jane easily admitted. It was times like that she took a bunch of them on, one after another, again and again and again.

But for now, it was the Irishman she wanted to paw her and diddle that place where she grew hot thinking on him.

A thousand soldiers! Ain't that some! she thought. Maybe it was just the unadulterated closeness of so much male equipage that gave her the heat she felt. She was the only woman—the only *white* woman—within hundreds of miles. And all these men to satisfy her longings with! Whoooooo, doggee!

She had to have men with her—in droves, herds, and flocks, whether they knew her secret or not. There were so many out here where she had cast her lot in life. Fifty, even a hundred, for every woman here on the edge of the frontier. All those prissy women at the mercy of those slick-talking men. Shit! Most men were nothing more than the lying devil himself!

Broke-down, skinflint merchants robbing the hard-working blind. Or they were flimflam scam artists a step or two away from their next killing, maybe only their next meal if they hadn't been caught and strung up in the last town they had hurried to leave in the middle of the night. Then there were the out-and-out criminals. Janey always stayed away from their kind. No telling what might happen with one of them. But the worst yet—worser still than the robbers and murderers was the men what was married back east, or in the Kansas and Nebraska settlements. The low-down snake-bellies that come out to the frontier to make their fortune in one town or another and didn't let a gal know he was really married and really wasn't about to make good on all his promises to that gal until after he had diddled her and was pulling his pants back up.

How she'd wanted to use her skinner and shave a few of them bastards so close that they'd sing sopranner in the choir and have to squat to pee just like she did!

Side-tongued-talking bastards!

But here she was, one of the few out here in this saint-forsaken part of Wyoming, by God. Not many respectable women ventured west past McPherson, north past Laramie either. And those cathouse girls that worked the settlements and army posts—why, they was lazy and made the men come to them. Especially those aging, ugly ones working their trade at Kid Slaymaker's Hog Ranch. To hell and gone with making the men come to her! Martha Jane Cannary knew what she wanted, so she damned well took it to where the men were!

If that meant hauling her love equipment clean up to Injun country to have a thousand of them all to herself, then—by damned—she would do just that!

After time among the rough men and crude life of Green River and Rawlins, South Pass City and Piedmont too, she had plied her way toward Deadwood, where she first learned of Crook's plans to march back north with a sizable army of soldiers and civilians. Men all! Hurrying south out of the Black Hills, she had forgone her long-standing whiskey revels at the McDaniels's Theater there in

Cheyenne and instead promptly hired herself a horse, setting out on the road to Fort Laramie. But it was there she decided to wet her whistle at John Collins's place and got herself pitched right off the military reservation.

Coming to the next morning, shivering and sick with the dry heaves, Janey licked at the cotton in her mouth and marveled that whoever had dragged her out here across the river and dumped her off had been kind enough to bring her horse along. She found the rented animal tied to a nearby cottonwood sapling, ogling her suspiciously as she stumbled its way. Unable even to think about food at that moment, much less look a square meal in the eye, Martha Jane dragged herself up into the saddle and headed northwest, weaving back and forth slightly as she set off, nonetheless fully intent on completing the ninety miles before she had to release her death grip on the saddle horn.

By some fortuitous stroke of fate she arrived, decked in mud-stained teamster attire and smelling as fragrant as any mule skinner ever had, just as wagon master Russell was rounding out his roster of bull-whackers. Martha Jane was hired, incognito, in disguise, in nothing short of heat for all that man-flesh and hanging-down love equipment!

Not that she didn't ever think of anything else. Janey had a soft spot in her heart for animals what was hurt or abused, and a special place for the sick. Out here on the frontier, there wasn't all that much disease—not in the way of anything other'n sniffles and a croup, or the tick-sick and the walking ague. But when something took hold of one of the labor or mining camps, it really took hold, and her help was sorely needed.

Like last year over at the work camps in South Pass City, where she had heard the news about the Robinson family's littlest girl took to her pallet with the black diphtheria. No one come around, not even the tonsorial doctor with all his colored bottles of patent medicines. He didn't want to catch the death that was surely waiting for the rest of the Robinsons, now that they all had been exposed.

But Janey came to their rescue. Like some angel. That's what the Robinsons'd called her when she came to their door, moved in, and started her healing. Sure enough, one by one they all come down with the death sentence. And one by one she had kept them away from death's own door.

It had even been a soldier like these with Crook who had bestowed the most famous of names on her. Teddy Egan himself—of the fighting Second—by God—Cavalry. Egan, that scrappy Celt, that handsome horse soldier who pronounced his name with the accent on the second syllable. E*gan!* he would beller out when drinking.

It was on that road to Custer City in the Black Hills, she repeatedly told all who would listen, that she had been given a new name of her own. Seems that Captain Egan found her a real blessing to have along when it came to fighting Injuns, she would tell listeners who bellied up to the bar to hear her tale. It was a name befitting a woman who already had a reputation for attracting lots of trouble, especially for the men she chose to call her "husbands," men most likely to die violent deaths.

Egan, so the story went, had said to her of a recent day, "Janey, you're a misdeed ready to happen, a kink in the rope, a calamity coming down the pike!"

So *Calamity* it became—and *Calamity* it would always be!

"I'm Calamity Jane and this drink's on the house!" she had roared more than one night in Cheyenne City at McDaniels's dance house or up to Deadwood and the infamous Number 10. No matter the place—any room filled with man-flesh had always roared back at her in joyous reply. Even that last night as a woman in the Black Hills before setting off to join up with Crook's army had been a memorable one.

"Calam's here—so let 'er rip!" she had cried out, swinging from the lamplit wagon wheel in the center of the saloon's ceiling.

Gunplay and smoke and all that drunken, weaving man-flesh all clawing after her to be the first to see her off to the Injun wars with one last diddle for the trail. Here at the edge of this land of prairie thunder and spring blizzards, whiskey that could kill you just as soon as Sitting Bull's warriors would, a land of high-water drownings and sometimes too much blasting powder in the hole, guns too quickly drawn on the wrong turn of too many cards scattered across a felt-topped table.

But, Lord—how Janey loved having so many men to herself!

"I'm Calamity Jane and you can go straight to hell right now!" she could shout if something didn't suit her just right.

"I'm Calamity Jane and I'll sleep where and with the man I wanna!"

She wanted that big Irishman now that they had reached Old Fort Reno by the Powder River. She hadn't had a man hard and fast between her legs in so many days—and it was time tonight.

Just the way she had yearned for Allegheny Dick and that Lieutenant Somers. The first had been no more than one of those fast-talking card shufflers, and the other was nothing less than a handsome soldier stationed far, far from a wife left back at home, a wife he hadn't cared to tell Janey about until he was off to a new duty station.

But both got their thrill and money's worth poking Martha Jane Cannary.

And now there was about to be a third to whom she would give her heart.

That big handsome Irishman would be the next to taste the forbidden fruits, the next to knock at heaven's door, the next to paw at her breasts and make hot, wet promises at her ear—if Calamity Jane had anything to say about getting him alone, getting him down in the willows along Powder River!

Chapter 12

3 June 1876

"*I don't see no Crow Injuns waiting for us, Seamus,*" Dick Closter grumbled.

The Irishman nodded, his eyes taking in the entire scene as they neared the south bank of the Powder River. "Bad sign."

"General's gonna be disappointed."

"Disappointed?" Donegan understood. "Crook's gonna be mad."

For the third time in his life Seamus Donegan was approaching Fort Reno from the south, moving down the Dry Fork Canyon until the column reached the Powder itself.

The bottomlands were covered with leafy cottonwood just coming into its glory beneath the afternoon sun. Two rows of tents stood out on the nearest bluff, a herd of animals grazing on the new grass close by. But—there were no Indian allies encamped. No Shoshone scouts. Not one Crow warrior.

The feeling of disappointment, perhaps bordering on despair, ran as tangibly as a chill wind through that assembly of a thousand men angling down to the Powder River with its black and brittle banks. Make no mistake, this was, after all, a place that symbolized what the army used to be in this high land. On the far bank above the column sat what was left of the abandoned post's adobe walls, their charred timbers poking out like the ends of blackened, broken bones protruding from open coagulating wounds. Rusting shards of shapeless metal, iron stoves and wagon wheels, cannon caissons and other debris, all lay in disarray. It had been a disordered and hurried retreat eight long years ago.

Despite all that time, the ghosts still clung to the charred remains of this post meant to guard the argonauts who had the Montana gold fields as their final destination.

Grouard led the column on across the Powder, which for the time being was running low and lazy, and therefore easily forded. Climbing the far bluff, the entire command went into an early bivouac, welcomed by the troops who had gone forward under Captain Frederick Van Vliet and Lieutenant Emmet Crawford.

Prairie shadows had lengthened and supper fires were glowing in their pits when John Bourke came round to the packers' camp.

"Ho, Johnny!" Closter called out.

Seamus turned to see the lieutenant approaching. Bourke had been a favorite of Uncle Dick's ever since their days with Crook's war on Cochise.

Bourke came to a halt by Closter's fire, rubbing his hands over the warmth. "Evening, gents. Seamus—the general wants to see you in half an hour."

Donegan looked up. "See me?"

Bourke looked at Closter and winked.

"So, Johnny—you figger Crook's gonna let this dumb Irishman go back to his lily-soft ways?"

"Could be," Bourke replied.

"Damn. And here Donegan was just getting used to actual' working for a living!"

"That what this is about?" Donegan asked, allowing himself to begin to sense some excitement. "I ain't gonna pack no more?"

The lieutenant shrugged, grinning. "Don't know anything about it, Seamus. But we'll find out in half an hour. You'll be finished with your supper?"

"S'pose I'll have to be."

"Grouard, Bat, and Reshaw will be there too."

"I'll be round. You can count on that, Johnny."

"Find the headquarters flag."

"Crook ain't never been hard to find, John," Donegan replied as the lieutenant waved and started away.

After wolfing down some half-boiled beans and a greasy slab of beef loin well salted, as well as several cups of steaming coffee, Donegan joined the discussion already in progress at Crook's headquarters tent.

"Good of you to come, Mr. Donegan," Crook called out as the Irishman strode up.

"From the sounds of that, I take it I'm late, General."

"Not at all. Come, join us," Crook replied.

Heads nodded all round that fire glowing on the faces tinted red beneath the deepening twilight, firefly sparks curling upward into the cool air from time to time as those soldiers, newspaper correspondents, and Crook's three scouts each paid the Irishman some sort of recognition.

"We were just talking about our mutual disappointment before we began the purpose of this meeting, Mr. Donegan."

Seamus asked, "Disappointment that the Crows aren't here?"

"Yes," and Crook nodded, staring back into the flames. "They were to be the largest contingent of auxiliaries. I had counted on them being at Reno when we arrived."

It grew quiet a few moments as the others allowed the general his time, allowed him to sulk in sullen disappointment once more. When next he spoke, it was only after he had let his eyes touch on every officer and civilian in that double-ringed hub of campaign manpower.

"One reason I did not rehire thirty quartermaster scouts for this march was that I had assured myself we would be joined by the Shoshone and Crow. And now I suppose I have no one else but myself to blame for all my high hopes."

Azor Nickerson, Crook's other aide, cleared his throat in preparation of saying, "General, you had been guaranteed both tribes wanted to get in their licks before we drove the enemy Sioux and Cheyenne back to their proper reservations."

"Even if I was—the truth is that I can't consider moving against the enemy without some auxiliaries to help us. In light of that, I am presented with a dilemma. One I have grappled with ever since arriving here this afternoon. My solution? Well, if the Crow aren't coming to me—I have no choice but to go out after the Crow and convince them to join me in this fight."

"Have you decided to send a battalion to their agency, General?" asked Captain Anson Mills of the Third Cavalry.

"No, Colonel," Crook answered, using the officer's brevet rank as a military courtesy. "I want my messengers to travel fast. They have a long way to go to find the Crow. Over Bozeman's Pass, right, Frank?"

Grouard nodded. "It's a long ride."

"Yes," Crook replied. "Besides, I plan on the rest of us proceeding north to a place where we can expect to eventually rendezvous with the Crow."

"Are you sending Grouard?" asked William B. Royall. "Our chief of scouts?"

"That's astute of you, Colonel," Crook answered, perhaps sensing some challenge. "Yes. As well as Pourier and Reshaw here."

"What?" Royall asked, his voice rising an octave.

"But, General—I must protest," Second Lieutenant Bainbridge Reynolds complained loudly.

Seamus figured the young officer might be counted upon to protest, as the son of Joseph J. Reynolds, the regimental commander Crook had brought up on charges, the colonel facing a court-martial still pending back at Fort D. A. Russell.

The young lieutenant continued his lamentation. "With all three scouts going to find the Crow—that will leave us without any guide for our march on north into the heart of Indian country!"

"I have a guide in mind, Lieutenant," Crook responded calmly, as if he were not going to be baited by the young officer. "A civilian. Someone who I am sure will likely remember our trip north last winter."

Donegan felt most of the eyes of those in that group slide his way before Crook looked at him from the far side of the fire.

"Do you think you know the way north from here to the Tongue, Mr. Donegan?"

"I . . . I suppose I can get us where you want to go, General."

"There, gentlemen," Crook said with finality. "Now we have a guide to take this column on north, with this wagon train and Moore's mule train, all at a snail's pace—while I hurry Grouard north at a gallop with Pourier and Reshaw."

"To find the Crow," Royall confirmed.

"Yes. And bring them back to meet us," Crook answered. He turned to Grouard. "You've already drawn your rations, Frank?"

All three scouts nodded.

"You each selected an extra mount to take with you?"

"Yes," the half-breed chief of scouts answered. "We figured we'd slip out when it got dark enough, General."

Briefly Crook gazed at the sky. "It's dark enough, Frank. And I suggest you travel at night to avoid being spotted by the war parties we all know are out and roaming about. But—that's something you're more savvy on than I." He held out his bare hand, shaking Grouard's, then Bat's, and finally Reshaw's in rapid order, one vigorous pump per scout before he moved on. "Good luck, and good hunting. I'll see you men in fourteen days."

"Fourteen days," Grouard repeated. "Yes—we'll bring them back, General." He and the other two turned away and were quickly swallowed up by the clutter of that camp on the bluff above Powder River.

Crook watched after them for a moment, then turned back to the group, his eyes immediately coming to rest on Donegan.

"I'll see you here at my tent for coffee at four A.M., Irishman. From here on out, you'll travel with headquarters. You can bunk in with Lieutenant Bourke here. Understood, John?"

"Yes, sir!" Bourke replied enthusiastically, smiling.

Crook nodded as if settled in all respects. "Four A.M. Not too early for you, is it, Sergeant Donegan?"

"No, General. Not at all."

"Then, with that settled, let's turn to another matter—"

Crook stopped, interrupted with the rising crescendo of the tumult suddenly rumbling their way: loud voices, laughter, and taunts generously mixed with a lot of whistling among the noisy shrieks of soldier catcalls.

"What is this disturbance?" the general demanded.

The officers parted slightly as Second Lieutenant Fred Schwatka appeared at the head of the gauntlet.

"Lieutenant Schwatka, M Company, Third Cavalry, sir!" He saluted smartly as he stomped to a snappy halt and clicked his heels showily.

Crook glanced quickly at Mills and nodded with approval before gazing once again at the young officer who had come to a stop before him. "What's going on, Lieutenant?"

"Sir?" and Schwatka's eyes quickly shot around the assembly. "Sir—we have a . . . a *situation* to report."

"Why report it to me, Lieutenant? You understand we have a chain of command?"

"Y-yessir."

Crook whirled on the M Company's commander. "Colonel Mills, go see to whatever problem—"

"Begging your pardon, General," Schwatka continued, swallowing, clearly nervous. "This isn't anything that was covered at the academy, sir."

"Improvise. Colonel Mills—see to this now."

"Mills? You say *Mills?*" a high-pitched voice called out from just beyond the circle of officers. More whistles and catcalls reverberated over the assembly. "Is my friend Colonel Mills here?"

Someone exclaimed, "Dear God! Is that a . . ."

By this time Donegan could make out the knot of soldiers approaching as they escorted a civilian prisoner into the heart of the officers' assembly. On either side of that escort came a gauntlet of more than a hundred soldiers immediately on their rear and lining both sides of the approach—every last one of the men waving, whistling, calling out in ribald good humor, every trooper hooting with unrestrained, even some raunchy, merriment.

"Get these men quieted down!" Crook hollered above the clamor.

Whirling immediately, the officers growled and barked, hushing the merry mob as they finally regained control at the very moment that escort brought the civilian to a ragged halt at the edge of the double crescent of officers.

The civilian pushed a hat back on his brow and exclaimed, "Why—it is you, Colonel Mills!"

"Do . . . do I know you, mister?" the captain asked.

"It ain't *mister,*" the civilian replied. "It's me, Colonel. You know me!"

"I'm afraid I can't place you, sir."

"Because you know I ain't a *mister,* and I sure as hell ain't no *sir,*" the civilian huffed, pulling aside the greasy flannel shirt he wore before cupping both hands beneath a pair of ample breasts that clearly strained against a dingy, sweat-stained red wool undershirt.

"Yee-god!" Royall gasped, standing closest to the civilian, as he fell back a step in shock.

"By the devil—he's a woman!" cried someone else.

"Not he—*she's* a woman!"

"I know Colonel Mills," the civilian hollered into the rising commotion, having to shriek it above the clamor of all those men shoving and jostling forward, craning necks and climbing on the backs of those in front to have themselves a look. Slowly the woman shuffled her clothing back in order. "The colonel was stationed—"

"I assure you!" Mills interrupted, the sudden surprise evident on the captain's face, the strain in his voice. "I assure every one here that I don't know you, ma'am!"

"Told you, Colonel—I ain't no sir and I sure as hell ain't no *ma'am!* I'm the toughest female hombre any man ever tangled with. Everybody's heard of me: I'm Calamity Jane!"

"You'll kindly explain what this is all about, Colonel Mills!" Crook demanded.

Martha Jane Cannary tried to take a step toward Crook, but was restrained by her two handlers. "Ain't you heard of me, Gennil'?"

Mills began to stammer. "I . . . I don't—" Then suddenly wheeled on his lieutenant. "What the hell's going on with this woman, Mr. Schwatka?"

"Captain, one of the men—Sergeant Kaminski—found her working among the teamsters."

"Working for Russell?" Crook asked.

"That's right, General!" Janey replied buoyantly.

"Is Sergeant Kaminski here?" Mills called out into the crowd beyond the ring of firelight.

"Here, Captain."

"Front and center," Mills demanded. "Now, explain to me how you found our stowaway down in the teamsters' camp."

The sergeant cleared his throat. "It weren't down in the wagon camp, sir." Charles Kaminski began his story by removing his black slouch hat. "I just finished supper and figured I'd take a walk along the river, up there where I'd seen a lot of trees. Go have me a walk and a smoke. Let my supper settle—a constitutional, Cap'n."

"Yes, Sergeant," Mills replied with undisguised aggravation. "So how did you run onto the woman here? How'd you catch her?"

"I caught *him,* Colonel Mills!" Calamity replied. "Caught him peeking on me taking a bath in all my naked glory!" She again cupped her breasts, kneading them provocatively for the crowd.

The hundreds cheered and hooted, whistling and stomping in their approval as they surged around the officers for a look at the well-endowed prisoner.

"Sergeant?" Crook demanded.

"General—I heard someone splashing in the river and singing," Kaminski continued. "In the fading light it didn't look like nobody I knew, so I walked on up closer to the edge of the bank so I could get round a clump of some willers and say howdy—and that's when I finally laid eyes on the person standing in the river, up to they waist in the water. Taking . . . taking—"

"A bath!" Martha Jane bellowed as loud as she did down in the saloons of Cheyenne City or up to Deadwood. "That's when your sergeant see'd my tits, Colonel. And nice ones they are." She held them out for inspection. "Don't you think, Colonel Mills?"

The crowd hooted more hotly now while Mills stood there, growing redder in the firelight as he shifted from foot to foot in frustration and anger.

"You're absolutely certain you don't know this woman, Colonel? Certain you have nothing to do with her being here?" growled Crook.

"Not in my life, General! On my honor as an officer!"

The general whirled on his officers. "Has anyone thought of getting Russell over here?" he demanded. "Bourke—go fetch the wagon master and we'll get to the bottom of this now."

"Yes, sir!" The lieutenant took off at a shot.

"In the meantime, Sergeant—you bring Miss Jane into my tent. Captain Nickerson, you'll accompany the prisoner as well. Until you are instructed otherwise by me, she's in your custody, Captain—until I decide what we're going to do with a goddamned woman along on this march."

Martha Jane whirled on her heel, lunging for Crook as she once more cupped her heavy breasts. In no way were they the breasts of a boyish adolescent. There was a full-bodied, curvaceous woman beneath those loose-fitting britches and flannel shirt, breasts straining against those red wool longhandles.

Still—Seamus decided as he inched forward into the firelight to get himself a look as the prisoner was herded past—this wasn't a particularly attractive woman. In fact, he could understand how it would be pretty damned easy for this Calamity Jane woman to pass for a man out here on the frontier. Plain as the unbroken prairie, despite all them curves.

"Why, Gennil' Crook," Jane gushed as Nickerson grabbed her arm and brought her up short from reaching the expedition commander, "I'll be happy to show your men just what we *could* do with a woman along on your march. All of it for the good of your soldier morale!"

The crowd catcalled even more profanely, even louder.

Calamity Jane appeared to have warmed up to her audience as well. "And I'll be please to start by showing you real personal, Gennil'. A poke for free, just so I can say I diddled the great Gennil George Armstrong Crook!"

"My name isn't Armstrong!" Crook bawled like a wounded bull.

Martha Jane smiled big. "Did I call you the wrong gennil, Gennil?"

"Nickerson!" Crook turned and roared. "Get the prisoner out of my sight!"

That's when the general's aide swung the prisoner around and shoved her toward the headquarters tent, muscling her past Seamus Donegan. Martha Jane Cannary's eyes found him in the crowd—not that he would have been hard to pick out in most any company. But for a fleeting moment she halted, dug in her heels, and bowed up her back, bristling as Nickerson tried to shove her off-balance and moving forward.

"You're the *Irishman*, ain't you?" she asked of Donegan, trying to lean close.

He smiled, amused, but also a bit confused by her question. Skeptical, he asked, "You know me too? Like Cap'n Mills?"

Calamity Jane shook her head and turned it slightly, her eyes fluttering as coquettishly as she could make them. "I don't know you yet—you handsome horseman. But I sure as hell wanna get to know you—know you real good!"

"Move on, woman!" Nickerson snarled behind her, finally succeeding in shoving Jane toward Crook's tent once more.

"Hear me, Irishman!" she called out to Donegan as she was hauled away, inch by inch, resisting all the way. "We'll get to know each other real good. I'll make you forget any of the chippies and whores at the Hog Ranch, or down to that red-light block in Cheyenne City. Calamity Jane will roll your bones like you ain't never been rolled before!"

Seamus watched the captain and two others herd their prisoner off as Mills himself came to a stop at Donegan's shoulder.

"Well, now—Seamus Donegan," the captain began with a bit of amused chagrin in his voice. "Seems we have an acquaintance in common."

The Irishman grinned, eventually looking over at the

officer. "You gotta be kidding, Cap'n. You're the one she claimed she knew."

"And you, Irishman," Mills declared as the crowd began to disperse, their officers ordering them back to their bivouacs, "it's you Calamity Jane wants to get to know in the worst way!"

Chapter 13

4 June 1876

"*I fought enough Injuns already,*" Finn Burnett said as he stood in the yard outside his small log home, squinting up into the early sunlight at the three horsemen. "Eight, nine years ago I fought enough Sioux to last me a whole lifetime, Tom. You take care of yourself. All you boys."

Tom Cosgrove held down his big, hardened hand and shook with Burnett, the first agricultural agent the Eastern Shoshone had on their Wind River Reservation. "When the great war ended, Finn—I thought I'd fought enough to last the rest of my life too. But now General Crook is marching out to fight the enemies of the Shoshone. Years back I married into the tribe, so I figure that makes it my fight too."

"Just be sure you come back, Tom," Burnett echoed, turned and stepped back to the narrow porch on the front of the log house where he had lived for two years.

"We're coming back, Finn. You can make a mark on that!" roared Nelson Yarnell, another Texan, and Cosgrove's lieutenant. "And we'll have us a little cheer when we finally got them Sioux run out of this country for good!"

The third man had always been a taciturn sort not much given to talk, so the most Yancy Eckles did now in taking his leave was to touch the brim of his worn hat and tip his head in Burnett's direction.

"Let's go fetch up our warriors, boys," Cosgrove said, reining his mount around in a tight circle and putting heels to its flanks. Make no mistake, this aging Confederate was a horse soldier. A Civil War veteran. Rode with no less than the famous Texas Thirty-second, C. S. of A. One of R. P. Crump's glorious and rowdy fighters. Most of all, Tom Cosgrove had been a Texan who had crossed the great river to hold the Yankees back.

In one battle after another, he had been shot at and unhorsed. He had felt the sting of Union steel and watched men go down, tumbling from their mounts with their heads lopped off, or completely cleaved in two like the bloody halves of a melon lying on the dead man's shoulders. It was a nasty, dirty way to make war—but it was war. And Tom had fought it, wounded and blackened by spent powder, following General R. P. Crump across the Mississippi to fight in one battle after another until the afternoon he was captured.

With the retreat blown by the twelve-year-old bugler of Crump's, Tom had instead turned back to try reaching a fallen friend, only to fall into the hands of the Yankees who were surging out of the brush and timber, hot on the heels of the withdrawing Confederate cavalry. Cosgrove never did make it back to that fallen friend.

But he did reach Camp Douglas in Illinois, up near Chicago. And there never was no place more Yankee than Chicago.

It was there Tom and the others were offered a way to get out of prison and go on fighting—but not for the Confederacy.

Seemed the Union was running out of men to put in Yankee uniform, and that made perfect sense to Cosgrove—what with the way he had seen the Union armies send ten, fifteen thousand or more to their deaths in one goddamned day. So the North was having to siphon off its manpower from the posts and forts out on the western frontier. But to keep the freight roads open, to maintain the telegraph link with California, the army needed manpower in the west. So the Yankees came up with a plan. An offer to those Confederate prisoners slowly dying of typhus and dysentery and scurvy in those prisons up north: "Volunteer to fight Indians out west; put on a Union uniform and we won't make you fight your former brethren; and when the war is over and your time is up—you can go back home."

Reluctantly, Tom Cosgrove finally took the oath, and with the hundreds of others boarded the boxcars that would take them west to a place in Kansas called Leavenworth. It was there they began their march across the plains to Indian country. A high, wild wilderness where those Confederate volunteers, those "galvanized Yankees" fought beside the Iowa and Kansas units to keep a lid on the warfare exploding across the Central Plains in the wake of Colonel John M. Chivington and his Colorado Militia marching down to massacre Chief Black Kettle's camp on Sand Creek in November of 1864.

It had been something altogether different, this fighting Sioux and Cheyenne warriors. Oh, Tom Cosgrove had charged into Union cavalry more times than he might remember—but those brown-skinned warriors mounted on their fleet ponies were a different sort of enemy altogether.

Besides finding he truly liked this Injun fighting, Cosgrove came to love that Wyoming country, in many ways like that country of Central Texas, where he had been born and whelped. Yet more than anything, the reason Tom came to stay on after he was mustered out of the U.S. Volunteers was his liking of the Shoshone tribe, who were in close contact with the army in those opening days of the great Indian Wars of the Plains.

Tom found him some Injuns he could like instead of hate, as he hated the Kiowa and Comanche who raided out of West Texas. Naturally enough, it wasn't long before Cosgrove ran onto a young Shoshone gal, as well as finding a place to give his restless heart some long-overdue sanctuary. R. P. Crump's old Confederate horse soldier had found himself a new home at long, long last among the Wind River Shoshone.

Down the road that would take him and the other squaw men to Camp Brown this morning, Cosgrove saw them waiting. Even at this distance Tom knew who the horseman sitting out in front of the others was.

"My, don't they look pretty, Tom?" asked Nelson Yarnell.

From here Cosgrove could see there were more than a hundred, all arrayed in their finery. That made his heart swell a little bit, knowing more had shown up for this journey after all—more than chief Washakie had first stated he would guarantee the soldier chief at Camp Brown.

Tom had been there when Washakie was called in to the soldier post, to hear that General Crook had wired his request for some Shoshone allies to meet him heading north on the Montana Road. The army was asking the Shoshone to join the general's soldiers who drive the Sioux and Northern Cheyenne back to their agencies.

"This is not just our fight," Tom had told Washakie. "The Sioux and Cheyenne are your enemies too." But in the end Cosgrove knew he had no need to remind the Shoshone chief.

Washakie had been a friend of the white man's ever since the white man had come to these northern Rockies. The first fur trappers had come to respect and count on the Shoshone, in large part because of this young warrior. Jim Bridger said he could rely on few men to cover his backside —and Washakie was one of them. Now the warrior was an old man, more than seventy-odd winters behind him, his hair streaked with the iron of those many snows.

Tom came to a halt with Yarnell and Eckles, in silence before the chief, waiting for Washakie to speak first out of respect for the venerable chief's reputation.

Washakie took a deep breath of that morning air, made all the more glorious by the rose-tinted streaks of early sunlight streaming into the valley of the Wind River. His entire face painted with narrow, vertical white streaks of earth pigment, a necklace of two shriveled Sioux fingers suspended at his chest, the chieftain peered about at the surrounding hills as if studying them, then finally approving of this place.

"It is a good fight you go to, Cosgrove," the chief finally said quietly as some of the ponies pawed and snorted behind him.

The feathers and scalp locks of the Shoshone braves lifted on the morning breeze in a radiant burst of color and motion. Tom felt himself damned proud to be going along to whip the Sioux with Washakie and Crook, that old Union warrior. They would be fighting side by side now: Crook, and most of them other Yankee officers the general would have marching north with him. Good to be fighting shoulder to shoulder with proven soldiers now, not agin 'em.

"We are ready to go with you now," Tom said.

Washakie wagged his head sorrowfully. "I'm not going with you today, Cosgrove."

That caught Tom by surprise. "Are you feeling your many winters?"

With a smile the old Shoshone replied, "No, more than anything I want to have a good fight with the Lakota and those Shahiyena. No matter my many winters—I want nothing more than to die in battle. Washakie will not die in bed." He turned to the younger warrior on the pony beside him. "For now, I am sending my son, Dick—to go on with you."

Tom's eyes went to Dick Washakie, then back to the chief. "You will come soon?"

Nodding, the old Shoshone answered, "When the Utes and Bannocks come. When Crook sent me word he wanted the Shoshone to join him, I sent runners to tell the Bannocks of this war on the Lakota. It would not be good for me to leave before they got here."

Cosgrove looked over the warriors behind the chief. "These others, they are coming with me now?"

"Yes. But because the Bannocks have sent a runner to tell me they will be putting warriors on the road to join us, I will wait. When they get here, I will bring them to follow Crook's trail. Until then, Luishaw will be the leader of my tribesmen."

With a nod Cosgrove acknowledged the middle-aged interpreter and famous warrior. Also known as Louissant in a French-inspired spelling of his name, Luishaw sat atop his spotted pony just behind Washakie with the other headmen who would be in charge of the warriors the ex-Confederate estimated to be at least a hundred in number. Norkuk and Rota, Aguina and Toahshur, along with Wanapitz and Weshaw, even Tigee, the one whites called Yute John. They had all counted coup on Blackfoot and Lakota, fought Northern Cheyenne and Arapaho over their many summers of raiding and pony stealing, defending their families and homeland along the Wind River.

"It makes my heart glad to see so many brave warriors coming with me to fight our enemies," Cosgrove said. "Each day I will look to the west where the sun sets . . . until I can look upon the face of my old friend Washakie."

The aging chief smiled broadly at that, his old eyes misting a bit as he nudged his horse forward, laying his hand over his heart as he did, then bringing the arm out so that it pointed to Cosgrove. The feathers tied to his scalp lock tussled in the rising breeze. It was still cold here as the bright yellow globe sneaked over the hills to paint the bluffs red-hued to the west.

"Do not fear: I will join you soon," Washakie said in bidding Cosgrove farewell, "to stand at your shoulder when we ride into battle against our enemies."

He had a pretty good idea where he would find the Crow.

Although Frank Grouard had raided the Apsaalooke several times in the years he spent among the Lakota, "The Grabber" had never gone as far west into the land of the enemy as he would have to go now.

Even though they had been outnumbered by their enemies on the north, south, and east for many generations, the Crow had time and again proved themselves as fierce and worthy adversaries. They would make good allies for Crook, Grouard knew in his heart. But as much as Three Stars, and even the Crow tribe, all wanted to defeat the Lakota—"The Grabber" himself wanted to crush Crazy Horse and Sitting Bull all the more, nourished by his own unrequited hate.

Three hundred miles lay before the three of them now, a long, long way to go through enemy country before he would reach the Stillwater River. Perhaps they would find the villages of Old Crow and Medicine Crow there. If not at the Stillwater, the three half-breeds would have to press on west, Reshaw and Big Bat had reminded Grouard. Likely to find the Apsaalooke bands camped at the mouth of Mission Creek. Pourier had traded among the tribe, working out of the Bozeman country from '65 to '68 when the army abandoned the Montana Road. Reshaw had spent some time among the tribe too. Ten winters or so before—in those years Louie came of age, when he came to know Mitch Bouyer.

Reshaw was talking about the man a lot now. How this Bouyer might be off scouting for the soldiers marching east from Fort Ellis across Bozeman's Pass with the officer Louie knew only as the Limping Soldier. Reshaw claimed this Sioux and French half-breed Bouyer would likely join any of the Crow who would guide the Limping Soldier's troops assigned to keeping the Lakota south of the Yellowstone.

No longer did Grouard call it the Elk River. After all, he had left the blanket, and was again among the white man.

Frank had suggested to Crook that it would be a good idea for the general to march his troops on to the northwest along the Montana Road, past the old Piney Creek fort* until he had reached the forks of Goose Creek. There, Frank said, with good pasture for the horses, timber for their cookfires, and plenty of water flowing down from the Big Horn Mountains, the soldier column could await his return from Crow country.

But first he and Reshaw and Big Bat would have to ride across three hundred miles of country haunted and hunted by the Lakota and Shahiyena. Frank prayed the enemy would not be out hunting for the three half-breeds. Prayed no wandering scouts had the slightest hint the trio had moved out after dark, leading their six strong horses, stripped of everything they would not use to save strength and to go the distance.

To bring the Crow back to Crook.

As the sky had seeped night-black to go a murky morning gray that dawn after slipping away from Fort Reno, the

---

* Fort Phil Kearny, Dakota Territory, 1866–68

three scouts went into camp near the Crazy Woman crossing. Hiding down in the timber, they waited out the rising of the sun. Then after the sun had reached midsky, they decided to chance killing one of the buffalo that grazed the nearby slopes. Since the shaggy beasts weren't in any hurry, it seemed doubtful there were any hostiles in the area to chivy the easily spooked animals. Bat went out alone and dropped a young cow, then immediately headed back for the shelter at the crossing. The three holed up for a long time until they were sure no one was coming to investigate the gunshot. Only then did they venture from the brush along the creek with their extra animals and butcher the cow.

Over a fire they kept as smokeless as they could beneath a leafy cottonwood to disperse any rising tongues of gray that would smudge the summer sky, the half-breeds hung the rich meat they had cut into thin strips. They had to jerk enough meat to last them for the rest of their long journey. None of them wanted to chance firing any more shots to bring down game, and no one wanted to risk making another fire. This was it, and it had to last for the dangerous ride yet to come that would take them into the land of the Crow.

At dusk they rode out again. But near dawn the next morning as they were crossing Clear Creek, the scouts surprised a grizzly bear at its breakfast in the willows. The great bear rose up on its hind legs, spooked and roaring fiercely before it dropped to all fours and charged their horses. As fast as a grizzly could move, there was no sense in trying to outrun the beast. Instead, there was one choice left the half-breeds. Only after more than twenty shots from their carbines did they drop the big silvertip.

With hearts hammering the half-breeds kicked their horses into motion, knowing full well they had to clear that stretch of country before they might be discovered. Minutes later as they climbed the north slope of the Clear Creek valley, they spotted a smudge of smoke against the sunrise. From the top of the ridge they looked down into the next narrow valley. There to the north, in the middle of the path they were taking, stood a cluster of lodges. What tribe, none of them knew for sure. But they could hazard an educated guess.

"This close to the old Piney Fort—I'll bet it's Lakota," Bat whispered.

Reshaw nodded.

"Let's make tracks," Grouard told them, agreeing.

He took them hard to the west, straight up Clear Creek into the foothills of the Big Horns. Turning north to push through the dark, cool shadows of the timbered slopes, they rode down the sun, reaching the waters of Piney Creek just as twilight deepened. They figured they could afford to ride down onto the prairie a few miles, perhaps make camp and get some rest after staying their saddles for more than a day.

But as they left the timbered slopes, they bumped right into a second hunting village and were forced to push on, riding the moon up and down again before reaching Little Goose Creek as the sky brightened the next morning. Here they finally took a chance on resting the horses, and while two men grabbed a short nap, one of their number kept his ears and eyes awake until all had slept a little in turn. By late morning the three moved out once more.

That day they ran across two more small hunting camps, each with a good number of lodges erected against the sky. It ate up a lot of valuable time dodging and back-tracking all that day and into the night. By moonrise the three reached Twin Creek and decided to rest until false dawn, when there would be enough light to move on safely.

"I'll take first watch," Frank told the others.

"All right, you wake me in three hours. I'll take second watch," Bat said quietly as he lay down on the warmth of the horse blanket his animal had worn for all those many miles. Then he pulled a thick Indian blanket over his head.

Both Pourier and Reshaw were snoring before Frank had dragged out his small canteen and pulled some of the jerky from a bag he kept lashed to the back of his saddle. Like that he sat, eating and listening to the night, watching the moon rise amid the slow, galvanic whirl of stars over-head. While the water eventually cut the dust and fear that coated his throat, the jerky landed like horse droppings in his belly gone too long without food.

But they were getting closer. Drawing near to the land of the Crow. And once there in the Apsaalooke villages, Frank promised himself a big steak, cooked just enough to braise the outside, with its middle a juicy pink. It was a promise to himself he meant to keep.

"Here they sleep, far from home. Far from civilization," John Finerty said morosely.

Seamus turned where he stood, watching the newsman come up in the dim, predawn light of that early morning. Finerty took the hat from his head and scratched his scalp, almost self-consciously, like a former altar boy finding himself back in church.

Donegan only nodded.

"You know any of them?" asked the correspondent.

"No. Up at Phil Kearny—I knew some of those men," he answered quietly, his voice prayerful here among the markers and headstones he had labored over in the predawn chill, setting them aright, figuring he could come here before anyone else would notice he was gone from the breakfast fires. First, coffee with the general, then, as the camp came to life, the Irishman had come here to listen to the ghosts before he led Crook's column into enemy country.

"Bourke said I might find you here," Finerty explained. "This isn't a walk a man should make in the dark, Seamus." And he flung an arm back to indicate the two hundred yards of dark prairie to the ruins of old Fort Reno.

"Sun's coming up soon. We'll be riding out, John."

One by one Donegan had counted them when he reached the cemetery earlier, moving slowly among their resting places: a single officer, and thirty-five soldiers, here beneath the thin topsoil that was the blanket of this unforgiving land, these fighting men left behind to take their final slumber. In the middle of this hallowed ground a memorial had been raised by their fellow soldiers serving at this post on the Powder River, but, like the individual headstone and markers, it had been torn down by the

Sioux as well. Seamus had done what he could to stack some of the cairn's stones back in place, then leaned against the broken slab, where some of the few words were still clearly etched:

ERECTED AS A MEMORIAL
OF RESPECT TO OUR COMRADES
IN ARMS, KILLED IN DEFENSE

But the rest of it lay shattered, the remaining words returning to dust, as were the mortal remains of those who had fought to open this road to the Montana gold fields.

"Privates Murphy, Holt, Clure, Riley, Morner, and Laggin, killed May twenty-seventh, 1867," Finerty read from a wooden slab he pieced together. "C. Slagle, Twenty-Seventh Infantry, killed thirty May, 1867."

Donegan commented quietly, "The Sioux and Cheyenne had been making things hot all along the road north."

"I heard you was up here ten years ago. Here at Reno?"

He wagged his head. "No. The northern post—C. F. Smith."

"Where they had the Hayfield Fight?"*

"Where *we* had *our* fight in the hayfield. Lasted most of the day, John." Seamus turned away, dusting his hands off on his canvas britches. "We'd better be getting back to camp. This column got nearly thirty miles to march today since Crook intends to make Crazy Woman crossing by nightfall."

"Thirty miles? That's pushing this outfit."

"The general will do just that from here on out," Donegan said. "He will force every last ounce of effort from the animals and his men. To get them into fighting trim by the time the cavalry strikes out on its own to go in search of the fight Crook so desperately wants with Crazy Horse."

---

* August 1, 1867: THE PLAINSMEN Series, vol. 2, *Red Cloud's Revenge*

Chapter 14

3–4 June 1876

Crook needed those Crow warriors the half-breeds had gone to fetch. Needed them in the worst way now that it looked as if the Shoshone weren't coming to join in this war against their old enemies.

As Donegan had led them away from the north bank of the Powder River, he heard the order echo back down the long, long column of infantry, on down the ranks of cavalry plodding in advance of the wagon and mule trains.

"Uncover!"

As they approached the frost-covered ruins of that little cemetery, the soldiers obediently took their hats from their heads. Two by two by two they passed that toppled monument crimson-tinted to a blood glow in the sun's first light.

"Eyes . . . *right!*"

In unison entire companies turned to gaze at the ravaged graves where their own had fallen almost a decade gone. Every one of Crook's soldiers got a good look now at how the enemy had desecrated this final resting place of those left behind when Reno was abandoned.

This is a good thing, Donegan had thought. Just what Crook wants them to see. Needs them to feel. To kindle some smoldering hatred for the Sioux and Cheyenne and what the enemy's done to the graves, maybe even to the bodies.

Seamus gazed over that country awakening with spring, lulled into a reverie most of that first day as they pushed away from Fort Reno, moving the column along at a good pace just the way Crook wanted him to. The general was going to whip his expedition into shape come hell or high water. And it was up to the Irishman to set the grueling pace for this march all the way to the crossing at the Crazy Woman. They needed to reach that creek. It was there he knew they would find the best grass all the stock required. There too was likely to be the first water they could count on finding after leaving Reno behind. Something more than those muddy, scummy buffalo wallows they had been passing throughout that long day.

For most of that Saturday the great, the granite bulk of Cloud Peak beckoned them onward, ever on to the northwest with its lofty white mantle seeping downward into the seductive, purple coolness of the Big Horn Range. More and more tracks of the nomadic buffalo herds crossed and recrossed the old Montana Road, as well as more frequent sign of unshod pony hooves. Warriors on the prowl: either to make meat, or to keep an eye on the soldiers advancing ever farther into this jealously guarded hunting ground.

At midday a few columns of smoke were sighted off to the northeast. Crook dispatched a company of cavalry to investigate each one. Each time the soldiers returned not having discovered any evidence of hostiles. Nonetheless, the general changed the order of the march and put Royall's second in command, Major Andrew W. Evans, out in the van with Lieutenant Reynolds's F Company of the Third Cavalry. Major Henry Noyes was sent to protect the rear with his I Company of the Second Cavalry. From here on out, Crook understood, the enemy could afford to be most unpredictable. That evening the general ordered the posting of extra pickets as the sun sank on their camp beside the cold, clear-flowing creek called the Crazy Woman Fork. As weary as the men were from their long, dry, and dusty march, Crook had no desire to be surprised at this legendary crossing.

"Damn near the whole day as I've heard others tell the

story, Donegan,"* Crook declared that night as they were discussing the trail the general would take on the morrow.

"And on past sundown into the night. Black as pitch when Jim Bridger and that cavalry patrol he was leading came onto us in the dark."

The general held out his coffee cup, and an orderly immediately moved forward to refill it as he said, "And scared away the Sioux waiting to finish you off with the next sunrise."

"Then, you heard the story."

"Most complete: with Reverend White's daring escape to carry word of the fight all the way back to Reno," Crook said with no little wonder. "Thirty goddamned miles to ride—alone—through God only knew how many warriors. Now that's bravery."

"And a fine-blooded racehorse under him too. Sometimes, General—bravery is nothing more than living to tell the tale."

There were no bugles blaring reveille in the chill darkness that next morning. Instead, Crook had ordered all trumpets put away now that they were inching deeper and deeper into enemy country. All orders were to be passed along through the chain of command.

After that long stretch of the day before, theirs was a short march this Sunday, something on the order of twenty miles. Along the translucent waters of Clear Creek the soldiers pitched their camp, and many tried their hand at hooking some brook trout from the wide, shallow flow of snow-melt gurgling over its rocky bed. It didn't take long before a few of the soldiers devised an even easier way to catch their limit: a pistol was fired into the thick of the wary trout, the concussion stunning several fish, which would float to the surface where the men scooped them up by hand and flung their wriggling catch to the bank.

After exploring the country for a few miles to the north, Donegan returned to camp and was dragging the saddle from the back of his gelding as John Finerty hurried up, excitedly pointing to a bluff across the stream.

---

* THE PLAINSMEN Series, vol. 1, *Sioux Dawn*

"Ho, Irishman! You're an experienced plainsman—by God, you ought to be able to tell me just what in the name of the Virgin Mary is that?"

Seamus glanced at the hillside, answered with a shrug, then strode away to drop the saddle beside his bedroll beneath the overhanging branches of the cottonwood.

"Well?" Finerty demanded.

"A burial scaffold."

"Sioux?"

Donegan shrugged again. "Who knows? But in this country it likely is Sioux."

"Bloody fantastic!" Finerty gushed. "Let's go have us a look, what say?"

They reached the top of the low bluff accompanied by a dozen soldiers who apparently spotted the scaffold about the time Finerty and Seamus crossed the stream.

"Well, Sam—what the hell is that?" one of the infantrymen asked.

"That? Oh, that's the layout of some damned dead Injun," his companion answered.

"Let's pull it down!" cried another.

"Tear the son of a bitch out by its roots!" was the unanimous echo.

As the soldiers of the Ninth Infantry put their shoulders to the task against the four supporting poles, Donegan explained the construction of the burial scaffold to the wide-eyed newspaperman. It didn't take much muscle before an empty buffalo robe lashed with strips of green rawhide tumbled from its six-foot-high perch to the raucous cheers of the soldiers, who quickly grew disappointed when they kicked open the dusty hide and discovered it empty.

"Now, who you suppose robbed us of the red bastard's body?" asked one of the soldiers.

"The Injuns?"

As a group, they turned to gaze at Donegan. He shrugged. "Sioux wouldn't do it."

"Don't make no matter," another soldier commented. "We was sent after firewood—and firewood we got right here. C'mon, boys. Let's take these timbers down for our mess fire."

As the soldiers slashed the rawhide thongs binding the

scaffold legs to the cross-members, Finerty went to examine the dried buffalo hide. Spilling from it were two blue blankets with red edging. Inside, the correspondent found a vest trimmed in beadwork, a single moccasin, a colorful shawl along with a quantity of bound horsehair.

"What you make of this, Irishman?" Finerty asked as he carefully picked up the edge of a piece of colorful cloth, its pattern still bright.

"Looks to be a plaid to me," Donegan replied, using the Celtic pronunciation: *played.*

"Why would one of these red bastards have a piece of a Scottish highland tartan in his burial robes?"

"Perhaps he took a shine to it, so bought it off some trader. Makes a pretty breechcloth, don't it?"

"Likely the bastard stole it from some settler, some traveler waylaid on his way west far from the protection of civilization."

Seamus turned away to watch the soldiers descend the bluff, dragging their kindling behind them. Finerty came up and stopped beside the scout.

"Don't give it another thought, Seamus," he said. "You saw how the damned savages desecrated the graves of our dead back at Reno, didn't you? Seems right and fitting that those soldiers returned the honor here."

"There wasn't no body left for them to tear down," Donegan reminded, then moved away, heading down the slope toward the camp on Clear Creek.

That evening Dick Closter boiled a delicious soup from three hapless tortoises he had captured along the streambank. It proved to be something Seamus had never before tasted, but found quite delicious.

"Not quite as tasty as my Maryland terrapin back to home," Closter said as they poured themselves some coffee after supper, stars winking into view one by one against the darkening canopy overhead.

"Seamus!"

"That sounds like Johnny Bourke," Closter declared.

The lieutenant scooted into the firelight. "General wants you come and talk to some fellas who wandered into camp just now."

"The pickets snagged some hostiles sneaking up on camp?"

Bourke shook his head. "These are white men."

At the headquarters fire sat two bearded, middle-aged men in trail-worn clothing. Nearby a pair of soldiers held the reins of their two weary horses.

"Donegan! Good," Crook called out as Bourke and the Irishman approached. "Here, come sit and talk with these fellas about the country hereabouts."

As Seamus settled at the headquarters fire, he introduced himself and set about talking with the two strangers, learning they were miners come down from Montana with a party of sixty-five gold-seekers that had made their way to the Black Hills before they deemed it prudent to return to the diggings in the Big Sky country.

"Things getting a mite too hot up there in the Hills," one of the miners complained.

"Not a week goes by but the Sioux don't rub out more'n one miner," the second added.

"The Injuns up by Last Chance are damned sight more sociable," the first declared.

The rest of the Montana party was a day behind, using this trail-hardened pair as advance scouts to blaze a road and locate campsites on their trek back to Montana.

He gleaned what he could of the precautions the miners' party was taking as they pressed toward Montana: rifle pits dug at each night's camp, a military rotation of the guard, as well as putting out some flankers for each day's march to prevent against surprise or ambush by any of the wandering war parties. With more and more frequency, the two said, they were coming across unshod pony tracks crisscrossing the country they ventured through with understandable caution. Most of the miners were veterans, Seamus had learned—men accustomed to what it took to move through an enemy's territory.

Eventually Seamus's curiosity could last no longer, and he asked, "Either of you know a fella by the name of Marr? Colonel Sam Marr?"

"You serve with him in the war?" asked one of the two miners.

"So you do know him?"

The pair looked at one another quickly. Then both shook their heads.

"No," said the one who had asked the question. "Just figured it was someone you served with, since you called him colonel."

That first flush of excitement that had momentarily filled Seamus rushed out of him now the way a fall from a horse would knock the wind out of a man.

"You might say we served together, but not in the war," Donegan explained. "Spent time fighting Injins up north on the Bozeman Road."

"You lived to tell your stories of it?" the second miner asked. "But you're back tempting your fortune and these goddamned savages to lift your hair again?"

Donegan laughed, then said, "It does sound like I've got some of the sense of a fool, don't it?"

A pair of the mounted vedettes moved slowly past on the edge of camp a few yards off. They were hailed in passing by the stationary pickets posted around the entire perimeter of Crook's army. The general was not about to allow any hostile raiding party to come in and run off the beef herd or any of his mules and horses as the enemy had done back in March.

"Well, fellas—we best be pushing on," one of the miners said as he stood.

They made their farewells to Crook and his staff, then shook hands with the Irishman.

"Maybe we'll run onto you up at Last Chance Gulch some time soon," the second miner said as he gripped Donegan's hand.

"I plan on getting there as soon as I can."

"Why not throw in with us now?" asked the first. "We could use a good trail guide like you. Besides, you go with us, you won't have to go looking for Injuns to fight like these soldiers always do."

"I'd like to, but I can't. Got a wife to get north with me when I do. She's down at Laramie for now."

"A passel of women in Deadwood," declared the first. "Not all of 'em whores either. Maybe you ought to take your wife there for the time being if you want to look for gold. She'll have more woman company in Deadwood than she would up to Montana."

With a shake of his head Seamus answered, "I'll finish what I started, and keep my word to the general over there. That comes first before I go digging for my fortune."

The two took up the reins to their weary horses and slipped back into the darkness, heading north by east.

A while later Colonel William B. Royall audibly growled and slammed his tin cup down on the stump where he roosted. "Dammit! Why in the devil didn't I think of it sooner, General?"

Crook asked, "Think of what?"

"Those two!" Royall leapt to his feet. "That pair masquerading as miners—why, they're no more than squaw men!"

"Squaw men?" asked Azor Nickerson.

"White men who live with Injun wives, in the Injun camps," Captain Guy V. Henry explained.

"You think those two were squaw men, Colonel?" Donegan asked in disbelief.

Royall nodded emphatically. "Damn right I do, Irishman."

"I had a funny feeling about them myself," agreed infantry captain Andrew Burt.

"They're probably on their way back to one of their camps right now," said Captain William H. Andrews of the Third Cavalry, "taking news of our troop strength and readiness with them."

"Shit," Seamus mumbled, wagging his head in baffled wonder. "You sojurs need some rest. Every one of you is seeing bogeymen everywhere you look."

"Mark my words, Irishman," Royall declared, "those two aren't miners at all."

"And if they aren't?"

"If I'm proved wrong, then I'll buy the brandy for you when we get back to Fetterman, Mr. Donegan."

"You make it whiskey—and you've got a wager."

"Of course! Anything at all," Royall cheered. "But just remember—you'll be filling my cup again and again with brandy, because there's not a doubt those two were sneaking, no-good squaw men. The lowest life form on the Indian frontier."

The soldiers were coming.

It was only a matter of time before they would try to attack the villages. Once more the white man would be a fool.

For over twenty suns the Crazy Horse people had been migrating away from Tongue River, following the Shahiyena, who led the growing procession ever closer to the Elk River, where scouts had spotted soldiers coming out of the land of the Crow. Crazy Horse and the war chiefs from the other bands kept their wolves coming and going every day now. Even when the camp had stopped for three suns to shoot the herd of buffalo found on the divide after crossing over to the west, into the valley of Rosebud Creek.

Three days later the encampment sent small war parties to harass the soldiers marching east along the Elk River—just to try the white man's resolve and strength. The Horse was reassured when the soldiers did not attempt to follow any of these small raiding parties.*

As a consequence of those forays, the great encampment lazily wandered a little farther up the Rosebud, not in any hurry. For three more suns they stayed put until the grass was eaten and the immense pony herds demanded another move.

"The soldiers are using People of the Raven for their eyes and ears, Crazy Horse," said White Cow Bull as he came up and took a seat in the sun.

Back in the shade of White Bull's lodge, Crazy Horse nodded in greeting to his warrior friend.

"The Raven People saw our encampment this morning," announced He Dog. "Some of them, along with a few white men."

"All were dressed in soldier coats," added White Cow Bull. "But we knew the Raven People from the way they wore their hair and their leggings. The moccasins they had

---

* Attacks on Colonel John Gibbon's Montana Column, May 22–24, 1876

on with long, trailing fringes. Only a handful were white men."

"And the army hasn't come to attack us?" Crazy Horse asked with a smile. "My friends, if those scouts did indeed look over all these hillsides where our pony herds graze, if they did see how long it would take to ride down this riverbank from the Shahiyena camp on the south to where Sitting Bull's Hunkpapa pitch their lodges on the north—then surely the soldiers will not even begin to consider charging down on us."

Unafraid, even unconcerned for the great encampment's safety, the Council of Seven Fires elected two days later to move a little farther up the Rosebud to Teat Butte—a place the Lakota bands and Shahiyena had been coming to camp for many generations. A place that always reminded Crazy Horse of Black Shawl's breast. How he had so enjoyed coupling with her.

But it had not always been so. Days gone in the past Crazy Horse had caused much pain among his people by stealing Black Buffalo Woman from No Water, her husband. Much, much bad blood among the Oglalla. Those were days of long ago, gone like spring snow-melt flowing away and never again to be cupped in his palms. Better to forget those days, those feelings and that passion. Better to forget that woman. Far better now for him to gaze at the snow gathered on the distant mountains, and know there would be more cold, clear snow-melt in the many summers yet left him.

After only one night spent at Teat Butte, the encampment moved the following morning another short march to Green Leaf Creek. Two days later the sky turned a sickly blue-and-purplish gray, like an ugly bruise lying over the land. It snowed, the wind whipping across the prairie and down through the narrow coulees as everyone withdrew to the warmth of their lodges and the scouts hurried back from watching the soldiers on Elk River.

That morning after the sudden snowfall, the Shahiyena sent out a few small scouting parties to the south, with the idea that they would ascend Rosebud Creek and probe toward the country where the soldiers had appeared in the Snow-Blind Moon to attack Two Moon's and Old Bear's camp on the Powder. Never again, the Shahiyena had vowed, would they be surprised by soldiers marching out of the south.

Then in the first days of Wipazuka Waste Wi, the Moon of Ripening Berries, Sitting Bull and some of the other headmen of the Hunkpapa had come to Crazy Horse's camp to tell the Hunkpatila leader that they had selected a special site one more day's march up the Rosebud.

"Tomorrow we will take this great encampment to the place where we will hold our annual dance to the sun, there to give worship to the Life-Giver," Sitting Bull explained to Crazy Horse.

"Each year you dance. Will you again this summer?" he asked the Hunkpapa medicine man.

"No," Sitting Bull answered. "But I plan to sacrifice my flesh at the bottom of the sacred pole. It is what I have been instructed by my vision helpers I must do. Tomorrow, when we arrive, I begin to prepare for my dream."

The Horse asked, "You have been told you would have another dream?"

"Yes," Sitting Bull answered solemnly. "I was instructed to have the sun dance at this special place. There I am told to take the fifty pieces of flesh from each arm as I sit beneath the sacred pole. Then I will sleep and be given my dream."

"And this dream of yours?" White Bull inquired.

Sitting Bull gazed at the other Lakota leaders gathered in the shade of the blanket bower where a summer breeze rustled the leafy cottonwood branches. Then he answered, as his eyes came to rest on the greatest Lakota war chief of all—Crazy Horse.

"My spirit helpers have told me this will be the most sacred dream of my life. They tell me . . . this is to be the most important dream of all time for all my people."

Chapter 15

5–6 June 1876

From Twin Creek, Frank Grouard, Baptiste Pourier, and Louie Reshaw moved north by west that next morning, hugging the base of the Big Horn Mountains. They had reached the no-man's-land where both the Lakota and the Crow hunted if they dared. This was contested ground, where any horseman spotted on a distant hilltop was likely an enemy out for ponies and plunder, or out for scalps.

They had gone but a few miles when Bat spotted a handful of horses tied in some brush down by the edge of a coulee not far off. The new day's sun was just then beginning to brush the backs of the Indian ponies with golden light.

"A war party," Bat declared.

"Out for ponies," Reshaw agreed.

"Those Crow ponies—or Lakota?" Grouard asked.

Pourier shrugged. "From here, who knows?"

"I don't want to go any closer—if those are Lakota warriors," Reshaw said.

"If they are Crow—they will know you both," Grouard said to Pourier. "What do the Crow call you?"

"They call me Left Hand," Bat replied, holding it up. "If they are not Crow—then all three of us are in trouble."

"Let's don't take the chance," Reshaw suggested.

They rode wide to circle round the raiding party, hoping not to awaken the warriors and alarm the strange ponies.

Late that afternoon the three reached the Little Big Horn and made their crossing as the sun eased down behind the mountain peaks. It was nightfall when they reached the banks of Soap Creek where Grouard decided they would make another cold camp for the night, with only the icy water from the swollen stream and the dried buffalo taken on the Crazy Woman to fill their bellies.

The next morning rumbled in early, replete with threatening thunderheads clamoring noisily off the Big Horns. Gusts of icy wind swept down off the nearby slopes, carrying frigid air from those glaciers frozen across centuries in the shadowy crevices of the granite peaks. They hadn't gone far when Pourier called out from the rear.

"Grouard! Pull off and hold up!"

Frank immediately reined into the trees that they had been hugging closely ever since moving out before sunup. He patted the neck of his mount as his eyes peered over their backtrail. "You see something?"

Bat nodded. "Something moved. Something not right."

"Dust?" Reshaw asked.

"No. Something . . . just moved."

Then they saw it at the same time. A good-sized war party in the distance breaking over the side of a hill, coming on the trio's trail, moving along as if the leaders were keeping a close eye on the tracks the three half-breeds had made that morning.

"How many?" Reshaw asked, licking his dry lips.

"It don't matter," Grouard said flatly.

"It does too matter," Pourier snapped. "We might have to make a fight of it."

Reshaw glared distrustfully at Grouard, snarling, "And I like to know how many I'm going to fight."

"It don't matter to me," Frank replied. "Because I'm not going to fight them here. I'm running for Crow country. You with me?"

Without another word Bat and Reshaw looked at one another, nodded quickly, and reined away with Grouard the moment Frank kicked his horse out of the timber.

They urged their mounts into an easy lope as Frank aimed for the broken country where they might not be so easily spotted by the war party racing down on their heels. For the rest of that morning and into the afternoon, the trio pushed their animals to the limit, ever closer to the Big Horn River, staying to cover as much as they could, when they could, but covering ground no matter what.

At the mouth of Black Canyon, Grouard told the others to wait while he pushed on to the brow of a nearby hill. In dismounting to look back across the broken country, Frank patiently waited, gazing across the immense, rolling land for sign of their pursuers. He waited, and waited some more. Still they did not show up.

"Maybe they give up," Reshaw contended when Grouard returned to tell the pair at the bottom of the slope.

"Could be," Pourier said. "Maybe they didn't want to get no closer to Crow country."

"We got lots of ground to cover," Frank said, and again turned toward the banks of the Big Horn, breaking cover.

They hadn't gone but a few hundred yards when Grouard spotted three horsemen on the gentle slope across the river. The half-breeds reined to a halt, and Grouard took his small signal mirror from a coat pocket to catch some of the sun that was playing dodge with the high thunderheads.

"Them Crow see this, they'll know we're not Lakota," Pourier declared.

"Let's just hope they know we're with the soldiers coming to attack their enemies," Reshaw added.

"I pray they remember you, Left Hand," Grouard said when the three horsemen across the river suddenly turned on their heels and disappeared over the hill.

With nothing else to do but to press on, as warily as they could, the half-breeds set out once more, ever watchful of the far bank on their left. Across the Big Horn.

As they passed the site of the abandoned Fort C. F. Smith, Bat pointed to a pair of horsemen slowly moving north along the west bank of the river. Again Grouard took out his army signal mirror and caught the furtive sunlight, signaling the pair. He got their attention, but they whirled and fled over the hills to the west, in the same direction the first three had flown.

"Damn," Grouard growled in exasperation. "I thought these Crows were hospitable, Bat."

"They don't know who the hell we are," Pourier grumbled.

Frank looked over his own dress and the clothing of the other two. "You mean we don't look enough like white men?"

Bat started chuckling as he gazed down at his own dress. "Sure as hell don't look like no Sioux, do I?"

"Let's get across the Big Horn and find that Crow village those horsemen been coming from," Grouard suggested.

"That river running pretty fast," Reshaw said when they rode down to the east bank to the edge of the water. "How you figure we get these horses across without swimming them?"

Pourier agreed. "I don't think I want to try that river—high and wild like she is."

Frank shrugged. "I guess we build a raft and take them over on it—one at a time."

All three dismounted in a copse of cottonwood and willow, deciding to have Reshaw cook up some stew with their dried meat while Pourier and Grouard attended to the felling of some saplings they would lash together for their raft. Reshaw had started his fire at the base of a cottonwood so the firesmoke would disperse through branches when Big Bat suggested they have a smoke before diving into their labors.

They sat on the bank of the Big Horn, cross-legged. Pourier took out his short pipe and charged it from a small tobacco pouch. He was just starting to light the bowl with a sulfur-head match when over his shoulder Grouard spotted a haze of dust rising beyond the hills.

He was on his feet, yanking on his coat and catching up his rifle as he hollered, "We gonna have company soon!"

Pourier wheeled at the moment the distant war party broke the skyline. "Sonsabitches did track us after all!"

Grouard hadn't waited to listen but was instead sprinting up the slope toward the other half-breed. He and Pourier were a long way from Reshaw.

"Louie! Get them horses caught up! We gotta skedaddle fast!"

Behind Frank, Bat was yelling.

"Frank! Frank!"

Grouard skidded to a halt and whirled. Pourier was not far behind, pointing back across the Big Horn to the west bank. Frank estimated there to be as many as six hundred horsemen making their charge down the far slope, all of them bristling for war.

Bat yelled, "Yonder come a lot more Injuns on the far side!"

"A lot more?" Grouard grumbled, angry with himself at getting caught in this trap. "That looks like the whole goddamned Crow nation!"

Reshaw was struggling to cinch his saddle on his mount as it pranced around, anxious at Louie's excitement.

"Forget it—just ride bareback!" Grouard hollered as he caught up the reins to his own mount, slapping the rump of two of the spare horses for good measure to send them flying.

"Only thing we can do now is fight it out," Grouard told the other two as they hammered heels to their horses and raced north for the banks of the Big Horn.

"Then let's turn and fight it out!" Bat shouted.

"No good to fight here. Up there. On the flat," Frank answered, pointing ahead where he figured they could make a stand of it in the open. "It's the only place where we might hold them off at a distance."

"Unless they wanna make quick work of us," Reshaw snapped. "Unless some of them bucks wanna come in and get their coups real quick!"

"They got to be Crow, Bat," Grouard said as they reached the flat piece of high ground and whirled off the backs of their horses.

"How the hell can you tell this far off?"

Grouard shrugged. "Can't for sure. Only thing—they're on the west side of the river."

"If that bunch is Crow—what about *those* sonsabitches?" Reshaw demanded, pointing to a war party tearing toward them from the south on the east bank of the river. "Gotta be Sioux."

"Appears we're smack in the middle of a little war, boys," Grouard replied.

Another half-dozen heartbeats and the warriors racing up from the south along the Big Horn finally reached the top of a low hill where at last they saw the far bank of the river for the first time. Skidding to a dusty, ragged halt, the twenty-five or more whirled about in tight confusion, yelping in surprise, brandishing their weapons and shouting among themselves before they suddenly turned on their heels and hastily disappeared back over the hill.

"I suppose they decided against helping us fight off them Crow," Grouard cheered, pointing at the far bank where hundreds of horsemen pushed their ponies down the edge of the Big Horn.

"Maybe the river will hold 'em back for a while so we can get a jump on 'em," Bat said.

"Or just hold 'em while we tell who we are and why we come," Frank replied.

"The bastards ain't stopping!" Reshaw shouted.

It made a sight. Those braids and feathers and scalp locks and all that fringe dancing on the wind as the hundreds of horsemen spread out, not slowing their fierce charge a bit as they forced their ponies off the bank and into that cold, rushing river fed by the melting snowcaps above them all.

"Like they don't give a damn about drowning!" Pourier grumbled.

"Horsemen like those ain't gonna drown," Reshaw growled in reply.

"You better figure on telling them we're friends, Bat," Grouard ordered, "or start telling me how you're gonna talk our asses out of this fix!"

As some bullets began to whine over the trio's head, the first horsemen into the river dropped out of sight beyond the east slope sinking sharply away to the Big Horn. All Grouard could see now were the rest of the hundreds still plunging into the icy torrent of the river, yelling their taunts, firing their guns at the three half-breeds on the far river slope.

"Goddamn—I said tell 'em who the hell you are, Bat!"

Shoving his horse aside, Pourier strode into the open, hollering for all he was worth above the clamor of gunfire and screeching warriors. He signaled with his arms—raising his left hand, striking it repeatedly with his right to make the ancient sign. Then the first horsemen across the river broke over the brow of the last rise, less than a hundred yards off, their ponies heaving at an ear-flattened gallop.

"If Bat can't stop 'em, Louie," Grouard instructed as he laid the barrel of his Springfield over the bare back of his horse, "get ready to take as many with you as you can before you go under."

"Left Hand!" Pourier was yelling in Crow as the snorting ponies bore down on the trio. *"Left Hand!"*

When they were less than fifty yards away, one of the leaders threw up a hand and began flinging his voice at the others. Gradually, the firing of the guns from the river faded as more horsemen broke over the lip of the hill. By now the warriors stretched across a half-mile-wide front, tearing along the slope that would carry them toward the trio.

"Left Hand!" Pourier continued to shout in the Crow tongue.

"Left Hand!" the warrior answered back, this time firing his rifle into the air. "Left Hand!"

"It's Old Crow!" Bat yelled over his shoulder at Grouard and Reshaw.

"You know him?" Frank asked.

Bat was almost crying, tears of joy in his eyes. "Hell if I don't!"

It happened all so quickly that Grouard could not quite take it all in at once: the first horsemen were upon them, swirling around them, fifty, then a hundred and more, each one shouting, laughing, leaping from their snorting ponies to come up and shake hands with Pourier, others who recognized Reshaw wrenching up his hand and pumping the arm for all it was worth in good white-man fashion. They were all running about, patting one another on the back in celebration—and laughing. Frank had never heard so much laughing from a bunch of warriors before.

About two dozen did not stop but instead rode on past in a haze of dust, pushing south at a gallop after the Lakota war party that had been dogging the half-breeds' trail since that morning. That furious pursuit gave Frank pause, thinking on all that laughter. He could not remember ever hearing so much gut-busting good humor before.

Then Pourier was beside Grouard, pulling him around to introduce him to a string of Crow war chiefs, and Frank was at long last able to have Bat explain to the warriors why they had come. Who had sent them. To say that "Lone Star" Crook desperately needed their help in defeating the Lakota and Shahiyena once and for all time.

"To drive them from your hunting ground, for as long as time flows beneath the stars," Grouard had Pourier explain to Old Crow and the other headmen.

The war chief shouted, repeating this momentous news to the rest, then set some of his warriors to work on a raft they would use to ferry the scouts across the Big Horn. In less than three hours the entire assembly was ready to push off as the sun began to fall behind the high peaks. While some of the younger warriors of the group swam the half-breeds' barebacked horses across the river, the three scouts were told to climb aboard the raft with their saddles and trail gear.

Grouard rubbed his aching hands, one in the other, as he quietly complained, "I ain't ever shaked so many hands in one place at one time."

"Crow always been a tribe enjoys to shake hands," Pourier replied.

"I'll say! For the three goddamned hours it took me to shake hands with all six hundred of them," Frank grumped. "Why—soon as we get back, we'll just have to tell Crook all about our great American handshaking tournament!"

From their camp on Clear Creek, it was a short sixteen-mile march past Lake DeSmet to the forks of Piney Creek, where ten summers before Colonel Henry B. Carrington began construction on his fabled post. Just past midday on 5 June, Crook's Big Horn and Yellowstone Expedition made camp on the extensive bottomland just east of the plateau where stood the ruins of Fort Phil Kearny. Soldiers and civilians moved out in hunting parties to make meat for supper. As the afternoon wore on, the hunters returned, bringing not only buffalo and elk back for the mess fires, but also beaver and antelope, pintailed grouse and sickle-billed curlew. Hundreds of fires winked into life, and the men gladly celebrated the bountiful harvest here in the land of ghosts. Not to be outdone, Crook himself brought down a cow elk.

That Monday became one of bittersweet remembrance for Seamus Donegan.

As the shadows lengthened, stretching down from Cloud Peak, the Irishman walked alone among the charred stumps of what had been the tall stockade, kicking at the fractured remnants in what remained of the brickyard, then followed what had once been the neat, graveled walks, now overgrown and nearly lost among the tall grass, coming at last to that scarred ground where the frozen, distorted, and mutilated bodies of the Fetterman dead had been consigned dust to dust once more.

Ten years of miles and faces swam once more before him that evening as his brimming eyes looked yonder to the firm height of Pilot Knob, where the infantry pickets would signal the approach of a supply train, reinforcements, or the attack on a wood train. It was there on the Knob, the place Carrington selected for the post cemetery, they had buried those who gave their lives in twos and threes from that July of '66 into the fall and early winter.

But it was here, right where Seamus now stood, in a fifty-foot-long trench below his dusty boots, that Carrington had buried the eighty who had fallen with Fetterman's fateful march over Lodge Trail Ridge. After all, Fort Phil Kearny was under siege. They had little choice but to bury their dead among those still living.

Turning, Seamus found the grassy slope of the far ridge turning a deep purple in the fading light. So different now in the first days of summer than it had been a decade ago, deep in the jaws of winter come to visit the northern plains. That brutal ride over Lodge Trail Ridge, to reach the battle site with the emotionally crippled soldier Ten Eyck. Discovering Jennifer Wheatley's husband in that tiny knot of fighting men he found at the bottom of massacre hill, those few who had done the greatest damage: sixty or more puddles of frozen blood he had counted around that small cluster of low rocks where the white men, civilian and a few old files, had gathered at the last, determined to sell their lives at a very high cost to the screeching red enemy.

"The Lakota talk proudly about that fight," Frank Grouard had told Seamus while they scouted together during Crook's March campaign to the Powder River. "In their winter count they call it the 'Winter of the Hundred in the Hand.' "

"A great battle they say, eh?"

"Yes. But not an easy victory," Grouard had replied. "In my time with the Lakota, I have heard them admit just how bad they were hurt in the fight. Many deaths."

"How many?"

"More'n a hundred all told. Not all killed time of the fight. Most of the wounded didn't make it through the cold. There was times they would talk about just how many of the Sioux and Cheyenne were killed by other Sioux and Cheyenne in the rain of arrows they were firing at the soldiers from both sides of the ridge."

"Caught in their own cross fire, eh?"

"Bound to be a lot in a close, dirty fight like that."

"Was their spirit worked up good?"

"They had blood in their eyes, Seamus."

Ah, sweet Jennifer Wheatley—Donegan thought now as he turned back to look over the ruins of the fort.

A road not taken . . .

Seamus squeezed off the painful reverie, just as he squeezed against the stinging mist threatening his eyes, scuffing off across the grass and gravel, cinders and charred earth, down the short slope to the east and onto the level tongue of bottomland between the Big and Little Pineys. He needed to find a friend, a smiling face, and a hot cup of coffee.

"The general sent Johnny Bourke to fetch you up. Wants to see you," Dick Closter announced as the Irishman strode into the packers' camp. "Right away."

"Crook?"

Closter looked at the others gathered around the fire. "Now ain't that just like a dense-headed mick for you?" He gazed back at Donegan, grinning. "What other general you think we brought along with us, Seamus?"

Chapter 16

6–7 June 1876

"*It's as simple as following a creek down to its forks, Mr.* Donegan," George Crook told the Irishman.

"Sounds to me you've made your mind up, General."

It was clear as summer sun the general had indeed set his mind on it the evening before, even prior to Seamus showing up to discuss the matter at his headquarters tent. Crook informed Donegan of his plans to send the Irishman on ahead of the column in the morning, on to the forks of Goose Creek with Captain Henry Noyes and ten troopers from I Company, Second Cavalry. Once there, Seamus was to help Noyes in scouting the immediate countryside for the most ideal location, where Crook would establish his base camp. The general declared he could be assured of plenty of water at the forks—no doubt of that. But Noyes and Donegan had to think of hard and extended use of pasture. And there would be the necessity of adequate firewood across the weeks Crook's campaign might take. All the while, Russell's wagon train and some of the infantry had to stay put, as the cavalry went in search of enemy villages.

"So you're the man I've picked to guide Captain Noyes in selecting that site for my base camp," Crook was reminding him again the next morning at sunup over coffee and some last-minute instructions for their rendezvous. "Now, you go do that. I think I can lead this column to meet you myself."

"Ain't far—just a little over eight miles, General," Seamus repeated, then glanced at Noyes, who appeared a little anxious to depart at the head of his ten-man detail.

"We'll be there shortly past noon. So, off with you. Good hunting, Major!" Crook sang out, addressing Noyes by his brevet rank.

With the thick broom bristle of a mustache upturned at the corners of his mouth, the captain called back, "You mean—good fishing, sir!"

Touching the brim of his hat with his fingers, Donegan tossed his empty cup to John Bourke and took up the reins to the piebald gelding. Settling the Henry over his thighs in front of him, Donegan led the eleven soldiers out, pointing his nose north by east, crossing the Piney and climbing the first slope out of Carrington's valley, moving along the rutted remnants of John Bozeman's Road to Montana Territory.

"This where Fetterman made his stand?" Noyes asked a few minutes later as they reached the far crest of Lodge Trail Ridge, completely out of sight of the old fort ruins as well as Crook's expedition column.

Seamus nodded, fighting down the stinging gall of the remembrance of this snow-blown ridge, bodies stripped and hacked, bloodied and dismembered, disemboweled and desecrated. Frozen. What few eyeballs remained in the hammered skulls staring at the gray unforgiving sky overhead. He had never seen anything like it before that cold December day. But in the nine and a half years since, Seamus Donegan had seen so much, much more.

"Where was Grummond's cavalry when they were jumped?"

Pointing down the slope, Seamus led them on. "Most of 'em were swallowed up about halfway down the hill, Cap'n."

"And the two civilians you mentioned at Crook's fire last night?"

"They were in the van—with a handful of some steady-handed veterans," he said, pointing to the grouping of low rocks near the bottom of the slope. "They never turned and tried to flee."

"Short work of them, I imagine."

The cut of his mouth and how the officer formed his words made it plain to Donegan that Noyes was a man much too taken with himself.

"No, Cap'n," Seamus answered. "I'd bet that little bunch was the first to be attacked . . . but likely the last to be overrun."

Noyes nodded and swallowed as he squinted back up the extent of the infamous ridge, this day drenched in bright summer light. "God bless 'em. Every one."

Donegan thought of crossing himself, knowing it would make the spirit of his mother proud. Here in this hard land, cast among the sort of dark-skinned peoples he thought pagan, the white man was more than ready to bring his own superstitions to bear on these primitives. So he did not make the sign as he once would have, and hoped his mother would understand a firstborn son who long ago had ceased to practice his catechism.

"Hold on, Irishman," Noyes called out minutes later as the scout urged his horse up the long slope to the west.

Seamus reined about and came back, again struck by the paleness of the soldier's skin, almost like a quality-folk bed sheet, fresh washed and line dried. "Cap'n?"

The West Point graduate pointed off to the north. Commissioned as part of the class of '61, Noyes fought with gallantry through the Civil War, breveted for meritorious service at Brandy Station, Virginia, and again at the capture of Selma, Alabama. "Aren't you taking us off in the wrong direction, Donegan?"

Down where Noyes was pointing, the creek drainage stood out plain as a green-bottle horsefly caught in liniment, with its leafy cottonwoods bordering the wandering path taken by the water course. Easy for most men to make just that sort of mistake.

"No, Cap'n. I ain't taking you off wrong. I've been in this country since '66. That's why Crook asked me to guide you, wasn't it?"

His pale skin flared red with anger. "What's that—if not what we should follow to the forks of Goose Creek?"

"Prairie Dog Creek, Cap'n Noyes."

"And the forks?"

"Got to go west a bit here. We'll reach Little Goose other side of this ridge. That's the one we follow right down to the forks."

"Then we'll be the first to find the best fishing holes, men—before the rest of the column comes up!" Noyes called back to his column of twos.

The ten cheered, some of them slapping their bedrolls where they carried their fishing equipment.

These sojurs are out on a lark, Donegan brooded to himself. Here we are, ready to stick our foot right into Crazy Horse's bear trap—and all they're thinking of is going on a fishing trip!

John Bourke had watched the clouds roll in off the peaks to the west. Now they were descending, roiling, turning blacker overhead as the wind picked up. Pretty clear the sky had them in for a hammering.

But that wasn't their only worry. The general had been adamant about taking what he believed to be the Bozeman Trail to descend Lodge Trail Ridge. But in following the meandering green path bordered by leafy cottonwoods and willow, Crook instead had mistakenly led his column all of eighteen miles, down Prairie Dog Creek right into some torturous country of scraggy, wildly crimson hills, pocked with thousands of prairie-dog towns, where the noisy animals chirked their protests at the passing soldiers and civilians.

And when the freezing, wind-driven rain finally tumbled over them, the expedition was much closer to the Tongue River than it was to the forks of Goose Creek.

"Lieutenant!"

"General?" Bourke replied as he brought his mount to a halt beside Crook's, rain sluicing down the brims of their hats.

Both braids of his red beard hung soppy in their twine against his old wool overcoat. He growled his order. "Pass the command we'll bivouac here."

With a quick, disapproving glance at the boggy bottomland here along the Prairie Dog, Bourke figured the general was as disgusted as any of them. The lieutenant swatted at a mosquito. There were a hell of a lot of the annoying bastards out for as hard as it was raining. "Yes, sir."

"We'll sort out what I did wrong in the morning, John," Crook said quickly, softly. Almost apologetically.

"It's all right, sir."

Crook shook his head, flinging rain from mustache, beard, and hat. "No. It isn't. But I'll find out what I did wrong when this blasted storm no longer has us tied down. Get the men under shelter and pass along my orders to put out double pickets and a running guard."

"Good idea, General. This is precisely the kind of weather the enemy likes when it comes horse raiding."

"Just be sure the company commanders understand their men are to be doubly watchful tonight."

"Understood, sir."

"And John—this march has started telling on some of the men," Crook said, the despair creasing all the more deeply those lines etching the flesh at the corners of his eyes. "Tell the company commanders to put their sick in the wagons if there's no more room in the ambulances. Tell them I plan to make for the Tongue River in the morning."

"What of you, General? How are you faring?"

"Me?" Crook asked, attempting to grin. "I'm fit as can be. In fact, while you get this expedition to bivouac for the night and get a pot of coffee going for me—I'm going out to look for something to add to my collection of bird's eggs."

"If you want, I'll ride on back and see what held up the column, Cap'n," Seamus offered, the rain battering his shapeless hat.

Henry Noyes peered up at the tall Irishman from under his soggy brim. "No, that won't be necessary, Mr. Donegan. We'll all go back together." He rose slowly from the patch of ground he had kept somewhat dry by crouching there at the edge of the willows under his gum poncho. "With the rain, our fishing's gone to hell, anyway. No sense in any of us staying put, sitting out the storm while we could be doing something."

"Like riding?"

Without answering the scout, Noyes turned away to the ten soldiers who were already drawing near when they saw their company commander getting to his feet. Behind them the mounts stood hipshot, heads hung, ears flicking with every hard pelt of the cold, wad-sized raindrops hurled down from the low sky.

"Tighten your cinches and prepare to mount."

"We're going somewhere, Captain?" asked Lieutenant Fred W. Kingsbury.

"To find out what's happened with the column, men. Even with this storm, Mr. Donegan says they should have been here by now."

Seamus glanced at the place the sun was falling, a pale blotch of light barely atop the peaks behind the bruised clouds. "A long, long time ago, Cap'n."

"Lead us on, Mr. Donegan."

"Aye, Cap'n."

The storm eventually rolled on east, yet left behind a cold wind slinking down from those glaciers in the Big Horns behind the dozen riders. As twilight fell, the Irishman could not help shivering, pulling his collar up beneath the soggy brim of his hat as they plodded east across this high land shrouded in clouds and gloom.

He tried to choose the best path for their weary horses, the ground grown slick and soft, even at the divide they crossed in dropping over to the Prairie Dog. It was nigh onto slap dark by the time Seamus spied the first of the bivouac's fires in the foggy distance. For some reason Crook was way off course, too far north and east. Probably realized it too late and had hunkered his men down here in the rain, Seamus surmised. Likely, though, the sort of man Crook was, the general hadn't even told his aides that he had made a mistake. Hell, Crook was from the old school: an officer never admitted a mistake. Such an admission would make him lose face before his men. Cause the entire command to lose confidence in the old man. That sort of candor could seriously affect morale.

Crook's silence about his error was likely every bit as dangerous as was the position the general had put his expedition in—here in the heart of enemy country. Having brought them to the Tongue River. In the dark. Not knowing where the hell he really was.

But there would always be morning, Donegan knew.

Seamus took Noyes and his ten soldiers half a mile closer toward the dim, murky firelight before halting them out in the dark.

"Why are you stopping us here?" Noyes demanded. "We can see the fires. Our column is camped right over there."

"That's plain as paint, Cap'n," Donegan admitted. "But I got a pretty good idea what Crook will do in putting out pickets and a running guard tonight. Just like he did last winter. You remember, Cap'n."

Noyes bristled, forced to recall that stain upon his record when he had allowed his men to unsaddle and prepare coffee while two other companies pitched into the enemy's village, sorely in need of reinforcement.

The officer's eyes narrowed, and that broom-bristle mustache twitched. "What are you suggesting, Mr. Scout?"

"We sit out the night here."

Noyes guffawed, raw and sharp. "Sit out the night? Here? We're all soaked and hungry, Irishman. In that camp are tents and dry blankets and fires to warm us."

"We can light our own fires," he replied. "I'm telling you it ain't safe to ride in there now. Telling you we oughtta go back to that draw we come out two hundred yards back."

"Why you say it isn't safe for us to go on?"

Donegan stared at the distant pricks of firelight through the drizzly fog as he explained. "Because I don't want to be the first man killed on this expedition."

"Killed?"

"Yes. Some green shave-tail shivering out there on picket duty, Cap'n. Not a one of 'em doesn't know we're in the heart of Injin country. Crook will have 'em all on alert tonight. Then in we come riding—bold as brass. No, sir. Go on ahead, you choose to, Cap'n Noyes. All you fellas—go right ahead and be the first men shot by some itchy-fingered shave-tail."

The ten grumbled and whispered behind Noyes as the captain quickly brooded on it.

"All right, Irishman," he snarled, swiping a drop of rain from the end of his pale nose. "Find us that ravine so we can make our own miserable little camp for the night."

"We'll ride on in come morning," Donegan added.

"Damn right we will, Irishman. Come morning—when our scout doesn't think we'll be mistaken for hostiles."

It was good to have the power of the sacred Buffalo Hat in their camp once more, Wooden Leg cheered.

Like the Seven Arrows of the Southern Shahiyena, the Hat would provide the protection of the Everywhere Spirit over this gathering of the Northern Shahiyena. With a little solemnity and much joyful celebration, Charcoal Bear had brought it to their first camp on Rosebud Creek. With this great medicine man of the Northern Shahiyena came the tribal medicine lodge as well as other sacred relics of Wooden Leg's people.

For their second encampment farther up the Rosebud, they chose the place where in recent years a despairing woman had climbed eastward up a coulee and found a tree, where she hanged herself. It was a thing not talked about among his people. To hang—so that the spirit could not free itself from her mouth. Suicide was something an Indian did not understand.

Wooden Leg was so young then, but even with the wisdom he had gained in the years since, he could not begin to comprehend. What sort of madness would lead the woman to condemn her spirit to such everlasting death? To trap her spirit forever in her lifeless body—when it could not be freed to walk the Star Road to Seyan? What sort of agony of the heart would lead a young woman to such madness?

At this second camp an old, half-blind man tottered through the village, crying out his news that scouts had seen Raven People spying on their camp.

"Were the Crows looking to steal our horses?" Wooden Leg asked his good friend, Little Hawk. He was not much older than Wooden Leg, yet was already a proven warrior in Charcoal Bear's band—one of those sworn to protect the Buffalo Hat.

"No. These Crow did not leave their villages west of

here to steal horses," Little Hawk replied. "These are Crow scouts for the soldiers marching along the Elk River. I have heard Lakota scouts say they have even seen the mysterious houses that walk on the water, smoke pouring from two great mouths above them."

"What wondrous things the white man brings to this land!" Wooden Leg exclaimed.

"But—the white man steals much more than he brings. Do not forget that, my friend."

At the next camp on the mouth of Green Leaf Creek, more Shahiyena arrived from the reservations. They brought confirmation of the scouts' reports.

"Many, many soldiers are being sent against us. From the west. The east. And soldiers are marching from the south."

Here along the west bank of the Rosebud the great Hunkpapa medicine man called for the annual sun dance. While only the Hunkpapa participated in the dancing and sacrifice, thousands gathered to watch and pray. By the afternoon of the fourth day, Wooden Leg tired of watching and praying, so he rode south to a site he remembered from his boyhood.

At the base of the tall hills he came to the deer medicine rocks where his father first brought him as a youngster who could barely ride on his own. Later Wooden Leg had made a second journey to these sacred painted rocks when he had learned some of the important lessons in a man's life. And now, at last, he was coming as a young warrior who had taken a vow to protect the lives of his people by laying down his own.

It was one of the most important oaths a young man of the Shahiyena could give before the sky and the Everywhere Spirit.

Dismounting there beneath the two towers of sandstone rock, where hunters of old would come before they went in search of deer and sometimes antelope, Wooden Leg went to stand between the two immense columns. Closing his eyes, he raised his face to the sun, spreading his arms, and asked for strength in his body, strength for his will. And wind to last him as long as this final fight with the white man might take.

Minutes later, as he opened his eyes, staring up between the two tall towers of sandstone, a long blackened streamer of dark clouds drifted across the sun, blotted out the afternoon's light. And a voice told Wooden Leg to return to camp.

There at the Hunkpapa sun dance arbor, the voice told him—the Everywhere Spirit was already delivering His message of victory over the soldiers.

Chapter 17

Moon of Fat Horses

The soldiers would fall into camp.

So it was foretold in Sitting Bull's prophetic vision. Having suffered for three days and nights, on the fourth the Hunkpapa medicine man had fallen into a deep sleep, his spirit taken to be with the Lakota's Great Mystery. Wakan Tanka told the Bull that He was giving those soldiers to his red children because the white man had failed to listen to Him.

Headfirst, the soldiers would fall into camp.

A wild celebration had begun that night.

But Wooden Leg had already departed the great encampment before sunrise that first day when the Hunkpapa shaman sat staring at the sun as Black Moon pricked fifty pieces of flesh from each arm.

With ten other hunters the young warrior had gone in search of buffalo. Riding east, they crossed out of the valley of the Rosebud and climbed the divide that took them into the valley of the Tongue, where they turned south, still looking for some sign of a herd.

"Too many have come this way leaving the agencies," Lame Sioux said, disgusted that they had seen no deer, elk, or antelope to hunt.

"Yes," agreed Crooked Nose. "They have driven the game from this part of the country."

Wooden Leg suggested, "I think we need to go farther south to find buffalo."

"Yes, let's go south!" echoed Little Shield.

Near Hanging Woman Creek they finally ran upon a small herd of less than half a hundred. That afternoon they killed three cows and a young bull. Nearby, the young warriors discovered a scaffold that had been desecrated, robbed of the dead warrior's most valued possessions. Nothing remained of the body or the poles, only the remnants of an old buffalo robe and some shreds of blue blanket. There was no way for any of them to know if it had been a Lakota warrior or a People of the Raven burial.

Then the hunters decided to cross over to the Powder River in search of a larger herd. In scouting ahead Lame Sioux crawled to the top of a hill to scan the country through which they would have to pass. He signaled excitedly—a soldier camp! The other ten came quickly up the slope and dropped to their bellies to have a look for themselves.

"I want to have a closer look," Wooden Leg said to the rest after studying the distant tents, and all those horses, his heart pounding.

"Me too," Crooked Nose said.

But Little Shield cautioned, "We must make ready. And go on foot."

"Yes, we should conceal our ponies very carefully," Lame Sioux replied.

"I remember a place," Wooden Leg declared. "We can hide the ponies and dress for our stalk on the soldier camp."

When they had made their medicine and completed their toilet, painting themselves and bringing out their talismans, the eleven crept over the hills and through the brush on foot to have a closer inspection of the soldier camp under the cover of darkness. It took half the night to make their noiseless approach through the rugged coulees and along the creekbanks.

"I don't see them anymore!" Crooked Nose suddenly

groaned when they again reached the hill where they had been that afternoon.

"Is this the right place?" Yellow Eagle asked.

"Yes—I remember! This is where I first saw the soldiers!" Lame Sioux protested.

Wooden Leg wanted to know, "Where did they go while we have been making our stalk?"

With nothing else for them to do now in the cold and rainy darkness, the young warriors decided to return to their ponies and sleep until dawn.

The late-spring sky still threatened overhead as the eleven awoke before sunrise. Now they rode without caution right to where the soldiers had last been seen and dismounted to prowl over the immense campsite. The carcass of a butchered animal was the first thing to interest Wooden Leg—one of the white man's spotted buffalo. With his knife he and most of the others pared off slices of meat still clinging to its bones. These they warmed in the coals of several fires they stirred back to life.

"Look, ho!" Yellow Eagle called. He strode up, clumsily, carrying a large wooden box across his arms. Its lid had already been pried open several inches.

"What did you find?"

"Maybe some bullets!" Yellow Eagle cheered as he started to lower the crate to the ground.

Crooked Nose pushed up and said, "Perhaps some powder."

When the box tumbled from Yellow Eagle's arms, the lid sprung, the top popped up, and some packets wrapped in waxed paper spilled across the ground at their feet. Each of them scrambled to claim one, tore at the smooth, silky paper, and found inside the army's hard bread, softened by yesterday's rain.

It was nothing to compare with the feast they could have enjoyed back in that great encampment of lodges and celebration. But that meal of the white man's spotted buffalo and his hard crackers nevertheless filled their bellies this cold, misting morning. It wasn't long before they packed away what they could of the hard bread and resumed tracking the soldiers down Crow Creek, northwestward over the low divide to the valley of the Tongue.

Late in the afternoon they saw the soldier encampment again.

Once more the eleven retreated up the river and at dusk prepared to make a crossing. Swollen with snowmelt and more than a day of rain, the Tongue lapped high and cold along its banks. Stripping off all their clothing, the young warriors tied everything in tight bundles lashed high upon their shoulders as they urged their frightened ponies into the freezing current. Upon reaching the west bank they immediately dressed, wrapped themselves in their blankets, and fell to the cold ground, where they slept until the dawn breezes awakened them to continue trailing the soldiers.

At first light, as the young warriors peered down on the enemy camp from a tall cliff, they bickered in hushed tones about what they could do that would bring them fame when they rode back to the Rosebud. Should they steal some of the big American horses? How else to count some sort of coup on the soldiers, to take something of value back to show the older warriors that they had been among the white man's camp?

Perhaps as important as anything else, they needed something that would impress the young girls. Wooden Leg wanted to see how their eyes would brighten when he brought in some of those big horses, a gun, an army blanket!

When the soldiers appeared to be preparing to move out, mucking about in the mud and boggy bottomland, Wooden Leg suggested, "I think it is time for us to take our news back to our camp on the Rosebud."

"I will stay behind," Little Hawk said.

"Why?" asked Crooked Nose.

"To watch what the soldiers do," Little Hawk answered. "To follow some more until we know just where they are going. Who else will stay with me?"

"I will," said Little Shield.

In the end three more elected to stay with Little Hawk, and five chose to ride back to the sundance camp on the Rosebud with Wooden Leg. The two groups made their hasty farewells at the top of that cliff, unseen by the soldier column that was forming up in the valley below.

Wooden Leg pointed them north by west, counting on the village still camping along the Rosebud. If the headmen had moved the great gathering because of their constant need of new pasture, then, Wooden Leg surmised, it would be farther upriver. Not downstream toward the Elk River, not toward that place where the Lakota had spotted the Raven People scouting for another band of soldiers.

That day two of the five who had stayed behind with Little Hawk instead turned around, hurrying to rejoin Wooden Leg's party. At twilight they killed a buffalo cow, butchering it for the liver, tongue, and the tenderest fleece that always lay along the hump. Just after dark that night they camped on one of the upper reaches of Rosebud Creek, daring to light a fire in hopes of warming from their bones the chill that had pierced them to their core these last few days. They sliced the warm liver and ate it raw while the tongue and slabs of hump rib sizzled over the fire.

All of them were excited about spotting the large army of white soldiers, even a little jumpy, especially two of the youngest. Most grew anxious that the soldiers would discover their tracks and follow their back-trail to the Rosebud. What great news to carry back to the village! Should they live to tell of it. Every few moments one of them would bolt to his feet and dash off into the dark, thinking he had heard a noise in the distance, fearing they had been followed. Once assured they had not been discovered, the warrior would return to throw more of the tender red meat down his throat and marvel again at the size of that immense soldier camp.

In the middle of their meal, well after moonrise, Little Hawk, Yellow Eagle, and Little Shield rode in, calling out from the darkness before they emerged into the firelight. Now all eleven were reunited.

"Are you sure?" Wooden Leg asked Little Shield.

"As certain as I am sitting here by this warm fire," he answered, holding his hands over the flames, rubbing them on his bare thighs to warm them as well.

"The soldiers are marching north, *aiyeee!*" cried Crooked Nose.

"Do not fear!" Wooden Leg snapped. "This is great

news to learn they are coming. Even though so many soldiers march against us—still our village is much stronger."

Around the fire, most of the heads nodded, and grim expressions slowly rose to smiles, their dark eyes widening to reflect the dance of the merry flames.

When all had eaten their fill, Wooden Leg and Crooked Nose agreed that for the sake of safety they should move on to find a place to sleep where they had not cooked their meal. They came across a place where their ponies could graze on the new grass beside the gurgling Rosebud. That night all slept soundly beneath a cold and clearing sky.

Even before the sun raised its head the next morning, the young warriors were up and moving out, riding down the Rosebud—anxious to make it back with their announcement. As soon as they spotted the first firesmoke above the outlying lodges, recognizing them for the Shahiyena of Charcoal Bear, the eleven eagerly kicked their little ponies into a gallop.

Tearing through the village, scattering people and causing the dogs to bark at the hooves of their ponies, the young warriors wolf-howled as they raced back and forth, hollering their announcement. Even some Sioux like White Cow Bull, an old friend of He Dog and Crazy Horse, were visiting camp that morning and were in a hurry to carry the news downstream to their Hunkpatila camp.

"We have seen many, many soldiers!" Wooden Leg gushed at White Cow Bull, who latched on to the single rein of the Shahiyena's pony as it pranced in a circle, wide-eyed with the noise and clamor and barking dogs.

"How many soldiers?" White Cow Bull asked.

"At least a hundred for every one of my fingers!" he told the Hunkpatila warrior.

White Cow Bull grinned, slapping young Wooden Leg's pony on the rump in exuberance. "The great mystery be praised! Sitting Bull's vision is come to the Rosebud!"

"What vision is this?" Wooden Leg demanded.

"You were not here when Sitting Bull was shown Wakan Tanka's gift?"

"No," he answered, dumbfounded. "We went hunting for buffalo, and found soldiers instead."

"So you know nothing of the great vision?"

"No! What vision?"

"Those soldiers you found, Wooden Leg!" White Cow Bull shouted exuberantly as he turned to hurry away. "They are a gift to us: soldiers falling into camp!"

"Damn you, Closter! You won again!"

As Seamus Donegan watched, one of the other packers bolted to his feet near Uncle Dick and stomped off grumbling. The old man had proved himself to be the expedition's best at whist.

Richard Closter turned to Donegan. "You play, Irishman?"

Seamus peered over the edge of his coffee tin at the white-haired packer. "If I did, I sure as hell know better than to play you, Dick."

"We bet thousands of dollars, you know," Closter said. "But just a few cents changes hands. C'mon."

"Believe I'll head over to take my bunkie John Bourke up on a game of checkers."

"You watch out for the lieutenant, now—he's good at that game!"

As planned, Donegan had led Captain Noyes's scouting detail into Crook's camp the morning of the seventh as the expedition was preparing to embark for the day. Taking the Irishman's advice with a curt grain of salt that he should head overland, Crook nonetheless instructed Seamus to lead them on down to the mouth of the Prairie Dog. The general rode off with Bourke, Nickerson, and a handful of others to sport after some buffalo while Donegan dragged the command another seventeen miles across the broken country to the banks of the Tongue River.

The best bottomland in that narrow valley lay beneath some impressive red-and-yellow-hued bluffs on the north bank of the Tongue, a restriction that required the expedition to string itself out for thousands of yards along the meandering bed of the Prairie Dog to assure proper grazing for the horses, pack-mules, and beef herd. A rumor begun by an officer attached to headquarters staff made its rounds of camp that evening with supper.

"Here's where they say Crook is planning to put his

base camp," Dick Closter announced as he stirred the kettle of white beans for the dozen packers in his mess.

"Here?" Donegan shrieked in shock. Then in disgust he threw down the oiled rag he had been using to clean and oil the Henry repeater.

"Why's that put a burr under your saddle, Irishman?" asked Tom Moore.

"He sent Grouard off to find the Crow. To bring them back to the forks of Goose Creek!" Seamus exclaimed. "So Frank rode off expecting to find the command one place, but now Crook is going to plant his ass down someplace entirely different!"

"That's all that bad?" Moore asked. "Grouard can find us."

Closter said, "Ain't no job at all for a handy scout like that half-breed to run onto us here, Seamus."

"Goddammit, boys. Don't you see? It ain't Grouard finding us that I'm worried about. I don't have a doubt in that man's ability—not after he kept us on that trail in the middle of a blizzard, in the black belly of night last winter, marching over the divide to locate that village on the Powder River. If he has to, Frank Grouard can find a gnat on a buffalo's ass a hundred miles from here."

"There's a lot of talk says Grouard and the others ain't coming back," Moore said glumly.

"I heard that palaver too," Closter agreed. "I suppose I'm one to figure he should be back by now. Word is that his hair's likely hanging from some Sioux belt right about now."

"Naw!" Donegan snapped, not wanting to even believe in the possibility. "Not Frank Grouard's!"

"Then tell me why in the hell ain't he back by now?" Closter demanded.

"That's a long bloody piece of trail through enemy ground he been asked to ride, Uncle Dick! If I know him, he'll take his time, lay low when he has to—and he'll get on back here when he can."

"So what's your damned worry about Grouard?" Moore growled.

"Like I said, I ain't worried about Grouard. It's them Crow," Donegan admitted. "Grouard's gone to sell them on the idea of helping Crook's soldiers fight their enemies, the Sioux and Cheyenne. Frank tells the Crow they can rendezvous with the soldiers at the forks of Goose Creek, about as far into Sioux country as them Crow will want to go to meet up with Crook."

Closter's head started bobbing. "So it's a twist in the cat's tail that we're still east of there, eh?"

"Here? Why we're right in the heart of enemy country," Donegan continued. "Not where Grouard guaranteed the Crow. They just might bolt on him."

"And turn back for home?"

"Then Crook will have to use Grouard and the rest of you boys to guide him to the enemy villages," Closter declared.

"Don't you fellas see? Crook doesn't need the Crow to *guide* him anywhere," Seamus declared. "Crook needs the Crow and Shoshone to join him in this fight against their enemies. The general needs those extra guns."

With the wooden spoon dripping bean juice on his dusty boot toe, Closter stood, a line of worry carving a crease between his thick eyebrows. "Ain't you told all this to Crook?"

"I did. He said he'd take it under advisement and let me know. But for now, appears like he's sitting here—just to save some face for getting himself turned down the wrong bleeming creek!"

Not long after supper, heralds came through camp to inform each of the companies that a military funeral was to be held for the soldier who wounded himself while out with Captain Meinhold's scout to old Fort Reno. Private Francis Tierney had finally died a merciful death after a week of painful suffering. While the men of Meinhold's B Company of the Third Cavalry performed the regulation roles in the solemn ceremony and formed the van of the funeral cortege, the ranks along each side of the procession swelled with cavalry troopers, infantry soldiers, packers, and teamsters. Even Calamity Jane Cannary was allowed to attend in the company of her guards from Russell's wagon train.

More than half the expedition stood, muted in gloom beneath a deepening, orange-lit sky, as Meinhold's men lowered the soldier's body into its grave beside the Tongue, an army blanket for a shroud, while Guy V. Henry of the Third Cavalry read from his copy of the *Book of Common Prayer.* When a lone bugler finished the last mournful notes of taps, that plaintive refrain echoing and reechoing from the bluffs hemming in the river, Captain Henry knelt beside the mound of dirt and was the first to drop a handful of fresh earth upon the body at the bottom of that cold grave as seven of the private's fellow troopers fired three volleys from the nearby slope. When the last echo faded from the nearby bluffs, Captain Charles Meinhold stepped forward, turning the first shovel of dirt into the soldier's final resting place.

It was a quiet, thoughtful walk back to camp for more than six hundred mourners as night eased down and the stars winked into view over Indian country. It took ten of Meinhold's men who remained behind to lower a flat boulder over the grave. By lamplight one of Tierney's friends inscribed his name upon the face of that stone as a memorial to one of their own.

"We leave him to his ever-enduring sleep," John Finerty pined quietly as he came up alongside Seamus in the heavy silence.

"Seen enough soldiers buried out here," Donegan replied as they moved back toward camp among the other mourners.

Finerty gazed at the hills growing black as indigo against the twilit sky. "I suppose you have, Irishman. Perhaps the burial of a man at sea is all the more lonely—but right now I am struck that the interment of a soldier in this great American wilderness is about the gloomiest of funerals I ever care to attend."

Glumly, Donegan replied, "John, sad truth is you will likely witness many more burials before Crook finishes this march."

"A shame, then, that Private Tierney should die by his own hand as this campaign is only beginning. The first of Crook's brigade to lay his bones beneath the terra incognita of Wyoming."

Chapter 18

8–9 June 1876

"*Why the hell didn't you have the general come get me?*" Seamus Donegan bellowed at John Bourke.

"So now you savvy Crow?" Bourke snapped back at the angry Irishman.

"A little!"

"Damned little, I'll bet! We aren't even sure it was Crow."

"Maybe I could've kept them talking long enough to find out who it was, and if they knowed something about Grouard."

Bourke gnawed on his lower lip a minute, as if he were considering it. "Maybe you're right, Seamus. A damn shame that Arnold scared the visitors off."

"Now we'll never know who they were, and what they came to tell us."

"Why you so sure they had something to tell us?" Dick Closter asked.

Bourke agreed. "Yeah—Arnold figures it was some Sioux warrior wandered up and bumped into us."

Donegan shook his head. "No, boys. We was being looked for. Just like I warned you. We're being looked for because we aren't where we said we was supposed to be. And now they heard that son of a bitch named Arnold answer them in Lakota—I'll bet they're high-tailing it back to the Yellowstone. Long gone now! Good and spooked."

Just past midnight on the morning of the eighth pickets along the banks of the Tongue heard the persistent howling of a coyote—the means used by many tribes of the northern plains to announce their arrival. A moment later the howls were followed by a single voice hailing the camp from the south side of the river. Thing was, that voice didn't speak in English, so the frightened picket ran to get his sergeant of the guard, and he went to fetch up the officer of the day, and that soldier, Swiss-born Captain Alexander Sutorius, decided to grab the first civilian he found who claimed he knew some Injun talk. Happened that it was a man named Ben Arnold who had been hired to ride courier service between Fort Fetterman and the campaign column, carrying mail, dispatches, orders. But for some reason early that Thursday morning, Arnold thought he recognized the Sioux tongue, then responded in kind—and lo and behold: nothing more was heard of that disembodied voice across the river, hidden by boulders and willow brush.

At dawn the following morning Bourke joined the Irishman in crossing the Tongue, where they found the moccasin prints of those mysterious night visitors, as well as tracks of five unshod ponies. They even discovered a weary, used-up animal some distance away from the river, likely abandoned by the unknown warriors who had hailed the camp only to be scared off.

"Crook figures it the same way you do," Bourke told Donegan later when he returned to the packers' camp as that afternoon of the eighth grew old.

"So the general finally believes that was a runner from the Crow?"

The lieutenant nodded. "Yeah. Which means he's gotten angrier and angrier all day about it. And ordered Arnold back to Fetterman."

"Fired him?" Closter asked.

"That was the man's last ride south," Bourke declared.

"What of that other courier come in today?" the old packer inquired.

"Dispatches from Fetterman."

"Any good news from headquarters you can tell us?" Donegan prodded.

"Sheridan wired that he's ordered up the Fifth Cavalry from Kansas to guard our rear—do what he can to block the roads north. Which is good to hear, because Sheridan also informed Crook that Agent Hastings has finally admitted that most of the able-bodied males of fighting age have already left Red Cloud, rushing north for this country. Still, some more good news did come over in a separate wire from Camp Brown."

"The post over on the Wind River?" Donegan asked.

"Informing Crook that over a hundred Shoshone were already on their way to join up with him."

"That oughtta perk up the ol' man!" Closter said.

"About all that could perk him up, what with the past couple of days," Bourke echoed. "We've heard the bad news that a wire's down somewhere between Fetterman and the Crow agency in Montana."

"So Crook didn't get word to the Crow?" Seamus asked.

"Doesn't appear likely."

"Then Frank Grouard is all on his lonesome to get the tribe sold on fighting alongside Crook when he meets the Sioux and Cheyenne. He's on his own."

Crook had designated that eighth day of June as one of rest for man and animal both. While many tried their luck with fishing, the rains of the past few days had swollen the creeks and rivers, building them to a muddy torrent unfit for any sport. Nevertheless, a group of infantrymen did fashion a crude seine across the Tongue, managing to snare a surprising number of shad to augment their diet of salt pork and beef on the hoof.

Late that afternoon a party of sixty-five miners trudged into the column's bivouac, on their way from the Black Hills and making for the Montana gold fields, just as the two mysterious miners had predicted days before. They asked to march along with the general's army, and Crook agreed, perhaps a bit more buoyant now that he knew some of his Indian allies were on their way to join up. If the Crow did not receive his call to arms and would not come with Frank Grouard's prodding, the general nonetheless would have something on the order of 130 Shoshone allies, along with the miners—another two hundred guns with which to launch his attack against the hostiles of Sitting Bull and Crazy Horse.

After bumping into the immense Crow war party, Frank Grouard had crossed the rain-swollen Big Horn River and rode some eight miles back to their village in the shadows of the dark-green foothills.

For much of the way Baptiste Pourier and Louie Reshaw had been talking with the Crow warriors, who competed with one another, all clamoring to converse in their own tongue with the two half-breeds. From time to time Bat would holler something of note to Grouard in English.

"Yeah, they saw our signal mirrors flashing," Pourier said. "But they didn't do nothing about it because they figured it was Sioux, figuring only Indians would know their signals."

"They thought we was Sioux?"

"Makes sense," Bat replied. "You saw that war party at the river yourself, Frank. The Crow knew the Sioux was in their country, coming from the same direction we was."

It did make perfect sense, Grouard grudgingly agreed, even if it got down in his craw a bit.

That evening, when they reached the large encampment, the Crow fed their three visitors before holding their first council. Beneath the clearing skies Grouard told the chiefs and headmen that he had come to enlist the help of their tribe, to ask for warriors to follow him back to the camp of Lone Star Crook's soldiers, who were marching to attack the enemies of the Raven People.

"He sent word for you to come over the singing wire—asking your agent to ask you to help him," Grouard said, then fell silent as he waited for Bat to translate into the Apsaalooke tongue.

"They say the agent never told them," Pourier explained. "Say he never got the message from Crook."

The Crow politely listened, then smoked ceremonially, and finally war chief Old Crow said they would all think on it until another time. From the looks on those dark faces gathered at that council fire, Grouard was sure he had failed to convince the tribe to send allies to join Lone Star at Goose Creek.

That following morning Frank bolted down his breakfast, then had Pourier wrangle a private session with Black Foot and Crazy Head, two of the leading warriors among the River Crow. It took some talking to convince the pair that Crook intended to drive the Lakota and Shahiyena back to their agencies, far from Crow country once and for all—but they finally agreed to believe, at least to the extent of calling another council so they could again propose joining up with the Lone Star soldier chief.

"If you decide you won't go with me," Grouard finally told the implacable warriors at that council, "I will be starting back tomorrow morning."

"Why are you in such a hurry?" Black Foot demanded sourly.

"Because Lone Star needs me. And I want to fight the Lakota. If the Crow do not want to fight them, at least *I* will help the soldiers drive your enemies out of *your* land. Any one of your warriors who realizes what a great honor it will be to drive the enemy from your hunting ground can join me when I return to the Lone Star. I will leave in the morning."

The headmen murmured among themselves, then eventually let Crazy Head make the announcement.

"If you will stay another day while we move our village to the banks of the Big Horn, we will send many of our young warriors with you."

This was about the best news Frank could have gotten after days of danger getting to the land of the Crow, days of frustration suffered since their arrival. True to its word, the next morning the village packed up and ambled slowly to the east, eventually stopping to make camp along the Big Horn River.

That night Bat came to Frank and told him the Crow were holding another council.

"I don't like the sound of things. We better get on over there pronto," Pourier urged.

Indeed, the Crow were reconsidering their decision. More than a few had voiced their fears of the Lakota, and now it seemed that contagious anxiety had spread among much of the tribe. Having heard enough to disgust him, Grouard bolted to his feet and shouted above the growing clamor—pointing at Big Bat.

"I am new among you. But my friend, Left Hand, has always told me the Crow were a brave people. Though small in number, the Crow always fought bravely against the mighty Blackfoot to the north, the Shahiyena to the south, and the overwhelming Lakota out of the east. But now, as I hear the frightened words of this council—I cannot see any of the brave Crow Left Hand told me about. Where are they? Do they live somewhere else? Tell me where I can find them—because I am going back to Lone Star's soldiers tomorrow. I will fight the Lakota since you will not!"

Turning on his heel, he pushed through the thick cordon of haughty onlookers watching the council.

Beneath the starry sky he stomped on toward the place where he had left his saddle and bedroll. At least he figured he could get a good night's rest before heading back in the morning.

"Grouard!"

Still fuming, he turned, recognizing Pourier's voice. Bat came up and stopped before Grouard, accompanied by an aging warrior.

"Grouard—this is Old Crow."

He only nodded at the warrior, then looked back at Pourier. "I'm going to turn in now, Bat. I got a long trail back."

"But Old Crow wants to talk," Pourier explained. "Wants to know when you fix on going back to Lone Star's soldiers."

He shrugged, eyes narrowing and words sharp as the edge of chipped flint. "Dammit—I already told 'em. Heading out in the morning."

Old Crow listened as Bat translated, while never taking his eyes off Grouard. After all that silence, the aging warrior spoke, and Bat translated happily.

"Says he'll go with you, Grouard! Can you believe that? This man's an important war chief—and he says he'll go back with us!"

At the same time, Old Crow turned to call into the night. A young boy emerged from the shadows, holding the reins to a fine war pony. Old Crow swung atop it as easily as any youngster and headed back into the village, haranguing the Crow—challenging them to join him as part of Lone Star's war on the Lakota.

"What are you afraid of?" he said, snarling at them. "It is our job to drive the enemy from our land. We must not have the white man do it for us. I will go—even if I am alone. Perhaps I am the last Apsaalooke!"

Early the following morning Frank took Bat and Louie down to the banks of the river and located the raft. As they were repairing it for their trip back across the Big Horn, Old Crow showed up with only three others.

"They want to know if you will wait to start back until tomorrow morning," Bat translated, with hope still written on his face.

Frank counted on that hope more than any of the promises these people had made only to break. "All right. Tell him the three of us will cross the river and camp for the night. After breakfast in the morning, we are leaving."

Between Grouard's threat to leave, and Old Crow's taunting challenge, something did the trick: by nightfall Grouard counted 159 Crow warriors on the east bank of the Big Horn River with him, each one outfitted with an extra pony and his finest weapons. They were ready to move out with the half-breeds at first light.

Lone Star would now have his Crow allies at his shoulder when at long last he stared Crazy Horse in the eye.

"That's a damned fine animal you have there, Captain," John Finerty declared the evening of the ninth.

Infantry officer Andrew Burt curried his fine-blooded gelding, one of the few possessions he had allowed himself during his long career with the army on the plains.

"Did he make you any money today, Mr. Finerty?" Burt asked, stroking the neck of the pale charger. "Or cost you some?"

John smiled. "I'm happy to report I made a little. But most of the men had no money to bet, though I did win a can of corn off one fella, and a can of tomatoes from an officer who bet against you. I—on the other hand—had the good sense to put my money on this magnificent horse of yours."

To combat the boredom in their bivouac along the Tongue River that Friday, Crook's soldiers had taken to amusing themselves with all sorts of diversions: foot races for the men, cold swims in the flooded river, as well as some heavy betting on a series of horse races. Burt had won the two races in which the captain had entered his gelding, which meant a lot of paper IOUs changed hands that evening around the mess fires.

"I'd love to give him the chance to really run for it," Burt explained as he curried the animal, "on a long, long race. Something cross-country, like a steeple-chase. Something—"

Bullets slammed into camp, whirring through the canvas tents, splintering tent poles behind Finerty, ringing off stove chimneys and ricocheting off cast-iron cookware. In a heartbeat all was pandemonium.

"*Sheol!*" Burt shouted as he whirled to find his men of H Company, Ninth Infantry, scattering across their bivouac.

"What the hell does *Sheol* mean?" Finerty inquired, drawing his head into his collar as he crouched behind some brush with the infantry captain.

"Just that, Mr. Finerty! The Old Testament term for *hell!* It seems all *Sheol* has broken out—"

Finerty recognized the unmistakable and sickening smack of lead slamming into flesh, followed by an aborted, painful whinny. A second slap, like a hand on wet putty, accompanied by a crunch of bone.

"Goddamn—"

Beside his wounded horse, Burt was slowly going down. Rushing to his side, Finerty found the captain unhurt. In disbelief Andrew Burt sat there, cradling the gelding's head in his lap, stroking the big blond animal's jaw as the eyes began to glaze, its legs quivering in the final throes of death. Blood seeped from a wound behind a foreleg, a faint trickle issuing from the bullet hole in its head, near that eye that stared up at its master.

"Captain?"

Finerty whirled, the hail of lead raining down from the hills across the river on the camp without letup, to find Lieutenant Edgar B. Robertson hurrying toward his company commander.

"Get the men formed up and behind cover, Mr. Robertson!" Burt hollered. "Seems we've got visitors!"

It was an ideal spot the hostiles had chosen for their attack. Only thing was, Crook had chosen it for them—down here in the bottoms with the steep hillsides rising above his extensive bivouac, those heights providing a commanding field of fire as the hostiles of unknown number continued to cause confusion and panic.

But Crook quickly had his aides and staff officers out of headquarters camp, with his orders sending all three companies of the Ninth Infantry off to support the pickets on the surrounding hills before they were overrun. Most of those camp guards had spotted some movement in the twilight just prior to the 6:30 P.M. attack. Two had even seen a force of warriors moving toward the bluffs en masse and on foot. Only moments before the first bullets announced the attack, those two had begun to circle their horses atop the ridges, a signal of impending danger that for the most part went unheeded in the camp.

Samuel Munson's Company C led out the infantry's advance, with Burt's H Company moving up to guard the right flank as they made their ascent. Company G, commanded by Thomas B. Burrowes, was forced to string itself out over the rugged terrain, consigned not only to guarding the rear of Company C but assigned as well to watch over the left flank of the counterattack. But whoever the attackers were, they had too much respect for the infantry's Long Toms and just what those "walk-a-heaps" could do with their Springfields. The warriors melted back beyond that nearest ridge, others scurrying upstream to hunt for a softer spot on the camp's underbelly.

From his cover in the brush willows along the Tongue, Finerty watched the action and occasionally got in a shot from his sidearm. Then he turned at the familiar nearby growl of the Third Cavalryman.

"It's about time!" Anson Mills shouted at the young staff officer running up to him out of breath.

"The general's compli—"

"Just tell me what the hell Crook wants of M Company!" Mills snapped.

"Mount your men, cross the river—and clear the bluffs," the lieutenant huffed breathlessly.

"Now you're talking!

"Sergeant Ballard!" Mills bawled as he sprinted toward the men of his horse troop. "Mount and follow!"

"M Company!" Alexander B. Ballard roared in kind as he reached his horse. "Prepare to mount . . . *mount!*"

"Move out in column of fours and cross as you can," Mills instructed them. "Re-form on the far bank at my command."

Crossing to the far side of the river amid a hail of bullets whining overhead, M Company coolly spurred their horses out of the swollen Tongue, through the thick brush, and to the foot of the barren slope.

"Dismount! Horse-holders to the rear!" Mills bellowed, watching the forty-seven shuffle through the drill as every fourth man strung his assigned mounts together by their link-straps, a fifteen-inch length of leather, snapped into the throat-latches, those rings on the bridles, leading his horses back down to the water's edge.

Under Captain Thomas B. Dewees, A Company of the Second Cavalry appeared out of the growing darkness to cross the river, dismounting on M Company's left about the time Mills ordered his remaining fighting men forward. "Skirmish lines! Form up, form up in skirmish lines. Bring them ahead, Sergeants—Ballard, Kaminski, Robinson, Erhard! All platoons on my lead: *charge!*"

As the dismounted horse soldiers scrambled up through the brush and over the rocks, scaling the slippery bluffs toward the unknown enemy hidden somewhere beyond, two more companies of the Third Cavalry crossed, dismounted, and began to follow up on M Company's right flank. Captain Sutorious's E Company, as well as I Troop under the command of William H. Andrews, all struggled up the bluffs as the hostiles began to fall back and back still, firing unsteadily at the advancing soldiers.

Finerty was struck in admiration, whistling low with approval as he himself finally waded into the freezing waters of the Tongue. The entire crossing of the turbid river by Anson Mills's M Company, its dismounting and rapid re-forming for the attack, all had taken scarcely more time than it had for that young staff officer to deliver his orders from General Crook. If this was Injun fighting, Finerty thought, by God—then Crazy Horse won't stand a chance!

As the newspaperman reached the far bank, the warriors were dropping back farther still, to a second ridge up from the river, putting them another thousand yards from the soldiers. From there the long-range battle rumbled for the next twenty minutes, with no harm inflicted on either side, while Finerty crawled up and took a position with Burt's infantry, the better to cover this duel at twilight. With his field glasses, the Chicago correspondent did his best to count the enemy as they appeared here, then there, on the distant crests. All he counted at one time, however, was an even dozen.

When Mills finally ordered an all-out assault on the Indian position, the warriors picked up and retreated once more. Just as M Company's captain decided he was not destined to bring his enemy to battle this day, the sudden sound of gunfire to his rear suggested that the hostiles might have made a flank attack on the camp.

Mills shouted his order to "About face!"

By the time M Company made it across the Tongue, Finerty was back in camp to tell the captain that a large party of warriors had circled the bivouac, evidently in hopes of driving off some of the horses and mules. Instead, they had been duly driven off by a stoic defense from the pickets thrown out by the Second Cavalry.

In less than an hour, from first shot to the last fading echo, the skirmish on the Tongue was over and night was sinking fast.

Crook's army had indeed reached the Tongue.

Already Crazy Horse appeared to be putting teeth into his warning that the soldiers must not go one step farther.

Chapter 19

10–14 June 1876

"*Crazy Horse made good on his word,*" *the Irishman reminded them that night following the attack as camp settled back into as much routine as possible.* "A promise made is a promise delivered on."

"How's that?" Bob Strahorn asked.

"Don't you remember?" John Finerty growled, furiously scribbling away at the notepad he held on his knee. "Crazy Horse warned General Crook not to cross the Tongue."

Strahorn nodded. "Yeah—I remember Bourke told me."

" 'At your peril, George Crook,' " Seamus added. " 'Cross the Tongue at your peril.' "

"Do the rest of you remember what the Irishman here said when he heard of Crazy Horse's warning?" Bourke asked solemnly, looking around that group of newspapermen. "Seamus told us, 'What you have sown on the wind, so will you reap on the whirlwind.' "

The casualties from the fight on the Tongue had been minimal. Two soldiers had been wounded, neither one seriously, by spent bullets. Besides Captain Burt's horse, two other cavalry mounts had been killed in the spray of lead from the far bank, as well as one of Tom Moore's mules.

Word had it that soldiers had seen two warriors go down during the fight, but the bodies had been dragged off by their fellow horsemen, so there was no way to know for sure. Estimates put the enemy force as high as nine hundred. But the Irishman warned John to be skeptical, not to trust the inflated numbers guessed at by officers who attempted to judge such things in the heat of battle.

"We're lucky that most of our horses were in among company rows for grooming, General," Bourke told Crook later that evening at headquarters. "If the mounts had been out to graze, the savages likely would have run off a good number of them."

"Doesn't it just go to prove what I've said all along, John?" Crook asked.

"What's that, sir?"

"The hostiles simply won't stand and face us, John," Azor Nickerson said as he elbowed his way into the conversation.

The general was nodding. "Exactly, Captain. The red bastards always scat from us. I can't for the life of me make them stand and fight!"

In the wake of the attack, Crook sent Lieutenant William B. Rawolle's B Company, Second Cavalry, across the Tongue to the high bluffs overlooking the camp, on the same slopes where the hostiles had opened fire. They were to protect the bivouac from an encore performance for the rest of the night. Just before midnight Rawolle's men discovered they had drawn the most miserable duty of all when the sky clouded up, blotting out both the stars and a pale rind of a moon. Less than two hours later it began to rain—a cold early summer soaker.

Having finished his work on the reports of the attack, Bourke hurried over to the packers' camp to look for Closter and Donegan. The lieutenant found them at a cheery fire, huddled beneath a shelter rigged with willow boughs and gummed ponchos, having themselves a rousing game of checkers on a crude muslin checkerboard. Both were having the best of time, their noses and cheeks radiating a rosy warmth that came from the inner man.

"Johnny! Get on in here with us!" Closter hollered.

"You come for some of Uncle Dick's brandy?" Seamus asked.

"Don't mind if I have a taste myself," Bourke replied.

"Did you hear of our fight with the tin Injun?" the old packer asked.

"The tin Injun?"

Closter nodded, but it was Donegan who went on to explain expansively. "Seemed from the looks of things—at least to those of us here in the civilian end of this camp—that you sojurs had everything well in hand."

"Very well in hand!" Closter echoed, slapping his knee and chuckling.

"Fine indeed, because as things turned out, me and some of the boys here had us a private duel of sorts with the famed tin Injin."

"So tell me about this fabled, mythical creature," Bourke demanded, taking Closter's tin brandy flask and tilting back his head, allowing the fiery liquid to slither down his throat.

"Over yonder," Donegan continued, pointing off across the Tongue, "where the infantry was throwing lead at the hostiles—Uncle Dick here spots one of the war chiefs riding back and forth on top of the near ridge."

"Back and forth just as smart as you please!" Closter added with a rosy smile.

"Up jumps one of the boys," Seamus said, "shouting to tell us that the Injin chief is wearing a tin hat!"

"A big tin hat!" Closter slurred, pantomiming a hat sitting squarely atop his own white hair.

"Back and forth," Donegan went on to explain, moving his entire body to the left slowly, then slowly to the right. "Back and forth again . . . and still again he rode on that ridge while them foot-sloggers fired lead balls his way."

"That's when I figured we should have some fun with him!" Closter interrupted.

"And what fun it was, Uncle Dick!"

"First that red bastard rode this way," Closter said, leaning to the right. "So I run that same way too, hollering out to the savage son of a bitch, a'waving like mad! Then he rode this'a way, so I run back to the left with him. Still yelling for to get his attention."

"It didn't take long before Uncle Dick had him a dozen or more packers running with him, all scampering back and forth along the bank of the river just like that tin Injin," Donegan explained.

" 'Head 'im off!' one of the boys shouts to me!" Closter went on to say.

" 'Nosebag 'im!' hollers another'n," Donegan said.

" 'Hobble the red son of a bitch!' put in another one of the fellas."

Seamus was close to sputtering, pounding his knee in glee as he said, "Pretty soon, I tell you—there was more'n two dozen packers running around on the bank as the lead flies over their heads, everyone bumping into one another, rolling on the ground, sprawled out laughing till they couldn't get up, John!"

"I should say, Johnny," Closter agreed. "We did get our money's worth of fun out of that tin Injun and his puny attack on this camp!"

Knowing George Crook was often one to hide his innermost thoughts and doubts, John Bourke believed the general was concealing some serious misgivings about the expedition to that point. No little wonder. For more than ten days his half-breed scouts had been gone, with no word of their whereabouts or their progress. On top of that, Crook himself had made a wrong turn and been locked on the Tongue instead of being camped at the forks of Goose Creek as he had promised the Crow. Besides, there had been no couriers come down from either Gibbon or Terry to the north, although Crook had undoubtedly wrestled with the thought of sending his own couriers through to either the Montana or Dakota columns, to establish contact, hoping to operate in concert.

Whereas before he might have hoped to have this all his own show—a chance for the Bighorn and Yellowstone Expedition of George Crook to do it all on its own—that dream had gone up in gunsmoke the evening of June 9.

Most disturbing of all, now Crook was certain the enemy knew of his column and the direction of their march. All chance of surprising the hostile encampment had disappeared before his eyes.

The commanding general expressed some of his concerns for his three scouts, as well as his anxiety of never having the Crow show up, all of it given voice in his dispatch to Philip Sheridan, sent by courier to Fetterman following the skirmish of the ninth. In that wire the general stated his belief that the attack served no better purpose than to cover the movement of the enemy camp, which, he figured, they would find on either the lower Tongue or the Little Rosebud.

Crook told Bourke late that night of 10 June that he had decided to push on, despite the handicaps he knew his expedition would face in bringing the enemy to battle.

On the morning of the eleventh, after giving his men and animals one last day to recoup themselves, the general ordered the command back on the trail, moving south by west this time: eleven miles of retreat back up the Prairie Dog before they struck cross-country for seven miles to the forks of Goose Creek, where Crook informed his officers he would establish his supply base.

From that station, the general told them, he would seek to strike out immediately against the hostile encampment.

Despite that frightening, frantic hour John Finerty had spent with the soldiers who went tromping after the hostiles who fired into their camp on the ninth, the reporter could still say Crook's campaign more resembled a summer outing than a military operation.

Few of the soldiers who had reached this Goose Creek encampment were mindful of their regulation uniform. All in all, the general was perhaps the worst of them all. The Chicago correspondent characterized Crook as a man who appeared to be more brigand than brigadier. What with that pith helmet he had put to good use down in Arizona Territory, and those two strawberry braids of his as Crook went loping through the hills and coulees in pursuit of new genus and species of birds, collecting nests and eggs with a zoologist's fervor.

Still, Crook was far from the only one. Both Andrew Burt and William L. Carpenter of the Ninth Infantry used all their free time to indulge their passion: collecting specimens from the butterflies that bobbed and weaved over the tall grass surrounding the exquisitely green campsite here at the forks of Goose Creek. As the earth warmed, the gramma grass reached for the sky for as far as a man's eye could see. Tall enough that not one of those spring days passed without its share of rattlesnake scares—poor soldiers shaken to their boots with the unexpected surprise of that warning that sounds like no other in all of the animal kingdom.

The cavalry camp itself lay along the Little Goose, running to the southeast. To the southwest along Big Goose Creek sprawled the infantry's bivouac. Between them the soldiers staged their daily horse races, an event made a little dimmer now by the deaths of Captain Burt's white gelding and Lieutenant Edgar Robertson's fleet-footed bay. Yet as the days crawled past, the boredom continued and the betting grew more furious on the races: cans of food or even the haunch of a doe taken in the surrounding hills as the coveted wager.

Not to be outdone, the packers organized their own betting events, mostly foot-races. While some soldiers played euchre and poker, checkers or whist, others fished in the clear, fast waters, and still more hunted daily to add variety to their army rations. Still, a majority of Crook's army enjoyed doing nothing much at all as they awaited the return of the three scouts. Lieutenant James Foster drew constantly, his sketches commissioned by *Harper's Weekly,* as did one of the packers named Stanley, both men capturing on paper life in that camp as well as the wildlife and verdant hills at the foot of the Big Horns. Anything that could be read, letters as well as old newspapers sent up from Fetterman, were passed around to kill time, until they disintegrated. Some of the newspaper correspondents fell to daily discussions of a Shakespearean play or an essay by one of the famous pundits back east as a means of keeping their minds occupied. And without fail every morning the sixty-five miners spread out along the creek banks, putting their pans to work rather than have the time go to naught.

Finerty grew as bored as the rest while they waited for the half-breeds to return, even bored enough to beg John Bourke to let him read some of the lieutenant's copies of reports written by those government explorers who had traversed that very area: Hayden, Raynolds, Warren, Forsyth, and Jones.

By the thirteenth even Crook could not conceal his anxiety over the long wait. He summoned Lieutenant Samuel M. Swigert to headquarters and dispatched him with a small detail of his D Company, Second Cavalry, to backtrack to Fort Phil Kearny in search of the long overdue Shoshone. Everyone knew the tribal leaders had sent word they were coming. So the question on every lip was, Where were they?

When Swigert returned to Goose Creek empty-handed that Tuesday evening, the thirteenth, Crook turned without a word and disappeared into his tent. He did not reemerge for the rest of the night, preferring to brood in private. Finerty imagined the general was nursing the same fear most everyone shared: each new day dimmed their hopes for the safe return of Frank Grouard's party.

By midafternoon the following day, Finerty was dozing, listening to the drone of mosquitoes and deer flies, his hat pulled over his face, stretched out on his back in a tall carpet of buffalo grass. At first the distant noise did not register, more than halfway to sleep as he was. Then something yanked on a cord of his consciousness, the way he would yank on a bell rope outside a brownstone house in Chicago. Men were shouting, laughing in joy and glee. Cheering something.

Likely another foot race, he thought, and allowed himself to drift back toward sleep once more. But only momentarily.

With the first cry of that word, Finerty bolted upright as if the earth had trembled beneath him.

"Injuns!"

Men were running for the banks, most of them stripped to the waist, every one snatching up his weapon. More and more soldiers flooded toward the far side of camp, joined by many of the civilians, who dashed to the edge of the creek, many pointing to the west.

Immediately on his feet, Finerty rubbed his eyes, clearing them to see the riders coming at a lope. But no great cavalcade. Only three—coming on there in the distance. Not at a charge. There was no shrieking as there had been the evening of the ninth. Most of all—there was no gunfire to announce an attack.

Three? he asked himself. Then it sank in. "By Jesus—it's Grouard!"

Dashing toward the creek, Finerty sensed a pang of regret for Crook. He had to find the general in that crowd gathering at the creekbank. Had to be there to see for himself Crook's reaction when the three half-breeds rode in . . . empty-handed.

As the trio of riders splashed across Big Goose Creek, Finerty's eyes opened wide, his jaw went slack in surprise. The crowd fell just shy of silent as near every man's attention was riveted on the middle horseman.

"What is he?" many were whispering hoarsely.

"Bet he's Crow," Finerty said. "After all, boys—Grouard went after the Crow."

Heads bobbed as the three riders splashed out of the creek and came to a halt on the bank. Crook emerged from the crowd already parting for the horses flinging water on those gathered nearby.

"Frank Grouard!" Crook called out, shading his eyes with both hands. He started to smile, then it disappeared, as if the general didn't know what emotion to express first. Happiness . . . or disappointment. "Damn—but I'd just about given up on ever seeing you again."

"That's no way to talk, General!" Grouard hollered back above the renewed clamor, a grin on his face. "Don't you never give up on me."

The general craned his neck, asking, "Why, where's Bat?"

Louis Reshaw answered, pointing back across the creek, north by west toward the end of the mountains near. "Bat stayed behind with the Crow."

Now at long last Crook smiled widely, rocking back on his heels and clapping his hands once in a little expression of victory. "The Crow! Why that's damn fine news to my ears, boys! Who's this we have here?"

Reshaw quietly said something to the middle rider before they both slid from their horses together. The half-breed walked up to Crook to make the introductions.

"General, this here is a powerful war chief of his people. He's called Old Crow." Reshaw turned to the warrior, saying something in the man's tongue. The warrior promptly held out his hand to Crook. "Old Crow, I want you to meet Lone Star Crook, soldier chief of the army that will drive the Sioux and Cheyenne far from this hunting ground."

After he shook the chief's hand, Crook asked, "Where's Bat?"

Grouard answered, "About ten miles back. The Crow didn't want to come at first. But Old Crow here talked the rest into it."

"Then you tell the chief I'm real grateful for that," Crook declared. He clapped his hands once and ground them eagerly. "So how many are waiting back yonder with Bat?"

"More than a hundred and fifty," Grouard answered. "They're still afraid of the Sioux. Mostly afraid that we might be in cahoots with the Sioux to decoy them all in here and kill them in a trap."

Crook turned, scanning the crowd. "Major Burt?"

The infantry captain stepped out of the crowd. "General?"

"Major, I want you to get mounted up."

"Mounted, sir?"

"I recall that you spent some time among the Crow."

"Yes, General. During my time up at Fort C. F. Smith."

"Exactly, Major. Ride back with Louie Reshaw here to meet up with the warriors hanging back with Pourier. Convince them that all is well, that their chief Old Crow has been well received."

"Certainly, General!"

"And, Major," Crook continued, "tell them we will have a proper military reception awaiting their arrival here."

Burt saluted smartly and said, "Yes, *sir!*"

As the infantry captain hurried off on foot to secure a horse, Grouard went on to explain. "There for a while I was afraid everything had gone up in smoke on you, General."

"What do you mean?"

"We was just about to head back from the Crow camp

that had just moved to the banks of the Big Horn—when a scouting party come in. Said they had run onto your soldier camp one night and called out to it."

Crook wagged his head dolefully. "Damn—then it was the Crow. I knew it! That son of a bitch Ben Arnold tried talking to someone who hailed our camp across the Prairie Dog."

"Except that the son of a bitch called back to the scouts in Sioux," Grouard grumbled. "Because of that it took a lot of talk from me and Bat to convince 'em that wasn't a big war camp of Sioux come to raid their villages. On top of that we had to convince the Crow you wasn't camping with the Sioux on the Prairie Dog. After we already told 'em we was to join up with you on Goose Creek."

Crook's eyes narrowed as he replied. "Only thing I can do about that mistake now is to make sure Arnold never works for the army again—and see that our chief here is made comfortable until Louie and Major Burt bring in Bat with the rest of the warriors."

Grouard rubbed his belly, as did the war chief. "How 'bout some food for us, General?"

Instantly Crook turned, pointing back toward his bivouac. "Frank, you bring the chief. Let's go back to my tent, where we can offer him something for his belly, something to drink while we're waiting. Now that you've got Old Crow here—I don't want to take the chance of running him off!"

Chapter 20

14 June 1876

"*Our first night after leaving the village we got as far as* the Little Horn," Frank Grouard explained to Seamus Donegan and the others who had gathered at General Crook's tent to await the arrival of the rest of the Crow warriors. It was now nearing three P.M. "Before we settled in for the night, I sent some scouts downriver to see if the Sioux were in the country. Next morning we took a chance on killing some buffalo we run onto. Spent most of the day drying meat for the trail, so we only made it as far as the head of Owl Creek."

"That runs into the Little Big Horn, right?" Donegan asked, his mind busy sorting out the topography and the course of those streams.

"Yeah," Grouard replied. "And then we pushed on into the Chetish Mountains. White folks call them Wolf Mountains. All this time I been figuring I would have to wait until I got to the Prairie Dog before I ran onto the soldier camp—because some Crow scouts come out to find your camp a few days back and got scared off. So don't you know I was some surprised to find the camp moved here to Goose Creek."

"You said it scared the Crow to discover Crook had moved his camp west of the Tongue," Donegan declared.

Nodding, Grouard continued. "That's right, Irishman. It was all the proof those warriors needed to believe that Crook's soldiers had got beat, or scared off, maybe even run on out of Sioux country. The Crow were ready to turn and bolt, ready to run home on us because they feared the Sioux, what with being so close and whipping the soldiers, were going to attack their villages and kill off their women and children for helping the soldiers they just defeated."

"Ain't hard to imagine how worries like that could get the Crow all worked up and ready to pull out on you, Frank," Donegan said.

"But we calmed the warriors down enough that they let Bat stay with 'em while me and Louie rode in here with Old Crow."

Seamus glanced at the aging warrior, who nonetheless stood tall and muscular before the admiring white men, nothing short of regal in the Indian's bearing. "Old Crow volunteered to come in with you?"

"He wasn't afraid," Grouard answered. "Told the others he would come in to the soldier camp just to prove to them how silly they was to be so frightened of the soldiers getting whipped."

Immediately upon reaching Goose Creek, Grouard had informed Crook that when he arrived at the village on the Bighorn River, he learned that at least thirty Crow warriors had already been enlisted by the army, gone to scout for the "Limping Soldier" marching east along the Yellowstone.

"General Gibbon," Crook stated, turning north to peer into the distance.

"Yes. When his soldiers were camped at the mouth of the Big Horn," Frank had explained, "the Sioux were sassy enough to ride right across the Yellowstone and raid the Crow scouts' pony herd. Gibbon tried to cross to the south bank of the Yellowstone, but didn't make it in the swollen river. Crow tell me Gibbon lost one horse before he give up and didn't try no more."

"Who's leading them Crow scouts?" Donegan asked.

"What difference does that make to me?" Crook inquired impatiently.

"Likely it don't mean a damned thing to you, General."

Donegan looked back at Grouard, eager to know. "They got an interpreter with 'em?"

"Yeah," the half-breed answered, his eyes showing some curiosity with the Irishman's question. "Why?"

"Who is it?"

"Bat told me it was a fella named Bwayer," he pronounced the name with a French twist.

"Mitch Bouyer?"

"Yeah. You know him, eh?"

Seamus nodded. "He was trained by Jim Bridger. I met Mitch back in the winter of '67. He was a sometime courier between Kearny and Fort Smith. Him and an old Crow by the name of Iron Bull. Met Bouyer and John Reshaw that winter."

"I know of Bwayer before," Grouard admitted. "Heard he was half-Sioux."

That seemed to prick Crook's caution. "Why's a Sioux half-breed scouting for Gibbon?"

Donegan grinned with those big teeth of his. "General —I'd imagine there are a lot of half-breed Sioux willing to guide for the army. Especially when such a man marries into the Crow tribe. Especially when their scalps are wanted on Lakota lodgepoles."

Seamus watched Grouard smile back at him with a look of some approval and a slight nod.

The half-breed said quietly, "I know how a man feels when his scalp is wanted something fierce by the Lakota."

Crook stroked half of his red beard, his blue eyes bouncing back and forth between the Irishman and the half-breed. "So Bouyer's Crows are with Gibbon now?" the general asked.

"Yes. Opposite the mouth of the Rosebud," Frank had answered.

"And the Sioux? Where do you think they are now, Frank?"

Grouard set his coffee cup down. "Likely back this side of the Yellowstone. The Crow figure their enemies are somewhere on the Tongue. Between the Yellowstone and Otter Creek country."

"What does Frank Grouard think?" Crook asked.

Seamus watched Frank heft that some in his mind before he answered, "No matter what the Crow say, I'm pretty sure the Lakota ain't on the Tongue, General."

"Where?"

"Up the Rosebud."

Crook asked, "Near the mouth?"

"No. Higher up."

"And what of the Little Horn? No hostiles there?"

Grouard shook his head. "No, General. The Little Horn is clear of Sioux. All over on the Rosebud."

The general signaled Bourke to pour some more coffee and sugar in Old Crow's tin cup. "Now, that's what I want to hear. Good news, at last! The enemy is closer than I had even allowed myself to think."

Crook had been making sure the war chief's coffee cup never went empty, nor was the Crow able to empty his tin mess plate of venison, biscuits with plenty of butter, or the stewed apples straight from an airtight the Indian had watched the lieutenant open with his knife.

"It was a grand idea asking for Captain Burt to go talk with them, Frank," George Crook said.

"Just hope what he say to 'em works," Grouard replied.

"It better," Crook said. "I've aged ten years worrying about you in the last ten days. Damn shame I didn't know about that wire being down to the Crow agency."

Grouard smiled darkly. "Oh, the Crow already knowed about your soldiers coming from the south. Knowed that you wanted some Indians to fight the Sioux and Cheyenne."

Crook looked highly skeptical. "How'd they know that without my telegram reaching the agency?"

"The Shoshone told 'em—Chief Washakie told the Crow he was sending a big war party to help you."

"How in the hell did the Shoshone get word to the Crow?" John Bourke asked, the coffee pot steaming in his gloved hand.

"Washakie sent four or five warriors north along the west side of the Big Horns to be sure the Crow knew you wanted 'em to come fight the Sioux with you. Those Shoshone warriors come this way with us. Back there now with Bat."

Crook wagged his head slowly, a slight grin growing in

the twin-wrapped beard. "Why, I'll be tied down and hornswoggled—"

"General!"

Most of those at Crook's headquarters stood as the commotion grew. Getting quickly to his feet, Seamus was able to see what had caused the bustle to stir the soldiers' bivouac. Atop one of the nearby hills a sentry waved a semaphore, signaling camp that horsemen were spotted to the northwest.

"Gentlemen!" Crook shouted, waving his arms for emphasis. "Form up your companies! Let's make an impression on these warriors!"

Bolting off in all directions, the company commanders got their troopers ready so that a real spectacle could welcome the incoming warriors. What a show it was: fifteen troops of cavalry, all at parade readiness, standing five feet from stirrup to stirrup at close order for a front of some four thousand feet across the wide, grassy bottomland just north of camp at the junction of the Goose creeks. At the same time on the far side of the horse soldiers stood the five companies of the "walk-a-heaps" across a full three-hundred-foot regimental front, their freshly oiled Long Tom rifles, with bayonets attached, gleaming in martial splendor beneath the afternoon sun.

"By damn, don't those warriors look pretty themselves?" John Finerty gushed there beside Seamus as they watched the horsemen approach Crook's parade ground.

Donegan had to admit, it was quite a sight to behold: more than 175 Crow warriors and that handful of Shoshone couriers, each with a spare pony in tow, coming in behind Reshaw, Pourier, and Captain Andrew Burt. Every one of the Crow had performed his personal toilet, making himself ready for this grand entrance dressed in his most splendid regalia. Feathers, stuffed birds, wolf-skin hats, and eagles' wings adorned the heads. Fringed war shirts and beaded blankets about their shoulders, leggings of blanket strouding and deerhide, complete with strips of porcupine quills and scalplocks, as well as long and flowing breechclouts were the order of the day. Every warrior clutched the very best weapon he owned. While most had a pistol stuffed in a belt, there were very few modern rifles among the Crow. Most, Donegan noticed, carried old muzzle-loaders. Even some old smoothbore fusils. Nevertheless, they were proud of their martial show as they entered that honored parade ground and marched slowly past the waiting cavalry and infantry of Lone Star Crook. Painted faces and ponies were streaked and daubed with earth colors, feathers and totems tied in manes or on those tails bound in preparation for battle. And bringing up the rear were three squaws—wives of the chiefs who had joined Old Crow in this journey: Medicine Crow, Feather Head, and Good Heart.

As the procession began to stream past, Finerty exclaimed, "They are a handsome people, Irishman! The most prominent cheekbones I think I've ever seen. Damned regal looking. Gad, will you look at the length of the hair on those fellas!"

"C'mon," Donegan said. "Let's mosey down where they'll set up their camp and see if we can find someone I know."

"Somebody you know?"

With a shrug Seamus replied, "I was up at Fort C. F. Smith in Crow country for the better part of half a year. Met some Crow during my time on the Big Horn. I figure my fight in the hayfield nine years ago wasn't far from where Grouard ran into those five hundred warriors on the riverbank."

"You're a man of many surprises, I'll give you that," Finerty said with no little admiration when the pair set off.

As the warriors quickly dismounted on a large patch of bare bottomland, turning their prized war ponies over to a dozen young boys who had come along to care for the war party's horses, they dispersed in all directions to begin erecting their war lodges—bending over young saplings, lashing together the tops to form small domes over which they threw blankets and buffalo robes. With the Chicago newsman beside him, Donegan slowly moved among the Crow warriors, studying each face for a moment, but looking only for the older men. It had been nine years, after all. And in '67 the face of the man he sought was already a well-traveled war map.

It took some time, but Seamus finally gave up. He had

seen them all, more than 175 copper-skinned faces—but not the one he had hoped to find. That evening just after six o'clock he found Baptiste Pourier just returning from an officers' meeting at Crook's headquarters tent.

"Bat!"

"Irishman!" the half-breed called out, turning and holding out his hand in greeting. "You been looking for me? I was over to the general's—hearing the orders for his march to the hostile villages."

Seamus replied, "Ready to march is he—now that he's got the Crow to go with him?" They shook. "You and me need to talk sometime. Nothing important. But right now —I need to ask you about a Crow warrior I been looking for in that bunch come with you. Find out if you know him. If he came along from the village on the Big Horn."

"So you do know someone in the tribe," Pourier replied, but did not continue until the Irishman nodded. "What's his name?"

"Iron Bull."

The smile around the half-breed's eyes slowly disappeared, and some sadness crossed his features as he looked away toward the western foothills where the sun was rushing to its nightly rest. "Iron Bull. Yes. I knew him too. He was a good friend to the white man. He had the power of the bull in his blood."

Already Seamus doubted, but had to ask. "You said he *was* a good friend to the white man. He—"

Pourier shook his head and turned back to the Irishman. "Yes, friend. Iron Bull is dead."

He took a deep breath. "In battle?"

"The Lakota, Seamus. On one of their many raids into Crow country each of the past three summers. Iron Bull staked himself at the edge of the village."

"And he went no farther?"

"No. Right where he stood, he took four of the bastards with him, Seamus," Pourier replied. "And the warriors rallied because of him. They came back from the far side of camp. Turned the Sioux away. Then buried Iron Bull with honors."

"I didn't know he was a war chief."

"He wasn't. Didn't want to be. Just—I figure he knew when it come time for him to stand. And not move on."

Putting his hand on Pourier's shoulder, Donegan eventually said, "I'm proud of what you did, Bat. Holding these Crow—like Iron Bull would have, don't you see? Because of you, they're here."

"And Lone Star Crook has his Apsaalooke warriors now."

Finerty hailed them as he approached, pointing to the southeast. "I figure the general has some more warriors coming to join up too."

It took but an instant for excitement to grow among the Crow warriors as well as the soldiers and civilians across the creek, each of the camps exploding into action. Hurriedly Crook once more ordered his cavalry into a regimental front; with both the Second and Third rallied, the blue-clad horse soldiers extended nearly a mile in length, a most impressive sight for the incoming horsemen. War ponies whinnied and danced against their picket pins in the Crow camp as Seamus, Bat, and the Chicago newsman joined the warriors in moving to greet the incoming procession.

"Look at 'em, will you?" Finerty asked. "Never thought I'd see such a thing—they're riding up in disciplined ranks!"

"I'll be damned," Donegan exclaimed with no small measure of approval. "Whoever trained them Injins had to be a horse soldier himself."

"Likely that white fella riding out front," Grouard said as he came alongside the trio hurrying with the rest toward Crook's headquarters.

"You got any idea who that is?" Donegan asked the half-breed.

"Crook already knows who it is, who's bringing them Shoshone in to join up," Grouard explained. "Got the leaders' names in a wire from Camp Brown."

Of a sudden the white man leading the procession shouted his sharp order and set off at a smart trot. The rest came on his heels as precisely as any company of frontier cavalry, prancing along in a column of twos, a pair of American flags flying from staffs above the first pair of warriors. Over the rest bobbed ceremonial lances fluttering with scalplocks and feathers, each man clutching a gleaming, well-oiled .45-caliber Springfield rifle across his lap as the eighty-one Shoshone loped up to Crook's headquarters behind the three civilians from Camp Brown on the Wind River Reservation.

The leader came to a halt right before the Sibley tent where Bourke had raised Crook's command standard that morning. His arm signaled to the ranks at his rear. The pair carrying the American flags turned on cue, the rest following as they came "left front into line." As they did, a pair of civilians brought their horses up directly behind their white leader and halted on the open ground between the commander and the wide front of flowing, fluttering Shoshone headdresses, each man resplendent in buckskin and bright blood-red wool, brass buttons gleaming in the sun and everything adorned with sprays of feathers.

"I haven't seen cavalry do that manuever so pretty in my ten years out west," Seamus remarked to those watching with him.

"That white fella trained them well, eh?" Finerty asked.

"I'll have to meet him," Donegan answered. "Chances be, we rode the same battlefield years ago."

"Yes," Finerty replied. "I'll have to get that man's story myself."

Above the quieting crowd a single voice now called out. "Do I have the honor of addressing General Crook?" asked the lone civilian out front of the Shoshone he had just brought in.

"You do, sir," Crook replied, taking a few steps forward before he came to a halt again. "Whom do I have the honor of addressing?"

With a salute that he snapped smartly away from his brow, the civilian answered, "Tom Cosgrove, General. Commanding—Shoshone volunteers, Wind River Agency."

"Mr. Cosgrove, a damn fine pleasure to meet you," Crook replied, saluting the civilian with a toothy smile. "Come down here and let me shake your hand."

Kicking his right leg over the saddle, Cosgrove dropped to the ground, strode quickly to Crook, and they shook.

The general asked, "You brought how many with you?"

"I have eighty-one who remained with me. With five who journeyed to the Crow. I expect they're here."

Crook's brow knitted. "I was told to expect more. Did some turn back?"

"About fifty, General. But I have eighty-six ready to fight."

"Do I detect some south in your voice, Mr. Cosgrove?"

The civilian beamed. "Yes, General. Texas. We might well have fought one another. R. P. Crump was my commander—Texas Thirty-second, sir."

Crook beamed even more, stroking one side of his wrapped beard. "Happy we never did meet in battle—not against you or R. P. Crump. From everything I heard during the war, you and that bunch of Texas Rangers were as nail-tough an outfit as the Confederacy ever put into battle on horse. Mr. Cosgrove—I'm damned proud to have you and your volunteers with us!"

Straightening as his chest swelled, Cosgrove replied, "I'm proud to lead in these Shoshone irregulars, General Crook. Trained 'em myself. They're ready to fight the Sioux. Ready as any man ever was to fight his mortal enemy."

Chapter 21

Moon of Fat Horses

Little Hawk's half-a-hundred returned to the great encampment opposite the mouth of Muddy Creek on the Rosebud, shrieking with joy, shouting with fevered excitement, broadcasting their accomplishment in that aborted attempt to run off some of the horses from the soldier camp.

None of their number had been killed, although two ponies had been wounded—so Wooden Leg had had a lot of fun.

But now the Shahiyena and Lakota camps were eager for war. No more horse raids. No more to simply harass the soldiers. The goal was to attack the soldiers marching from the south, to sting them bad enough that they would choose to sit on their hands instead of marching to attack. Which was just what they had done to the soldiers up on Elk River. They had run off the pony herd belonging to the Raven People scouting for the soldiers. They fired random shots into the soldier camp, forcing the soldier pickets to hug their camp closely. It was good. Those soldiers were sitting tight, refusing to budge, on the north bank of the river.

All they had to do now was convince this second soldier column to turn back to the south.

Ever since Wooden Leg's eleven had brought in the news of another army on the Tongue River, the Shahiyena's medicine men had called for hunters to bring them all the horns they could harvest from buffalo bulls. With these the shamans were constructing special headdresses: caps of curly buffalo fur, the two horns reattached on either side, decorated with special earth paint that would guarantee the warriors who wore such a sacred headdress would be bullet proof.

But with the coming of news from far-ranging scouts that the soldier column was on the move again, this time to Goose Creek, the time for battle was at hand. Sadly, less than sixty of the powerful headdresses were ready for the Shahiyena warriors.

"Wooden Leg, you must come!" Crooked Nose hollered. "Crazy Horse is about to address the war council. They are planning our fight with the soldiers. Join me!"

It was a night Wooden Leg knew he would long remember, watching the unadorned war chief standing at the center of that great council of chiefs. Hundreds upon hundreds upon hundreds more of warriors gathered like the oaks of a mighty forest around that ring of old men and counselors. Along with Sitting Bull, still weak from his sundance ordeal, the mighty Hunkpapa were represented by Crow King and Black Moon. Big Road of the Oglalla was there to offer his wisdom. Spotted Eagle of the Sans Arcs. Miniconjou chiefs Touch the Clouds and Fast Bull. Inkpaduta, leader of the uprising in Minnesota, sat among that council to represent the dwindling numbers of the Santee and Yanktonais. And for the Shahiyena, Old Bear, Two Moon, and Charcoal Bear.

Standing alone to address them, Crazy Horse spoke.

"We have stopped the soldiers to the north. They are afraid to cross the Elk River to fight us—their hearts are like water. And now our wolves have gone to the south to see and count for themselves the soldiers who march against us. They say the ground is black with them, their white tents like great patches of old snow spread across the prairie at Goose Creek. Now more of the Raven People have joined Three Stars's soldiers. We are told the Snakes are on their way to join in this fight against us."

"But we knew they were our enemies," Big Road said.

"Yes," Crazy Horse agreed. "What stings me most is that our wolves tell me they saw two guiding the Raven People back to Three Stars's camp. Two of the French trader's sons who will guide the soldiers against our villages: the one called the Big Bat; and my old friend . . . the Grabber."

Instantly there arose a great outcrying for the half-breed's blood, a call for his capture and painful torture as partial repayment for his betrayal. Eventually the Horse quieted them.

"I say we do not wait for the soldiers to attack our villages. I say our warriors ride to attack them!"

The crowd responded mightily, challenging the chiefs.

"What is the village to do without the warriors here to protect us?" asked one of the old men.

Another shouted, "Yes—what if the Raven People or the Snake attack us while our warriors are away fighting the soldiers—what then, Crazy Horse? Would you have our people scattered across these hills like the dust from a puff-ball?"

"He is right," cried a third reluctant chief. "We must keep our mighty warriors here. Let them stand as a wall around our camps. As a fortress between the people and those soldiers of Three Stars when they attack!"

"This is talk of women!" Big Road hollered back at them, standing at the edge of the inner circle. "You speak like old, frightened women!"

"Let's go right now!" came the cry from the hundreds of young warriors gathered in a great ring around the council.

More and more took up the cry as the first began to turn and press backward, perhaps eager to catch up their war ponies and ride south. Then, with one gesture from his hand, Sitting Bull dispatched his many, mighty *akicita* to stop the impetuous warriors.

His voice still weak, the Bull told the assembly, "Wait. There will be fighting soon enough. First I would hear the words of Crazy Horse. My heart tells me the Hunkpatila war chief has words that will inspire the hearts of warriors all."

"Hoye! Hoye!" the crowd rumbled their approval.

The Horse waited for the clamor to grow silent. When only the insects were heard scritching among the green branches of the rough-barked Rustling Trees along the creek, he spoke again.

"I say the older warriors and chiefs will remain behind in camp—to guard our women and children and the sick ones. I would ask Black Moon and Crow King to remain behind . . . to lead the older warriors if the need should arise to defend our camps. While they remain here with the older men, I will take the rest—they will follow me south!"

There arose a sudden and exuberant outburst as nearly every voice was raised, warriors singing their blood songs and vowing on their lives to carry death to the soldiers.

Crazy Horse quieted them, then continued, "But you must heed my words: this will be a far different kind of war we must fight. Some of you will remember the winter we spent near the Piney Fort. Those of you will remember how I told you then that we must no longer fight only to count coup. Instead, we knew we had to fight to kill. These many winters later, the white man once more sends his soldiers against us. These too are men without homes. Men without wives and children. We warriors have both homes and families to protect.

"Like the fight of the Hundred in the Hand . . . this too will be that sort of battle.

"The soldiers are coming to kill us, our families. To kill our women and children. We, then, must drive them away for good. If we cannot drive them from our hunting ground . . . then we must kill them. Kill them all."

That evening after the council proved no different from all the previous nights through the last three moons as the village slowly moved from camp to camp. Families feasted other families, there was dancing and singing and celebration as men brought out their weapons, cleaning the guns, sharpening the axes, hawks studded with long nails, knives, and buffalo lances. Everywhere the girls stood waiting in their best blankets as the young warriors strutted through the many camp circles, showing off their finest regalia, singing out their exploits. And those yet unproven warriors? They shouted loudest, proclaiming just what they vowed to accomplish in their first battle against the soldiers.

Sadly, there were a few who did not share in the full measure of these festivities as the warriors prepared to ride south to victory. In each village were those who saw this summer's gathering as the last any of them would share before being rounded up, corralled, and driven in for all time to subsist on the white man's flour and moldy pig meat. While chiefs like Sitting Bull and Crazy Horse proclaimed the camp would fight to the last man, vowing that the white man would never divide and conquer their great assembly, promising that the Lakota and Shahiyena would stay free and roaming forever . . . nevertheless there were those who recognized this summer's fight as the final swan song before their great peoples went down to defeat.

Their few voices, however, were silenced, drowned out with the merriest celebration. A few of the gloomiest of the Lakota people were even preparing to leave, taking down their lodges and packing up, when Sitting Bull's camp police, the *akicita,* showed up to slash the bindings on their travois, to bully and threaten those who would depart. No one would be leaving the camp, the *akicita* declared. Sitting Bull would not allow it. For now there would be a united front against the coming white assault on this last great hunting ground.

So united and celebrating, readying themselves for the coming fight, the village moved on up the Rosebud a few miles each morning. Then yesterday the Shahiyena chiefs had turned away from the Rosebud, leading the wide march of travois twelve miles west up the divide of the Chetish Mountains,* to Sundance Creek,† which would take them down toward the valley of the Greasy Grass River‡ on the far side.

With each new sun the ponies grew sleeker, made stronger on the tall grasses nourished by the spring rains.

Even old Black Elk, the aged cousin of Crazy Horse, had come in from the Red Cloud Agency at long last. His

---

* Present-day Wolf Mountains

† Present-day Ash Creek

‡ Little Bighorn River

arrival brought great joy—for the venerable old man was proclaiming that this time he had come to fight to his death, preferring that to selling away the Paha Sapa to the white men as the agency chiefs were preparing to do.

"Better," Black Elk told them, "to die fighting the white man than to sell the bones of your relatives to the white man."

Hopo! There would be much honor in the coming fight!

And a good day to die!

It was one of the funniest damned things Seamus had seen in his life!

One hundred and seventy-five of Major Alexander Chambers's infantrymen gathered in the bottomland near the Crow and Shoshone camps, each of those foot soldiers volunteering to ride into battle, but first required to break to saddle the wary mules recruited from Charlie Russell's wagon train. Captains Andrew Burt and Gerhard Luhn, as well as some veteran sergeants and old files among the infantry companies, offered to teach the "walk-a-heaps" soldiers what they could about riding a cantankerous, half-broke mule.

First order of the morning was getting each stubborn animal to take the regulation army bridle, followed by cinching on the clumsy McClellan saddle doubly secured by both surcingle and girth straps. As the reluctant novices rose into their saddles, the fun began.

Mule ears went down as tails and heels shot up. Squeals and cries and heer-awwws reverberated along the forks of Goose Creek. Saddled backs bowed as the animals uncorked all their nasty best beneath the wide-eyed, airborne infantrymen. Off the soldiers flew into that summer blue sky, flung out of the saddle in pairs or groups, catapulted this way and that to a wild chorus of cheers and hoots from bystanding cavalrymen. For a mile in each direction the bottomland was agog with apish mules, jack-toyed soldiers, broken saddles, and cheering, guffawing spectators.

It wasn't long before many of the warriors came to watch. As one after another of the rebellious mules unhorsed their hapless riders and tore off for the brush, the

Crow and Shoshone allies swept in to grab reins, swinging up and into the white man's saddles to show just what a superb horseman was the warrior of the plains. Every time applause broke out from the bystanders—all boredom bucked right out of Crook's camp.

Donegan nonetheless brooded. If Crook had intended to mount his infantry on the mules all along—why, the general had gone and wasted more than a week, his men and those stubborn mules idling as they waited for the allies to show up.

While a thousand soldiers hastily prepared for the final march on the enemy village, the 262 allies were every bit as busy. Before sunrise Captain George M. "Black Jack" Randall of the Twenty-third Infantry, Crook's military chief of scouts, had dispatched five Crows to ride north, searching for sign of the enemy in the country drained by the headwaters of the Rosebud. Meanwhile in their camps that morning of the fifteenth, both Crow and Shoshone cleaned their weapons, sharpened knives and axes, freshened the paint on their ritual clothing, and looked to their war ponies with special attention.

Near midday they lined up in orderly fashion near Quartermaster John V. Furey's wagons to receive their four-day rations and ammunition. Those warriors who needed guns received what the army could spare of government weapons, as well as the forty rounds of ammunition allocated to each Indian scout.

Just as important, Captain Furey issued every one of the 262 Crow and Shoshone a long strip of bright-red cloth each warrior was instructed to tie around his upper arm.

"This way," the interpreters told the warriors, "in the heat of battle the white soldiers will be able to recognize you as an ally and can see you are not their enemy."

That afternoon the tribes wagered on foot races they held on a course 150 yards long.

Excitement was growing high among both white and red allies, all anxious for the final assault on the enemy. Crook himself made no bones that he was spoiling for a fight after the disastrous Powder River debacle. That martial fervor was highly contagious: what marked that army gathered at Goose Creek was that each man shared a common belief in his invincibility. Spirits soared.

Despite the jovial air to the bivouac, Donegan kept to himself there at what John Bourke had christened "Camp Cloud Peak," composing what Seamus knew would be his last letter to Samantha for some days to come—at least until they had engaged the enemy and returned to Crook's wagon camp here at the forks. Perhaps he might even write his next letter from the banks of the Yellowstone when Crook joined up with Gibbon or Terry in a week or so. Along with the sixty-five Montana miners, twenty of Tom Moore's packers had volunteered to ride along with Crook's soldiers and allies to give battle to the villages of Sitting Bull and Crazy Horse. The rest of the mule skinners were staying behind with Russell's teamsters at the wagon corral.

To keep from letting any of his own gnawing doubts about an early return to Laramie come through what he was expressing, Seamus instead told his wife of Crook's plans as the general prepared to cut loose to strike the Sioux.

He wrote that just after the bugler had blown "retreat" the night of the fourteenth, Crook had summoned his officers and scouts, as well as Tom Moore and wagon master Russell, to headquarters. There beneath his own battle flag, the expedition commander issued his terse orders.

"Day after tomorrow, we're cutting loose from the wagon train," he declared. "Each of you company commanders will see that your men carry four days rations of hard-bread, coffee, and bacon in their haversacks or saddle pockets. One hundred rounds of rifle or carbine ammunition for each belt or pouch. Tents are to be left behind, packed in the wagons. Only one blanket per man. Gentlemen, make no mistake: we are stripping for pursuit of the enemy."

"You'll be leaving us behind, General?" Russell asked.

"Yes. Quartermaster Furey will be left in charge, along with a guard of one hundred infantrymen who are unable, or for some other reason do not want to make, the ride north."

"Ride, General Crook?" inquired Major Alexander Chambers. "My infantrymen?"

"Yes, Colonel," he said as he turned to Chambers. "All of your foot soldiers can ride."

"If you can break those mules," Tom Moore declared sourly.

"I'm leaving that up to you and Russell, Tom," Crook said, clearly bristling. "You've got tomorrow to get it done."

"Tomorrow?" Russell grumped.

"Make the most of your time, men. This column is pulling out before dawn on the sixteenth."

This time Crook turned to Captain Furey, expedition quartermaster. "Major, I suggest you select the most defensible place as early as possible tomorrow and get your wagon camp moved to it. I am recommending the junction of the creeks—where you'll have water on two sides, and it will be easy to fort the wagons on the third side."

"Very good, General."

"You will await word from me after our attack on the Crazy Horse village," Crook explained to his quartermaster as well as the rest. "If we are successful in driving them away, we will load what dried meat and other food we can confiscate in their camp, and march north to effect a junction with Terry or Gibbon. Perhaps both, if they themselves have joined up on the Yellowstone."

It was not long after Crook had adjourned that brief meeting that Cosgrove's Shoshone had come riding in from the south. So that night a great bonfire had roared near headquarters, where the general held a grand council with his new allies. In a huge crescent, two men deep, the officers of the expedition arranged themselves. Opposite them sat the war chiefs and headmen of the Crow and Shoshone battalions. Near him at the center Crook had his staff, his three half-breed scout-interpreters, as well as the chiefs of the two tribes who had each selected one spokesman to parley with Lone Star Crook. The warriors from both tribes laughed heartily whenever one of the translators made a mistake.

Clearly it was a time of joy for these red horsemen,

Seamus thought. A time to be forming alliances in hopes of destroying an ancient enemy.

The Lone Star now led some 1,325 men against the Sioux and Cheyenne: cavalry and infantry, Crow and Shoshone, packers and Montana miners too.

Repeating his orders of earlier that evening to the allies, the general went on to ask if the Indians had anything they wished to ask, or to add. When both Old Crow and Luishaw requested that they be allowed to scout for their old enemies in their own way, Crook agreed.

"You can search for the Sioux and Cheyenne the way you always have," he told them. The general stood near the center of the council, his hands in his pockets, appearing half-bored with the long proceeding of multiple translations. "It is of no concern to me how you do it. The only thing that matters is that you find the enemy for me. You do that—my soldiers will do the rest."

Nodding with approval at the general's words, Old Crow asked to speak a few words.

"Lone Star has heard the heart of his Indian brother. These are our lands. They have long been our lands. The One Above Spirit gave this land to our grandfathers' grandfathers. But in recent seasons the Lakota and the Shahiyena came here to steal the land from us. They hunt in our mountains. They fish in our streams. They steal our ponies. They have murdered our women and children."

Wails and laments arose from the circle of warriors.

"What white men have done these things to us?" Old Crow continued his speech. "The face of the Lakota is red . . . but his heart is *black!* Yet the heart of the pale face has ever been red and true to the People of the Raven."

Now the warriors answered with loud grunts of approval.

"The scalp of no white man hangs in our lodges," the chief added. "But in Lakota lodges white scalps are as thick as quills on the back of a porcupine. Yes, Lone Star will lead us against our enemies. Our war is with the Lakota and only them. We want our lands back. We want their women for our slaves—to work as our women have been forced to toil in their villages. We want their ponies for our young warriors, their mules for the burdens of our women.

These Lakota—too long they have trampled upon our hearts. And now we shall spit upon their scalps!"

Cries and yelps became deafening.

"Lone Star can plainly see our young men have come to fight. No Lakota shall ever see the back of a Crow warrior. We do not retreat. Where Lone Star's soldiers go, there will my warriors be at their shoulders. Is Lone Star now content? Together we shall make war on our enemy!"

The old chief and Crook shook hands amid a rising crescendo of cheers from soldier and warrior alike as the general's council adjourned.

When the conference broke up near ten-twenty P.M., Seamus was sure the entire camp would grow quiet. After all, there had been much excitement for the civilians and soldiers that day what with the arrival of the allies. Certain that the Crow and Shoshone would be weary from their long trip to join the soldiers, Donegan had rolled up his mackinaw for a pillow, pulled his blanket to his chin, closing his eyes.

—and immediately opened them when the first peal of an ear-splitting war song cracked the night air like a thunderbolt. Drums suddenly joined in, with a chorus of at least two hundred more voices adding their strength to the celebration both tribes were holding in their camps. A few warriors passed back and forth from village to village on horseback, screeching out their prayers asking for many Sioux scalps, beseeching the Almighty to avenge the deaths of loved ones at the hands of the enemy they were now stalking. Some prayed for Sioux plunder, the spoils of war. Others pleaded for Sioux ponies.

Near his bivouac, Seamus listened as the lowing cattle grew restless with the noise before suddenly bolting for the hills about the time a soft summer rain began to fall. No great loss he figured: the herd had been whittled down to all of six.

As the allies continued their dance in the cold rain, the second of Crook's soldiers passed to the ages. A victim of an unknown malady, Private William Nelson of the Third Cavalry went to his Maker with the ringing of war songs in his ears. A wild and fitting requiem for any fighting man come to breathe his last in Indian country.

At sunset on that night of the fifteenth, Seamus walked with John Finerty and Bob Strahorn at the rear of the long funeral procession winding its way toward the brow of a grassy hill where Nelson was to be buried with full military honors. After Captain Guy V. Henry again read the service from his *Common Book of Prayer*, seven of Nelson's fellow soldiers from L Company fired three volleys over the open grave.

It was but a matter of heartbeats before Donegan felt the ground shudder with the thunder of hooves as more than two hundred Crow and Shoshone galloped up in a swirl of noise and blazing color, screeching and brandishing their weapons—certain that the soldier camp was under attack by the Sioux.

But, as Donegan explained in his letter to Samantha, as soon as Pourier made the allies understand that the soldiers were burying one of their own, the warriors fell silent as if suddenly struck with a common coup stick. In a great crescent they sat atop their ponies at the far edge of the gathering for what remained of the ceremony, their feathers and unbound hair fluttering on the breeze as the sun sank red and lonely behind the Big Horns.

Nowhere near as lonely as he was for her.

Chapter 22

When You See Our Mountains

Unlike most of the other tribes on the Plains and in the Rocky Mountains, there were no moons among Luishaw's Shoshone. Only the cycle of the four seasons. Now in spring as the snow slowly began to disappear from the high peaks of the Wind River range, he realized why the old ones lost back in time had given this season its mystical name.

Which made him remember the season yet to come. A season made for fighting.

It had been two years this summer since he had last gone into battle against an enemy village. While he had gone to fight a skirmish now and then, it had been a long time since Luishaw had enjoyed the danger, the thrill, of fighting old enemies.

Back to the year called Seventy-Four by the white man, Luishaw's Wind River Shoshone had tired of the frequent raids on their pony herds and outlying villages by the Arapaho, who repeatedly slipped over the Big Horn Mountains from the east to do their evil. Through that spring and into the early summer, the enemy had come boldly into the Basin to strike, but always fled quickly before the soldiers from Camp Brown could catch them, even to bring the enemy to fight.

But then in the summer of Seventy-Four two of Washakie's sons discovered where the Arapaho had camped in the foothills of the Big Horns. They returned to the reservation to tell Agent James Irwin and the commanding officer at Camp Brown, Captain A. E. Bates, of their discovery. Without delay the white men agreed to crush the arrogant Arapaho raiders once and for all.

To this day Luishaw was still very proud of the part his Shoshone played in the fight that followed. For all those winters left him, the war chief would repeat again and again the story of the time they had the Arapaho in their grip, the time the army allowed the enemy to escape.

Riding out at the head of 125 warriors who wanted to join Bates's soldiers as well as the agency surgeon, Thomas Magee, Luishaw shared joint command of the warriors with the squaw man named Cosgrove. As they neared the foothills, the forward scouts spotted a column of dust rising some fourteen miles distant. The scouts put their ponies to the gallop only to discover that the Arapaho were fleeing. In returning to the column, the scouts brought with them articles of clothing the enemy had abandoned in their hasty retreat. Hungry for this long-awaited victory, the Shoshone prodded the soldiers to hurry their march.

Instead, Bates held a council with his officers while Luishaw and Cosgrove fumed. The enemy would be far, far away by the time the soldiers were ready to resume their march.

Then the scouts had returned a second time, their weary ponies in a lather, reporting that the Arapaho village was taking refuge in a narrow gorge a short distance away. Plans were laid, Bates stating he would take his soldiers on a frontal assault on the village while the Shoshone were to go over the nearby hill and down the bluff to cut off the enemy's route of escape.

But Norkuk, the tribe's best interpreter, did not fully understand the excitable captain's anxious, Gatling-gun manner of speech.

Instead of going ahead to take up a position that would seal off the enemy's escape, the Shoshone followed the soldiers into the village.

While 112 lodges were eventually captured, the soldiers

did not easily drive the enemy from the gorge. One of the Shoshone, Peaquite, slashed his way into the hottest part of the battle, where he received a fatal belly wound. With what little time he knew he had left, the warrior drove his coup stick in the ground, then lashed his ankle to it as he repeatedly sang his death song.

Another courageous warrior, Aguina, was shot through the lower arm, the ball exiting from his palm to cut off his middle finger. Ever since that day, he showed that missing finger to one and all, always talking about what total victory the Bates Battle should have been for his people.

As the fight raged on, the Arapaho who had been driven from their lodges eventually gained the slopes of the gorge above the village, where they began raining fire down on the soldiers and Shoshone alike. Atop the high bluffs some were even lighting signal fires to alert the Lakota and Shahiyena believed to be somewhere in the nearby country, come in kind to raid the Wind River Reservation.

Under such intense resistance, Bates ordered a retreat, afraid of defeat as their ammunition ran perilously low. For the soldiers, this had not been a battle to be proud of.

It was natural that Luishaw now hungered for the coming fight with Sitting Bull's warriors. This was destined to be a fight of which legends were made.

For over fifty winters the Shoshone war chief had lived, and had survived many fights with these old enemies. Understandable was it that his prayer this morning as the Lone Star got his column underway to the Rosebud was that on this march the white men would not give up and retreat when victory was within their reach.

Luishaw prayed that this time the white men would stay in the fight until their battle was won, and their enemy beaten.

"I'm afraid Crook and the rest of his officers still don't have idea one what hellcats these Sioux and Cheyenne can be when it comes to having their backs forced up against the wall," Baptiste Pourier said to Seamus Donegan that morning of 16 June as the expedition began its march away from Goose Creek.

The Irishman nodded. "Even John Bourke. Seems every

last one of these sojurs figure the wild northern tribes will buckle under quick. They're bragging that the Sioux and Cheyenne won't be able to take a steady drubbing like the army had to give Cochise's Apache before they gave up down in Arizona Territory."

Bat smiled grimly. "The Sioux and their friends up here will give back ever' bit that's throwed their way. Stupid shame the army figures it handed Crazy Horse a bad blow last winter, enough a blow to weaken 'em."

"But you see things through a different keyhole, don't you, Bat?"

"Damned right I do, Seamus. The Crow tell me that the Sioux and their friends are as many as the blades of grass. So the way it lays out to me—these tribes we're hunting never been stronger. We're marching into a hornets' nest."

"These Crow and Shoshone see it the same way?"

Pourier shrugged. "I suppose. Maybe they're coming along hoping the army will make good on all its promises to 'em. About like me. But we'll just have to wait and see." He shrugged, then continued. "They told Crook about the two dead horses they found up north."

Seamus asked, "Dead horses?"

"Buzzards was circling over 'em. South of the Yellowstone. Old Crow said both had iron on their hooves. Been shot."

"Anything of the riders?"

Bat shook his head. "Old Crow figures the horses was rode by a couple of couriers sent from the soldier chief on the Yellowstone to Crook with some message."

"And that's why the old chief's warriors figure Crook ain't heard from Gibbon or Terry."

"Superstitious balder-shit, boys!" John Finerty swore in a gush as he brought his horse in alongside Donegan's gelding. "Crow or Shoshone, Sioux or Cheyenne or even Apache—it don't make a goddamn bit of difference! An Injun's an Injun. Nothing's changed in two hundred years, fellas. He's still the same mysterious, untamable, barbaric, unreasonable, childish, superstitious, treacherous, thievish, murderous creature he's been since Columbus first set eyes on him at San Salvador!"

"Damn you, Finerty!" Seamus growled, having watched

Pourier turn his horse aside and kick it into a lope without a word of farewell.

"To hell with that damned half-breed, then, Irishman. You're a white man, and there's nothing gonna change the fact that Big Bat won't ever be as white as you and me. Doesn't matter, Seamus. Whether friendly or hostile, the Indian is still a plunderer. He will first steal from his enemy. But if he can't get enough of what he wants that way, he'll steal from his friends."

"You been lallygagging around with that Davenport fella too much," Donegan grumbled, speaking of the correspondent for the New York *Herald*. "A born coward and redskin hater, both. Together that's a bad combination."

"Shit, Donegan. Wake up and admit there's a new world on its way here to the frontier. The day of the noble redskin is over. Not even you can tell me that the Sioux aren't the full-fledged descendants of Cain himself. They're the veritable children of the devil!"

"I've heard enough of you myself. Think I'll find some more suitable company."

"Suit yourself, Irishman!" Finerty shouted at Donegan's back. "Mark my words: goddamned Indians are all alike. No matter the tribe. Most of 'em greedy, greasy, gassy, lazy, and knavish!"

Seamus hurled his voice back over his shoulder, "Gonna find me a little better class of company, I might add!"

If he seemed grumpy that Friday morning, Seamus Donegan had more justification than the ignorant ramblings of the inebriated journalist from Chicago. What with the drumming and dancing, singing and chanting coming from both the Crow and Shoshone camps the night before, he had found it next to impossible to fall asleep.

When the scalp dances quieted just before first light, Donegan was belatedly discovering a bit of peace for himself as there arose a new assault on his senses. Groans and yelps, cries and wails of lamentation brought the Irishman upright as better than a dozen old shamans began their ride of the entire length of the camp, all but naked and garishly painted, waving their rattles and beating hand-drums, shaking feathered wands decked with scalps, all calling at the top of their lungs for the Almighty to grant them victory, to award them many scalps and enemy ponies.

Stirred from their war lodges by the medicine men, both tribes began to eat their fill of army rations before they went about any final ministrations to their chosen war ponies, rolled up their blankets, and freshened their face paint.

Without benefit of bugle calls, the entire command was fully awake at four A.M. and in the darkness worked like an oiled machine to break camp for the trail. Tents were struck and packed away in Quartermaster Furey's wagon corral. Those hundred or so foot soldiers who were staying behind were left the responsibility of putting out the mess fires where the cavalry and infantry, packers and miners, had guzzled swallows of scalding coffee and bolted down the choking dryness of their hard-bread before the order was sent up and down the company rows just past five A.M.

"Prepare to mount!"

As the sun peeked like a blood-red rose at the horizon far to the east across the rolling prairie, they heard that singular word that would carry them to the hostile villages.

"Mount!"

Atop his own black charger Crook instructed Grouard to lead the cavalry out in the van, fording Big Goose Creek,* rain-swollen and muddy, then marching the column of fours just west of north for some six miles before fording the Tongue River, the Deje-agie of the Crow. As Cloud Peak and the other granite spires of the Big Horns slowly fell away behind them, the thirteen hundred ascended a ridge that paralleled the river, moving through a region where the waving buffalo grass brushed the bellies of the horses. Behind the ranks of cavalry plodded two mules: one laden with crates containing Surgeon Albert Hartsuff's hospital supplies, the other packing pioneer tools. On their heels came Tom Moore's packers and mule-train, among them the sixty-five civilians on their way to

---

* Present-day site of Sheridan, Wyoming

the Montana gold fields. Bringing up the rear were the hapless but daring infantrymen turned mule-whackers. On the left flank rode the Shoshone battalion, half of them under the leadership of Tom Cosgrove, the others following Luishaw, each one carrying some sort of long wand replete with windblown streamers. Along the right of the column pranced the war ponies of the Crow, the tails and manes of each fine animal daubed with red or orange paint. The headmen and shamans of both tribes led them all, wailing and singing, continuing to beat their hand-drums to invoke total victory in the coming fight.

As the grass thinned and the country became less verdant on the divide that took them up from the Tongue and west over to the headwaters of the Rosebud, Crook had his command disperse across a much wider line of march so they would not raise so much dust, possibly alerting the hostiles they believed would be camped but a few miles to the north. Word had it that the general hoped to take his force within twenty miles of the village, then press upon it with a forced night march so that he could attack with full surprise at dawn.

On that march from Goose Creek the expedition's engineering officer, Captain William Stanton, not only kept a written record of the compass readings of their line of march, but in addition had rigged an odometer to be drawn by one of Tom Moore's mules. Because his two-wheeled gig had more the appearance of a peddlar's wagon, loaded as it was with some of Stanton's personal creature comforts, the soldiers who passed by the captain from time to time throughout the day's march called out in great humor, making sport of the "drummer's wares."

"Mother's pies! Get your mother's pies!" one would bawl, eliciting laughter from every man in the immediate area.

Later another soldier would cry out, "A bottle of horse liniment! My kingdom for some horse liniment!"

Their spirits still high, the soldiers and civilians fully believed themselves to be invincible as they marched ever closer to the headwaters of the Rosebud. Even the air rising to their nostrils that morning came scented with the delicate perfume of prairie flowers like the blue aster and owlclover, as well as the purple gayfeather and yellow ladyslipper, in addition to the profusion of pale, pink rosebuds dotting the verdant meadows and slopes fed by the torrents of snow-melt.

Just past noon Crook ordered a halt on the divide of Spring Creek. Dispersing somewhat, the command sought to relax in what shade they could make themselves beneath the increasing warmth of the summer sun. Seamus watched Frank Grouard ride past, waving in greeting to the Irishman as the half-breed led out a dozen of the Crow auxiliaries, moving north by west with orders to scout a few miles into the distance, where the allies had spotted a small herd of buffalo blackening the narrow valley.

Donegan dragged his wide-brimmed hat down over his eyes and laced his fingers across his chest as he stretched out in the grass, hoping that evening Grouard would share some hump-ribs of any buffalo the half-breed brought down on his hunt.

It was a good sign, this. The herd of buffalo in the valley—right here along the trail they were taking to attack the Lakota village of Sitting Bull and Crazy Horse. The Grandfather Above was giving these animals to the Crow as a blessing. Giving them also to the Shoshone and Lone Star's soldiers too.

But Plenty Coups knew the buffalo were meant as a gift to his Crow.

He had joined this hunt with the half-breed called Grabber, the one who was the chief of Lone Star's scouts. Plenty Coups figured the Grabber had to hate the Lakota as much as his own Raven People hated them.

The Crow war chief was not a young man, but neither was he old. He had an unremarkable face, though it encompassed a firm mouth and chin, a wide and noble brow above the commanding nose. Of average height, with the chest of a bull and the long arms of sinew and muscle, he had tested his body against his enemies and the animals of this land. Twenty-nine winters he had lived, fought, loved—and distinguished himself among his own people. The People of the Raven. The Apsaalooke.

They were, after all, every one of them his children. He

had been told just that many years before when he was but a child himself. The dream had come to him, on the wings of a spirit helper—to tell him he would have no children of his own blood and body; yet all Crows would be his family.

That sacred dream had pointed the way for the rest of Plenty Coups's life. He had followed that footpath without faltering.

Plenty Coups was born in the summer at the place his people called "The Cliff That Has No Pass" on the Yellowstone. One of his grandmothers had married a Shoshone. So he considered it good fortune to be riding with Luishaw's warriors against the Lakota, even if the old chief Washakie was not here to lead his tribesmen into battle.

It was natural, after all, to feel such strong kinship with the Snakes—for Shoshone blood flowed in Plenty Coups's veins.

Earlier that spring the Limping Soldier* had come to the Crow villages to talk to the chiefs about joining his army in its war against the Lakota. When the soldier chief asked for some wolves to scout for him, the Raven People sent thirty. They went with the soldier chief to his camp on the Yellowstone to await the arrival of The Other One† and the Son of the Morning Star.‡

It wasn't long after those thirty scouts departed that Left Hand and the Grabber arrived at the Big Horn River, saying Lone Star wanted some scouts for his march on the Lakota. It was a good thing to help the soldiers, for the white man was strong and without number, like the stars in the sky in his own country. Besides, the Crow had struggled for generations against the Lakota, Shahiyena, and Arapaho anyway. To defeat these old enemies would be a great thing. Many warriors finally heeded the words of Old Crow and decided to follow Left Hand and the Grabber back to Lone Star's camp.

Plenty Coups knew he would long remember his first sight of that soldier camp: row upon row upon row of tiny white tents nestled down in the tall green grass like white

---

* Colonel John Gibbon, Commanding, Montana Column

† General Alfred Terry, Commanding, Dakota Column

‡ Lieutenant Colonel George Armstrong Custer

snowberry blossoms, men in blue here and there and everywhere, more horses and mules and white-topped wagons than he had ever seen before, all corralled in the great vee formed by the forks of Goose Creek. Then they rode down the slope to the soldier camp while some of the white men came together marching in step and others mounted horses matched by the same color, all those big American horses seeming to dance to the music called from the tin horns and the drums.

To amuse and entertain the white men, the Crow chiefs called out to their warriors: the brown-skinned horsemen immediately put their ponies at a gallop, rushing forward to perform a mock charge on the soldiers, firing their guns and shouting.

It had been great fun. A time to make the heart of Plenty Coups swell and grow strong to see so many going against his old enemies, the Lakota.

Left Hand had told the Crow something important—that Lone Star had decided to march north even though he was still expecting an overdue message from Limping Soldier or The Other One up on the Elk River. Lone Star had been three days waiting here for word, but now he would press ahead with his own soldiers.

Lone Star asked Plenty Coups to go with the Grabber to scout the country ahead toward the Rosebud. The war chief was to pick nine others as well. The eleven slipped away from the great wagon camp earlier that morning than most of the soldiers still in their blankets and tents. Ten had painted themselves and donned wolf hides before they followed the Grabber quietly past the outlying soldier pickets and on up the first slope that looked down on the forks of Goose Creek.

Turning one last time to gaze back at that little camp in the gray of false-dawn, Plenty Coups had found his chest swelling in pride.

"Yes," Plenty Coups said with great confidence to the Grabber, who rode near him, "we can whip the Lakota, all the Shahiyena, all the Arapaho in the world!"

Out there beyond the far edge of the soldier camp, in that cold predawn darkness, they first heard one, then another Lakota wolf call out. The Lakota did their best to howl like the gaunt-legged predator, but a warrior knows the difference between the howl of a man and the howl of a wolf. No matter how good the imitation, for some reason a man's call always makes an echo. Later as the wild rose light began to spread out of the east, and Plenty Coups's warriors rode on toward the north, they spotted Lakota scouts from time to time on the crests of the hills.

Plenty Coups waved to the enemy, signaled them. His heart was buoyant—if not downright cocky and spoiling for this fight—simply because he was certain the Lakota were soon to suffer a grave defeat. It was nearing mid-morning when he first noticed the buzzards circling a patch of pale sky far ahead. Below that patch of sky Plenty Coups and his scouts discovered the carcasses of two big American horses, each with the U.S. symbol burned in the hide of the rear flank. Iron hooves further confirmed that these had been soldier horses.

"Where are the riders?" asked Fox Just Coming Over the Hill.

"They are with the Lakota now," Humpy said tragically, wagging his head. In some ways many would see this short, deformed man as a pitiable creature—but Humpy was instead a brave and accomplished warrior.

"Better to die quick in battle, than die slow in a Lakota village," Fox replied.

"It's no wonder now," Plenty Coups said to the others as they were leaping back atop their own ponies. "No wonder Lone Star has not received any message from the soldier chiefs on the Elk River."

The Grabber only nodded and moved them out, not speaking a word nor making a sound save for the muted hoofbeats of his pony loping through the tall grass.

Later they came across some buffalo grazing on the slopes of the valley, black as sowbugs against the deep green of the new grass. Stopping his scouts to watch the herd for a moment, Plenty Coups saw some of the black forms racing down the slope. Immediately he knew why the beasts lumbered in their hurry—for this was not something buffalo would do, perhaps only in the season of the rut.

Hunters!

Those horsemen in among the herd could only be from the enemy's village. From the way the distant riders wore their hair and painted their ponies, he knew they were not Lakota. These were Shahiyena hunters.

The other nine were yelling now, at the enemy in the distance and at the Grabber, working themselves up to go in pursuit of those hunter horsemen, racing their ponies back and forth along the slope to give them a second wind just about the time the Lakota saw the Crow on the far hillside. Both sides reined up in shouting distance, taunting the enemy, hurling insults back and forth as well as exposing their manhood—as if to say how they would desecrate the bodies of the enemy dead they would kill that day.

Even though the Shahiyena outnumbered the Crow scouts, they did not rush the Grabber and Plenty Coups's warriors. He thought there must be a reason—

"The Shahiyena must surely know of the soldiers coming behind us," the Grabber said, making sign talk with his hands.

As the Shahiyena turned their tails and slapped their bare rumps in a parting gesture to the Crow, Plenty Coups signed, "Let us go kill some buffalo. No hurry now, for we know the enemy goes north to the Rosebud."

"Yes," the Grabber signed. "It is good. We shall feast tonight. And fight our enemies tomorrow."

Chapter 23

Moon of Ripening Berries

He felt the blade slide between his ribs, the metal so cold it actually seemed hot, as if the soldier behind him had held it in the fire only a heartbeat before lunging for him with the long weapon.

Crazy Horse jerked upright, blinking into the darkness of morning-coming. Heaving, to catch his breath. As cool as it was at this time of the day, he wasn't surprised to find his naked skin damp, beads across his brow.

In the firepit the coals lay dead, the camp quiet beyond the hides stretched over the ring of lodgepoles that were his sanctuary. His woman lay sleeping still, her breathing heavy. He had not awakened her this time.

His own heart hammered beneath his ribs like a captive bird beating its wings against a cage now that the hot flush of fear surged through his veins. Filling his entire body with its terror.

This was the only fear Crazy Horse had ever known.

The awful nightmare had returned again. Here on the eve of the battle they would take into the lap of the soldiers marching out of the south against this great village camped on Sundance Creek.*

---

* Present-day Ash Creek

Not often did it return. Only at certain, mystically powerful times in his adult life would the same terrifying vision revisit him, come to haunt the Hunkpatila war chief. Now again that they had reached the season known as Wipazuka Waste Wi.

Yet what pained him much more than the soldier's long rifle-knife sliding past his ribs to puncture his kidney was the fact that it was not other soldiers who held Crazy Horse as he was mortally wounded. What agonized him most about his recurring nightmare was that Oglalla warriors imprisoned his arms. His own friends helped to kill him.

Time and again he professed to his people that no gun had been made by the white man that could kill him.

"No bullet fired by these soldiers marching north from Goose Creek will kill me when I ride into this battle," he repeated to his warriors, seeking to drive them into a fighting fury.

But there remained something he did not say to anyone, not his wife, nor his best friends: the only thing Crazy Horse had ever feared was his own people, dying like a trapped animal in their clutches.

When all he had ever wanted for his Oglalla was for them to be truly free.

With a corner of the shaggy, fire-fragrant buffalo robe, he swabbed some of the stale sweat from his body, then rose quietly, taking his war shirt and leggings with him as he ducked from the lodge. He dressed outside rather than chance awakening his wife, Black Shawl.

His war pony snorted, picking up the man's scent even though he had picketed the animal on the far side of the lodge. Crazy Horse went immediately to the magnificent creature that seemed so much to be his namesake. The war chief stroked the pony's muzzle, more to calm himself. Its coat would soon become a brilliant red when the high sun rose that day over this land. The pale slash it bore between its eyes as well as the two stockings on the gelding's forelegs made the animal stand out in any company of horse-mounted warriors.

Turning, Crazy Horse went to a nearby copse of trees, letting his moccasins feel their way across the earth for what his eyes could not see in the starlit darkness. He knew he had not slept long without looking overhead at the positions of the star patterns, simply because his eyes felt so gritty . . . then his toes felt the humped earth. Kneeling, he confirmed that he had found the mound of dirt thrown out of the burrow by a pocket gopher. Scooting on his knees, he found two more burrows nearby. Now he scooped earth from the mounds into both hands and returned to the pony.

Slowly he poured some of the loosened dirt along the spine of the pony as his spirit helper from the lake had taught him long ago. Then on each leg he rubbed the fresh earth in those zigzagging thunderbolts. And around each nostril to bring power to its lungs. Back to the rear flanks with what little he had left in each hand, spotting the hips with hailstones.

This completed, Crazy Horse dropped to his knees and felt for some drying grass. His fingers selected three stalks dry enough to suit him. Each of the short blades of grass he stuffed into his hair: one behind each ear, and the last in his own forelock. Rising again, he stroked the war pony's muzzle once more.

Today they would ride south, together. Perhaps tomorrow to reach the soldiers. His medicine was strong, made all the more potent with the arrival of his cousin Black Elk, come from Red Cloud's agency down on the White Rock.

It made the gall rise in his throat now to think of what his old friend of many winters ago was doing to betray the Lakota: joining with Spotted Tail in agreeing to sell the Paha Sapa to the white man. Still, it gave Crazy Horse a little spark of pleasure to imagine how the aging Oglalla chief must feel of late: Red Cloud's own son Jack had abandoned his father's reservation, had journeyed with Black Elk to join Crazy Horse's free-roaming Hunkpatila this summer.

What a thing this was! Jack Red Cloud fleeing his father's reservation, stealing away with his father's rifle—a beautiful silver-mounted Winchester repeater the white man's government had presented the Oglalla chief during one of his trips far to the east to the land of the great father, given Red Cloud for keeping his people at peace.

Now it seemed that special weapon with the white

man's talking marks engraved upon it would be used to kill some of the great father's soldiers when Crazy Horse led his warriors against them. Yes, he thought, he would lead the hundreds south to give a proper greeting to Three Stars's soldiers who were guided north by Yugata, The Grabber.

Thinking of the one the white man knew as Frank Grouard made the Horse's heart heavy with sadness. For whenever he thought on The Grabber, he immediately thought on his friend He Dog. The half-breed Yugata had married He Dog's sister against her brother's wishes. There had been bad blood between them until The Grabber finally fled. Where, no one knew.

Until a short time later in the Sore-Eye Moon, Yugata led Three Stars to the Powder River, where they destroyed Old Bear's and Two Moon's camp, where the half-breed called out for Crazy Horse and He Dog to come fight him with honor.

The Horse had not been there—or he would have gone boldly forward to rip the heart out of the one who betrayed the Lakota who had taken him in, asked him to become one of their own. No matter that Yugata had also betrayed Sitting Bull and the Hunkpapa's whiskey and powder trade with the Slota, the Red River Metis. Mistakes can be made.

So much sadness for He Dog—his sister should never have married The Grabber.

The heart of Crazy Horse ached for his old friend, He Dog, for He Dog was also Red Cloud's nephew. He felt truly sorry—for He Dog's heart was made small knowing for some reason his uncle had lost the brave blood of a warrior. The old man clung to the white man's reservation on the White Rock River, agreeing to sell away the sacred hills where the young men went to speak with the spirits and renew the strong blood of their people.

"Once the fighting starts, there is no stopping it," He Dog said quietly, his words reaching out of the predawn darkness.

Crazy Horse turned suddenly, surprised at the disembodied voice.

He Dog stepped into view out of the murky starshine.

The Horse took a step toward him, feeling his face begin to smile. "I could not sleep."

He Dog moved on past Crazy Horse slowly, staring at the ground. "No, there is no stopping it now, my friend."

He paused by the magnificent animal and stroked Crazy Horse's pony along the withers for a moment before he continued. "I thought I could get my family, the sick and old ones, away from the fighting."

"And you learned that once this fighting with the white man starts, there can be no escape."

"Yes. Everyone gets hurt by it," He Dog replied. "Not just the ones who fight. Not just the ones who want the blood."

Crazy Horse wagged his head sadly. "I cannot understand why it is—but the little ones, and the women—they are hurt when it is the warriors whose job it is to protect our families."

He Dog nodded, then shuddered with the chill sweep of a breeze presaging the coming of dawn. "Many times I've thought on this since returning to the Hunkpatila after the Powder River fight. It seems I have but two choices: to take up the gun like all the others before me and I myself have always done. Or to join Red Cloud and Spotted Tail at the Soldiers Town—walking on their knees with the grease on their lips and the flour on their fingers."

"A man might as well die and be no more."

"Yes," He Dog replied. "To live on the reservation would be worse than death."

"So, my friend—is there really a choice?" Crazy Horse asked.

"No. For a man of the People. There is but one path to take."

"*Hetchetu aloh!* This day we ride that path, He Dog!"

He smiled at Crazy Horse. "Yes. Today we ride that path together."

"Don't think for a moment that Crook would chance disciplining the Crow and Shoshone," Seamus Donegan told the handful of newsmen gathered at his fire that evening of the sixteenth. "He can't dare make them angry at him for fear of them leaving us here on the doorstep of his great battle."

"But all that shooting they did in the buffalo herd!" John Finerty exclaimed.

"Damned right," echoed Reuben Davenport, reporter for the New York *Herald*. "If the hostiles didn't know we were marching for their village before today, they know now."

Seamus wagged his head and pulled the hump-steak from the fire to test its doneness. "Oh, them red h'athens know, fellas. Don't doubt that Sitting Bull's hostiles already know we're knocking at their back door."

"But to go and have a sporting holiday in that buffalo herd," complained Joe Wasson, correspondent for not only the New York *Tribune*, but also the Philadelphia *Press* and the San Francisco *Alta California*.

"I agree," growled T. B. MacMillan, a soft-edged man, not the sort who should be sent out west as a correspondent for the Chicago *Inter-Ocean*. "They're supposed to be scouting for Crook—not hunting buffalo. This fighting with Indians is something I'll never understand."

"Likely you won't," Seamus replied sourly as he poked a finger against the length of buffalo intestines he had coiled around a green willow wand, which he had suspended over the coals of his fire to roast slowly in the way of the warrior and plainsman. "Hard to understand, is it now? Well, boys—to the Crow way of looking at things, the more Sioux buffalo they can kill, the less Sioux buffalo the enemy will have to eat. To shoot all those buffalo like they did this afternoon, why—it's just another way the Crow make war on their old enemies."

"And those enemies aren't far off, are they?" Finerty asked.

"No," Seamus answered, pointing into the night with his long skinning knife, shiny with grease and the juices of warm flesh. "Grouard figures since them hunters took off to the north when he rode up with the Crow scouts, the village sits just up the Rosebud."

As the half-breed had taken his guides to explore the trail ahead at noon, Crook temporarily dismounted the expedition to await Grouard's return. Seamus had glanced up the slope as they waited, finding Captain William Stanton heaving the shattered remains of his odometer-cart down the uneven creekbed. The terrain had grown exceedingly rougher as the morning wore on, until the engineer's equipment finally could take no more and broke down.

"There'll be music in the air now, for sure," William Andrews had exclaimed prophetically to his fellow captain, Swiss-born Alexander Sutorious. "Wherever you see buffalos, there too you will find Indians."

Donegan had turned back to find practically all the troops stretching out upon the tall grass to relax beneath the noonday sun. He had tried closing his eyes, but the chanting and thumping of the hand-held drums proved to be too much. With some of their number accompanying Grouard and Plenty Coups on a ride north, the rest of the Crow, and Shoshone as well, joined in holding an impromptu war dance, complete with drumming and screeching, which was interrupted only when a handful of Grouard's trackers returned at a gallop to announce that they had spotted some of the enemy. As well as a herd of the enemy's buffalo.

As soon as the scouts had delivered their news to the chiefs, it seemed nearly the entire auxiliary force hurled themselves atop their ponies and raced the animals back and forth across the slopes of the nearby hills to give them a second wind in expectation of bringing the enemy to imminent battle. When a handful of the Crow suddenly bolted away to the north without looking back, the rest took off at a wholesale gallop, wading into the herd, where they gleefully brought down as many as they possibly could until the buffalo stampeded, disappearing beyond the far hills.

"Steady, men!" came the command repeated up and down the line to deter any tempted white hunter. "Maintain your ranks!"

When the order came to remount after that noon break, Seamus climbed into the saddle near John Finerty. Grumbling about the heat, the Chicago correspondent carelessly clambered atop his horse, dragging back the hammer on his sidearm as he did so. When finally released, the hammer fell, the pistol fired, and its echo reverberated from the surrounding hills as the newsman leapt to the ground, stumbling back a few steps in shock.

"You're shot?" Donegan asked as he flew to the ground and rushed to Finerty's side.

Here, then there, the newsman slowly pressed his hands over most of his body. "I . . . I suppose I'm not," Finerty replied in utter amazement.

The soldier column pressed on once they discovered they were not under attack with Finerty's accident, jittery as everyone was with rumors of hostiles spotted nearby. Inspecting the correspondent's saddle as the cavalry troops passed by, Donegan and Finerty discovered the bullet had chipped part of the cantle, lodging in the earth near the horse's hooves. The leather on the saddle still smoked slightly from the muzzle-flash.

"Sonofabitch—and Mother Mary!" the reporter hollered as he ran his hand over the damaged saddle. "To hell with George Crook and these red bastards he's chasing. To hell with Wilbur Storey and Clint Snowden! To hell with their wanting to send me traipsing out here across this saints-infernal wilderness!"

"Damned lucky, you were," Seamus grumbled.

"Lucky indeed!" cheered old Lloyd, Captain Alexander Sutorious's black servant, as he rode up to satisfy his own curiosity. "My, my—but it appears you wasn't made to be killed by bullets, Mr. Finerty—or that would've fixed you for certain!"

"I'm not talking about this stupid newsman shooting himself!" Donegan growled back at the gray-headed Negro. "I meant it's damned lucky he didn't kill his horse! A beautiful animal—why, it would've been a goddamned shame to kill a mere innocent bystander so thoughtlessly!"

"Go to hell, Donegan!" Finerty grumbled as he dusted off his clothing after stumbling out of the stirrup.

"Finerty!"

Donegan and the newsman turned to find Captain Guy V. Henry galloping up.

"Colonel!" Finerty called out, addressing the officer by his brevet rank.

Henry brought his horse to a sliding halt. "Good God, man! I heard you were wounded."

"I don't think so."

Now the officer smiled, his eyes the sort that ignited with any merriment. "Well—by jove—if you don't know for sure, it's about time you found out!" Henry roared, chuckling lustily as he reined about and galloped off to rejoin his D Company.

Throughout that afternoon the command came in sight of no sizable timber to speak of. What stunted cottonwood and willow there was lay along the emerald streamers bordering the courses of every little brook tumbling down most slopes toward the many valleys resplendent in the delicate pink of the wild rosebud, the pale blue of the native phlox, and the radiant yellow of the ten-petal blazing-star. Snow-melt gurgled along every pebbled bed, a springtime melody given harmony from the brush by the multitudes of meadowlarks and wrens, as well as other songbirds piping their warning of the rattlesnakes the soldiers spotted from time to time slithering through the tall grass along the line of march.

After completing thirty-five miles, twenty-five of it in sight of those grazing, meandering buffalo, Crook had ordered his command into bivouac on the headwaters of the south fork of Rosebud Creek about seven-twenty P.M. while the sun continued to sink low beyond the Bighorns. As the first outfits to make camp, the cavalry formed three sides of a hollow square surrounding a small lake at the bottom of a natural amphitheater itself surmounted by low bluffs on three sides. When the first of the infantry began to arrive about eight o'clock to complete the fourth side of the general's defensive camp, the horse soldiers quickly gathered to watch what they expected would be quite a show from what they had dubbed the "mule brigade." Denied the chance to watch the foot soldiers-turned-mule-whackers put to the trail that morning at departure, the cavalrymen hungered as much for the evening's entertainment as they did for a hot meal.

Coming up in good order behind Major Chambers, and Captains Burt and Luhn, with little difficulty, the infantry began to re-form along their side of the hollow square in admirable form.

The major bellowed his command, "Halt!"

As if on cue, and in most disharmonious unison, the 175 plucky pack-mules-turned-riding-stock blared their noisiest protest yet at the long day's hot march, perhaps their impatient expectation of shedding the saddles so they could give themselves a good, hearty roll in the dirt and grass. At the noisy, unanimous braying of the mules and their sheepish, shaky handlers, the cavalrymen instantly filled the valley with their laughter.

"Sonofabitch!" the furious Chambers swore as he wheeled on the hundreds of cheering, laughing troopers. "I'll not be humiliated again in this way by the likes of you ignorant bastards! Shut up!" he shrieked.

Stomping a foot when he found he could not get hundreds of horse soldiers to stop laughing, the major bellowed, "To think of it—me! Forced to ride these goddamned mules: the devil's own creation! Shut up, I said. I order you! For Crook to treat me this way! Go away, damn your blue hides!"

Grown mortified at the laughter, Chambers whirled around and around, flinging his arms in the air, shouting at the horse soldiers for quiet, to disappear. Then of a sudden the major ripped his campaign sword from its clips at his belt and flung it to the ground in disgust.

Leaving the infantry in the care of Burt and Luhn, Chambers stomped off in disgust, muttering to himself.

"Crook will not see my face again until he personally apologizes to me before the entire command! He can fight the goddamned red savages by himself for all I care now, after this indignity!"

Having directed his soldiers not to light any mess fires, but finding that his order had no effect over the Crow, Shoshone, and even some of the civilians, Crook issued instructions for a double rotation of pickets to be posted on nearby hills and bluffs, as an attack by the hostiles might prove a very real possibility.

The anxious bivouac settled down to fitful sleep while the weary stock grazed on what grass had been left behind with the passing of the buffalo herd. It wasn't long before the allies resumed their nocturnal celebrations, complete with drumming and war chants. Before turning in, the general sent Grouard and Cosgrove to the Crow and Shoshone to ask that some scouts ride out under cover of darkness and feel their way into the country immediately ahead. Grouard returned to headquarters to tell Crook the Crow refused to go.

Tom Cosgrove did little better, but finally convinced a half dozen of his Snakes to join him on his probe into the night as the wind died and the sky clouded up, rank with the smell of summer moisture. Off to the west, the Irishman watched the distant flares of green phosphorescent heat lightning hurled into the night sky as he finished his late supper.

About the time Seamus turned in, it began to rain, nothing more really than a light drizzle that seemed to swirl mistily around a man, although there was no breeze to speak of. Still, all in all, the moisture came as a relief after the heat they had suffered that long day marching north from Goose Creek.

He was still awake when Finerty returned to camp and hurriedly climbed under his single blanket.

"This goddammed thing isn't worth a piss at keeping a man warm in this rain!" the newsman grumbled as he spread his gum poncho over his blanket and flung his sopping hat on the far side of his damaged saddle.

"Lay still, Finerty," Donegan growled. "You're bound to get warmer."

The correspondent sighed. And in a moment replied, "Sutorious says we'll have a fight tomorrow. What do you think, Irishman?"

"Doesn't take a side-show fortune-teller to sort it out, John. We've spotted the enemy hunting buffalo. The Sioux can't be far now."

"How much farther we got to march?"

"Not far." Donegan sighed, suddenly thinking on Samantha. "Whether Crook pitches into their village, or they pitch into us—Sutorious is right. It'll be tomorrow. I can smell a damned bloody fight in the air."

Chapter 24

17 June 1876

"*Rout order!*"

One by one the company sergeants echoed the call back down the long column of cavalry. When the order reached the infantry, Captains Burt and Luhn were there to explain.

"Means we're to march in close order!" Andy Burt bellowed into the predawn darkness.

Gerhard Luhn amplified Burt's explanation. "Four feet from your mule's head to the croup of the mule in front of you!"

"Croup?" cried a plaintive voice somewhere down the line that disappeared into the darkness. "What's a croup?"

"A mule's ass! At least the ass of the mule in front of you, soldier!"

Then even the infantry sergeants were taking up the call.

"Close it up! Close it up—rout order!"

Crook had stirred them from their blankets at three, so he could be marching by five. Tom Cosgrove's handful of Shoshone scouts had returned after midnight in the cold drizzle to report finding a large wickiup, an old gum poncho within, as well as the ashes of a warm fire outside.

A temporary shelter likely used by the buffalo hunters they had bumped into earlier that day, Crook surmised.

Over a quick breakfast of coffee and hardtack, Donegan and Grouard had agreed: the column was being watched by the occupants of that wickiup, likely had been watched from the time the soldiers left Goose Creek, until they were driven off by Cosgrove's Shoshone.

The first muddy streaks of dawn were staining the east as Crook's camp came reluctantly to life. While the soldiers joked and talked around their tiny fires, it became painfully evident that those wild celebrations the Crow and Shoshone had shared the past few nights were now over. In the darkness of this fateful morning, Lone Star's allies were instead stonily silent.

An hour behind Crook's schedule, the infantry was the first to move out at six. They were soon followed by the cavalry, then the packers, with the Montana miners bringing up the rear. Marching down one of the Rosebud's narrow forks, the scouts soon picked up the main channel of the South Fork of the Rosebud itself and led the soldiers on through the hills where the creek flowed almost due east before making a sharp turn back to the north. It wasn't long before the rapidly moving cavalry had overtaken the infantry and assumed the lead that early morning. Where the Rosebud tumbled north as crooked as a corkscrew, the march slowed somewhat, the surrounding terrain growing more rugged with every mile. First the column was forced to hug the base of piney bluffs, a mile later forced to squeeze through a perilously narrow defile, unable to see more than fifty feet in any direction. Then suddenly the river valley would open, giving the troops a good view of a sizable piece of country ahead before another mile would drive them once again to skirting the base of another harrowing ridge, pinching George Crook's command through the eye of another narrow canyon.

Just past seven-thirty Crook's vanguard, both Mills's and Noyes's lead battalions, had come a full three miles north, marching down both sides of the narrow creek, finally to skirt an impressively high ridge that rose to their immediate right.

Off to his left Donegan spied the weaving course of the north fork as it came tumbling in to join the south fork to carve out the pebbled bed of the main channel. The widened Rosebud took another sharp turn to the east, flowing nearly another three miles through a valley that widened slightly about half a mile before it again abruptly turned back to the left at a place well-known on the northern plains as the "Big Bend of the Rosebud." From here the famous creek flowed almost due north by the compass needle, straight for the Yellowstone.

Reaching a midpoint between these two bends in the creek, Crook decided to order a brief halt that would allow his scouts more exploration beyond the hills rising to his front. After Grouard found hostiles out hunting buffalo before noon yesterday, surely—the general reasoned—he must be getting close to the enemy village. Best to feel their way carefully north from here. Especially now that one of the Crow had reported seeing earlier this morning what he took to be Sioux herding some ponies ahead of the column on a path that would take them into the hills to the north.

Where everyone knew the enemy villages would be found. If not today, then they would reach them tomorrow. And attack the following dawn.

Go carefully from here on out, Crook had to reason. He had already pushed his expedition some five miles through very rugged country this morning. And it was getting close to eight A.M. Besides, the general had to notice that the stock hadn't recovered from the wear and strain suffered in yesterday's thirty-five-mile march.

Dispatching some two dozen Crow scouts, along with a lone Shoshone warrior named Limpy, to push into the hills to the north, looking over the ground for more signs of the enemy camps, Crook ordered his cavalry to dismount there in the gently sloping bottomland, allowing them to loosen the cinches on their saddles and relax. Then he dispersed some pickets to take up position on the hills a few hundred yards to the north of the stream where the rest of the troops went into temporary bivouac.

Anson Mills rode by Donegan, nodded, then stopped at Crook's impromptu headquarters, where the general stood shuffling a deck of worn cards as he peered at the country immediately in front of their line of march. There by a spring that fed the Rosebud, Crook finally became aware of the captain and looked up at the mounted Mills as if discomfited by this interruption to his deepest thoughts.

Saluting, the cavalry officer asked, "Permission to make coffee, General?"

Crook looked away again, absently shuffling the cards as he continued to gaze to the north, then put a flat hand up to shade his eyes. He turned back to Mills. "Permission granted." Watching the captain rein about and move back downstream to his company, the general hollered for one of his aides. "Nickerson—pass the word. The command can unsaddle and put the stock out to graze. We might well be here awhile waiting for those scouts."

It was eight A.M.

Not waiting for the general's orders, many of the old files among the cavalry and infantry had already scurried down to the willow and alder lining the creek, scrounging the grass and reeds for kindling to start their small fires. Kettles were dipped in the clear, rushing waters. Lucifers were struck and coffee rations combined by the messes gathering around each fire in small knots. After removing the saddles from their mounts and picketing their horses and mules, soldiers and civilians alike stretched out in the grass, lounging in the sunshine, eager to enjoy the relaxation in what was turning out to be one of the most beautiful days of the campaign.

Noyes's lead battalion of five companies of the Second Cavalry relaxed on the north side of the stream. To the west of them sat Van Vliet's two companies from the Third. The entire "Mule Brigade," all five companies of mounted infantry, along with Tom Moore's packers, were west of them, including most of the Crow and Shoshone, who preened their ponies, freshened their war paint, and watchfully eyed the surrounding hills.

On the south side of the Rosebud, across from Noyes's troops, lounged Mills's battalion of four companies of the Third Cavalry. Immediately west of Mills sat Guy Henry's four companies of the Third.

It had taken some time for the last of the expedition to reach the valley after Crook, who rode at the head of the column, ordered his halt. By the time they were all making coffee, the entire command stretched for more than a mile along the clear, sluggish creek.

Finerty strode up pulling a pad and pencil from the pocket of his mackinaw and plopped nearby. "By mercy, Irishman—I just remembered that it's the anniversary of Bunker Hill."

"What's this Bunker's Hill?"

"*Bunker* Hill," John Bourke corrected as he squatted among the rest at Donegan's fire. "The day of a great battle the colonials had with the British."

"Colonials? In the Revolution, eh?"

Finerty nodded, turning to Reuben Davenport. "An anniversary to celebrate, right, Davenport? When we began in earnest to throw bloody King George out!"

"Here's to freedom!" Bob Strahorn echoed, then peered at Donegan suspiciously. "What's with you, Seamus? Don't care to salute this day of freedom?"

With a shrug Donegan replied, "Not sure how I feel. Seems like we've got no right."

"Got no right?" demanded Finerty in that grating voice of his. "Got no right to celebrate freedom?"

"That's what I'm saying, newsman," Seamus growled as he clambered to his feet. "Here you are celebrating *freedom* when this army is about to take away what these hostiles love most: *their* freedom."

Rising in a whirl, Donegan stomped away, pounding the grass and dust from his canvas britches with his gloves, his eyes turning west, back up the valley until he spotted the half-breeds. Better, perhaps, for him to have his coffee and this stretch among those men. Strange, too, to think on it now as he moved through the grazing horses and mules, skirted the tiny knots of civilian and soldiers clustered at their smoky fires—he realized he was becoming less and less used to the company of those who called themselves civilized . . . more and more comfortable in the company of achingly honest, unadorned, unpretentious, and straightforward men of these high plains. Men who could not fail to make the distinction between the right and the wrong in a course of action.

The day was too perfect, the air too clean and the sky too bright, pristine of the merest hint of clouds, for Seamus to allow any man to ruin it for him.

"I knew the one called Clifford," Frank Grouard was saying to Big Bat as the Irishman came up to the fire where the half-breeds sat with a handful of the miners. "Met him of a time, back when I was hauling up to Fort Hawley."

"He's a scout for some time now," Pourier went on with his story as Seamus settled among them. "Mostly been around the wild tribes. You ever run onto him while you was with them up here, Frank?"

"Nope, not while I was with Sitting Bull or Crazy Horse."

"Got him a Lakota squaw. Lived with one band or another for some winters now. Anyways, I heard him say that if it ever come down to a big war between the white man and the Sioux, the warrior bands know of some country up hereabouts where they could go and take refuge and never be pulled out. Never get beaten."

"Country like that? Where?" Louie Reshaw asked, doubtful and disdainful.

Bat replied, "Hank Clifford said it was on the Rosebud. Yonder to the north somewheres. Deep canyons and high cliffs, rough country where the Lakota say they can hold off three or four times their number in soldiers."

"Maybe need a whole lot of cannon to blast 'em out, eh?" asked one of the old miners.

"Lots of artillery and grapeshot'd do the trick," echoed another one of the fortune seekers.

The whole group fell silent for a few moments, most turning their head this way and that to study the countryside.

"Got to admit, the going's been getting tougher ever since we left Goose Creek," the first old miner observed.

"Yeah," the second agreed, "Injuns get in rough terrain like this—be hell for any army to pry 'em out again without that artillery."

"There's a place called Dead Canyon, not far up yonder," Grouard informed the group.

"Dead Canyon?" Reshaw asked.

"Only heard of it. Never been there myself," Grouard replied. "Heard tales of it being deep, and dark."

"We ain't marching in there, are we?" growled a miner.

Grouard shrugged. "We can only tell Crook what he should and shouldn't do. The rest is up to him."

"Sonofabitch!" one of the miners grumbled. "Sounds like that Clifford fella was right. The red bastards are probably laying for us right up there in that Dead Canyon."

Another of the civilians grew animated. "Yeah! Crook marches this army in there—ain't none of us coming out!"

Still, those fears were not generally shared by those come here to the valley of the Rosebud. Here and there, up and down the gentle slopes, the soldiers and civilians laughed and lounged in the sun, talked and told stories, smoked their pipes, or played cards and checkers. Another ten minutes passed as some of the Crow challenged a few Shoshone to race their ponies in sport.

Now a full half hour gone, spent here waiting for the Crow scouts to return with a report. Not far away Captain Andrew Burt was raising his talented voice in song, fragments of the tune carried to Donegan sounding familiar. Crook himself sat down for a rousing game of whist with Bourke and Nickerson at the spring about four hundred yards back from the head of the column.

To the Irishman as he looked over the whole assembly, all in all, the morning's halt seemed more befitting of a summer outing than a military campaign.

It was closing on half past eight.

Seamus lay back in the grass, feeling its cool, tickling caress on the back of his neck when he swept his long hair aside. He thought of Samantha. To enjoy her here, oh—to see the look in her eyes as she took in the rugged beauty of this valley.

Distant, scattered echoes of gunfire drifted over the ridges to the north.

Donegan rose on one elbow, straining to listen over the laughter and chatter, over the singing and the clamor of the allies' pony races nearby.

"Them damned Crow again," someone grumbled behind Seamus.

Another voice replied, "Yeah—shooting more buffalo."

A third added, "Red bastards gonna go and scare off the goddamned Injuns before we can pitch into 'em."

More gunfire interrupted the talk. Concentrated shots this time. Seamus sat up.

That was not the sound of a buffalo hunt.

He glanced over at Grouard—found the half-breed gazing at him, his eyes half-lidded. They nodded together as they rose from the cool grass. Nearby Pourier and Reshaw were getting to their feet as well, and some of the curious packers and miners were beginning to mumble among themselves.

One of the civilians asked, "What the hell's going on, Donegan?"

Another pried a louse from his beard and inquired, "Something wrong?"

Closer . . . steadily closer . . . came the gunfire reverberating from the ridges and hills immediately to their north.

"Something is wrong, boys," Seamus declared almost too quietly to be heard. He turned, finding the piebald gelding on some good grass a hundred yards away. He hadn't taken its saddle off, only loosening the cinch and dragging the bit from its mouth so that it could graze more easily.

"Frank—what say you and me go take a ride?"

Grouard nodded, acting every bit as calm as the situation demanded of them both. "Let's go have us a look, Irishman."

As the sun had reluctantly weaned itself from the sky yesterday, the hundreds upon hundreds of warriors began to stream from the village on Sundance Creek. In large bands, in small groups, pairs, and some men on their own—the painted horsemen mounted up and tore south into the night behind their war chiefs.

Vowing to protect the great encampment filled with their women and children.

They would stop Three Stars's soldiers.

Wooden Leg rode with the Shahiyena following Young Two Moon, son of Beaver Claws, as well as his uncle, Two

Moon himself, and Spotted Wolf, the hero of their fight on Powder River. With them rode one woman, the sister of Chief Comes in Sight. Among them were the six-times-ten, warriors chosen by Charcoal Bear and the other shamans to don the powerful buffalo headdresses that would make their wearers bullet proof.

Some of the riders carried new rifles, the .44-caliber repeaters white men preferred to call "Winchesters." Others had only old one-shot rifles, smoothbores, and fusils. Some brought their Spencer repeating carbines and old Sharps military guns. In addition, most carried war clubs and quivers on their backs, filled with the short bows and the reassuring rattle of arrow shafts.

After making a grand procession that extended around the perimeter of that entire encampment, groups of Lakota warriors started out by different paths to the south while the Shahiyena war leaders chose to push on into the twilight via the banks of Trail Creek, striking the Rosebud eleven miles north of the Big Bend. There the hundred Shahiyena rested awhile, making medicine for the coming fight.

One of the older warriors had carried an ancient lance point with him from the village. On one side of the pink stone, a shaman had scratched the figure of a man wearing a hat with its brim turned up and his head pointed down. A small group quietly sang to the pink stone as they waited for sunrise. During the special prayer, Wooden Leg clutched his eagle wing-bone whistle in both hands and sang his own war song. Next to him swayed another warrior, a man who hummed his own medicine chant. His name was Black Sun, and he wore nothing but his moccasins and half of a blanket lashed about his waist, a stuffed weasel skin tied to his unbraided hair.

The air smelled sweet here before dawn: the perfume of the rosebuds, the heady wildflowers of blue and purple, orange and white, all in bloom across the slopes, the dawn scented by blossoming crabapple and sweetplum.

The Lakota who followed Crazy Horse out of the camp selected another route: marching up the south fork of Sundance down to Corral Creek, which would eventually feed into the Rosebud. Strictest with his group, the Hunkpatila war chief resurrected an ages-old practice from the buffalo hunts by assigning his *akicita* to ride along the flanks of the mighty column as a means of preventing any hot-bloods from charging ahead and thereby alerting Three Stars's soldiers.

Still another, but smaller, force of Lakota chose to reach the upper Rosebud by moving over Sioux Pass. In this group rode the great Hunkpapa shaman, Sitting Bull. Weakened by his recent four-day ordeal and loss of blood, the medicine man struggled to stay atop his pony during the furious night ride to confront the soldiers. Time and again others suggested Sitting Bull turn back, that he had no business riding into the coming battle.

Steadfastly, he refused.

"My body may be too weak for me to fight the enemy," he told his companions beneath those clouds hovering over Sioux Pass as the sky began to drizzle a cold rain. "But I will come so that I may pray during the battle. So that I can offer my words of encouragement to our young men as they slaughter Three Stars's soldiers."

Yesterday Wooden Leg had followed the admonishment of that proven warrior, Spotted Wolf, and kept his war pony near at hand.

"Young one, better to tie up your pony near your lodge. Be sure you do not let him eat too much grass. If your pony's belly is not full, he can run a long, long way. But if you let him eat his fill, he will grow tired on you when the battle is but half-finished."

"Thank you, Spotted Wolf," Wooden Leg replied.

The older warrior smiled. "I tell you this because I like you. Because I want you to take a leading role in the coming fight."

"I will," Wooden Leg said confidently. "Many scalps will be mine."

The sky to the east turned gray in the passing of the storm, and the morning's stars winked into life behind the dissipating clouds. Now the various Lakota and Shahiyena warrior bands flowed together once more just north of the Big Bend of the Rosebud. All the smaller groups approached with caution, coming in with the warning hoot of the owl to let the others know.

The hundreds. Maybe as many as ten-times-ten-times-ten again. Who could count for sure? Many of them had been hardened in conflict with the Raven People and the Snake, had experience riding into battle against the soldiers. Some of these, however, had fought only with the white agents on the reservations, struggling for rations and allotments to feed their families. Now that the white man's promises rang hollow, with as much weight as a hollow caterpillar's cocoon, these men had brought their families north to the land of the free tribes. For perhaps the first time, they would fight in earnest.

It made Wooden Leg's heart swell with such fierce pride as he rode along with the many while the sun rose in the east. Not far to go now—and they would hurl themselves into the teeth of Crook's cavalry. Horse soldier against horse soldier.

Among the Hunkpatila waiting beside the creek for the sun to arise there arose some quiet talk in a tongue that Wooden Leg did not understand, although he was made very curious by the tone of the voices.

The one who was known as Jack Red Cloud was making a great show of removing something from a large, special pouch tied over his shoulder. From the soft skin pouch he unfurled a magnificent headdress so long that when he put it on, the double-trailer of eagle wing-feathers still dragged the ground. Wooden Leg wondered how so young a Lakota warrior could have earned so many coup-feathers. Wondered why this Oglalla with the shiny, silver-mounted Winchester wore the headdress of a mighty chief.

Even the young man's fellow Oglalla and Hunkpatila appeared in sympathy with Wooden Leg's feelings, so it seemed. Many turned away, refusing to give Jack Red Cloud his admiring audience, every veteran warrior clucking his tongue in grave disapproval that Jack should dare to wear a headdress clearly not won with his own exploits in battle.

It was here in this meadow near the Rosebud that the Shahiyena camp police told the hundred that the war chiefs wanted everyone to wait a while longer. Little Hawk, the discoverer of the soldier column, advised everyone that the soldiers must be close by, not far down the Rosebud. Acting on that advice, the Lakota and Shahiyena chiefs selected two young men from each tribe to ride forward and inspect the country immediately to the south from a high hill Wooden Leg could see off in the distance.

"If you spot the soldiers, do not allow them to see you," Crazy Horse instructed these forward scouts. "Return to me and report how many soldiers you have found. How many of the Raven People and Snake horsemen you count."

Before those scouts had gone but half the distance to the far hill, a few of the remaining warriors began to slip past the Lakota's *akicita* and Shahiyena Dog Soldiers. The excitement grew contagious, more than any man could bear. In a matter of heartbeats all the hundreds were urging their ponies forward at a walk. Wooden Leg rode among them, sensing the sharp tingle of anticipation like the coming of prairie thunder that would raise the hairs along his arms. His breath grew short, the thrumming of his heart at his ears—exactly as the rest of these young men must sense their own rising hunger for battle.

Far ahead the chosen four reached the slope of the distant hill about the moment Wooden Leg thought he saw a wavering along the skyline.

Two . . . then three . . . perhaps more figures. Horsemen!

They swirled in the wavering shafts of heat as the morning's new light warmed the earth.

The distant horizon swam with liquid figures darting this way and that.

Try as he might, squinting and rubbing his eyes—he could not make out the objects. Perhaps only more of the buffalo herd that blanketed this country.

Then there arose a murmur among the warriors around him. Rising voices. Louder talk and pointing.

Then the first, distant shots.

Gunfire!

The immediate cry of war songs from the front of their wide procession.

And the instantaneous, mad pounding of heels against pony ribs.

The hammer of thousands of hooves against the ground.

Their great battle had begun.

Hopo!

Chapter 25

Moon When the Grass Is Up

He was the last to turn and flee in the face of the bullets the Sioux flung their way.

Just staring down the slope at those hundreds upon hundreds of onrushing horsemen would be enough to make any man's heart falter.

That sight only gave Plenty Coups the resolve to stay long enough so that he could cover the retreat of the others as they began their race back to Lone Star's soldiers.

At first they had plunged right into the enemy horsemen—even though outnumbered three to one. But those first gunshots exchanged between the swirling, taunting, chant-singing horsemen seemed to draw more and many more of the Lakota like flies to a buffalo carcass. After a short, hot fight, with far too many of the enemy rolling over the hill toward his scouts, Plenty Coups's Crow were forced to retreat. Almost as one he got them to disengage the Lakota, turn, and flee.

The first of their scouting party passed him like the wind. A diminutive warrior with one leg deformed and shorter than the other. The only Shoshone who went with the Plenty Coups's Crow to probe to the north—Limpy was already screeching his warning to the distant troops even before he had raced back the long eleven miles to reach the top of that last ridge bordering the Rosebud valley.

One by one the others sailed by Plenty Coups in a blur, then came the last to fly past. Already dangerously wounded, the face of Alligator Stands Up was tormented with pain, bright blood falling to splatter the warrior's bare leg and moccasin as he dashed past.

Still Plenty Coups stayed his ground, struggling to hold his pony steady, to control the animal despite its fright as he brought up his old Starr Carbine, long ago a present from the soldier chief of old Fort C. F. Smith. But that was before the Lakota drove the white man to abandon his posts near the country of the Apsaalooke. And Andrew Burt was now one of those serving under Lone Star.

Aiming carefully at the first oncoming rider, he told his heart to quiet itself, conscious of holding his breath as he squeezed the trigger—just as soldier Burt had taught him to do.

Slamming his shoulder, the carbine roared. Plenty Coups shifted the reins, swapping them with the carbine, and furiously kicked his pony in the ribs. The last thing he saw as he whirled about was that first Lakota falling into the grass, arms up as the horseman spun off his pony, tumbling through the air like cottonwood down on a summer breeze.

Flying over one crest after another, he kept his pony stretched out in the chase—hearing them coming, coming, coming behind him in a great angry mob. Sensing the air around him singing with death, now and then he caught the hateful hiss of Lakota bullets snarling past his ears. Over every new hill and down into each of the gently rolling valleys. One by one he raced back toward the valley where the others would ready Lone Star's soldiers for the enemy's charge.

As he reached the ridgetop and hammered his heels into his weary pony's flanks even harder, hurtling down the gentle slope, Plenty Coups gazed wide-eyed from left to right at the white men still sprawled in the grass around their coffee fires or lying in the boggy meadows under their improvised awnings of blankets laid over willow branches. Here, there, and everywhere he looked, the horses and mules remained unsaddled, up and down that entire mile of creekbank.

But suddenly a handful off to the right side were standing, shading their eyes, looking at him. They were not army, these white men.

A moment more and four of them were turning to sprint toward their grazing horses.

Plenty Coups knew who those men were.

"Sioux! Sioux! *Otoe* Sioux!"

The small Snake warrior with the short, crooked leg flew right past Donegan and Frank Grouard in a blur of color, his head down as he raced arrow-straight for his tribesmen, continuing to shout his warning in Shoshone, Crow, and English.

"Sioux! Sioux! *Many* Sioux!"

Still, it didn't take a plains linguist to figure out that the enemy had to be hot on the scout's tail. Already saddled up, the Irishman and Grouard reined up near the top of the slope as the rest of the scouts flooded over the crest and tumbled past them.

"Sioux! *Heap* Sioux!"

In heartbeats the Crow scouts were in among the soldiers now, white men and allies clambering up, bursting in all directions as they raced for their horses and mules, yelling and shouting, animals rearing and bucking, braying and snorting, breaking away—white men cursing, crying out in confusion. In fear. Even terror. A cacophony fit for the pits of hell itself.

"Sonsabitches caught us flat-footed!" Seamus screamed at Big Bat as they reached the creek bottom again.

"C'mon!" Pourier shouted. Flinging up the stirrup fender, he yanked on his cinch, dragging the saddle off his mount.

"Where you going?" Donegan demanded as he watched the saddle land with a thud in the grass.

Bat was already sailing onto the pony's bare back, hauling back on the rawhide halter. He yelled, "The Crow!"

Donegan wheeled his piebald about, glancing at the black-hatted general riding up the long slope to the bluffs, where he would likely assess the situation. At that moment the Irishman had to agree with Pourier. Bat's impulse seemed the only thing to do as the soldier camp sprang to life—but only a confused, stuttering, maddened life.

Grouard stayed beside him.

"Back up there—c'mon!"

Shaking his head, Donegan said, "No! This bunch doesn't have a chance we get hit by all them Lakota at once!"

"What you figure to do?"

"Bat's right!" Donegan shouted. "We got to get the Crow and Shoshone moving—it's Crook's only chance, Frank: hold the Sioux at bay until he can rally his men, form them up, and counterattack."

"Let's go!" Grouard said, kicking his horse into motion.

As they neared the allies, Pourier began pointing, shouting, "Look at that!"

Atop nearly every rocky ridge and grassy bluff now, Donegan suddenly saw. The skyline to the north was black with them. Every last one of them screaming and flying toward the valley on those straining ponies. Feathers streaming, hooves kicking up tufts of the new emerald-green grass and clods of damp earth from the high ground. Nostrils flared and eyes bugged as the little animals carried the Sioux and Cheyenne over the ridgetops like a spring torrent flowing over a beaver's winter dam, tumbling ever down toward Crook's troops scattering, rushing, cursing—desperately trying to ready themselves for the enemy charge. Only three of the infantry companies were moving in something resembling good order. Officers had them formed up and were getting them spread out into skirmish formation. Making sure the green soldiers did not bunch up as the enemy came on.

That hundred or so would be the first to feel the heavy blow of the charge, their officers bellowing among them, ordering them not to buckle. To stand and face the enemy.

"Three to five yards," Donegan whispered to himself, remembering just how Confederate infantry would disperse its men with intervals in the ranks, ready to receive a Union cavalry charge. Depending upon how many men and how much ground a regiment, a battalion, or even a company, had to cover. How much ground those foot soldiers had to hold. It looked like Burt's men. Luhn's too —their infantry spreading out in a clatter of shrill, barked orders, noisy haversacks slapping against gunbelts and Long Toms, bayonets jabbing the summer-blue sky like stalks of brittle buffalo grass.

By the Mother of God—those youngsters were going to get their baptism of fire!

But, he thought . . . wasn't it always that way?

Up on the slopes a hundred yards or more beyond the allies, the first of the Sioux had already reached Crook's outflung pickets. In a blur of color and sound, warriors screeching and soldiers screaming for help as they fired and reloaded—the enemy horsemen washed over the sentries in a great, darkening red wave. Most of those soldiers bravely held their tiny patches of ground. Using their Springfields as effectively as they could, firing, then swinging the rifles like clubs or lunging, jabbing with the long bayonets as the painted, bellowing demons from hell swept past, around, and even right over them.

Bedlam! Satan had torn open the gates of hell. That fallen angel freeing his banshees on mankind!

"What's that son of a bitch doing up there now?" Donegan growled, seeing George Crook bring his black stallion to a halt atop a rise to the north of the troops, almost due east of where the hostiles were sweeping over the slopes in greater and greater numbers.

For those few opening minutes amid the first shots and numbing confusion, the general left his command to fend for itself, sort out a rally, form on its own, while he went to look things over. Still, he must have said something to his officers before he dashed away, Seamus decided.

Turning, the Irishman found Anson Mills in among his Third Cavalry battalion as they struggled to get resaddled and formed up. The captain kept motioning to the south, his bellow indistinct at this distance, with this much ear-numbing noise.

Whirling at the frightening nearness of the war cries, the hair standing at his neck, Donegan found his heart suddenly choking his throat as the Crow and Shoshone swarmed past him to meet the oncoming enemy tearing down from the high ground to the northwest. As a scattering of shots from the enemy whined overhead, the Irishman gazed one last time behind him, across the creek. Guy Henry's battalion struggled among their horses to catch and get the mounts resaddled. Already the first of Van Vliet's two companies to get mounted on the far bank were streaming to the bluffs south of their position.

Good, Seamus thought. High ground what needs covering.

Sawing the gelding's reins, he brought the piebald around and drove the small brass spurs into its flanks. It leapt away, head bobbing low as it raced for the slope where Burt and Luhn had their infantry already climbing, huffing and heaving up the hillside to reinforce the pickets already overrun—where three, now four, and quickly five separate bands of warriors poured over that high ground, swirling around and around the helpless guards.

As the foot soldiers spread out in an ever-wider skirmish line, surging forward in a foragers' charge with their officers hollering above the onrushing din of shouts and war cries, gunfire and noisy mules braying behind them at the creek, the infantry began to turn the first of the warriors, forcing the red horsemen to seek out weak, vulnerable gaps in the blue line hurrying to hold back the massed charges pouring into the valley.

On the far right war cries grew in a frightening crescendo as an even more massive wave of hostiles swept through the wide gap at the end of the ridge, riding some ten abreast and heading for Noyes's battalion of the Second Cavalry. The big mounts still reared, fighting the horseholders, the troopers battling to get blankets and saddles on, to shove bits back into the mouths of chivvied horses as the warriors swept down on them—blowing the high-pitched, eerie whine of their eagle wing-bone whistles, flapping pieces of red, blue, and green blanket, snap-snap-snapping shawl-sized pieces of stiff rawhide. Firing pistol, carbines, and rifles into the cavalry herds to frighten and stampede them.

It surprised Seamus as he reached the bottom of the steep slope that Noyes's dismounted cavalry got off a concerted volley into the massed charge pouring through that gap. Noyes had formed some of his troopers at the last moment and ordered the first volley when the enemy had come to less than 150 yards of their disciplined ranks. Already on their knees, the first squads now threw open the trap-doors to the Springfield carbines as the second squads hurried up three steps through the gaps, kneeling in turn, and aimed. They fired a second volley directly into the teeth of that wide, red, screaming front. It was not until a third burst of concerted gunfire that the Sioux and Cheyenne finally turned, the first ranks of those horsemen making it as close as fifty yards to the Second Cavalry position.

Then the enemy was sweeping past the outnumbered Crow and Shoshone, countercharging to blunt the enemy's attack. Flooding past the allies like spring runoff tumbling past a boulder in the middle of a stream, Sioux and Cheyenne horsemen were making for the creekbank west of the bivouac, left of the position where the packers and miners had been relaxing in the morning sun. Pushing toward the creek with every intention of rolling on across the Rosebud toward the bluffs to the south, where the first of Van Vliet's men were soon to be outnumbered and overrun. Hearing the oncoming charge, they turned to their right as the screeching, whistles, hammering hooves, and gunfire rumbled their way across the stream. Strung out as thin as spider's silk, those two desperate companies didn't even have the time to form up to receive the charge. They began to return the enemy fire without so much as an order from Van Vliet. But it worked.

First one, then another of the warriors reined up in a fury, shooting back into the teeth of the soldiers still scrambling to gain control of the slope, to hold on to those bluffs south of the Rosebud.

Seamus watched breathless for a moment, his heart hammering in his ears. Afraid of what he might see happen before his eyes as the hordes converged on Van Vliet's battalion.

But in the space of another half-dozen heartbeats, those few stalwart Third cavalrymen turned the enemy horsemen back, denying the brown-skinned horsemen that high ground.

Honor regained! he cheered them.

Dignity and honor earned now in this battle for glory on that few acres of high ground—the honor of the Third redeemed once again after that enemy village beside the ice-bound Powder River. Three months to the day—and these soldiers long vilified for the disaster of Reynolds's battle were here and now redeeming their good name, and that of the Third Cavalry.

"There must be two thousand or more of 'em!" Pourier shouted as he brought his snorting horse to a halt beside the Irishman.

"No need trying to count how many there are, Bat!" Seamus replied. "We'll never know, anyway: they swarm over us here, then disappear to flow back over another part of the line. We'll likely never know how many we're fighting. The way they're jabbing at us here then there, it makes it look like there's thousands coming at us."

"Coming at the weakest part of the line!" Bat replied, pointing at the allies mixing in among the hundreds of Sioux.

"Blessed Mother in Heaven—Crook owes the lives of his men to these Crow and Shoshone."

"They're circling us!" Pourier growled, then was gone, firing his pistol at the long line of horsemen pouring down the creek drainage for Van Vliet's battalion.

As Seamus turned back to the north, the Sioux and Cheyenne flung themselves down the grassy slope against the Crow and Shoshone, throwing all their strength against the overwhelming numbers. In a swirl of dust, the allies met the hostiles face to face, pony to pony, even hand to hand. With clang of weapons, grunts of men and muscle, the snorts and cries of horses, red man fought red man for those terror-filled moments. Out of the growing clouds of dust loped ponies without riders, some animals crippled, others with only blood-laced pad saddles slung from their bellies as they clattered in frightened retreat down toward the boggy bottomland by the creek.

But in that desperate twenty minutes, the allies had turned the enemy.

Although outnumbered two, three, even four to one, the Crow and Shoshone courageously hurled themselves into the breech, pouring into that suicidal no-man's-land between the oncoming red waves and the unprepared blue line. Only they blunted the hostiles' charge, falling back, countercharging, but never buckling as they absorbed assault after assault just long enough to allow Crook's soldiers to re-form, resaddle, hurry into position.

Twenty to thirty long, numbing, bloody minutes before the cavalry and infantry began to have any real effect in the battle.

Had it not been for these garishly painted Crow and Shoshone scouts, Seamus brooded as he chambered another round into the Henry repeater and took aim at another warrior wearing a buffalo-horn headdress—we'd be wolf-bait by now.

Crook's allies damned well saved our hash!

Chapter 26

17 June 1876

"*Dear God—see to Nannie and the little ones! Care for them every one if I don't ever make it back home to* their arms," Anson Mills whispered, his prayer lost in the crushing clamor of that battalion of five companies he led across the Rosebud.

For some unexplained and mystical reason that Mills had long ago come to accept, the captain's Negro servant had heard the enemy coming, far away—even before the Crow scouts had raced back over the hills with their shrill warning. Anson trusted old black Henry with his life. Knew in his heart that the former slave had better ears than he ever would.

Racing toward the heights south of where his battalion had been relaxing, Mills saw them. At least the black, swirling, onrushing masses of them less than a mile away. Rushing back down the hill, Anson had been intent on reaching Crook for orders. But he had never reached the general.

Crook had already hurried off to make an observation from the heights somewhere up there to Mills's left when the order came from Royall. Not much of an order, carried by that lieutenant from North Carolina, regimental adjutant Henry R. Lemly.

Just simply, "The general's compliments—your battalion will charge those bluffs on the center."

Mills sensed the flush of instant exasperation. "Beg pardon, Lieutenant?"

Lemly licked his lips. "Sir, you are to mount, cross the stream, charge, and drive the Indians from the opposite hills."

To Captain Anson Mills of the Third U.S. Cavalry, who now hammered a saddle as he raced across the shallow creekbed of the Rosebud, that order translated to nothing more complicated than "Take the high ground. Hold it. Turn them back and *hold* the high ground."

It remained for Mills to choose the route for his own four companies, and two more temporarily assigned him from Guy Henry's command, B and L. Raking his eyes over the ground quickly, the captain instantly decided: sweeping to the far-right flank seemed like the best, perhaps the only, way for him to take them into the breech.

"Right front into line!" Mills bellowed as the troopers behind splashed up and onto the north bank of the creek to re-form. "Left front—oblique!"

It was a beautiful thing, watching the companies and their like-colored mounts flow left, others right, going four deep, lieutenants and sergeants taking their outfits across a wide three-hundred-yard front. Something to stir the horse soldier's heart seeing the last of them urge their protesting mounts into position here on ground a bit more suited to his charge.

In a matter of seconds he would lead these two hundred cavalrymen into the maw at the end of the ridge where the enemy was pouring through—with guidons snapping and iron-shod hooves clattering across the uneven ground, their mounts charging up the slope toward the high ground above the gap, where they plainly saw a frightening cavalcade of horsemen streaming from the north.

"Move out on me—center guide!" the captain hollered, rising in the stirrups. "Bugler! Sound the charge!"

Captains, lieutenants, and sergeants prodded the last of their men into formation. All but a few of the troopers hurriedly slid their short-barreled Springfield carbines behind them on the black leather slings, yanking up the mule-ears on their holsters and drawing out the preferred weapon of choice in a charge: the .45-caliber Colt's revolver. An easier weapon to handle on horseback . . . at least until he ordered them back to their feet.

Trumpeter Elmer A. Snow brought his shiny horn to his lips and stuttered those stirring, brassy notes into the summer sky, and a hundred voices were raised as the big horses shot away from the Rosebud in the first massed charge of the battle.

In a matter of heartbeats and a few leaps of their mounts, that wide blue front was a spare eight hundred yards from the enemy, and closing. Already the acrid gunsmoke stung his nostrils in that warming air, the morning breeze beginning to whip Anson's black mustache, to water his eyes as he led these proud men of the Third Cavalry into history.

The air rang with gunfire and the snarling orders barked back and forth among the six companies just as the hostiles closed on five hundred yards, beginning to break to left and right as they poured from the gap like dried beans spilling from a coarse sack all over Nannie's floor back at D. A. Russell.

How much she does with so little, he thought as his blood pounded at his temples.

How Anson Mills prayed he would see his sweet Nannie again—when this day was done. How desperately he prayed, leading his battalion toward the first of the two ridges north of the creek. Behind him his men began to cheer ever louder, to scream back in answer to the horn's brassy blare. Working themselves into a blood-lather as they came ever closer to the painted enemy.

Of a sudden he realized the buckskin troop was missing.

Captain Andrews's I Company!

Turning in his saddle for an instant, Mills couldn't find them anywhere on the slope below him.

Where they had gone in moving up from the creek bottom to begin his charge on the first ridge, he didn't know. All that was certain was that he was now left with only five of his original troops of cavalry . . . as well as those hundreds of yards of broken ground to cover.

They were out of the bottom now and into the open to do it—only man against man and animal against animal—surging forward on horseback and making some damned fine targets of themselves, having to lean far forward in their saddles in dashing up the steep ascent.

Worrying about Andrew's company, Anson's attention was brutally yanked back to their front.

On that rugged, broken ground the first of the horses were stumbling, falling, going down and spilling their riders. Toppling over on some of the men, crying out almost like wounded children. Over and over they tumbled backward.

In the space of taking another ragged breath, Mills suddenly found the Sioux and Cheyenne were there among their disordered charge, sweeping onto the troopers, rushing up and over the low rise from the north—pouring through that wide bottleneck between the terminus of two ridges. At less than fifty yards both forces surprised one another, the warriors and the cavalry all reaching that rocky terrain unsuited to fighting from horseback at the same time.

"Charge! Don't falter, men! Pitch into them!"

Seizing that moment of shock, Mills led his cavalry right in among those astonished hostiles. The gunfire, the surprise of that massed front, the clamor of that noisy charge of dusty blue horse soldiers immediately turned the enemy back onto themselves just south of the gap.

They fell back, farther and farther back, firing as they went, back even more as they retreated up the slope toward a second ridge rising to the northwest another half mile off.

Between the two forces now lay some rugged, uneven, broken ground pocked with boulders and turkey-tracked by shallow coulees carved by torrential spring rains. Terrible ground, where their horses would stumble and pitch their riders. Here too was the last cover Mills's men could take if the tide of battle turned—here were the last big boulders.

And here their mounts became almost too much to handle for those frightening moments. How close they were to the retreating enemy. What with the screeching and gunfire, the flapping of the blankets and rawhide strips —all around Mills the mounts fought their riders. Every bit as frightened and confused as his troopers.

Reining about suddenly, Mills shouted, "Battalion dismount! Horse-holders to the rear!"

Raggedly they began to obey, going afoot and clumsily handing off their mounts.

Screaming above the ear-numbing war cries, Anson Mills commanded, "Throw out skirmish lines! Back there —protect the mounts behind those rocks!"

Every fourth man now dropped to the rear, struggling with the frightened horses, clinging with all his strength to the long link-straps buckling four horses together as the animals clattered to the rear, toward what little cover the battlefield provided.

When the companies had their skirmish lines thrown out, it was time to order, "Forward on my command. Watch that near ground for stragglers!"

As a body the troopers surged forward in a crouch, making themselves as small as possible as even more of the horsemen swirled out of the gap toward the broadening front of dismounted soldiers. The hostiles came in swarms at Mills's battalion, not massing in their entirety as they burst out of the bottleneck—but clotting in swarms of twenty and thirty or more—coagulating in one wave after another that washed toward the ragged soldier line . . . then raced noisily west, past the left flank of the blue wall. In drawing away, some of the horsemen even rose from the backs of their ponies just enough to pull their breechclouts aside and slap their copper bottoms.

Such impudence from the enemy only served to anger Mills all the more—that, and his missing company. "Where the hell did Andrews go?" he growled under his breath.

At the top of that first ridge, their gallant charge ground to a halt as the soldiers broke up, taking position among the smaller boulders, each one just enough cover for one man, perhaps two at most, to fight behind. From there all the way to the bottom of the second and higher ridge, Anson Mills saw the heaving ground strewn with the sandstone boulders.

Eight hundred . . . perhaps as much as a thousand yards to go across that deadly no-man's-land. Where the men would be out in the open as they charged forward. But at a crawl. Taking that ground yard by yard, foot by foot. Inch by precious inch.

Mills hollered out his orders, hearing them echoed back down both flanks as he began to crab forward for a better look at the battlefield, a better look at his enemy. On they came, those red horsemen who poured through the gap and threatened to roll over Anson Mills's Third Cavalry.

Surprising his battalion for heart-stopping minutes, they rolled forward, screeching and firing their guns, raising clouds of dust as they plunged as little as fifty paces from the blue line of soldiers scattered irregularly beneath that bright summer sun. Close enough for Mills to make out individual designs painted on the screeching faces, see the small totems tied in the black hair or lashed around an upper arm, or beneath the jaw of the ponies. Close enough for the captain to tell the difference between a feather fluttering stiffly on the morning breeze and the brown, red, or blond-haired scalplocks these warriors boasted from every rifle muzzle, war club, and shield as they dropped to the far side of their little ponies, every single one of those daring horsemen making as small a target as possible as they rumbled down on the boulderfield.

Their advance ground to a halt under some sporadic and ineffective fire from those first warriors taking up position along the ridge to the west. Without stop, wave after wave continued to charge through the gap where they swept to the left, clattering up the broken ground to that ridgetop where most of the brown horsemen dismounted and began firing down on not only the infantry and Noyes's cavalry, but Mills as well.

Nonetheless his battalion held, taking the brunt of every charge and turning it back as the warriors closed in. Mills's men yelled out to one another, cheering when they forced aside the fevered knots of ten or twenty or more warriors preferring to stay out of range of the soldier guns.

"Shoot the goddamned ponies!" someone shouted off to the captain's right.

"Drop the ponies!" another voice raised the call.

As if they had heard the soldier talk, the warriors swerved en masse to the left of the cavalry line like a great, tumbling tide of hellish noise careening down upon them. . . .

And Mills suddenly found the ground to his immediate front open and uncontested once more.

It might prove to be a trap, he fussed with himself—like getting into that Powder River village had been, only to find themselves pinned down by the warriors in the bluffs above them.

But now, he argued too, if he made sure these men didn't string themselves out, if he kept their flanks close to the center and none of them tarried, Mills figured they stood a good chance of making it to the top of that second ridge to the northwest.

"Order the horse-holders forward!" He turned to fling his orders back at Lieutenant Augustus C. Paul. "We won't remount. Going to charge left front across the open ground."

As their mounts came forward, the men jostled among the horses and the holders. The sergeants and lieutenants hurried back and forth before the companies, forming them up. As his men began to shape up their line four deep across a wide front for the charge on foot across the broken terrain, their mounts immediately to their rear, Mills again had the nagging sense of something desperately wrong, something grossly out of order, peering back as he did across both flanks of his command. It wasn't just Captain Andrews's troop any longer. Now he was missing B and L Companies. Leaving a gaping hole along his left flank. Anson was unable to spot them anywhere behind him.

Where they were gone in the middle of taking that first ridge, he didn't know, having last seen them to his left on the north side of the Rosebud the first time he formed up the six companies.

All that was certain now was that Mills was left with only three troops of dismounted cavalry and a few hundred more yards of broken ground to cover to reach the bottom of that second ridge. His men would have to break out into the open now to do it, pushing forward with his horse-holders coming noisily on their rear.

Mills grinned grimly: at least this time they didn't have to worry about leaving their bloody coats behind in the snow before they charged the enemy. Not like the Powder River fight Colonel Reynolds had botched and nearly cost the lives of every man with him.

Mills whirled and gazed back downslope once again, wondering where the hell those three companies had disappeared to. Growing more than curious. Now he was angry.

He sensed the bile rising in his throat as the first of his men joined him in weaving through the rocks and boulders there atop the first ridge, staring across all that open ground in front of them. All too clearly did Mills remember how the other outfits had abandoned his and Egan's companies to their fate when he and Teddy got themselves pinned down under that snowy mesa. It had been enough to make a man chew a rusty nail.

Where the hell did those three companies go?

Chapter 27

Moon of Ripening Berries

He held nothing back, ordered not a single warrior to remain in reserve. How could he? Crazy Horse wondered.

So, so long had they desperately hungered for this fight.

When his four wolves bumped into the enemy scouts who outnumbered them, the Raven People warriors drove the four back, back farther still across the hills in a running battle until they finally came in sight of Crazy Horse's hundreds. His *akicita* tried desperately to hold the eight-times-ten in check. But failed.

The excited horsemen flowed past the camp police like spring snow-melt rushing past a rustling tree fallen in mid-stream. Yelling out their bravery songs, crying their war chants, making their own medicine strong—they every one raced after the Raven People and Snakes, right up that final slope that brought him here to the top of this bluff where he finally looked down on the soldiers of Three Stars.

Reaching this creek valley, they felt the countryside vault beneath them, heave and roll, growing sharply broken as it fell away on either side from this ridge. In streaming up the slopes, his horsemen were forced by the raw texture of the land to peel off into four distinct bands. On over the top of the ridge these four waves poured, across the high plateau, then down the far slope toward the soldiers in the boggy bottomland.

Without much delay beyond their first shots, the pickets atop the slopes started to fall back in the face of the horsemen. Those who chose to stand their ground were swallowed up, lost beneath the pounding hooves and whirling clubs, war axes and lances glittering, glinting, flashing in the new day's sun.

The only ones to turn the charge were those Raven People and Snakes. With the bright-red strips of cloth tied around their arms, they mounted and rushed into the fight, covering the retreat of those pickets who ran and stumbled, fell and picked themselves back up to flee some more, dragging their long rifles as they bolted past the Indian horsemen charging up the slope right into the teeth of Crazy Horse's attack.

Now, as half his force, hundreds of warriors, were checked far to the east where they had been pouring through a gap between the hills, Crazy Horse turned finally, looking north. Wondering where the Hunkpapa were. When they would arrive. He knew they were coming. With his own eyes he had seen Sitting Bull helped atop his spotted pony before leaving at the head of the Hunkpatila column.

But where they had gone in leaving Sundance Creek, he did not know. When they would arrive was of far greater consequence to this fight now that the element of surprise was gone like puffball dust, now that the white man was no longer confused, unhorsed, and on the defensive, now that the soldiers were regrouping and making a counterattack.

He ground his teeth—angry enough to shake a fist at the sky, cursing the Hunkpapa for the long trail they took, for not being here to throw themselves into this fight.

Their medicine man was tired, weak. Sitting Bull should not have tried to lead his tribesmen.

But it mattered little now, the Horse decided. The fight was already at hand, and the rest of his warriors were already in the thick of it, rolling this way, probing along the soldier lines . . . then reining away in another wave to jab and punch at some new place atop the miles of rolling, broken country.

If Sitting Bull wanted his vision victory over the soldiers—best he get his Hunkpapa here to assure the white man's defeat.

A bullet sang past Crazy Horse's ear, snarling like an angry wasp. He stared down the slope at the foot soldiers clutching their long rifles like their mothers' breasts—frightened like babes, they were.

Another shot nicked the decorative trailing fringe on his right legging. The pony pranced sideways. But in leaning over to inspect the animal, he could find no blood, no wound.

He sat up straight once again, his chest swelling in pride and the certainty of his invincibility.

As sure as his dream-makers had made him that he would not die by a white man's bullet, not at the hand of the white man at all.

As frightening as would be his death at the hands of his own people, with the long soldier knife driven into his back—that fear nonetheless released Crazy Horse for now. For he knew this was not his day to die.

Wait! . . . there in the far distance. Off among the dark green of the trees to the north. He saw the first flashes of color in the morning sun, the first rise and fall of the motion of ponies coming on the lope.

They had heard the noise of the battle. The rattle of gunfire. Now they must realize they are late. He cursed the Hunkpapa.

Then gave thanks—for there was more than two-times-ten-times-ten coming now to reinforce his horsemen.

Hopo! May the Great Mystery be praised! It was a good day for them to slaughter the white man!

That long, thin line of Apsaalooke and Shoshone stretched, here and there they gave a little ground—but they did not break.

Along with the half-breeds and the three squaw men from the Wind River Reservation, Captain George Randall, Lone Star's chief of scouts, rallied the allies, exhorted them, moved back and forth along the wide front as the hostiles poured down on them, all the time intent on plugging any of the holes in their line which the Lakota and Shahiyena could use to charge down on the soldiers still milling in confusion at the creekbottom.

Plenty Coups heard the next wave coming. The hooves pounded closer, ever closer. Those shouts and screams and taunts yelled to frighten the young men among his Raven People. To lure his warriors and those of the Snakes into doing something foolhardy. But this was not the time for foolishness. If they kept their heads about them, they would hold the enemy long enough for the soldiers to come up behind them with their long-range rifles. Then, and only then, would the day be won.

For now, it was up to a couple hundred allies to hold back these innumerable Lakota and Shahiyena.

As Plenty Coups's scouts had raced back to the creekside camp in that chase of more than ten miles across the broken country, "Black Jack" Randall had reacted immediately. Perhaps quickly enough to avert what Plenty Coups feared was certain disaster as he reached that last ridgetop only to discover the white men unprepared to receive the enemy charge that was coming hot on his heels.

Between Randall and the man called Cosgrove, they got the allies spread out and countercharging back toward the few soldier pickets falling back in a thin line, barely ready to receive the onrushing hostiles. The enemy's ponies came within five hundred yards before they pulled off, whirling, milling . . . but then charged in again. Coming closer this time.

And fell back under the fire from the allies armed with the white man's powerful weapons. The Lakota circled once more and came racing down on Plenty Coups and the rest. Each time, the horsemen rode a little closer, became a bit more daring, charging into the muzzles of the allies' guns, screeching and dropping off the far side of their ponies.

It wouldn't be long, the Apsaalooke war chief realized, before his enemies made a daring ride right through this thin line of defense. Like powerful gusts of strong spring wind, the knots of horsemen slammed against the Crow ramparts: ten, then as many as thirty, charging in bunches, hurling arrows and shooting their guns. But Randall's line did not break under all the pressure that first fifteen long minutes.

Then Cosgrove and the captain were among the allies, shouting in English and Snake and Apsaalooke. Gesturing, cheering, getting the scouts on their feet.

"The scalps are yours! Every pony is yours!" one of the white men shouted.

"Remember your women and children!" the other white man hollered. "Kill these Sioux for them!"

In an instant Plenty Coups was leading the rest, setting off at a ragged sprint toward the enemy as the Lakota were caught regrouping for another charge. If they could surprise the enemy this way, then they might catch them off balance. It was good, this plan: rather than fight nothing more than a defensive war, why not take the offensive, push back at your enemy until he folds?

Then Plenty Coups saw him through the waves of dust and the thin layer of murky gunsmoke. As if the entire battlefield fell quiet while he watched only that single warrior coming on among the others in their new charge.

How could any man miss him? Plenty Coups wondered.

A long double-trailer of eagle wing-feathers spilled away from the Lakota warrior's magnificent bonnet. The midmorning sun glinted brightly off that shiny rifle—it appeared to be a repeater. What a prize that weapon would make hanging in any man's lodge! As well as the warbonnet. Any man who wore such a bonnet had to be an accomplished, courageous warrior.

Still, more than the rifle and bonnet, Plenty Coups wanted that great warrior's scalp.

Skidding to a halt, he dropped to one knee and brought the soldier carbine to his shoulder. Snapped the hammer back a second click to full cock and laid the front blade on the man's chest . . . just as the warrior dropped to the far side of his pony. All Plenty Coups found in his sights were the ends of the feathers radiating from the crown of that magnificent headdress.

Angrily he slowly lowered that front blade, laying it down in the vee of the rear sight and holding on the vee in the broad chest of that warrior's pony. With a gentle squeeze of the trigger the rifle roared. Without so much as waiting to see for sure, Plenty Coups was already on his feet racing for the warrior as the Lakota's pony stumbled, reared, then fell back to crumple on his forelegs, giving out completely and rolling to pitch its rider forward.

With a half dozen others Plenty Coups heedlessly raced for the warrior struggling to shake the cobwebs from his head. He looked up, blinked dust from his eyes, and saw the enemy sprinting for him. Clambering to his feet, his legs wobbly at best, the warrior turned and took off.

This was not the way of a warrior of many honors!

He has forgotten the bridle, Plenty Coups thought as some Apsaalooke riders dashed past their war chief on horseback, racing for the unhorsed enemy.

It had long been a symbol of cool-headedness, a sign of ultimate courage, for a man to calmly remove the bridle from his pony fallen in battle.

But this one, this Lakota warrior with the magnificent bonnet that spoke of great war deeds—he did not act with courage and disdain for the enemy.

He ran like a young jackrabbit.

In a matter of heartbeats the four Apsaalooke riders overtook the Lakota and began whipping him one at a time in turn with their rawhide quirts. As Plenty Coups sprinted up, one of the riders reached in and ripped that beautiful bonnet from the warrior's head.

"It is mine now!" the happy man shouted to his companions. "See how great a prize it is!"

Only then did Plenty Coups see this was not an older warrior, proven in battle. With the bonnet taken from the man's head . . . this was no man—why, this was no more than a youngster! No more than twenty winters could this young one count in his life!

The little jackrabbit cowered from the Apsaalooke horsemen who swirled about him, holding both hands over his head as if he expected the enemy to club him.

"You are only a boy!" growled another of the laughing horsemen as he wrenched the rifle from one of those hands held over the Lakota's head.

How Plenty Coups had wanted that bonnet, coveted that rifle. And mostly the scalp of a great Lakota warrior.

But now they could all see the enemy was nothing more than a boy.

"Go! Run, boy!" Plenty Coups taunted the youth, parting some of his fellow warriors as he raced up to join in the humiliation.

"A child like you has no business wearing so great a bonnet as this!" another Crow snarled.

Although the Lakota youth did not know this foreign tongue, he nonetheless understood the shame heaped upon him by his enemy. Before their eyes he collapsed to his knees, his eyes filling with tears as he stammered, stuttered some unintelligible words, gazing up at his tormentors as he beseeched them, hands outstretched, pleading for mercy.

"We must go!" shouted one of those near Plenty Coups.

As one man all the warriors looked up—saw the wide front of Lakota horsemen racing down on them.

"They think we have killed this little gopher!" roared Plenty Coups.

He looked down at the youngster, yanking him off his knees with one hand and shoving him away, toward the onrushing horsemen.

"Go, my scared little jackrabbit. Tell Crazy Horse and Sitting Bull we spared your life. Remember we kill only great Lakota warriors. We Apsaalooke will never kill children. Go now! Back to the safety of your friends!"

"Come—Plenty Coups! Now!"

He turned to an old friend reining up behind him. The man's nervous pony danced beside Plenty Coups, its rear flank knocking him backward.

Bull Snake hollered, "Get up behind me! We must race back to our side!"

With a smooth vault Plenty Coups pulled himself up behind Bull Snake as they burst away like teal-headed ducks spooked from the slick surface of a winter pond. Back toward Randall and Cosgrove, the Snakes and the thin line of their own tribesmen.

One of the riders ahead of Bull Snake had that beautiful bonnet out at the end of his arm, laughing and holding up his trophy for all to see.

Another shook that shiny repeating rifle overhead in triumph.

Now Plenty Coups felt a twinge of regret, some sadness at not having taken the enemy's scalp.

He looked back over his shoulder at the youngster lunging away on foot, racing for the Lakota horsemen. Only then did Plenty Coups realize that he had won something perhaps even better than a man's scalp.

He had robbed the young warrior of his pride, his manhood, his warrior spirit by letting him live, forced to awaken each day to his humiliation at the hands of the Apsaalooke.

Those three companies left to Anson Mills blunted every assault and charge by the enemy horsemen, turning them one by one by one. With every wave the hostiles flowed past the left flank as his cavalry plodded toward the second ridge. It was there the warriors turned to the west, melting into those rugged slopes that eventually rose to a conical hill.

But now there were no warriors east of the gap. Mills's troopers had swept the country clear.

Dismounting his men at the second ridge, the captain gave orders to pursue the enemy fleeing west, his intention being to join with those three companies of infantry under Chambers and Noyes's three troops of the Second Cavalry, who were spread out along the middle of the battleground now a half hour or more into the fight.

About an hour had come and gone since the Sioux and Cheyenne first made their frightening appearance at the top of the far hills where the allies held the enemy in check for that desperate thirty minutes until Mills got away and Van Vliet could charge south—so Crook's men would not be completely surrounded.

In forcing the warriors into motion along the ridgetops, Mills's charges had allowed those six companies of infantry and dismounted cavalry at the center to advance once more, taking some of the pressure off the center of the fight.

With the red horsemen pushed and harried on their own left flank by Mills's battalion rushing in from the east, as well as being harassed by Mills's galling fire as his men drove the warriors back, back toward the ever-higher ground, the hostiles ultimately had to relinquish their withering fire on the troops pinned down in the middle of the battlefield. Noyes was the first to get his cavalrymen up and moving out on foot, although the fire from their carbines proved ineffective against the warriors from so great a range. Even with their Long Toms, Major Alexander Chambers's infantry didn't have much of an effect against the enemy.

"Keep pushing, boys! Keep pushing them!" Mills bellowed, urging his three companies forward as the enemy fell back.

That ineffectiveness of the infantry's long-range weapons must have made the warriors turn in their retreat once they reached the highest ground below the sweeping slopes of the conical hill a mile west of the gap they had just fled. What bullets the soldiers were firing—for there was a deafening racket from the ridge below the Sioux and Cheyenne there atop the slopes—were falling harmlessly to the rear of the enemy warriors. Natural that the red men turned, taunted, and dug in as best they could at this new vantage point, returning fire on Noyes's dismounted troopers, Chambers's infantry, and Mills's daring unhorsed horse soldiers.

Then for the moment that enemy gunfire slackened. The bullets landing in front of his battalion's position appeared to wither away. If Captain Anson Mills didn't know any better, it looked as if many of the hostiles were turning their attention to the west now.

Through the gunsmoke and the dust, he peered down the slope, straining to see back toward the bottomland near the creek. Now he caught sight of those three missing companies.

At the moment Mills had turned to lead away his six companies from the creek bottom to began his assault on the first ridge, Colonel William B. Royall had evidently commandeered Andrews's I Company. There was no other explanation, for there was I Troop—down there with Royall.

"Damn him!" Mills grumbled under his breath, cursing his regimental commander. Without informing me!

Anson wondered if Crook knew. . . .

Then he realized that Royall must have returned to the rear of his formation as Mills was pressing up the slope to that first ridge, come back to steal the other two companies—B and L.

Down by the Rosebud, Royall had all his cavalry troops mounted up, forming for their charge, four deep. Anson thought he recognized the colonel's bay as it pranced smartly along that front, side-stepping as it jumped from time to time while bullets sang down the slope from the warrior positions.

As Royall ordered his battalion out, it appeared that the colonel was taking them far along the left flank now, off toward the west where Mills had seen Guy Henry already go, pushing far to the left and west rather than charging due north, directly into the face of the enemy. Perhaps Henry and Royall were going to attempt circling behind those warriors falling back to mass on the heights around that conical hill.

As much as he detested Royall for robbing his battalion of those three companies, Mills nonetheless had to admire the colonel grudgingly for what the man evidently had in mind. By taking his strike force west behind Guy Henry, Royall could support the thin line of the Crow and Shoshone spread out there on the immediate left of the packers and miners who were hunkered down just to the left of Chambers's infantry, who for now were pinned down at the middle of the battlefield with Noyes's dismounted Second Cavalry. And having themselves a very hot scrape of it.

What had every appearance of a stalemate could now be broken, Mills figured as he rose to a crouch and waved his men forward. If Guy Henry and William Royall succeeded. If . . .

And for the time being, Anson Mills would do what he could here on the east.

"C'mon, boys! Let's show these red bastards they can't pin us down here!"

Yes, the stalemate along more than a mile of battlefront could indeed be broken—if the right push was made with that cavalry moving out behind Royall and Henry.

If—and only if—they didn't get themselves swallowed, chewed up, and spit out first.

"You don't mind, I'll ride with you, Major," Seamus shouted into the bedlam at Captain Guy V. Henry.

The soldier looked the Irishman down, then up. "If you're any good with the repeater and you'll take orders—you're welcome to ride along . . . Mr.—?"

"Donegan."

"All right," Henry said, his voice filled with exasperation as he surveyed what he had left of a battalion. "Now that Colonel Evans ordered those two companies of mine to go with Mills—I'll gladly take any gun I can, Mr. Donegan. Crook wants me on the left, five hundred yards over there. To prevent the enemy from turning on our flank."

As second in command of the Third Cavalry behind Royall, Major Andrew W. Evans had relayed the commanding general's hurried orders in those first moments of the battle, carrying the bad news to Captain Henry: Evans was reassigning Companies B and L to Anson Mills's charge that Crook had ordered on the eastern flank of the ridge.

Here on the west Seamus cheered as he struggled to control the nervous gelding beneath him. "Colonel Henry, we get these boys of yours to lay down enough fire, we can damned well turn these red bastirds!"

"Lieutenant Reynolds!" Henry called out to the officer in charge of F Company. "Left into front on me, oblique to that far point at the end of the ridge!"

As Henry wheeled about, he found his bugler, Frank Ropetsky, and gave the order to blow the charge. Then the captain put the brass spurs to his mount, both companies bursting into motion behind him—yelling, cheering, shouting for no better reason than it served to work a man up into battle readiness, got his blood running hot, and just might give pause to some of those warriors who were clotting on the heights off to their right. The ones pinning down Chambers and Noyes.

Still farther to the east there arose a louder rattle of gunfire. Seamus could only assume it came from the fight

Anson Mills was making of it with his battalion and those two companies Evans had commandeered from Henry.

It took little enough time to cover that rolling ground sweeping up from the creek bottom toward the far western extent of the ridge, at least what they could see of it as they galloped in a wide circle to the left. Throwing up his arm, Henry ordered a halt.

"Looks like we've come west far enough," Donegan said to Henry and Reynolds. "You want, Colonel—I'll have a look top of that hill just to be sure we got around their flank."

The captain nodded, squinting into the bright light. "Permission granted, Mr. Donegan."

Tapping the brim of his slouch hat with his fingers, Donegan reined about and spurred his snorting piebald up the gentle rise. Atop that heaving ridge, he saw the blackened mass of gathering, swarming warriors off to the east on the slopes of the conical hill.

Without waiting for any of them to find him silhouetted against the skyline, Donegan whirled about and raced down to the horse soldiers.

"The Injins still to the east, by that tall point. Looks to be Crook is holding 'em at bay in the center."

"Then we have come far enough," Henry declared with little satisfaction, looking again at the strength of his diminished command with harsh criticism in those slightly bugging eyes.

"May I suggest we push back east and take up positions that will put some pressure on the hostiles?" asked Lieutenant Bainbridge Reynolds.

"Suggestion noted," Henry replied with a bit of a grin. "We will do just that—as long as we can be sure the hostiles won't flank us, won't come up behind us or the other battalions."

"I'll volunteer to close the file on your march east," Donegan offered.

"You're a civilian," Henry flared, eyes narrowing. "I can't order you to do anything you don't want to do, Mr. Donegan."

"I just offered, Colonel. Every column must have a rear-guard."

With approval Henry replied, "Very well, sir. You will ride with me."

The captain turned to his lieutenant. "Mr. Reynolds, your F Company will take the point. D Company will bring up the rear—with Mr. Donegan and me closing the file . . . together."

Chapter 28

17 June 1876

"*Goddamn!" John Bourke growled in that knot of harried* officers arguing, snapping, formulating battle plans on the north bank of the Rosebud. "This officer corps is caught flat-footed like a bunch of shave-tails!"

"Not us," Alexander Chambers retorted, whirling on the lieutenant. "Not this officer corps, Mr. Bourke!" He flung his arm out, pointing up the ridge to the solitary figure slump-shouldered atop his black horse. "Your Brigadier General George Crook—that's who's gone and got our bangers caught on a rock!"

John shut up, more than a little concerned—downright scared with the way the enemy swarmed over the pickets and those two hundred Crow and Shoshone who were barely holding their first and only line of defense against a total massacre for the moment.

"Caught with our pants down," grumbled Thomas B. Dewees. "Down around our ankles!"

Though Bourke would never confess it to another soul, from the look he had seen cross Crook's normally impassive face as the general leapt into the saddle to tear off up the slope, the old man was more than a little worried himself.

Not that Crook could be scared of the Sioux. Not really

scared of having a tough fight of it either. More likely, John figured, the general suffered a numbing dread that he would relive the one great mistake, the one horror of his military career: Cedar Creek—a dozen years before—when Phil Sheridan himself had to come pull Crook's hash out of the fire after Jubal Early slipped in through his lines during the Shenandoah campaign.

And now, by God, Crazy Horse had gone and done the same damned thing!

In that vacuum caused by Crook's absence, much to Bourke's dismay, Captain Azor Nickerson swaggered about, shoulder to shoulder with Chambers and Evans to begin barking orders, running here, then there, among the commands for those first few minutes that stretched into half an hour. When Colonel Royall finally rode up to find out why he hadn't received instructions from Crook and immediately wrenched control of things from Nickerson's novice paw, John felt nothing short of relief.

Sending Nickerson off in one direction and Major Andrew Evans in another to mobilize the cavalry, Royall calmly, coolly began to issue orders designed to wrest victory from what clearly had the appearance of the jaws of defeat.

The first matter was to dispatch Van Vliet's battalion to take the high bluffs south of their position on the far side of the creek—to get soldiers there before the warriors could sweep across the Rosebud and secure that high ground. Van Vliet was to hold that position pending further instructions.

Gazing up the slope to the flat top of those bluffs, Bourke again realized that Van Vliet had the most perfect and commanding view of the battle just then beginning: his very own "orchestra seat." Still, here in the thick of it was exactly where John wanted to be, and nowhere else.

Just how long it would take these men beside the Rosebud to get saddled and formed up to go on the defensive, never mind making a counterattack, Bourke had despaired, sensing a darkness seep into his jubilant mood as each long and noisy, frantic minute passed, waiting for his general while the allies struggled to hold the enemy at bay.

And he found himself praying this would not be the

Powder River all over again: the Indians taking the heights, pinning the troops down below, fighting so fiercely that the soldiers were driven off, abandoning some of their dead and wounded.

John cursed the evil of that despair, scolding himself sharply for allowing the return of those frightening memories. This was, after all, a different fight. And for God's sake—George Crook himself was here!

To the shouts and cheering of many, the general was suddenly back among them.

"These red savages wouldn't be attacking us if we weren't within striking distance of the villages, men!" Crook bellowed, his voice like strikes of cold iron above the bedlam. "They came upon us from the north. Because of that I divine they mean to delay us, to cover the retreat of their village."

In a matter of seconds he spat his orders like a Gatling gun. Most important, he dispatched Chambers to push ahead to the base of the slope with his infantry in support of the Crow and Shoshone who were having a hot and noisy time of it. The foot soldiers were the first to be ready, the first to move out.

Immediately Companies G and H of the Ninth Infantry under Captains Thomas B. Burrowes and Andrew Burt hurried forward to secure the ridges just north of the spring where minutes before Bourke had been playing whist with Crook and Nickerson. At the same time, the remaining three companies of infantry, D and F of the Fourth under the command of Captains Avery B. Cain and Gerhard Luhn, as well as Company C of the Ninth Infantry, with Captain Samuel Munson in the lead, moved north in the same general direction, throwing out an active skirmish line. Traipsing along on their far left flank came the ragged and undisciplined civilians—packers and miners—all hurrying forward in the shadow of the infantry like hangers-on, carrying their big-bore weapons.

"Nickerson, you'll go with the infantry," Crook shouted above the noise and confusion.

"General?" Nickerson squeaked with clear disappointment.

"Go with the goddamned infantry!" Crook snapped. "If I need something—I'll send for you."

The wounding crossed the older man's face. "Very well . . . General."

Nickerson turned on his heel to scurry off to join Captain Luhn's F Company. After twenty yards he glanced back over his shoulder at Bourke, plainly glaring his dark disapproval in not being left behind with Crook, who had ordered Captain Henry E. Noyes and his dismounted cavalry up to augment Chambers's infantry, moving the dismounted troopers off to act as skirmishers along Cain's right.

Wheeling about, the general dispatched Captain Guy Henry off to the left to hold a low rise south of the Rosebud. At that very moment the three companies of able skirmishers in Captain Cain's battalion were firing by volleys into the onrushing warriors swarming against the allies in their front: feathered bonnets streaming and faces painted, dust and clods and tufts of the new grass thrown up by hundreds of hooves along the brow of the slope, as first one squad, then another and another, dropped to a knee, aimed, and fired, then reloaded while another squad moved forward and halted, knelt and fired, maintaining the pressure on the noisy hostiles, who were struggling in a seesaw duel against the Crow and Shoshone.

Finding they could not easily penetrate the stiff resistance of the allies, the hostiles flowed to their left for a few moments, there to encounter resistance not only from Noyes's skirmishers, but also from the new pressure of Anson Mills's troopers inching up toward the gap after securing that first ridge.

Crook's entire battle front was stretching now, thinning to something more than a mile across the entire face of that pine-studded ridge beside the Rosebud.

By damn, Bourke cheered himself, we just might have this thing wrapped up before any man can work up a sweat!

Their long-distance battle raged back and forth with little damage done to either side while Mills brought his dismounted cavalry across the rise of the first ridge to the base of the second. Bourke watched Mills push on, his skirmishers crawling toward ever-higher ground—which left the gap behind them. Unprotected.

The warriors must have seen the very same thing as opportunity dropped right in their laps. Once more the gap—that funnel that poured into the creek bottom where the soldiers had been resting—was open and uncontested.

Crook realized it almost as quickly as did his enemy.

"Captain Dewees!" he cried, summoning the Second Cavalry officer to his side. "Take your A Company forward as dismounted skirmishers and bring along G and H of the Ninth. Inform Captains Burrowes and Burt that you're taking all three companies east . . . over there." The general was pointing.

"That gap, sir?" Dewees asked, nodding.

"Exactly. Seal that son of a bitch off for good, and sit on it until you receive further orders. Do not leave your post without my personal instructions."

Dewees saluted, his back snapping into a rigid shaft. "Understood, General."

Bourke turned away for a moment, sensing—more than really hearing—the growing volume of gunfire coming from the south. On those tallest of heights overlooking the valley of the Rosebud, Van Vliet's men were having a lively time as the warriors repeatedly attempted to overwhelm the two cavalry companies. And now, with Dewees going east and Henry's cavalry riding west, that long mile of front was stretching even more.

In the time it took to get the battalions mounted and moving out from headquarters, Crook's battle with Crazy Horse had strung itself thin as a cat-gut fiddle string along a front nearly three miles wide.

At first Wooden Leg, like others, thought the scouts for the soldiers were Snakes and Pawnee. It wasn't until the Shahiyena were in the thick of it, riding around, among, and through the enemy warriors, that he and the others discovered they were not fighting the Scalped Head Pawnee. Instead, these were People of the Raven. The ones the white man called the Crow.

For as long as it would take a man to eat his breakfast and smoke his pipe, Wooden Leg had hung close to the Lakota, who fought the Snakes and Raven people up and down the rugged slope while the first of the blue walk-a-heaps marched forward and finally brought their far-shooting rifles into play.

He had a soldier gun, captured in the Sore-Eye Moon battle on the Powder River—but the barrel on his was not as long as the barrels on the guns carried by these soldiers hurrying up from the meadow below the ridge. During that early part of the fight, Wooden Leg leveled his soldier rifle at one of the enemy's scouts, killing a Snake who wore a spotted war bonnet. He did not try for the bonnet and scalp: the enemy's body lay too close to those walk-a-heap guns.

Within minutes of the arrival of those far-shooting soldiers, most of the Shahiyena and many of the Lakota were forced to withdraw from the ridgetop. As they dropped back, they rode off in a wide circuit that took them east toward the gap between two of the tall bluffs.

"This will take us right down to the creek," war chief Little Wolf cheered them just before making their charge. "We will ride down upon the soldiers and attack them from behind!"

But about the same time as those warriors were beginning to burst through the gap, the soldiers were climbing up from the creek bottom, many of their big American horses stumbling, spilling on the rough terrain, pitching riders in their colorful, noisy charge. Once the soldiers were stopped, it came down to making bravery runs—racing back and forth in front of the soldiers on their sprinting ponies. Although both sides shot at one another without much effect, Wooden Leg was most proud that the Shahiyena and Lakota were courageous and wild enough to ride close to the enemy, dropping to the far side of their ponies until the last moment. And with each retreat after such a bravery run, many of the younger men would suddenly spring back into full view of the enemy and bare their bottoms.

It was the worst of taunts to make before any adversary,

white or red. To expose such a defenseless part of one's body—as if to say those soldiers could not even hit that broad, brown target. As each subsequent wave of warriors circled back toward the second ridge rising beside from the gap, the others would cheer and the laughter would be great. For now the battle seemed like such great fun. Even Buffalo Calf Road Woman, who had come from the village with her husband, Black Coyote, and her brother, Chief Comes in Sight, rode in among the soldiers, taunting them with her bare buttocks, then retreated to laugh with the rest of them.

Such a good day—only ponies had gone down so far.

Then the soldiers regrouped for a charge on that second ridge. A great cry arose above the warriors, and again they rushed the pony soldiers. In this furious countercharge the Shahiyena and Lakota forced the white men to dismount and send their big horses to safety behind them. As they did, a few brave warriors closed in and began making coup, striking where they could, clubbing soldiers as they dropped from their saddles.

Even Wooden Leg emerged out of the dust and gunsmoke, swinging his bow to come between a soldier and his big gray horse, striking the white man across the shoulders. The young warrior rode off in triumph, knowing he had dented the shiny brass horn the soldier carried behind his left arm.

During these fierce moments among the soldiers and their mounts, one of the enemy's horses became frightened and ran away with its rider, carrying the soldier right toward the Shahiyena and Lakota lines. As much as he tried to rip back on the reins, the horse continued on, fighting the bit, its head turned nearly backward as the scared, bareheaded soldier plummeted toward certain death. As it galloped ever closer, one of the warriors shot the horse in its chest. Gradually the animal slowed its race as it neared the Shahiyena where the warriors swarmed out to pull the soldier from the horse and club him, a dozen or more racing in, each to count coup and stab the white man.

Hot was their blood that day.

Dismounted, the soldiers dug in behind the rocks and

humps and coulees scattered across that rough ground. And now the battle changed. What had been fun quickly turned grim. What had been reason for laughter now elicited cries of despair and anger as they all watched friends fall, some attempting to crawl away, out of range of the soldier guns. As the sun climbed in the sky, more and more ponies lay dead and dying on the ground. From time to time one of the Shahiyena rode in to rescue another warrior hurled from his pony, perhaps a friend who lay wounded in the grass. They dared not leave a single body on that battlefield, knowing how the Snakes and Raven People would mutilate their enemies.

Chief Comes in Sight was one of those Wooden Leg saw fall.

On horseback Chief Comes in Sight and White Elk had passed one another dangerously close to the soldiers twice before, and now they began another death-defying race before the enemy guns—White Elk riding in from the east and Chief Comes in Sight from the west nearest the gap. Just after they had passed, taunting the soldiers, a bullet struck Chief Comes in Sight's pony. The animal started down in a blur, hurling its rider over its neck as it fell, tumbling in a heap—less than four arrow flights away from the enemy's scouts. Bullets immediately began to fall around the dazed warrior, kicking up tiny spouts of dust, splattering leadenly against the face of the bluffs behind him.

While Wooden Leg held his breath, the brave warrior shook his head—then calmly strode back to his fallen pony and began removing the bridle from its jaws.

Instantly a great cry went up among the Shahiyena, so great that it echoed from the red bluffs hemming in the gap. That echo had not died before there came a noisy rush behind Wooden Leg. He turned in time to see the sister of Chief Comes in Sight flying past him, urging her pony onto the open battlefield, riding low along the animal's neck as she raced under the muzzles of the soldier guns—heading straight for a trio of Raven People scouts who were galloping out from the soldier lines to count coup on the unhorsed enemy.

Buffalo Calf Road Woman shot by her fallen brother like the wind, reining her pony about in a savage turn, then dashed back to Chief Comes in Sight as the white man's bullets fell about them both. Her pony pranced around the solitary warrior. Pranced around him again, shying each time she tried to urge the animal close to her brother. Now they could hear the yelps and cries of the Raven People warriors. Without fully coming to a halt, the young woman held out her arm as she went past a fourth time. Her brother grabbed hold and pulled himself up on the pony's rump just as Buffalo Calf Road Woman kicked the animal into furious motion, lumbering with its heavy load for the warrior lines.

In a matter of heartbeats the pair was among their cheering friends, who pulled them both from the wide-eyed, weary pony. It was again a good day for brother and sister, for those Shahiyena and Lakota who had watched one of their own snatched from certain death by an incredible act of bravery.

"These soldiers are angry now that they cannot kill us," Little Wolf declared to some of those around him.

"See—some soldiers are going west," Contrary Belly said at the edge of that group. He pointed at the distant slope.

No more than half-a-hundred soldiers were mounted up and moving west along the front of the bluff away from the creek bottom.

"Let's go stop them," Little Wolf suggested.

"Yes," Wooden Leg agreed with the war chief. "If we don't stop them, they will circle back around on the Lakota at the top of the ridge."

"These few will be easy to stop!" Young Black Bird cheered, rallying many of the Shahiyena.

"Besides," Little Wolf added, "I want to fight soldiers who stay on their horses—to fight like warriors. These white men who hide behind the rocks like gophers are not worthy adversaries."

"Let's go fight the horse soldiers!" Contrary Belly shouted as more than six-times-ten of the Shahiyena turned their ponies west.

"Let's go count coup on the pony soldiers!" Wooden

Leg cried as he followed Little Wolf up the back side of the bluff.

The war chief nodded. "We can have a lot of fun surprising the white men!"

"Yes," Wooden Leg replied. "To pop up where they don't expect us to be!"

Chapter 29

17 June 1876

It was as if they were sprouting right out of the ground. From behind every bush and boulder. Materializing magically out of the bottom of every shallow coulee.

On foot or horseback.

Like an overwhelming red wave, they hurtled toward Guy Henry's two companies of the Third.

Minutes ago Colonel Royall's charge at the center of the battle line had taken some of the pressure off the desperately thin left flank of Major Chambers's infantry, where the packers and miners had been skirmishing under growing pressure for some frightening moments until the cavalry arrived.

But to Seamus Donegan and those men riding with the Henry battalion, it seemed all Royall had accomplished was to plop a huge boulder down in the middle of a spring torrent: the hostiles didn't back off; instead, they merely rallied all the more fiercely as they flowed to the left and right of the colonel's impediment.

And now Royall was forced to ride back to the creek-bottom camp, leaving his battalion on a knoll to hold the line with those foot soldiers and civilians the best they could. He went personally to order up the remaining troops of the Third to fill the breech suddenly left open when the Crow and Shoshone began withdrawing from the fray with their wounded.

"Look at them red bastards, will you!" grumbled a young soldier near Donegan. "Running back for cover when things get hot."

"When things get hot?" the Irishman snapped. "Those Injins likely saved your hide, sojur!"

The corporal whirled at the voice, finding the civilian nearby. "Looks to me they're running scared as jackrabbits, I say."

"Taking their wounded and dead to the rear, you loud-mouthed greenhorn. Crook owes his life to them. You as well."

"Owe my life to a bunch of yellow-bellied redskins backing out of the fight?"

When the soldier began to belly laugh, an old sergeant swung the butt of his carbine squarely into the younger man's middle.

Crumpling in half, pain graying his face, Corporal William Blair demanded in a raspy squeak, "What'd you do that for?"

"Get you to shuttup, Blair." Sergeant Patrick Flood flicked a glance at Donegan, then went back to growling at the young soldier. "Listen to the man—and be thankful our Injuns was there to fight Crazy Horse when we wasn't ready to do it ourselves."

"Halt!"

The order came from the front of the column where Henry threw up an arm. Off to the right and down the slope came Colonel William B. Royall with his three companies of the Third: Meinhold's B, Andrews's I, and L Company under Captain Peter D. Vroom. He halted his battalion near Henry, who saluted the regimental commander.

"Colonel," Royall addressed Henry by his brevet rank, tension and anxiety in his breathless voice, "you'll join your battalion with mine."

"Colonel, yes, sir. Our objective?"

Royall pointed. "We've been ordered to charge the flank of those hostiles, making things hot on Crook's center."

Henry nodded. "Very good, Colonel. We'll fall in behind."

Rising slightly in his stirrups, Royall turned, spotting the far guidon whipping in the breeze, flinging his voice over the entire battalion to order, "I Company—take the left flank! Center guide on me—forward!"

Sending Captain William H. Andrews's troops to the far western end of their line of march, Royall led a total of 225 officers and men, five mounted troops of cavalry, on their ascent of that rugged slope at a fast canter, north by east until he reached a high point only a half mile from where Crook was marshaling his own infantry and civilian forces against the hostiles, who were themselves concentrated on the brow of that conical hill to their rear and the series of boulder-strewn ridges to their immediate front.

As Royall's men broke the skyline, many of the hundreds of hostiles now turned their attention to the south and west.

Firing intermittently, the colonel's troops were suddenly finding their advance grinding slower and slower as they crossed to the last fifty yards at the top of that rugged ridge. There they suddenly reached a wide, craggy ravine that separated them from the hostiles firmly in control of the far heights. Rushing to a palisade of sandstone that resembled the ramparts of an ancient Celtic castle on the far side of the ravine, many of the hostile riflemen began to pour fire across the canyon at the cavalry.

Ordering his battalion to dismount into skirmish formation, Royall was determined to prevent the Sioux from sweeping their left flank and gaining the rear as they scurried in black masses along the far heights.

On his own volition Captain Andrews had already detached Lieutenant James Foster with eighteen men from I Company during the last few hundred yards of their march to reach the precipice of that deep ravine.

"Take a platoon and ride to that point, Lieutenant," Andrews had ordered. "Clear away the enemy from those heights on the left."

Foster led his platoon away from the battalion, reining west to begin his wide sweep to the left. The nineteen horse soldiers watched in growing frustration as the warriors dropped back, from ridgetop to ridgetop, as the lieutenant pushed the hostiles farther and farther, decoying the small group of soldiers . . . until Foster's little command was more than a mile from Royall's column. Far out of the reach of any aid.

Just about the time Royall reached the high ground near the rugged ravine with the rest of his two hundred, the enemy realized it had a small force cut off from the main body of soldiers.

As the battalion clattered to a halt, Donegan's eye was caught by the dark movement of distant platoon against the new grass and the pale summer sky. More probably he sensed the spidery movement of the warriors moving in on them of a sudden—more than a hundred horsemen hurrying to cross that far slope to the southwest, scrambling up out of each one of the rugged fingers splaying off the deep ravine, working quickly to encircle the lost platoon.

"Cap'n Andrews!" Seamus bellowed in alarm as he brought his horse to a skidding halt near the officer charged with protecting the left flank.

"What is it?" the soldier replied brusquely, looking the civilian over.

"Yonder," and he pointed. "You're about to get those men swallowed up!"

Andrews shaded his eyes, whispered in a gush, "Dear God in heaven!"

Rising in his stirrups as the rest of Royall's column was getting the order to dismount, Captain Andrews looked over his company, then shouted at the horseman he knew could make the ride.

"Private Weaver!"

"You're going to send that boy to alert Foster?"

Andrews glared at Donegan. "I am. That *boy* can ride!"

Donegan wagged his head dolefully. "No. The boy stays—I'll go."

With a sharp wag of his head, Andrews said, "No. I'll not have the blood of a civilian on my hands."

Seamus replied, "But you'll have this man's?"

Andrews's face went gray with worry. "I don't know a damned thing about how good a horseman you are. But I do know Weaver. The man's the best we have in this regiment—"

"Captain?" Herbert W. Weaver saluted his company commander.

"Weaver—Lieutenant Foster is on the far heights." Andrews pointed to the southwest.

"I see him, sir."

"Can you reach him and order him to return—to fall back immediately?"

Private Weaver tugged the dirty kepi down on his forehead and nodded once with a grim smile. "I'll get through, sir." Without a look back, he reined about sharply and spurred away, his mount kicking up clods of dirt and grass.

"But will they get back?" Donegan grumbled.

By the time Weaver reached the platoon, having to race across a long route that took him around the head of the deep ravine, Lieutenant Foster was already painfully aware of his gloomy predicament. The hostiles were closing in from two directions. And one of them was the way Weaver had made it to the small platoon. Their planned escape route had been shut tight.

Reacting quickly, Foster ordered, "Stay together at all costs and ride like the wind, boys! This doesn't have to be a pretty retreat—just save your hair!"

The lieutenant's brash countercharge right into the teeth of that closing noose surprised the converging warriors, who fell away from the suddenness of the troopers' attack, firing their pistols and shouting to beat the devil. Only by putting their mounts into a full gallop did Foster's lost platoon make it back to Royall's command intact and with only two men wounded.

But as those twenty riders reached the main body, more than a hundred warriors rushed into the wake, gaining possession of that ground to the southwest of Royall, which effectively began the all-but-complete encirclement of the colonel's battalion.

In the meantime William B. Royall had other fish to fry —matters most grave as the enemy he confronted across the ravine began to grow in numbers, shifting from east to west as Royall's men dismounted, making their appearance and taking up positions among the boulders on the high ground.

"Horse-holders to the rear!" Royall ordered. "Company commanders will remain mounted. See to it your men are rallied and reinforced when needed."

As every fourth trooper brought out the fifteen-inch leather link-straps and led his horses back to the rear, two straps clutched in each hand, it stirred Donegan's old soldier's heart to see those six officers—Royall and his five company captains—exhibiting such conspicuous bravery before their troops, staying the saddle, moving back and forth among their men.

In a matter of moments the enemy responded to the arrival of the horse soldiers. The flow of warriors began to seep like spring runoff down from the slopes of the conical hill toward this new adversary, hurrying almost due west toward a high point of ground, streaming into the protective cover of the numerous coulees at the head of what is today known as Kollmar Creek. Clearly, they intended not only to conduct a long-distance shooting match with these new arrivals—but Seamus Donegan believed the Sioux plainly intended to flank Royall's command.

This sort of broken terrain might well let the enemy do just that.

Digging in at the eastern end of a series of rocky sandstone outcrops and ledges, the colonel's battalion could go no farther on horseback, could do no more in driving the enemy off. Here they were stopped, blocked by the deep ravine from mounting any further charges. But here just as well, they would have to sit while the enemy had the luxury of both time and the terrain, to work slowly but persistently around the far heights, ever closing their red noose all the tighter.

It became more and more evident as the minutes rolled by, one by one adding up to a first hour of heated fighting, that the hostiles were quickly seizing every advantage offered by the broken ground.

"Don't fire less'n you got yourself a target!" shouted First Sergeant John Henry, who, though not ordered to, had chosen to remain on horseback among his men of

I Troop. "Make every shot count, fellas—or save your cartridges till you can do some good!"

As the minutes crawled past, inching by into a second hour, the gunfire increased, the rattle and clamor of battle swelled as the growing pressure on Royall's left flank began to tell on the battalion. The enemy concentrated at some point across the ravine, fought for a few minutes, then withdrew to pop up somewhere else along the colonel's front. Time and again they confounded the troops until they made their first rush—in they came, the air filling with wild whoops and the crackle of the hostiles' repeaters, accompanied by the whine of .44-caliber lead singing over the heads of the soldiers.

But the blue line held in those frantic seconds, pouring their fire into the enemy waves until the hostiles were forced to turn in frustration and retreat to their rocks and ravines just beyond the end of the sharp-sided slope. In their rush to regain cover, the warriors had abandoned one body—a brown-skinned rider who had made it within fifty yards of Donegan at the skirmish line. As the horsemen turned back, the Irishman quickly rolled onto his back and dug into the pocket of his breeches, dragging out a handful of the dull brass. One at a time he shoved them into the loading tube under the Henry's barrel, and when he could load no more, he locked the barrel back in place, peering at the far slope.

As the naked horsemen made charge after charge on Royall's battalion, the white men counted at least one of their number wounded with each new assault on the skirmish line. Not only did that mean another gun lost along their defensive front, but two more men were stolen from the firing line, needed to drag and carry a wounded comrade to the rear, where Surgeon Hartsuff had established his field hospital near the trees in the creek bottom. Seconds and heartbeats collided and tumbled, congealing into minutes, an agonizing gathering of time as the numbers of Sioux coming west from the heights swelled, and swelled again.

"There's gotta be more'n five hunnert of them bastards trying to overrun us now," a soldier said nearby.

Seamus nodded. "At least that."

He glanced up from reloading the Henry repeater and peered across the canyon at the high ground to the west, where it seemed so long ago Lieutenant Foster's patrol had nearly been eaten alive. Steadily, surely, the hundreds were working around to the south end of the ridge. Royall's command was now all but encircled by the enemy.

"Look yonder," and Donegan pointed to the southwest as the hostiles rolled closer, ever closer around their unprotected left flank. "Right now I'll lay you three to one we're facing at least seven hundred, what with that bunch circling round us to the west."

"These men don't need any of your gay Irish optimism, Mr. Donegan!" growled Guy Henry as he brought his mount to a halt near Seamus.

"I'm just like any man here, Colonel Henry—like to know what I'm up against."

"Doesn't make a damned bit of difference," Henry snarled, reining about so that his back was to the Irishman as he moved off again down the skirmish line. "A hundred, five hundred, or a thousand—our job is still the same, *Mister* Donegan. Any old sergeant of cavalry would do well to remember that."

"A sergeant of cavalry?" asked John McDonald, the corporal squatting on the far side of Donegan. Wagging his head, the soldier glanced left, then right, up and down the skirmish line quickly, every man kneeling or lying some three to five feet apart. "I don't see no goddamned sergeant anywhere near us—"

"Colonel Henry's talking to me, boys," Seamus replied, feeling chastened.

"Talking to you, is he?" asked a soldier.

"Sergeant is it now?" responded the second with a peat-heavy brogue.

Donegan snorted. "I'm nothing more'n a bleeming chuckle-headed civilian now, fellas."

"Not if a man like that Cap'n Henry calls you sergeant —means he must think you was some sergeant."

A voice called out, "What's he know of you, mister?"

With a shrug Donegan glanced at the sun and figured it must now be going on ten o'clock, maybe a little after; then he replied, "Got no idea what Henry knows of—"

"Here they come again!" came the shrill alarm from the far left side of that thin skirmish line as the warriors vaulted out of the coulees and from behind their boulders, kicking their ponies into a blur of color and motion for another charge on Royall's position.

"By God, boys!" hollered a soldier to Donegan's right. "Let's show these red devils what the Third is made of!"

In the next breath the Springfield carbines began to boom above the more distinct cracks of the warrior guns as the horsemen came on, sweeping out of the southwest.

"That's right! Here's to reclaiming the good and gallant name of the Third Cavalry, by Jesus!"

Some of the men crouched in the open, using their .45 Colt's revolvers as the warriors drew closer and ever closer.

"Drop these sonsabitches—and seize the day!"

"By damn—this'll take the stain from the honor of our regiment!"

The air hung heavy with gunsmoke by the time they had turned another charge.

"Hold your fire!" reverberated the order up and down the line.

"Don't waste ammunition!" was its echo.

"Kill all them red devils, I say!"

"For the glory of the Third, by Jupiter!"

"To the glory of our Third!"

It was nearing mid-morning when Lieutenant Henry R. Lemly rode right through the red gauntlet and reined up, dismounting on the run even before his horse had skidded to a halt near Anson Mills.

"Colonel!" the lieutenant called, using Mills's Civil War brevet rank.

"Mr. Lemly—what word do you bring me from the regimental commander?"

"I come from General Crook, sir. He sends his compliments. Requests that you respectfully remount your battalion, face about to the west, and take that hill."

Mills peered off into the distance where Lemly pointed. "That tall one, eh?"

Lemly nodded and said no more.

"Lieutenant Schwatka!" Mills called out to his own adjutant. "Inform the company commanders we are about to make another charge."

"Mounted?" asked Fred Schwatka.

"We are," Mills answered. "Order the companies to cease fire and bring up their horse-holders."

As Schwatka hurried off, the captain turned back to Lemly. "You want to go with us?"

"I was given no instructions not to return to the general."

"Then, by all means—I suggest you get while the getting is good, Mr. Lemly. This hillside is going to come alive with the enemy in a very few minutes."

"Thank you for the suggestion, sir," the lieutenant replied quickly as he yanked on the reins, bringing his horse around so that he could leap into the saddle. He tore off at a gallop to the southwest, down the slope of the hill that took him back toward the infantry under the personal command of Crook himself.

A moment later Lieutenant Schwatka sprinted up, chest heaving. "Company commanders have been informed of the charge, sir."

Mills stood, peering momentarily through the small field glasses he had carried with him since the final days of the Southern Rebellion. A present from his beloved Nannie. From what he could see in the mid-distance, the slope was far from suited to any sort of charge—on foot or mounted. But if they began by angling to their own left and moved southwest for a couple hundred yards, then they just might be able to cross that tongue of ground and race almost due west into the face of the enemy guns.

The trick would be angling across that full front of those guns before they turned back into the teeth of the Sioux and Cheyenne. If his men could stay in the saddle, running the gauntlet across that rough ground until he could finally wheel them west—they stood a ghost of a chance.

As his battalion began to taper off their fire in preparation for the charge, the enemy took it as a sign of weakness and immediately put renewed pressure on his men. Nothing could possibly be gained by waiting a moment longer.

"Prepare to mount!" Mills flung his voice left, then right. "Prepare to mount!"

The call was immediately taken up by the three companies left him. Horsemen hurried among their mounts, unlatching the link-straps, dragging the animals into one wide front, four men deep. He had already placed E Company under Captain Alexander Sutorious in the center of their skirmish line. Ordering Lieutenant Joseph Lawson's Company A to the left, Mills now placed his own M Company on the right flank, where he figured the fire might just be the hottest as they plunged across that tongue of deadly ground.

"Mount!" he bawled. The order rang off the nearby ridges, making it sound as if there were far more than three companies leaping into the saddle at that moment.

The squeak of leather, accompanied by the rattle of bit-chains and the snaps on those carbine slings the troopers used to carry their Springfields, sent a shiver up the veteran horse soldier's spine.

"Left front into line! Right flank guide and pivot on me!" Mills raised himself in the stirrups and found his bugler right behind him in the first of the four rows.

"Mr. Snow, let's have you give us the charge!"

The notes of that first stirring stanza were barely freed of the horn's brassy bell as Mills and others shouted that soul-stirring call and those three companies shot away, brass spurs digging in and horses heaving, on this—their third charge of what had already been a long and bloody morning.

From the start of the battle Crazy Horse had kept moving, here . . . then there. Constantly separating his warriors when they first tended to bunch up in fighting the Snakes and the People of the Raven. He ordered some west to circle around the broken ground near a deep ravine in hopes of striking the soldiers from behind, maybe drive off their horses from the creek bottom.

With none of their big American horses left them, the soldiers would then be at the complete mercy of his splintering tactics.

Many of the rest he had sent to the east, to sweep down

on the soldier camp through an opening gap in the bluffs. It was there that the fighting had quickly grown every bit as hot and dangerous as the first eye-to-eye combat they had with the scouts on the slope of the ridge.

Failing to drive off the cavalry horses, he next intended—having caught the soldiers unawares in the creek bottom—to herd the confused white men toward the boxed end of the Rosebud Canyon where the valley walls rose more sharply. There the Three Stars would not have room to maneuver his horses. In that place Crazy Horse's warriors would hold the white men penned in that corral just like the enemy's stupid spotted buffalo. To slaughter them slowly, and surely—by firing down from the heights.

But by the time Sitting Bull's Hunkpapa warriors arrived that morning, the battle with the soldiers had already become three distinct fights: the continuing skirmish with the walk-a-heaps in the center; the ebb and flow of the running battle with the soldiers near the gap to the east; and far to the west where the Shahiyena had gone as well as a growing number of his Lakota who were pouring south, down from the high ground, working hard to encircle gradually a large number of pony soldiers.

Now he heard a subtle change in the battle sounds from his left—to the east near the gap. The heavy booming of the soldier guns was tapering off. He would not let himself believe the warriors had destroyed all those white horsemen.

No, for some other reason the enemy had ceased firing.

By the time he reached the ground near the end of the ridge, the pony soldiers were already mounted and moving. Their soldier chief had them charging toward the southwest across the wide front of his warriors ensconced among the rocks and brush. It appeared the horsemen intended on retreating back to join the walk-a-heaps at the base of the ridge.

Because of this, many of the Lakota and the few Shahiyena left among them all raised a cry of victory, believing as Crazy Horse wanted to believe that they had indeed driven the enemy from that portion of the battlefield.

"It is good!" White Cow Bull said to the war chief.

"Why is this good?" Crazy Horse asked, watching the pony soldiers gallop along the wide front across that tongue of broken ground.

"We drive the white man away from this ground—I think that is very good!"

Crazy Horse shook his head. "It is not a good thing, White Cow Bull. More than anything, I wanted to divide the pony soldiers from the walk-a-heaps. I wanted to carve each band up into smaller and smaller bunches."

"We can still defeat them, even if they are together," White Cow Bull said, bristling.

"Can you eat the whole hump of a buffalo cow in one bite?"

Reluctantly White Cow Bull shook his head. "No. It would take me many bites."

"That is what I am trying to tell you. We must cut these white men into smaller and smaller bites. That is the only way we are going to swallow them."

At that instant the cheering all around him sharply changed tone and became cries of dismay and surprise. The soldiers had suddenly turned, riding right into the face of their guns. They were not fleeing to rejoin the walk-a-heaps down the hillside at all.

The pony soldiers were charging directly into the maw of the Lakota guns.

In a trickle at first, like the beginning of a soft summer rain, the first warriors far down the slope began to rise and retreat, hurrying back among the rocks. Then the trickle became an ever-increasing flow as the pony soldiers heaved closer and closer, racing across the broken ground. A few of their big horses stumbled, fell, pitching riders into the grass beneath the wholesale fury of their charge.

Still, on they came.

"To the hill that is shaped like the tip of a bull's horn!" Crazy Horse rallied his warriors, guiding his pony in among them.

Then he turned and halted, watching the soldiers coming until the last of the warriors had fled past him.

If it was not Three Stars himself . . . then just who was this daring soldier who had driven his warriors from this part of the battlefield?

As the air began to hum with the nasty snarl of bullets, Crazy Horse calmly reined about, knowing his life would never be forfeit to a white man's gun. The dream had told him. The dream of dying at the hand of his own people.

So now he had to find another fight for his warriors. Perhaps the struggle going on far to the west—at the broken, scarred country cut with deep, sharp-sided ravines. There another battle raged. The Shahiyena had started that fight by attempting to surround the pony soldiers and their big American horses. The Miniconjou and Sans Arc had gladly joined in.

Perhaps now . . . yes! Now it was time for his mighty Hunkpatila to come to the aid of the rest, to throw the weight of the great numbers Crazy Horse could bring to bear on that distant fight.

Now it was time to swallow up those pony soldiers, chew them good. Then spit out their battered, bloodied bodies one . . . by one . . . by one.

Chapter 30

The Season When Things Grow

Luishaw's most fervent prayer had been answered.

The enemy was retreating.

The soldiers were fighting back, throwing everything they could at the Lakota and their Shahiyena friends.

In and out of the raging battle the Shoshone war chief slashed his way, firing his weapons, singing his war song, cheering those of his warriors who grew tired, perhaps grew doubtful that this would be a day of great victory for not only Lone Star's soldiers, but for the Wind River Shoshone as well.

"The Lakota are falling back, Luishaw!"

He turned to find Aguina, a brave warrior brother, hurrying toward him. As he always did, Luishaw's eyes fell to Aguina's hand clutching the soldier rifle, the middle finger gone. Two years now—a wound he carried in proud remembrance of the Bates Battle against the Lakota. When the soldiers had quit the fight too soon.

"I am glad, my friend," Luishaw replied, watching the enemy as they were pushed back, and back still farther by the pony soldiers' charge. Retreating to the west, toward that conical hill.

"You were afraid, I know it," Aguina said quietly as the battle rumbled along the slope above them. "Afraid these soldiers might give up and go back home as they did before."

"Like our last fight against these enemies." He reached out and laid his hand over Aguina's.

The warrior glanced down, and a look crossed his face as if he understood what his war chief was telling him. "We lost some of our own pride that day, Luishaw. Forced to run away with the soldiers."

"Not today, my friend. There will be no running for the soldiers—and none for the Shoshone this day!"

"Your eyes are always searching the enemy," Aguina commented a few moments later as the Lakota continued their retreat far to the west. "You are looking for Sitting Bull?"

Luishaw smiled grimly. "I would be proud to meet him in battle."

"And Crazy Horse."

He smiled and nodded. "Especially Crazy Horse. While Sitting Bull is a powerful magician, it is the other one . . . this war chief who has killed many Shoshone—the one I want most to meet in battle."

"If you do not mind, my friend—I want to watch your fight with Crazy Horse. It would be something to see."

The grim smile grew on Luishaw's broad face. "Indeed it would, Aguina. It would be a fight our people spoke of for many generations to come."

For much of the two hours the fighting had seesawed back and forth between the soldiers and the hostiles. There had even been those terrifying moments when it seemed Crazy Horse's warriors were reinforced and the overwhelming weight of the hostiles drove Crook's infantry back to the willows along Rosebud Creek. For some of the soldiers, all had seemed lost—until Mills began his timely second charge from the far east end of the battle line and Royall began his circling push far to the west along the left flank. That seemed to divert enough of the Sioux and Cheyenne just long enough to allow the general to rally his infantry at the middle.

They had countercharged, eventually regaining the slopes of the bluffs. Then the top of the ridge itself. And finally the highest hill* east of the conical knob, that tall promontory where the enemy horsemen were driven by Mills and Crook together. From that high ground they had turned, beginning to harass Royall's cavalry.

Something of a breathing spell settled over the rest of the battlefield.

John Bourke watched Captain Samuel Munson approach, crabbing across the open ground at a half crouch, as if he were about to pitch forward on his chin at any moment.

"General, we need the mules," the captain declared when he came huffing to a stop in that knot of officers.

"Very well," Crook replied after a moment of thought. "I was thinking the same thing. Perhaps we can use them to make a mounted charge on the center of their line. At least on part of it—drive them back. To keep the savages off balance. Yes, Captain. Permission granted: bring up the mules."

Munson saluted and was gone, waving an arm toward his C Company of the Ninth Infantry as he headed downhill. They moved out behind him in ragged order across the slope.

Not that many minutes later the warriors evidently noticed the activity among the mules grazing in the bottomland. Not only had Munson gone to fetch his own company's animals, but John Bourke saw that Captains Burt and Burrowes had shown up on a similar mission. All three officers ended up evacuating their wounded from the morning's campsite, loading everything they could to bring with them as they reclimbed the slopes to Crook's headquarters. They returned with not a moment to spare as the Sioux rushed Crook's position from not only the west, but the north as well.

There along the western flank Tom Moore's packers and those sixty-five Montana miners put their powerful rifles to work as never before, firing from their redoubts among the red rock interlacing the ridgetop. Earlier that morning upon reaching the heights, these civilians had

* Known today as Crook's Hill

hurriedly built their own ramparts and lunettes, piling up what stones they could, using any deadfall that could be safely dragged to the scene. Now their big civilian weapons —from Civil War Spencers to the latest lever-action repeaters, from Remington rolling-blocks and Sharps sporting or buffalo rifles to the latest in needle guns—all laid down a deadly fire the hostiles were unable to match with their old muzzleloaders and light repeating carbines, much less with bow and arrow. Their sort of warfare dictated that they move in close enough to the enemy to overwhelm; and not accomplishing that, then at least draw close enough that they could loose their rain of iron-tipped arrows that would arc down from the sky in a hail of terror.

But the Sioux were able to do neither that morning as they tried rushing the civilians hunkered down among their rocks on the north rim of the bluff. Nor could they get close enough for their bows.

Crazy Horse was forced to rally his horsemen to the western end of the ridge.

John Bourke saw them in the distance. He didn't have to explain to any what was happening, much less George Crook. It grew plain enough when the gunfire along the north of the ridge dissipated and slacked off quickly as more and more of the hostiles left that central theater and rode far to the end of Crook's flank. Now, but for the rapidly growing gunfire heard coming from perhaps as much as two miles or more away, where Royall had taken his mounted companies to junction with Guy Henry's battalion—this battlefield had become suddenly and eerily quiet.

"If those savages mass on Royall now," Crook grumbled dolefully, "he's done for."

It was there on the flats just below the eastern slopes of the conical hill that Crazy Horse gathered his hundreds, formed them up, ready to make their charge.

Seems he had still one more surprise in store for Three Stars that day.

Ten-times-ten Shahiyena, no more than that. But now more and more of Crazy Horse's Lakota had come to join the fight against the mounted soldiers on the far western end of the long ridge.

In the distance Wooden Leg heard the gunfire all but die away. The soldiers had made their charge up from the gap, had dug in like badgers protecting their burrows. Nothing much was going to change that, thought the young warrior.

As things quieted to the east, the bloodiest action began to shift to the fighting around the pony soldiers who had taken up their positions across the deep ravine from Wooden Leg and his friends. The war cries of the arriving Lakota became a constant and growing thunder as the horsemen rode up from the north and northwest slopes, rallying, come to try these soldiers.

It was just as Crazy Horse had guaranteed it: they were dividing Three Stars's soldiers into smaller bands so that they might be more easily overwhelmed and swallowed up. What they had failed to do near the gap because of the pony soldiers' tenacious charges was nonetheless beginning to work its magic here along the western end of the slopes, more than a mile away from the gap.

Just moments ago two small bands of soldiers had returned to the main group. Both bands had attempted to clear Lakota sharpshooters from some nearby hilltops, only to come close to being surrounded and chewed up. As heavy as the fighting was, only two soldiers were hit, dragged back to the main group that was beginning to come together at the end of the line: the terminus of the ridge where they were forced to halt like a frightened herd of the white man's cattle. Wooden Leg knew enough that when the enemy began to bunch up and mill around like that, much of the warrior spirit had gone out of the pony soldiers.

By working from rock to rock, the warriors in the advance had closed to within effective range of their rifles and were beginning to pour some deadly fire down on the soldiers—from the southwest, the west, and now the north as well. Swarming in ever-greater numbers, they nearly had their enemy surrounded. Every small crevice in the rocks, every outcrop, every tall tuft of grass hid more than one rifleman as they poured their bullets down on the bluecoats.

Overhead the sun relentlessly climbed in the sky. From time to time Wooden Leg could hear renewed fighting from far east. Sometimes he could hear the echo of gunfire from the tallest heights in the entire valley, those slopes south of the Rosebud where some of the Lakota fought half-a-hundred pony soldiers. But those sounds never lasted very long.

As the morning grew old, the real fighting proved to be here in the west.

Where the Shahiyena and Lakota were slowly tightening their red noose around the pony soldiers, ever tightening until these white men would have no way out.

"**F**ancy finding you here where there's no chance for whiskey, Irishman."

Seamus turned to find Reuben Davenport crawling up behind him to his small shelter of low sandstone rocks.

"No flat-backed New York City chippies here for you, Davenport!" Donegan cheered. "Get your arse in here afore some bleeming Injin shoots you where you sit."

"When'd you get here, Donegan?"

"I been here from the start. Rode in with Colonel Henry."

The reporter wagged his head, peering over the top of the boulders. A bullet sang overhead, another ricocheted off the rock, sending lead and chips and sandstone dust over them both.

Davenport swiped at his eyes. "I came with Royall to join up with Henry's bunch."

A grim smile crossed Donegan's face. "Not the place to be right now, I'm afraid. We're having the hottest time of it."

"I can see."

"Face it—you're not a fighting man, Davenport. For God's sake get back to a horse and go rejoin Crook's command."

The correspondent looked about, mostly to the south and east, where the only avenue of escape was closing—then sighed, slightly nodding. "Wish I could, Donegan. But it looks like it would be sure suicide for any man to try riding back through that for now."

"Gonna get worse before it gets better. You're a reporter. Not a man has to lay his life down like these sojurs."

"I can handle a rifle as good as many of these!"

He realized he had pricked the man's pride. "I'm sorry. I just meant . . . you got no business sticking your neck out like this."

"Listen, Irishman," Davenport began, swiping the back of his hand across his lips and reaching into the back pocket of his britches. "I volunteered to come on this expedition for the New York *Herald.* And the position of a newspaper correspondent on an Indian campaign is to go in with the rest: Royall, Henry, whoever. I've learned one thing so far today, found it out for myself: that there is no such thing as a rear, unless with some reserves Crook would hold back. But, you see, Irishman—Crook's thrown everything he's got against Crazy Horse, hasn't he?"

Seamus had to agree and nodded once. "If he hadn't, we'd been overrun—caught with our britches down the way we was." Then he peered over the top of the rock for a moment.

"Besides, Donegan—if a journalist does not share the toil and the danger with the soldiers he followed on the march, his mouth is all but shut, isn't it? If I stayed behind where it was safe, what could I possibly say to an officer who challenged me by asking: 'What the deuce have you got to say about it? You were skulking in the rear, Davenport—and got everything by hearsay. We don't give a bloody damn what you think!' "

"No picnic, eh?" Seamus snorted.

"I'll say," and he finished fishing out the thin German silver flask. "Want a taste?"

"Surprised to see you carry liquor on you. Never knew."

"Never had a real reason to want a taste until after supper. Until now."

"Just pass it here and don't think of asking a second time." Donegan took the flask, biting down on the cork to pull it from the neck.

"How quickly I've learned that to go on an Indian campaign, I must go ready to ride forty or fifty miles a day, go sometimes on half rations, sleep on the ground with little or no covering, roast, sweat, freeze, and make the acquaintance of every sort of vermin or reptiles that may flourish in the vicinity of my sleeping couch."

"Here—and thank you," Donegan said, licking the last drops from his shaggy mustache as he handed the flask back to Davenport. "A hard lesson that—to learn that a soldier on an Indian campaign must have the heart of a lion and the stomach of a mouse, eh?"

Davenport upended the flask, swallowed heartily before he spoke. "And finally, I must be prepared to personally fight Sitting Bull or Satan himself when the shooting begins —for God and the United States hates noncombatants. So thus is it that I, who am peaceably disposed, am now placed in the position of an eyewitness to the bloodiest fighting in the history of the Third Cavalry."

"Peaceably disposed, are you?"

He laid a hand on his chest and said, "Me? Truth is I'd rather be wrapped legs entwined with a soft-skinned, lilac-smelling wench along the Bowery right now, Seamus, me boy! Make love and not war, I always say."

"But here you are, right in the thick of it."

He took another drink, then brought the flask away from his shiny lips, his eyes gone misty as he asked, quietly, "You'll see that I live to tell my story, Seamus?"

Seamus had watched even the grim edge of humor disappear from the newsman's face. Saw that for all the bravado and the facade his words might give him in civilian life—this dirty fight just might prove to be one of the crossroads in Reuben Davenport's character. It was one thing to rant and rail against the hostiles in print, back in civilization. It was quite another to lay your body and possibly your life on the line in these little-known wars against the wild tribes, out here in the wilderness.

"Yes," Donegan said finally as he reached again for the flask from Davenport, for one more swallow of that elixir. "I'll do all that's in my power to see that we both make it out of this alive. You to tell your story to the folks back east. And me, once more to hold someone very, very dear in my arms."

Now that Captain William Andrews's men had vacated the two forward positions before they could be overrun, the hostiles had taken up the abandoned high ground. All attempts Royall made to pursue them met only with frustration as the Sioux and Cheyenne confounded the colonel's cavalry. When the horse soldiers charged, the warriors fell back to the next ridge. As the cavalry turned to rejoin the main command, the red horsemen wheeled about and surged back on their rear guard, counterattacking.

As aggravating as their seesaw contest was, what was causing even greater despair among Royall's troopers was the increasing failure of the infantry on their right to keep a concerted pressure against the hostiles. In fact, to many it seemed that Crook's center was slowly, inexorably, giving ground—permitting the enemy to concentrate their firepower in turn on the western end of the ridge. Chambers's skirmish line had ground to a halt, and burrowed down.

And the warriors knew it.

Almost as if ordered out in some disciplined wave of red horror, the horsemen burst from cover, warriors on foot in their midst, pouring from southwest, west, and north, spilling down on Royall's line from nearly all points of the compass. Into that growing cloud of dust and gunfire the ponies raced, circling at the last minute, warriors dropping to the far side of their animals, firing beneath the ponys' necks as those on foot worked their way from rock to rock to gain a sniper's vantage point, from which they set up a fire hot enough to keep many of the frightened soldiers down behind their rocks where they could not fire on the warriors on horseback.

"Why doesn't Crook move his infantry to help us out?" Davenport gasped in exasperation as he plopped down on an elbow and began shoving cartridges into his pistol.

Gazing east, Donegan saw there was no movement along the rest of the ridge. No offensive taking place on what little he could see of the rest of the battlefield. "I got no other choice but to pray Crook's got a damned good reason he's not throwing his support over to Royall."

Closer and closer the horsemen were able to cross that

broken terrain, gaining ground on the left and rear of the cavalry lines strung out dangerously thin in places, soldiers concentrated in fevered knots of spastic firing in others. From the west the hostiles swept around to gain the south, running unopposed for the first time. Yipping and screeching now that they held that ground, uncontested.

The soldiers had drawn back, on the defensive. Fighting for their very lives. Surrounded.

"We're going to get overrun soon—I can feel it," Davenport said quietly, then licked some of the brandy from his lower lip.

It wasn't that his words dripped with fright. To Donegan it sounded no more than resignation to an incontrovertible reality. "We'll get out. Royall's bound to withdraw soon. He has to."

"If he doesn't?"

Seamus didn't want to say it. Saying it would somehow be like admitting it.

Looking down in the creek bottom now, he watched the enemy horsemen sweep across that ground where Crook's army had rested early that morning, where the infantry itself had only recently come to retrieve their mules. The copper-skinned riders galloped right over a lone Shoshone youth left to guard a small herd of ponies. Shooting the boy, they drove the Snake horses south across the Rosebud, splashing back to the west and around to the north again beyond the far ridge, where they disappeared in a fading cacophony of victory.

Quietly, he admitted only, "I've been in worse fixes than this, Davenport."

"Pray tell where, Irishman?"

"On the Crazy Woman Fork."

"Place we crossed? Between Reno and Fort Phil Kearny?"

Seamus nodded. "The next year in a corral beyond all help, near Fort C. F. Smith."

"Surrounded?"

"Yes. And a third time on a little sandbar island in the middle of a nameless river a year after that. Then out to Oregon country—where the Modocs could have butchered us all at a place we came to call Black Ledge."

"Jesus Christ," Davenport whispered in a hushed tone of reverence, his eyes wide as tea saucers. "Tell me of those, Seamus. For God's own sake—tell me that you've been in tighter places than this."

"Aye—I have been, Davenport. If you'll look closely now—and squint your eyes just so . . . you'll see me own guardian angel resting on this shoulder."

The reporter finally smiled, a little less grim. "All right, Seamus. Now you can tell me about those times things were worse than this. And I'll just scoot a wee bit closer to you here, if you don't mind. Figure I might as well share that angel you've got perched on your shoulder."

"Hang close to me, Reuben Davenport. No guarantees, you understand—but me sainted mither in heaven knows just how bleeming busy I've kept this good angel working in the past."

A few minutes later Davenport asked again, "We'll make it out?"

Grinning, Seamus patted the newsman's shoulder, much as one would gently embrace the hand another man would lay there for reassurance. Sensing the presence of his sainted mother at his side, Donegan answered, "Aye, we're going to be fine now."

Chapter 31

17 June 1876

When Crazy Horse sprang his unexpected surprise on Crook, the general found his soldiers totally unprepared for the ferocity of the Sioux charge. For the second time that morning, it fell to the Crow and Shoshone to repulse the attack and prevent what might become a ringing defeat, if not a total massacre.

"Damn these gutless sonsabitches!" Tom Cosgrove grumbled to Ulah Clair, a Shoshone half-breed at his side, cursing the nearby infantry. The two had been fighting elbow to elbow all morning, the half-breed interpreter helping the former Confederate relay his orders to Luishaw's warriors.

"Ain't that general ever gonna get his soldiers up and pushing these red bastards back?" Nelson Yarnell snarled nearby.

Cosgrove shrugged. "Don't look like it, boys. For the life of me I can't understand how these blue-bellies ever beat the South with soldiers like these."

Yancy Eckles spat a stream of tobacco and growled, "Shit—with a general like this'un!"

"How did they win the war agin' us, Tom?" Yarnell asked. "With officers what won't lead . . . and soldiers what won't follow?"

While Yarnell was a heap of a talker from the word *scat,* Eckles on the other hand rarely said much at all. Cosgrove figured his old friend from Texas must indeed be worked up something fierce for him to put that many words together at one time.

"Yancy, you and Nelson just be glad we got these Snakes with us what wanna fight, boys."

Eckles tapped Cosgrove's arm. "Lookee there now, Tom. Maybe we misjudged these blue-bellies."

"Could be," Tom replied thoughtfully as he watched the action on the nearby slope. "Looks like a few of 'em got some balls anyway."

Cosgrove noticed how two officers in dusty, sweaty blue were in and among the Crow at that moment. Randall was the only one Tom recognized and knew by name. A major, he thought. The other, why—Cosgrove had seen him mostly hanging close by Crook's headquarters for the past three days since the Shoshone come in to join up with the general's campaign. So what was a white-handed, soft-bellied general's aide doing with "Black Jack" Randall, rallying the Crow, getting them to their feet?

Yarnell asked, "What they up to, Tom?"

"I don't know," Cosgrove answered, slowly coming to his feet too as the enemy came closer and closer, bullets singing overhead. "But I'm fixing to find out. Ulah—get me the chiefs."

The half-breed Clair rose to a crouch, crabbing away as he sang out, "Luishaw!"

Cosgrove saw the war chief turn when he was called. His eyes went to the white man's, then back to Clair as the interpreter reached the Shoshone chiefs. Like most of the others, Luishaw was naked to the waist, wearing only a breechclout and moccasins, and that headdress: eagle feathers standing straight up, fully encircling his head from brow to crown, a long trailer draping from the rear flank of the spotted war pony he sat upon, cheering the marksmanship of his tribesmen.

"Ulah! Bring Norkuk and Tigee. Get the word passed to the rest. We're throwing in with the Crow!"

"Whoooeee, Tom!" Nelson Yarnell exclaimed. "Just like a real rebel countercharge!"

"You goddamned betcha!" cheered the taciturn Eckles.

Cosgrove whirled, waving his arm, impatient and not waiting for the interpreter to translate his order, realizing most of the Shoshone could plainly see the Crow getting to their feet and beginning to rush back to the rear among the rocks where they started to remount their ponies. Behind the squaw man came the first dozen. Then twice that number, and finally the rest were up out of their rifle pits, following the three white men, Ulah Clair, and Luishaw. Catching up their ponies, it seemed every one of them was shouting, singing, chanting—working each other up with war cries and bravery talk.

A man married to a Shoshone knew enough of the tongue to catch some of it. Stuff about the spilled blood of mothers and fathers. Another cried out about the blood of their own—invoking the spirit of that boy killed minutes ago down in the valley. Come here on this journey for his first fight, the youth had asked Luishaw for permission to join in the battle—wanting no longer to be treated as only a herder. The chief had allowed the youth to go down to the spring at the creek bottom, where he could paint himself as a warrior, say his medicine song, then return to fight with the men of the tribe.

It was there beside the Rosebud that he had been overrun by the Sioux when Crazy Horse's warriors started eating ground in their charges off the slopes of that conical hill.

Talk of the young boy, talk of their families and loved ones left behind—all of that was enough to get these Snakes ready to ride bravely into four, maybe five times their number.

That, and Tom Cosgrove standing in the stirrups leading them out to join the Crow and the young aide to General Crook what was boldly coming up to ride the point alongside the old Confederate.

Lord, those Shoshone were yelling like there were two or three hundred of them.

As Captain George M. Randall set the Crow in motion, John Bourke galloped off to join the Snakes in this countercharge meant to blunt what Crazy Horse was throwing at Crook's infantry. Reining his mount in beside the squaw man called Cosgrove, the young lieutenant realized there was likely nothing that would now stop any of these warriors, Crow or Shoshone, every last one of them galloping hot on the heels of the white men leading the allies back into the teeth of the oncoming Sioux.

Charging straight toward a weak place in Captain Avery Cain's skirmish line, the hostiles clearly intended to ride right on over the infantry and tumble the foot soldiers down into the creek bottom, fragmenting Crook's troops even further. In a fury the Sioux plunged past the miners and packers back in the rocks, toward the infantry down the slope, clearly headed for the boggy flats near the Rosebud.

Riding with Cosgrove's Shoshone, Bourke joined the Snakes who poured into the breech along that left flank at the absolute last moment—crashing right into the enemy's front lines, pony ramming pony, war club swung against coup stick, muscle straining against muscle, the air filled with screeches and war cries as the Crows came up with Randall, throwing their weight into the snarling countercharge.

Coming under sniping fire from the enemy last March in the Powder River fight, even fighting Apache down in Arizona Territory—none of that had begun to prepare John Bourke for the ferocity of the fighting as the outnumbered Crow and Shoshone hurled themselves into the naked Sioux horsemen. Across a front of some two hundred yards of grassy ridgetop the antagonists clashed, many of them dismounting, others spilled in that first noisy collision, on their feet now to fire into the opposing ranks, while still more of Crazy Horse's cavalry came up from the rear, continued racing toward, then in and among, the enemy, dropping to the far sides of their ponies.

John decided this had to be the pit of hell itself: not only the shrieks and cries of the men—red-skinned all—but the wails of the ponies struck by bullets as well. Above the clanging of metal and wood, bone and iron, rose the occasional racket and rattle of gunfire. Still, what struck the most fear in him in those few frightening minutes was the fact that the majority of the fighting was done close enough to see your enemy's eyes, close enough to smell his sweat.

Closer than John Bourke had ever been to a hostile warrior.

Then Randall had his Crow flowing to the left flank—pushing, jabbing, breaking through the Sioux charge with a renewed countercharge of their own.

Bourke turned and waved, rallying the Shoshone with Cosgrove, leading them toward the right flank of the Sioux, along the edge of a trough immediately to the southwest of the conical hill. The hostiles fell back, then turned to flee. But in the space of a few heartbeats the enemy suddenly wheeled and flung themselves back at the outnumbered Shoshone.

At that moment Bourke realized he had been joined by a handful of soldiers who were in that charge with the allies. Third Cavalry bugler Elmer A. Snow from Anson Mills's own M Company spurred his mount into the fray.

"Lieutenant!" Snow hollered, coming alongside.

"Snow!"

"General says for you to get your b—," but the trumpeter quickly swallowed down the epithet. "General Crook says for me to tell you that you got no business charging in with our Injun scouts, sir."

"Too late now, Private!" he answered, flicking a look back down the far slope to where Crook likely was watching the whole clash of red man against red man. "What the hell are you doing at headquarters anyway? You're Mills's bugler!"

Snow gulped. "General's 'bout ready to send Colonel Mills's battalion downriver to attack the village."

"Damned right!" John cheered. "Let's get these Sioux pushed back, bugler—then we'll go back to headquarters together and march on the village!"

With a grim attempt at a grin, the trumpeter nodded. "Y-yes, sir."

How quickly the dust rose on the warming air, stinging Bourke's eyes, burning his throat as they rode in to push back the Sioux. The white men and the allies were all yelling orders, and John wondered just who the hell was really listening. Yet all that was important for the moment was that the Snakes around him were flinging themselves into the veils of dust kicked up on every side by skidding, sliding, slashing pony hooves.

Just how the allies knew who was the enemy, Bourke did not guess. It was bedlam. To him every last one of these Indians looked the same. Despite the red arm bands given out to the friendlies, the lieutenant found it hard to make them out in the billowing clouds of dust, in the heated fury and the adrenaline surging through his veins, the mind-numbing confusion and color-graying blur of the hand-to-hand skirmish. Nigh onto impossible to tell Crow from Sioux, Shoshone from Cheyenne.

So sudden was the allies' charge, so fierce was their fighting, that the Shoshone were once more able to turn the Sioux around, even though they found themselves pitted against odds of two or three to one. With mighty cheers and the cries of their victorious blood songs, the Snakes harassed the rear guard of the retreating Sioux as the hostiles fled on past the conical hill now secured by the allies. On, on to the west Crazy Horse's warriors were forced to retreat toward the next high ground, that farthest point reached earlier by Captain William Andrews's I Company with Royall's battalion before the colonel had ordered Andrews to retreat and rejoin his command.

Ever on Bourke and Snow and the Shoshone pushed, firing into the backs of the distant and retreating enemy, until the lieutenant reached that high point far west of the conical hill. Here he could suddenly look down on the enemy milling about on the broad slopes to the northwest, and was instantly impressed with their numbers. There was no real confusion among them, for to the lieutenant they seemed to re-form for another countercharge. With the noise of the battle quieting some as the hostiles retreated, Bourke had time now to sense the pounding of his own heart.

What exhilaration from the chase! he thought. To have the enemy on the run at last!

But as he turned about in the saddle there on the high ground, the young lieutenant was shocked to find himself with but bugler Snow and a half dozen of the bravest of the Shoshone.

They had outrun their support. Indeed, as he watched, the rest of the allies were already returning to Crook's skirmish lines more than a thousand yards away, having accomplished their task of repulsing the Sioux charge. His zeal had once more landed John Bourke in the fire.

He wheeled about again, looking back at the hostiles—this time the hair stood on the back of his neck. Along the slope to the northwest where the hundreds had been chased, those uncounted Sioux now cried out as one, kicking their war ponies into motion. They had spotted their outnumbered quarry.

Adding to the danger, more enemy horsemen suddenly appeared to his immediate left, likely having wheeled away from Royall's right flank. In but a matter of heartbeats those fifty or more screaming Sioux would threaten to cut them off from ever reaching Crook's lines.

On nothing more than instinct the two soldiers and the handful of Shoshone put their carbines to work until the Springfields were emptied and the onrushing enemy was no more than thirty yards off, still coming at a full gallop.

"We're going to have to run for it!" Bourke shouted, waving, spurring his mount savagely as he and Snow took off among the Snakes.

Crouching low in the saddle, John hadn't covered much ground when he heard the familiar sound of lead smashing through bone.

Snow groaned audibly.

Turning, the lieutenant found the bugler's face gone white, his reins fallen, flapping in the wind. Hauling back on his own reins, Bourke wheeled his horse alongside the bugler's, finding that a Sioux bullet had smashed through both of Snow's elbows at the moment they set off. Now unable to hold his reins, Snow draped across the withers, weaving faintly, desperately holding on to consciousness and clutching his mount the best he could—when suddenly Bourke slapped the animal's rump, flogging it again and again and again, driving it ahead of him until they crossed the infantry skirmish line with the Sioux screeching like unleashed demons on their tails.

Only when Andrew Burt's boys opened with a devastating fire from their Long Toms did those hostiles turn aside and beat their own retreat, a spare few yards from the heels of those two soldiers' horses. Grabbing Snow's reins just short of the bridle, Bourke finally brought both animals skidding to a halt near headquarters.

"You there! Get him down!" barked the lieutenant at some of the foot soldiers. "You—get me a surgeon! Get a surgeon up here on the double!"

Then Bourke was crouching over Snow, the young bugler's face grown even pastier, a color that reminded John of the dough rising in his mother's bread pans back home. Quickly his nervous fingers slipped some of the buttons from their holes on the front of Snow's tunic.

Then he whispered down to the trumpeter, "We got a surgeon coming, soldier."

The private's eyes fluttered closed as he groaned, then slowly opened once more. He tried out a brave smile.

Bourke turned to gaze up at the crowd of infantry gathering around him. Through their crush he saw Crook coming on foot at a lope along the side of the hill.

"Is that goddamned surgeon coming?" John bellowed.

He tore his folding knife out of his pants pocket and began to slash open the bugler's right sleeve. Soggy, bloodied wool always made for a hell of a mess.

"That was some ride," Snow murmured softly. "Wasn't it, Lieutenant?"

Tearing his eyes off the shattered elbow, purplish bone protruding from the oozing wound, Bourke looked down into the bugler's green eyes, trying his very best to grin. "A fine, fine charge you made, Private. Damn—but you're right. That was a fine, fine ride indeed. A finer one I've never seen!"

In such fierce fighting, with bullets flying this way and that, Plenty Coups was almost glad the soldiers with Lone Star did not shoot from behind their rock barricades.

They would not be able to tell who was good Indian. Who was enemy.

Already one of his childhood friends was seriously wounded, shot by the Lakota while he repeatedly made his victory runs back and forth in front of the enemy positions near the conical hill.

But Bull Snake was far from being out of the fight. After he was shot through the thigh, just above the knee, the Crow warrior dragged himself from the carcass of his dead pony to a nearby tree, where he propped himself up to watch the ongoing battle. There he sat, yelling encouragement to his fellow Apsaalooke warriors as if it did not matter that his leg was irreparably shattered, did not matter that he was slowly bleeding to death.

It was such bravery that Plenty Coups vowed long to remember.

He himself had lost his pony a few minutes ago, as the Lakota fell back into the ravine, then suddenly wheeled about to countercharge the Crow and Shoshone. A bullet struck the animal just behind Plenty Coups's thigh. After nothing more than a twitch, the pony began to ease down, staggering to its front legs before it collapsed completely. Then, by thrashing with its forelegs, the animal attempted to rise.

He knew its back was broken. Shattered by a Lakota bullet.

He had listened while the noise of the enemy's war cries grew as they swarmed back onto Randall's Crow. For those few warriors still out front, there was barely enough time for retreat. Among the rocks at the edge of the bluff, Plenty Coups spied a small hole and began sprinting for it. Bullets snarled around his flying feet, slapped the rimrock where he dived for protection. In that hole he stayed as the Crow and Shoshone swept back down on the Sioux in ferocious hand-to-hand fighting, driving them back out of the ravine.

When he finally emerged, he found ponies and soldier horses scattered across the battlefield, some standing here and there while dead and wounded animals littered the rolling terrain where Indian had struggled against Indian. As Plenty Coups hurried to catch up one of the abandoned animals, the Sioux again put renewed pressure on the allies, converging from the high ground to the west. Scout chief Randall ordered a retreat, bringing his warriors with him, sweeping past Plenty Coups, running for the soldier lines.

As the high slope cleared in the wake of his tribesmen, for the first time Plenty Coups saw the lone soldier on foot

—left behind as the others retreated. Now the white man turned, finding himself alone as the Sioux began to rush forward in increasing numbers above the soldier on the grassy slope.

Halting near Plenty Coups, Randall whirled, realizing he had one last soldier to extricate from danger. "Von Moll!" he bellowed like a wounded bull. "Get out of there, Sergeant—now!"

John Von Moll took off on a dead run.

Sweeping in suddenly from behind a nearby rise, the enemy horsemen enveloped the lone soldier as surely as the fading echo of the scout chief's words was swallowed up by the Sioux cries of victory. Plenty Coups turned, ready to leap into the saddle at the same moment he was rocked by the thunderous approach of pounding hooves.

Like the darting flight of a wasp, the lone horseman shot past Plenty Coups.

It was Humpy, one of the bravest of the Apsaalooke warriors, lashing his little pony with that elk-handled quirt, riding straight for that knot of Sioux that had completely encircled the lone soldier, who held them momentarily at bay with his carbine.

Through the enemy ring Humpy dashed, and in that moment of confusion reached the sergeant as Von Moll fired his last cartridge at his screeching tormentors. Frantically throwing open the trapdoor breech on his Springfield to extract the empty cartridge, the soldier discovered he had no ammunition left.

Watching Humpy's gallant rescue, scout chief Randall shouted, "C'mon! Now's our chance!" as he motioned the Crow back toward the stranded sergeant.

Patting the back of his war pony, Humpy held a hand down to the soldier, who tried to leap aboard.

By now the scattered Sioux had regrouped and were closing in again. Von Moll flung aside the dead weight of his carbine and made it up on the pony's flanks, looping his long arms around the small Crow warrior's chest as Humpy sawed the animal's head about in a tight circle, kicking it in the ribs as he brought it around.

While the war pony struggled back toward the Crow lines with its burden, soldier chief Randall ordered his Apsaalooke warriors to retreat, following the Snakes who were falling back in face of the renewed Lakota offensive.

The enemy had indeed begun to press hard once more, pushing east across the open ground as the allies fell back. It filled Plenty Coups with regret to look behind him and see the terrain they were now forced to give up, thereby letting the enemy regain the slopes of that conical hill once more.

Didn't Lone Star realize the danger of allowing the Lakota possession of those heights? From there, after all, they could fire down into the walk-a-heaps doing their best to find something to hide behind.

Lone Star would have to make up his mind soon, or Plenty Coups knew this battle would be lost. If the soldiers came to fight—then they would have to take that hill and hold on to it.

But if Lone Star's soldiers did not come to fight and win, then the Crow might as well go on home now. Go home to protect their families and pony herds when the victorious Lakota spread across this land that had once been Apsaalooke hunting ground.

If Lone Star's soldiers had not come here to the Rosebud to defeat the Sioux for all time to come—then the Crow would have to fight alone, to protect their own.

"Private Lemly!" George Crook shouted, wheeling about when he was sure Bourke had made it back to the infantry's lines with that wounded bugler.

"Sir?"

"Front and center, Private!"

"Yes, sir!"

"My compliments to Major Van Vliet," Crook began, using the officer's brevet rank. "Carry him my instructions to rejoin my command."

"Certainly, sir," Lemly said, turning a moment to glance to the high bluffs across the Rosebud before he left to catch up his horse.

It was the highest ground overlooking all of the battlefield. And at the moment not only were some Sioux still pressuring Van Vliet's two companies, enemy horsemen were also beginning to pour down off the slopes of the conical hill, plunging into the head of Kollmar Creek on the north side of the Rosebud.

Royall's young adjutant asked, "Is that all, General?"

"Just tell him to make it double time," Crook added. "I'll need him to replace Mills and Noyes." He watched the soldier's eyes squint as he gazed into the east, finding the battalion forming up for its march on the village.

"You've dispatched them to another part of the fight?"

"Leaving momentarily—to the enemy camp, Private. Now—get Van Vliet in here and quick before these Sioux seal up that bottomland along the creek and he'll never be able to cross. We'll be pulling in all the units to follow on Colonel Mills's rear and support his attack on the village."

Lemly saluted. "Yes, sir! I'll do my best."

He returned the private's salute. "I know you will. God's speed, son."

Chapter 32

17 June 1876

"*The single most important reason I marched this expedition* out of Fetterman more than two weeks ago was simply to find the goddamned village of Crazy Horse!" George Crook had explained to Anson Mills more than an hour before. "To find that village—and destroy it!"

Crook had gone on to expound in precise detail the direction of his thinking: why he believed the village to be in his immediate front, perhaps no more than seven or eight miles north down Rosebud Creek.

Having to contend with three separate battles along some three miles of battle line, the general nonetheless still believed he had his situation under enough control to detach Captain Mills with the three troops of the Third Cavalry under his immediate command to make a charge on the village. Despite Crook's assurances to the contrary, Anson Mills realized there remained some very solid reasons for the general to be concerned about the progress of their fight over the last few hours.

Crook had the infantry under Burt and Burrowes dug in along the southwest side of the ridge, while in those rocks on the north rim of the bluffs he had posted the Montana miners and Tom Moore's packers. Although casualties had been minimal to this point, the expedition surgeons had set up their open-air field hospital on the slope just south of where Crook established his headquarters.

Having been summoned by a courier, Mills reached that bustle of activity around the general and waited, listening in as officers came and went with reports. Only then did the captain realize they were fighting a battle that had stretched itself across better than three miles of rugged Montana terrain. Perhaps most worrisome to George Crook was Royall's predicament on the far left. Five troops of horse soldiers—one full third of the general's cavalry—were more than a mile away, all but out of sight and contact, off fighting what had the makings of a tough scrap of it.

Now as Mills stood waiting, the general dispatched Royall's orderly, Henry R. Lemly, to carry word to his cavalry commander: immediately rejoin the left side of Crook's line in preparation for withdrawal and a march on the village.

That done and with Lemly on his way, the long-whiskered general finally turned to Mills.

"As I was explaining when you came up," Crook declared, "to my way of thinking, the only reason these bastards are fighting the way they are would be to protect the flight of their families in that village. We're close, Colonel Mills. Damned close. And I want your battalion to assure that those Crazy Horse people don't escape me again. Like they did to Reynolds on the Powder River!"

"That fiasco was a most bitter pill for me to swallow, General. I was there when the colonel ordered his retreat."

Crook screwed up his lower lip and chin within that strawberry-blond beard, then nodded. "Yes, Colonel. Now we both have a chance to redeem the honor of your regiment. Gibbon and Terry and even Custer are off somewhere in the north—doing God only knows what. But we've hit the bonanza! It's our Wyoming column that's struck pay dirt!"

Mills couldn't help but catch some of the contagious excitement radiating from the unkempt expedition commander in his nondescript private's uniform and battered, floppy top hat, faded from months in the sun and miles on the trail.

"Frank?" Crook called the half-breed over, then turned back to Mills. "I'm sending Grouard with you. He'll be your guide. No one knows this Sioux country better than Grouard here. Frank, take a dozen of the Crow along with you." Then the general turned back to the officer, both his hands balled into fists he shook before him. "Take that village, Captain. And hold on to it until I bring up the rest of the command."

Returning with the scout to his battalion, Mills asked, "Do we follow the creek, Grouard?"

The half-breed nodded. "It takes you straight to the many old campsites used by the Crazy Horse Lakota."

A grim smile formed on Mills's lips as they reached his men. He was confident Grouard would get him there. After all, the scout had performed some pretty amazing feats in locating the Crazy Horse village once before—last winter, in the middle of a blizzard, during the black of that subzero night. Here, with the sun in full glory overhead and with nothing more difficult than the banks of the Rosebud to follow—for a moment Mills wondered why Crook was sending Grouard along with him at all.

Why, a blind man could stumble across that encampment by accident!

This was nothing short of the plum assignment a cavalry commander waited years for: to capture the most feared and respected warrior chief on the northern plains. Maybe even Sitting Bull as well. Mills allowed himself to imagine how Nannie would feel, there to watch as he was promoted to major.

Hell! Capturing Crazy Horse would net him a sure lieutenant colonelcy! And from there it would be one easy step before he commanded his own regiment. Perhaps even his beloved Third . . . after Crook's court-martial moved that white-headed incompetent Reynolds out of the way.

Forming his three companies into a column of fours well below the crest of the ridge in the hope of concealing his intentions for as long as he could from the enemy, the captain led his cavalry out on a right oblique, southeast toward the bottomland beside the creek where Grouard took them toward what was widely known as the east bend of the Rosebud. After covering less than two hundred yards, the last of Crook's infantry had disappeared from the captain's view. With every moment the rest of that broad battlefield fell farther and farther behind them as well. As they marched smartly toward the end of the ridge where the creek turned back to the north, the rattle of rifle fire grew more and more faint.

As the dusty column drew close to the bend, a few hostiles appeared on the crests of the hills to their left and in their front, feathers, headdresses, and long hair lifted on the hot breezes. But otherwise silent, watching the horse soldiers.

"Lieutenant Paul," Mills called back to his adjutant after ordering a brief halt. "Take my compliments to Captain Sutorious. Ask him to mount a charge with his full company and drive those warriors from their position on those hills."

"Yes, Captain."

In a handful of moments, Alexander Sutorious, the Swiss-born captain who had come up through the ranks, was leading his E Company past the remaining two troops of cavalry, ascending the gentle rise until he called a halt and formed his sixty men into a broad company front. They set off at a gallop for the distant horsemen dark as pitch against the skyline, making a picturesque charge against those two dozen or so warriors watching the progress of Mills's command. The warriors fell back, beyond the crest as the horse soldiers struggled up the slope. At the top of the highest rise Sutorious halted his troopers for a few minutes.

Mills decided they were delaying to be sure the warriors were skeedaddling from the far side.

As he led his E Company back to rejoin Mills, Sutorious pulled off and came to a halt before the battalion commander while his troops continued on past to resume their place at the rear of the column.

"Mission accomplished, sir," Sutorious said, his words heavy with his Prussian-Swiss accent.

"That was a pretty charge, Captain. Well done. Let's be on with our march on the village."

Behind Grouard and the twelve Crow, they again moved out down the west bank of the Rosebud but only went another half mile before a courier came galloping up to the head of the column with word from Captain Noyes that he was hurrying his five companies of the Second Cavalry to join Mills. After ordering another brief halt here, Henry Noyes appeared around the base of the hills. Leaving his five troops back in the line of march, the captain came to the van to report to Mills.

"The general's compliments, sir."

"Major," Anson addressed Noyes by his brevet rank, looking past the captain to see that newsman Finerty and John Bourke among the arriving battalion. His eyes went back to Noyes. "Crook sent you?"

"It wasn't long after dispatching you to march on the village that the general decided it would be a good idea to reinforce you with my battalion. We are at your disposal."

Mills smiled mechanically at the officer around whom so much controversy swirled because of that cold day beside the Powder River. Noyes had ordered his men to dismount, build fires, and boil coffee while Mills and Teddy Egan were pinned down in the enemy village, in desperate need of reinforcement. "I am much pleased to have your troops along, Major. If you are ready to fight—I'm sure we'll get our share of it today."

Noyes stiffened somewhat, yet it seemed he made a conscious effort not to show affront. "Thank you, Colonel. It will be a pleasure fighting alongside you and the men of the Third."

"Your companies can take up position as rear guard as we resume our march, Major."

"Very well, sir."

Noyes saluted and reined away, loping back along the length of the column of fours as Mills ordered his attack force back into motion, marching into the gentle east bend of the Rosebud. He now led eight full companies of cavalry—more than 475 men—surely more than enough to capture the enemy's village with most of their warriors off battling Crook and Royall.

Just after the creek had turned back north, Mills sent orders to Noyes to take his five companies across the creek and to move parallel beside his own three companies of the Third. Now they were marching on both sides of the sluggish stream, with flankers thrown well out on left and right to prevent a surprise ambush. As well, Anson Mills ordered twenty troopers from Lieutenant Joseph Lawson's A Company of the Third to stay close where they could act as couriers who would maintain contact between both battalions in Mills's attack force.

They put two more miles behind them after the bend in the creek before Mills ordered another halt, calling his eight company commanders to the front of the march while the troopers dismounted and tightened girths. There, in the still, hot air of that midday, coming out of the saddle at a spot where they could still hear the distant but heavy gunfire from far to the west, Mills pointed out how the valley was beginning to narrow.

"Looks to be no more than one hundred twenty-five, maybe one hundred fifty yards wide at the most," Captain Noyes observed.

"The village got to be close now," Sutorious said.

Mills only half listened. The greater part of his attention was fixed on the Crow scouts who had gone ahead a few hundred yards to probe the shrinking shadows of the canyon. Catching Grouard's eye, he signaled the half-breed over.

"Are those guides of yours as nervous as they're acting?" the captain asked.

Grouard nodded. "From what I understand of their talk—they don't like the way the canyon is . . ." And he motioned with his hands, as if searching for a word.

"Getting smaller?" Mills asked.

"Yes," the half-breed answered.

"Are they scared of ambush?" Noyes inquired.

"Forget the Crow—how about you, Frank?" Mills asked, reading something on the half-breed's face that Grouard wasn't doing much good in concealing.

"Yes," he eventually admitted. "It could be a good place for an ambush."

"We saw those warriors on the hills back yonder," said Lieutenant Lawson of A Company, Third Cavalry.

Mills turned to Sutorious, asking, "Could those same

redskins who fled your men have gone north to set up an ambush, Captain?"

"When I drove them off," explained the affable Sutorious, "they did go north. I watched them for a few minutes until they disappeared beyond the hills. Could be they ride this far."

"Maybe they watched until you drove them off," said Thomas Dewees of the Second Cavalry. "Then went to tell the others."

"Could be," agreed Lieutenant William Rawolle. "Maybe they figured out that we're coming for the village, so they rode off to tell the rest who are waiting for us up there."

"Damn right," growled Lieutenant Samuel Swigert. "Waiting for us in ambush."

"That's why we haven't been opposed," Captain Elijah Wells, commander of E Company, Second Cavalry, spoke for the first time. "They want to sucker us down that goddamned canyon!"

"Wells might be right," Noyes declared. "You said those Injuns just fell back when Sutorious went after 'em. They want us to keep going."

Dewees grew animated, saying, "That canyon is where they want us to go!"

"Hey! Listen!" John Bourke hollered above the hubbub and mumbling.

For a moment that knot of officers fell quiet, straining to hear what sounds the hot air carried: distant but growing gunfire from the west, its rattle and crackle, rise and fall, floating over the pine-studded hills.

Mills wanted the matter brought to a head. "Grouard —do you think we're riding into a trap?"

As the officers all turned on him, the half-breed did not flinch. Calmly, he nodded once. "Lots of brush. Trees down. Deadfall all over that canyon yonder. A bad place to go riding into. Yes. Up there a trap waits for your soldiers."

"Dammit—isn't there a better route?" Mills snapped. "Another way to approach the village without going through this canyon where there may or may not be some trap prepared for us?"

With a shrug Grouard replied, "I could lead you up

those hills, out of the valley to the west." He pointed, then shrugged again. "Probably the same way Crazy Horse brought his warriors south to run into Crook."

Mills snorted, grinding a heel into the grass of a deep, emerald green. "All right. That's what we'll do. Give that route a try, gentlemen. Unless there is some dissent I've haven't listened to?"

Waiting a moment, Anson glanced at the faces of the captains and lieutenants, where he read some resolve, as well as a great deal of relief that he was not asking them to plunge on down the creekbed toward a possible surprise ambush. Finally he said, "Let's get your sergeants to ready your outfits for an attack on the village at any moment. Make sure cinches are tightened, weapons are loaded, and we'll resume the—"

"Riders coming in!"

They all turned as one when the voice called from back along the column.

"Now who the hell do you think that is?" Noyes asked as they watched to the south, catching their first glimpse of a pair of horsemen flogging their mounts in the direction of Mills's rear guard.

"Afraid I'm not so much concerned about *who* they are, Major Noyes," replied Anson Mills, his ears growing more attuned to the distant firing that had become more and more distinct, "as I am worried about just what news they're bringing us."

"Sweet Mither of God!" Seamus Donegan bellowed when he heard the news. "Royall might as well put a gun to his head right now!"

"I'll ask you to keep your voice down, and your opinions to yourself, Mr. Donegan!" snapped Guy V. Henry.

The Third Cavalry captain had just finished telling his battalion how William B. Royall's orderly, Lieutenant Lemly, had dared to ride alone through the enemy's bullets to deliver Crook's orders to the colonel, demanding that Royall's troops immediately begin to extend their right flank so that the battalion could reengage with the left of the main body of Crook's line. There, Burt and Burrowes were dug in and having a fierce time of it against repeated assaults by enemy horsemen.

Little did Crook or any of the rest of the infantry officers at the center of the ridge know just how fierce Royall's end of the fight had become.

Instead of issuing his command to begin an orderly withdrawal of all five of his cavalry troops, Royall inexplicably sent his adjutant, Lieutenant Charles Morton, with orders for Captain Charles Meinhold to take his B Company, Third Cavalry, east down a ravine so that they could join up with Chambers's infantry under Crook's main command. Royall then sent word to his remaining four company commanders, Henry, Reynolds, Vroom, and Andrews, to extend their front even farther to the right so they could fill in the gap left by Meinhold's departing troops as Company B began its perilous descent down the ravine toward Crook's hill.

"There's too many holes in our line—and they're all too bleeming big!" Donegan grumbled as he peered over the broken ground.

"Royall already argued with himself over it," Guy Henry explained. "We all agreed that to make a wholesale retreat to the right as Crook ordered would risk the certain loss of the whole battalion down in that ravine."

As the most exposed segment of Royall's battalion, Henry's D Company held on to the far left flank of the colonel's thinning line only by the skin of their teeth and a fingernail.

"By the devil—I see you've decided your men should fall here with the Sioux surrounding us and closing in, rather than lose them in that goddamned ravine where they can at least try to make it back?" Seamus snarled, his voice rising in nasty exasperation with pig-headed officers.

Henry was clearly angry, his voice growing louder, "You don't understand—"

"With you blathering officers it's only a matter of deciding what ground, isn't it, Colonel? Deciding just where your horse sojurs are going to fall and die!"

"You've got no right to—"

"We're bloody close to being doomed right now."

A moment before, the captain's face had been crimson

from the neck up. He now went pale as a Sunday tablecloth. His lips a thin line of controlled emotion, Henry gritted out the words, "I'll have you resume your position along the line, Mr. Donegan."

"Mark my words, Colonel—someone must convince Royall he's making a mistake sitting on his hands right here," Seamus continued, even though Henry was waving for a few soldiers to hurry over. "You can get these boys to drag me away for now—but I've fought alongside William B. Royall before. You ask him. He knows me. Knows I make sense, Colonel."

Just as five soldiers got there to latch on to the Irishman, Henry suddenly motioned them away again. "You know Royall? Fought with him?"

"Down to Summit Springs when Carr pitched into Tall Bull's Dog SOLDIERS."*

"That was seven years ago," Henry replied as if shaking it off. "Take my word for it, Mr. Donegan: Royall's a different man now."

"Listen—your own company is the most exposed. Your men have the most to lose. Won't you even talk to the colonel about my idea?"

Henry finally nodded. "All right, I'll go and make your case."

"He'll remember me and Bill Cody."

"I said I'll go!" Henry snapped, his eyes raking the battlefield where the enemy pressed his horse soldiers, inching forward screeching and howling, blowing their whistles and rattling pieces of rawhide to spook the horses being held not far down the slope. "Time for you to get back on the skirmish line, Mr. Donegan. It's there I can most use your gun."

"Aye, Cap'n."

As Seamus scurried back to the far left of the dangerously thin line, he caught a final glimpse of the last of Meinhold's B Company disappearing down the ravine, heading southeast across that open, unprotected ground toward Crook's line. First to move out were the horse-

* THE PLAINSMEN Series, vol. 4, *Black Sun*

holders and their frightened charges. Under the harassing fire from the Sioux, Donegan saw one of the horses go down clumsily as the troopers fought a rear-guard action against the warriors surging in upon them once the hostiles realized the small group was detaching itself from the main body.

With howling ferocity the Sioux fell upon the company's left. Pushing his flankers out, with the rest of his men inching slowly from one crest to the next in skirmish formation, Meinhold made painful progress. Then just before those harried troops disappeared from view into the jaws of the ravine, Donegan watched a bullet strike one of the soldiers, his carbine tumbling from his grip, his right arm useless. Two others immediately scrambled to help drag along their wounded bunkie before the trio disappeared over the slope.

"We gonna make it out of here?" asked a frightened soldier.

"Sure we are," Reuben Davenport replied before Seamus had a chance to utter a word. He glanced at Donegan. "Aren't we, Irishman?"

No sense in letting them know what the odds were. He quickly looked over the dozen or more soldiers all staring at him, waiting for his answer. Never any sense in dwelling on the odds.

"Why, boys—we'll be drinking whiskey back at the wagon camp inside of two days."

A voice bellowed its order from the right along the line. "Pulling back!"

"We're retreating?" Davenport asked, some sudden worry clouding his face like summer thunderheads.

A new voice to the right shrieked, "Goddamn—the line's giving way!"

"Oh, Jesus!" someone else cried out in supplication.

Seamus squinted beneath the wide brim of his hat as the order came relayed down the line from company to company, platoon to platoon. Across the rugged ground to the south and west of them, the warriors were up and moving forward in greater force than they had all morning.

"Appears we are pulling back, fellas. Them Sioux spotted Meinhold's retreat—so that's only made them red bastards all the more bold."

He jammed the worn stock of the Henry repeater to his cheek and brought one of the enemy horsemen into his sights. Squeezed the trigger.

"For sure—we're pulling back?" Davenport asked as if it had become a prayer.

Seamus nodded, bringing the repeater away from his cheek and twisting the receiver at the muzzle so that he could reload in preparation for their retreat. "Yeah, Reuben. Maybe Crook's got plans for us to march on the village too."

"March on the village?" Davenport wheedled, his eyes widening.

"The one named Lemly—lieutenant what brought Crook's orders back to Royall—he said the general's planning to send some companies north along the Rosebud with Mills to attack the Crazy Horse village," Donegan explained.

"Say, fellas," one of the older soldiers grumbled nearby, "don't you wish you were in on that charge?"

"By damned—wouldn't that be a hot time!" another old file gushed. "Wish I was in on that goddamned charge. Get in some licks, I would."

"With Crook ordering Royall to pull us back in retreat," Seamus continued to explain to the newspaperman, "I'd wager what the general has in mind is wanting every last man with him when he goes to support Mills when he jumps that Injin camp."

For a moment Davenport seemed almost disappointed as he replied, "Damn—but that's where the real action is gonna be now: with Mills blasting into Crazy Horse's camp!"

"Glory bless—but you're a chuckle-headed idiot!" Donegan snarled at the civilian.

"What the devil do you mean?"

"Here's the stand where things are hottest, you stupid son of a bitch! It's action you want? Just you keep your head down and your eyes skinned when we start moving back, Reuben Davenport. We ain't none of us yet come out of this fix alive. Not by a long chalk we ain't."

Chapter 33

Moon of Fat Horses

Back and forth across the broken ridges their battle against Three Stars had raged. A few warriors lay dead, carried back to the women wailing on the slopes of those hills to the northwest. Many more were wounded, flesh torn or bones broken by the bullets from so many powerful soldier guns.

Yet what hurt Wooden Leg the most was the sight of all those ponies lying crippled, or dead. Carcasses scattered for almost as far as his eye could see.

Already it had been a costly fight—but still the sun had fully half its journey yet to go across the sky.

Just as Crazy Horse had told the old ones—those counselors, the headmen and chiefs—this was to be a far different fight than any they had fought before. This time they had resisted fighting as individuals in pursuit of personal coups. This time each man became one of the whole, following the commands of the battle chiefs as the tide of the long, bloody struggle waxed and waned back and forth, like the tossing of the tall stalks of buffalo grass in the summer breeze.

"You have the scalp, Wooden Leg?" Crooked Nose asked breathlessly as he brought his pony alongside.

"Yes." He took the damp scalp from the narrow thong

around his waist where he had hung it. Long black hair, tied with a few small significant ornaments, the flesh a dark, angry red as the blood dried in the hot summer wind.

In the beginning only the white man's scouts came out to fight against the Shahiyena and Lakota. Finally the white soldiers came themselves. Eventually, at that most crucial point in the battle, the Raven People and Snakes again threw themselves into the bloodiest fighting—pony to pony and hand to hand. Face to face against ancient enemies.

Wooden Leg still had the smells in his nostrils: the stink of a pony's riven entrails as they spilled across the dusty ground; the fetid odor of the Snake's sweat-slicked body as he and Wooden Leg grappled at the bottom of the ravine gorged with dust and powdersmoke and the noise of men dying. Then the Snakes and Raven People and four white men had turned and hastily retreated. The Lakota joined the Shahiyena in flowing back upon the fleeing enemy. They counted many coup on that chase near the tall, round hill.

With the soldiers' scouts chased off again, they returned to the fight with the soldiers far to the west.

Like a cradleboard swinging from a tree limb on a gentle spring breeze, this fight in the west flowed first one way, then the other. All along the slope the soldiers lay huddled where they could take cover, strung out in a thin line. A few of the blue-clad men moved among the others on horseback. It was those daring soldier chiefs that Wooden Leg and Goose Feather tried hardest to hit. The courageous ones who shouted orders to the others as they rode back and forth, back and forth among their men. Surely, to have the scalp of so brave a soldier chief would be a great thing, Wooden Leg thought.

"Look!" White Shield yelled nearby, pointing as he arose behind a rock, exposing the top half of his body to the soldier guns.

For the most part the soldier guns did not fire in his direction. Amazed, Wooden Leg and the others stared at the white men. Then he knew why.

Someone announced, "They are moving their horses!"

"I want a horse!" cried another.

"Don't let them take the horses away! They belong to us!"

The young men called back and forth to one another as they waited those precious heartbeats—perhaps trying to sort out what it was the soldiers were doing for certain. Then it became as clear as mountain runoff.

"They are retreating!" Brass Cartridge bellowed, waving his arm in the air, in his hand the soldier rifle he had taken from one of the Raven People scouts he had killed early that morning.

"Quickly now! After the soldiers!"

Behind them and on all sides of the Shahiyena came the foreign Lakota tongue, a smattering of which Wooden Leg understood, having spent time off and on among the Hunkpatila Oglalla, known as the Crazy Horse people.

They were among the Shahiyena now, hurrying forward as the long line of soldiers inched backward across the open, rugged ground. Sometimes the white men knelt and fired back at the warriors. But they always clambered to their feet and backed up a little farther until they stopped and wheeled and fired their guns again, each muzzle making a little puff in the hot air of this midday. Firing repeatedly until a murky gray cloud hung just over the white men, staining the summer blue of the wide domed sky here on this ridgetop.

As the Shahiyena and the Lakota swept down on the soldiers from three sides, it was as if the warriors had the white men spewing out between the jaws of a great, menacing beast. And nothing so fired the heart of a fighting man as the sight of his enemy fleeing in the opposite direction. Everywhere the air filled not only with gunfire—but also with exultant shouts of victory.

"Do not let them get back to the others!"

Recognizing the voice, Wooden Leg whirled about, finding the unadorned Oglalla war chief reining up among them on his pony, waving his repeater in the air.

"Keep them from reaching that hilltop!" Crazy Horse shouted.

Instantly a wide throng of warriors swept sharply to the east to cut off the intended path of retreat. Going with them, Wooden Leg fired and ran, fired and ran some more. Slowly, slowly it was working. The white man's retreat was grinding to a halt. He could even see the horses and their struggling holders now at the center of that tightening bunch of soldiers milling about near the southern end of the ridge. They weren't moving near as fast as they had been. Come grinding to a halt now.

Having met with the stiff, fierce, bloody resistance of the Lakota and Shahiyena warriors Crazy Horse threw squarely into the path of their retreat.

The white men were surrounded.

"Good God, Colonel Mills—but you've covered some ground!" Azor Nickerson exclaimed, his voice raspy as his horse splashed out of the Rosebud, having crossed the creek to reach the battalion commander charged with attacking the village of Crazy Horse.

"At least five miles, Captain," Anson Mills replied peevishly. He quickly eyed the orderly dismounting beside Crook's aide-de-camp, a youngster rubbing his buttocks and thighs. "What the hell are you come to tell me?"

"The general's compliments—"

"What the hell word do you bring? More companies? Is Crook in my rear as he promised?"

Nickerson swallowed, his brow knitting with worry. "No, Colonel. Crook sent me to check your advance."

"Check? Check my goddamned advance?"

"Don't listen to him, Colonel," Henry Noyes suggested acidly.

There arose a murmuring of assent to that.

For the moment Mills ignored them. He glared at the soldier dressed in showy buckskins. "Turn back, Captain Nickerson? Are you absolutely certain that's what you and your orderly galloped five miles, alone through country crawling with Indian horsemen, to tell me?"

"Yes," Nickerson replied, wiping the back of a hand across his parched lips.

"Why, pray tell?"

"As soon as your battalion detached itself, the enemy resumed its attacks on the middle of the line—"

"Where Crook is fighting?"

Nickerson nodded. "Yes. But the greatest strength has been thrown against Royall. The colonel's getting cut up something bad. He and Henry and Vroom—all severely pressured and taking great casualties. That's convinced the general that Crazy Horse had thrown his reserves into the fight on Royall's front."

"Reserves? Crazy Horse has reserves?"

"Yes—with every minute there seems to be more and more Indians riding back and forth across our front. If he leaves to come reinforce your rear, the general doesn't think he can protect his wounded much longer with what forces he has to leave behind."

"The situation has changed that much since we left?" Mills asked.

"Yes," Nickerson replied. "Crook says he won't be able to follow you, to support you with the rest of the command. Right now—it's all he can do to hold the enemy at bay. Therefore, the general respectfully countermands his previous order to you and requests that you come reinforce his weakening front."

"Royall's?"

With a shrug Nickerson replied, "Crook said nothing about going to Royall's aid. The general wants you to come reinforce his position at the middle of the ridge."

"But the village!" Mills began to protest. "We almost have it. I'm certain we can hold it—even without Crook's reinforcement."

Nickerson stiffened. "I have clearly stated the general's orders, Captain. Are you in need of clarification?"

"I am not in need of clarification, Captain Nickerson!" Mills grumbled, finding himself perched at the top of the horns of a dilemma.

"We can't go back, Captain!" Sutorious growled. "We got the goddamned village in our reach!"

"To hell with Crook's orders!" Dewees echoed.

Rawolle argued, "But the savages have an ambush laid for us up there!"

"To hell with you! And Nickerson too!" Elijah Wells bellowed. "I say let's march on the Crazy Horse camp!"

"I can smell that village—it's so damned close!" agreed

Swigert. "Don't go back when we can end this war right now!"

"Shut up! All of you!" Mills snapped, his eyes lidded, breath coming quick, his heart already climbing to his throat.

This was exactly the sort of position in which he had never dreamed he would find himself. On the brink of victory, a good and gallant soldier following orders with aplomb and dispatch—only to receive new orders that made little or no sense, orders from a commanding officer miles and miles away, someone who, for all intent and purpose, knew little about what was possible, what was probable, what could be just within reach.

"Grouard!"

The half-breed rose slowly, sidled up to the circle easily as if he did not care the slightest for what he knew was to be asked of him. "Colonel?"

For a moment as the rest of them buzzed and mumbled behind him, Mills stared north, down the valley of the Rosebud. Then he pointed and asked, "You're sure the hostiles could find a place to ambush us up yonder?"

"The canyon narrows, like I told you."

"Yes," Mills answered quickly. "With the deadfall and brush, you said. Yes. Yes." Then the captain turned on Grouard, his nose inches from the half-breed's. Gripping the scout's upper arm, Mills pleaded, "So what you're really telling me is that if we tried going this way, we never would reach the village?"

Grouard nodded, opening his mouth to say something when Mills brushed right on past him and returned to the crescent of officers.

"All right, gentlemen," the captain said, and removed his hat to swipe his brow before returning the hat to his head. "I have no idea why we are being recalled at the moment of our greatest victory for the Third Cavalry. And for the Second Cavalry. For total victory on the northern plains against the wild tribes. Be damned, I haven't the slightest notion—but I am a soldier who follows orders."

Turning, Mills flung his voice over his shoulder. "Grouard. Get up here. I want you to tell me what you think of climbing over those hills there to the west of us."

"Into those? Those hills?" Nickerson asked, pointing. "The general wants you to return by—"

"By damned, I am returning, Captain Nickerson!" Mills barked. "By what I believe to be the fastest route possible."

"I misunderstood you, Colonel," Nickerson retorted. "The general does indeed intend for you to take the fastest route, over the hills if possible."

"He said that?"

"He did," the adjutant answered. "Crook needs you to fall on the rear of the savages who are ready to swallow up Royall and Henry."

"Hot damn!" Sutorious exclaimed, rubbing his hands together eagerly. "A rear-guard fight!"

"Let's ride, Colonel!" Wells cheered as more of the officers voiced excitement at the prospect of riding in to catch the unsuspecting enemy by surprise from the rear.

"Get these men mounted!" Mills bawled above the hubbub.

"Prepare to mount!"

The squeak of stirrup fenders and the rattle of bit-chains rose above the quiet summer gurgle of the Rosebud as eight companies of horse soldiers prepared to charge on a new enemy.

"Mount!"

They swung into the saddle and moved out, five companies joining the three after crossing the shallow stream, the droplets flung into the hot air like tiny crystals of dew that darkened the coats on all the horses, slapped the dusty boots that rose nearly to the knees of those men who would ride to the relief of George Crook's beleaguered and overtaxed front.

These were the dusty, sweaty men who would eventually raise the bloody siege of those weary, harried, frightened soldiers who were at that moment preparing to make a second frantic retreat behind Colonel William B. Royall.

"I must go, Colonel Royall," Azor Nickerson had declared more than an hour ago just after the colonel's battalion had retreated to their second position along the bluff.

"General Crook wants me to carry orders to Mills's battalion marching on the village."

"Marching on the village!" Royall had fumed. "For God's sake! When we could use those men? If Crook doesn't get us help soon—"

"Colonel," Nickerson interrupted, "that's precisely what the general has in mind: I'm to recall Mills and Noyes from their march on the village so that they can fall on the rear of the warriors who have applied all this pressure to your left. Lieutenant Lemly is with your command?"

"I asked that my adjutant stay after he delivered the general's orders to connect with his left flank."

Nickerson nodded grimly. "Crook was concerned when the lieutenant did not return."

"It was on my own responsibility that I kept Lemly here. If nothing else, he is to be commended for taking his place along our skirmish lines."

Crook's aide-de-camp sighed, peering down at his hands a moment, then asked, "If I may be excused, Colonel?"

Royall saluted and turned away, not watching Nickerson and his young orderly swing into the saddle and kick their mounts into a fury as they sped southeast down the slope into the Kollmar Creek drainage. With deep regret the Irishman wished he were riding off with Crook's couriers—even if it proved to be suicide.

Through every one of those long, agonizing minutes that had swollen into more than an hour, Seamus Donegan peered to the north and east in the direction of the Rosebud lying just beyond the green-blotched hills. If Mills was indeed marching north when he was recalled, that was the country where he would appear with his eight companies.

Eight companies, Seamus marveled.

And here Royall sits while the fringes of his command are chewed on just the way coyotes chewed on rawhide rope and packsaddles and latigo. Nibbling all the way around the edges as the colonel's three remaining companies shrank, drawing closer and closer together like drying rawhide itself, the sun beginning to slip past midsky.

After the warriors had spotted Meinhold's company escape toward the Kollmar Creek drainage, they swiftly invaded that portion of the ridge, pressuring Royall's right, effectively sealing off that route to further escape. Now the red waves loomed nearer to the northeast as well, there at the head of the ravine running down toward the Rosebud.

To reach this, his second position of the morning, Royall had been forced to squeeze his remaining troops of cavalry through the one portal left open to them—turning their faces almost due south to retire to the crest of a lengthy ridge jutting out toward the Rosebud itself, just southwest of that head of the Kollmar. In their harried, frightening retreat that covered more than a half mile across the gently sloping and open ground, the horse soldiers followed the horse-holders, turning on command as squad leaders ordered fire by volleys into the warriors who swarmed at them from nearly every direction at once.

To Donegan it was nothing short of a sainted miracle they had retreated without suffering a single casualty in all that fighting.

To finally reach the end of the ridge. Here was the end of the line.

Royall could go no farther: they had come to the far western edge of the crest where the bluff fell sharply to a deep, wide canyon. Here the only cover for the retreating soldiers was a low strata of brownish-red sandstone boulders where the men bunched up and again turned their fire at the enemy.

Royall ordered Captains Vroom and Andrews to hold the ground along the north slope—which meant the troopers now faced the position from which they had just retreated. Didn't seem to be many soldiers in those four remaining companies who were immune to the growing despair brought by looking back to see that the ground they had just abandoned only moments before was now overrun and swarming with an army of red ants.

With Captain Henry's two remaining companies, D and F, Seamus fought his way to the south slope where the battalion struggled in a hot fire-fight until they were eventually able to take refuge among the few rocks at the precipitous ledge falling abruptly into the deep chasm. They had slashed and shot their way to the boulders not a moment too soon. Had Henry's men tarried any longer in securing their position—the Crazy Horse warriors would have been there to greet the soldiers at the edge of the chasm.

Hunkered here, Donegan grew thankful for what breezes stirred among the rocks and tall grass along this southern slope of the ridge. Any wisp of air on the move hurried the clouds of gunsmoke and stinging red and yellow dust on its way. Just to the east of them milled their frightened, chivvied mounts—more than a handful for the horse-holders. Not long ago Royall had called forward half of those men so that the holders who remained in the ravine with the mounts now had responsibility for eight animals latched together with the swivels on their link-straps. Pushing and bumping against one another, whinnying, jostling with eyes wide as runny egg whites in a cold cast-iron skillet bottom, the horses stuck their nostrils high into the wind to snatch any scent of the Indian ponies and grease-smeared naked bodies painted with frightening, mystical symbols.

Seamus brooded: if our horses just don't bolt completely . . . damn! But Royall has to make a decision soon or—

"I'm sending the horses away first—again!" Royall shouted above the clamor of the noisy mounts, the rattle of gunfire, and the screeching of the warriors who paraded back and forth along the ridgetop just out of range while others crept in closer, ever closer through the grass, from rock to rock and tree to tree. Some of the copper-skinned horsemen even dared to make courage runs along the entire stretch of Royall's shrinking front. Blowing their eagle wing-bone whistles, yip-yip-yipping like a damned coyote, taunting, luring, almost seductive in a primal way.

More than a handful of the young soldiers had growled in exasperation, standing to try a shot at those distant riders. When they did, such frustration, daring, and anger only earned them a renewed rain of gunfire from the warriors sidling ever closer from the north and west, as well as the southwest along the base of the ridge.

"Are you sure we're ready, Colonel? As soon as they see us falling back, they'll rush us again," declared Captain

Guy Henry. Bug-eyed, he glanced at the Irishman as if for confirmation.

Royall followed his subaltern's eyes, looking at the civilian himself. "The captain's right, isn't he, Mr. Donegan? Why wouldn't they rush us? They'd like to separate us from our horses, wouldn't those bastards? To keep us from joining with Crook's left."

"Our only chance is to go now, Colonel Henry," Donegan pleaded. "We wait—it ain't about to get any better."

"I disagree, Colonel," Henry argued. "We've learned that Crook has sent for Mills's battalion. I say we sit tight and wait for them to fall on the enemy's rear, which will take some of the heat off us."

Donegan shook his head when Royall looked back at him. "This is it, Colonel." He swallowed: just saying it would be hard. "You'll likely take some casualties retiring across that last defile—to make that far ridge yonder where there's infantry and the Crow. But what men we lose is for the sake of the rest."

"You're saying if we don't get out now—this entire battalion is lost?"

"Look for yourself. All of you. The Sioux are wrapping us in a tighter and tighter corner until there'll be nowhere to go. I ain't one of your officers—but I do know a hard scrape when I see it. No better choice but to tighten our cinches and get while the getting is good."

Royall bristled. "I'd prefer this to be thought of as a charge rather than another retreat—"

"This ain't nothing like Summit Springs, where you and Carr was able to get the jump on those Dog Soldiers."

The colonel's face went gray with concern, his cheeks sallow with the weight of command and the gravity of their predicament, perhaps realizing not all of these men would make it to the end of that far ridgeline where Chambers's infantry was spread in ragged skirmish lines with the Crow and Shoshone.

Eventually Royall sighed in a quiet gush. "Here we are, gentlemen—without a prayer of taking the offensive. All right. I suppose the best I can hope for now is nothing more than to retreat with our wounded . . . and our lives."

Chapter 34

Moon of Ripening Berries

His gut burned with hate, boiled with rage.

Crazy Horse watched as the young Hunkpatila boy of fourteen winters spun off the bare back of his pony, landing with a spray of dust where he lay dazed, easy prey to their old enemies. This sort of bravery run was something for an older, more accomplished warrior.

But those Raven People and Snake scouts!

Crazy Horse ground his teeth in anger. As much as he hated the white man and all the misery he had caused the Lakota people, the Horse hated the white man's Indians just that much more.

In making their daring ride, two youngsters had charged too close to the enemy's lines. Too far east along the top of the ridge.

As the pair of horsemen had broken over the crest of the hill in harassing the retreating soldiers, they had strayed too close to the walk-a-heap soldiers, as well as those Indians who fought alongside the white men. Spotting the two riders, the scouts for the soldiers opened up a deadly fire, finally knocking one of the boys from his pony. Turning on his heel, the other youngster galloped out of range, down the north side of the ridge, frightened right out of the fight.

As the unfortunate youth slowly rose to his hands and knees, shaking the confusion from his head and touching the bloody bullet wound along his side, the soldier scouts descended on him.

Crazy Horse had watched the enemy strike in a flurry of clubs and knives, the muzzles and butts of their rifles, falling upon him like starving ants converging on a juicy morsel dropped from a steaming kettle in a lodge.

The Horse knew there would be little left of the body to take home to his family. Only the words he could say to the boy's mother, to the father—that their son had died fighting for his people, as bravely as any full-grown warrior. Died not only in a struggle with the white man but against ancient enemies as well.

A noble death.

No matter how noble, it did little to stop a mother's tears, or a father's rage.

He himself knew of a father's rage. His only child—a young, beautiful daughter—died of the white man's terrible spotted disease. That's what came of knowing the white man. That's what came of hanging about the soldier forts and the trading posts. Better to keep the white man as far away from the villages as the warriors could.

That's why they had decided to attack the soldiers, rather than chance letting them draw any closer to their camp.

Because of that he kept reminding himself all morning long that this could not be the great battle Sitting Bull had envisioned. No soldiers were anywhere close to their villages. No soldiers were falling headfirst into their great gathering of lodge circles.

Although they had the soldiers in the middle of the battle fought to a standstill; although many of the pony soldiers had inexplicably disappeared down the Rosebud; and although he now had most of his warriors closing in on the white men they had surrounded far to the west end of the ridge—although this was indisputably a great victory for the Lakota and Shahiyena . . . this fight on Rosebud Creek was nonetheless not the greatest of victories Wakan Tanka had promised to give His people.

No soldiers were falling into camp here.

Instead, the white men had huddled up against the steep slopes of the ridge with nowhere else to go. For so long they did nothing but fight back like cornered mice. There was no manhood in cowering as they did.

But now—with a sudden flurry of movement, some of the white men they had surrounded were breaking off from the rest, leaving their horses and companions behind, hurrying toward the crest of the ridge.

"Hopo!" Crazy Horse cried, wheeling his pony in a circle, raising his repeater to get every man's attention. "We could want nothing better!"

"We fought to cut the soldiers into little bites so that we could chew them up," He Dog shouted. "Let us now go grind their bones in our teeth!"

"Hoka hey!" Crazy Horse called as the hundreds rushed in for the kill. "Go after them! Remember your families! Cut them off! Remember your children! Kill these soldiers—kill them all!"

"I judge there to be more than five hundred warriors closing in on Royall now, General!" Alexander Chambers declared without taking the field glasses from his eyes.

George Crook ground his hands together, murmuring, "Dear God in heaven."

"If they succeed," Chambers continued, finally tearing the field glasses from his face, "the colonel's men will be cut off from us, perhaps cut off from all chance of our support."

Crook wagged his head, looking over his infantry and the allies, knowing how suicidal it would be for him to order an attempt to go relieve Royall's battalion. He had to fight the grip of despair, hold off the melancholia. "What can be keeping Mills?"

As if prompted by this sudden shaking in the general's self-assurance, Major Chambers turned to train his field glasses a little east of north.

It gave Crook pause to realize he now was something less than confident of winning this battle with Crazy Horse. Ammunition had to be running low after nearly half a day of fighting. The hillsides were littered with the dark carcasses of dead and dying cavalry mounts and the mules that had carried his infantry to the Rosebud. After some four hours of fighting, his expeditionary force was not only strung out along more than three miles of ridge, but more than a third of his cavalry was nowhere to be found among the hills to the north. He simply could not allow this trembling in his own self-confidence to shake the optimism of his officer corps.

"You see anything, Colonel?" he asked of Chambers.

Continuing to adjust the focus, the major studied the ridgetops, the crests of the hills, the open meadows stretching between the stands of emerald green pines. Without a word he worked his field of view slowly down the slopes toward the flats in the valley to their immediate north.

"No, General. I don't see a thing of the Mills battalion."

Crook drew himself up and sighed, turning back to listen to renewed, heavy firing from Royall's position. It seemed some men were breaking off from that spur to the south, ascending the ridge. It seemed like the perfect act of suicide.

"Then I have no choice but to conclude that Mills is beyond giving us any support, Colonel Chambers," Crook admitted, turning away from that skirmish to the west. "Much too far away to get here in time to support Royall's rear guard."

"Burrowes and Burt are extended thin enough as it is, General."

Nodding, the general turned to Chambers, leaning close, confidentially, asking in a low voice, "Would Mills possibly disobey the orders I sent with Nickerson? Would he find some reason to continue on to attack the village?"

The major's eyes darted about, like those of a man put on the spot and not sure if there was any right answer to such a question. Finally he answered the older man before him. "From what I know of Colonel Mills—what I've heard of his gallantry in the war and on the Powder River —I don't think disobeying is in the man's constitution, General. I've heard others testify that he's as fine a soldier as they come."

With a wave of his hand, and a brave attempt at a grin, Crook replied, "A little on the excitable side of things, the colonel is. But I agree. I don't think Mills is the kind who could ever justify disobeying a direct order."

Chambers seemed relieved to be taken off the hook.

Crook sighed. "Colonel—how I hope I can rectify my mistake. Before this enraged enemy, I've gone and committed the second major blunder of my career."

"Blunder, sir?"

"The worst blunder a commander in the field can make: splitting up my forces and placing each of these components out of supporting distance of the others." He turned to peer off into the north. "Where the devil can Mills and Noyes be?"

"Colonel Chambers? General Crook? You wanted to see us?"

They both wheeled at the call from Andrew Burt. At the captain's side came Thomas Burrowes. "Gentlemen. Thank you for coming on the double. We have a dire situation here—"

"Royall's detaching some of his men, General!" Captain Burt interrupted with a shriek.

"Do you know how many?" Crook asked.

Burt answered, "Maybe a troop—at the most."

"It will be a miracle if they aren't cut up," the general replied. He reached out to take the field glasses from Chambers, squinting into the sunlight atop that crest as he adjusted the focus so he could watch the black, distant figures ascending the gentle rise to the rugged head of Kollmar Creek.

"You needed us in a hurry, General," Burt prodded.

"Yes," Crook answered, turning back to the infantry commanders. "Move your commands as far to the left as you can—"

"Begging the general's pardon," Burrowes broke in. "We're stretched out there like Nettie's pantaloons already, sir!"

Taking a deep breath, Crook continued, "Push your men as far to the left as you can, expeditiously. As daring a move as you can make it."

"What are we to accomplish, General?" Burt inquired.

"I want you to lay down some covering fire for Royall's men."

"I've got Meinhold's company with me," Burrowes declared.

"Yes. Good. Take them with you, every man you can spare," Crook said, wanting to watch that hill through the field glasses, but he dared not. "I don't know why in hell it's taken more than two hours for Royall to obey my order to rejoin the left of your line."

"From what Captain Meinhold told us," Burrowes replied, "it wasn't the easiest retreat to make."

"Dammit, Captain!" Crook snapped. "It hasn't gotten any easier for the rest of Royall's men because of his flat-footed shilly-shallying!"

Both infantry captains fell quiet as Crook fumed.

Then Burt asked his question, trying out a stiff upper lip, "General, some of my men say that they get so hardened to this sort of thing."

Crook asked, "Hardened? To what sort of thing, Captain?"

"To this constant firing, the noise and commotion of battle, so that they don't mind it."

The general shook his head. "What's your question, Burt? Do you have a point?"

"I suppose I wonder whether you feel like I do in a position of this kind, General," Burt replied.

"Suppose you tell me how you feel, Major." Crook used Burt's brevet rank.

"Why, to be perfectly honest about it—"

"Speak frankly, Major."

"Just that—if you were not in sight, I'd feel like running the hell away from those goddamned savages."

Crook snorted explosively, a wry smile inside his reddish-blond whiskers. Then he started laughing, and could not stop when the other three men joined in. Finally, the general said, "Well, speaking frankly, gentlemen—sometimes I feel exactly that way myself."

Then Crook turned to peer to the north beneath a hand he held to his brow.

Fidgeting, Burt finally inquired, "Is that all, General?"

"Yes, Major. I thought you and Burrowes would already be on your way! Be quick about it. And take those allies with you. Every gun you can. Support Royall's retreat in any way possible. Now, go—or all is lost!"

This time it was Burrowes who replied, "Yes, sir!"

Crook listened as the two captains trotted away, training the field glasses now to the west of north, resolved to look once more where that tiny company of soldiers had gone to protect the head of the deep ravine.

Where the brown-skinned horsemen were converging in greater and greater numbers, inching in on that little band that had circled up, their backs all to the center, every man of them slowly backing up . . . step by step by step as their circle shrank and shrank.

It would be a damned death-defying retreat, George Crook thought, if—

If any of them made it out at all.

"Captain Vroom—you will lead your company and precede the rest. Take that crest," William B. Royall ordered, pointing to the head of Kollmar Creek. "You must take that high ground and hold it against attack while the remaining companies begin their retreat behind the led horses."

"I'm to fight a rear guard, Colonel?" Peter Vroom asked.

"Yes, you are."

"Yes, sir." Vroom saluted and turned to leave, hurrying off at a crouch to form up his men.

All told, Royall reached his third position with something on the order of 200 men. By sending L Company's 55 men to the crest, Royall had left himself with perhaps 150, less when one considered that one soldier of every 8 was struggling with the horses. Surrounding these men swarmed more than 500, perhaps as many as 700, horse-mounted warriors. Easily three-to-one odds. Maybe even greater.

Donegan always hated himself for thinking about the odds. But he would hate himself all the more if he didn't get said what was suddenly eating away at his craw.

Seamus called out to Royall, "Colonel—you're gonna have those men exposed up there."

"Exactly what I want, Donegan," Royall retorted. "I

want them to take a little heat until I get the rest of this outfit mounted and moving. Buy us some time—"

"You'll have your wish before you know it," the Irishman replied, watching Vroom's company hoof it up the slope across the bare ground, naked of any cover but for the season's first growth of grass. "See there, Colonel?" He pointed. "The Sioux been keeping their eye on us. And you've just gone and give 'em the sort of bait they like to swallow."

Royall's jaw clenched tightly as he whirled, calling out to his adjutant, "Lemly!"

"Colonel?"

"Ride, Lieutenant. Go to Crook and tell him we're coming but we're in desperate need of his support. Ask him for covering fire from the Chambers's infantry. Got that?"

"Yes, sir."

Lemly was gone, catching up a mount among the horse-holders, reining away out of the dust and confusion, down the side of the narrowing ravine toward its bottom that would take him straight to the mouth of Kollmar Creek.

True enough was the Irishman's prediction: the anxious, milling, blood-eyed horsemen had been watching Royall's battalions, waiting for the white soldier chief to make just such a blunder as this.

Waiting for the soldiers to weaken themselves further by splitting up even more.

Donegan knew the Sioux and Cheyenne could hope for nothing better.

Wasting no time, and likely smelling victory in their nostrils, the screeching horsemen burst from their lines, scattering across the open ground like a bag of dried white beans, a hundred or more spilling toward Vroom's company.

Seamus was up and rushing after Royall as the colonel prepared to remount his horse. "If you're gonna move out with the rest of your men, you better start doing it!"

"We've fought together before, Mr. Donegan—but that does not give you the liberty—"

"We don't have time to argue, Colonel!"

Royall glared down at the civilian. "You'll do well to leave the commanding to me, Mr. Donegan!" he shouted, then stuffed a boot in the hoop of a stirrup. Once in the saddle, Royall wheeled, pointing east toward the wide ravine, his voice above them all now. "Company commanders—get the horses moving first! Horse-holders lead out! Andrews—take your I Company in the advance!"

Up the grassy slope near L Company the thunderous rattle of gunfire was growing, becoming a steady, pounding, mechanical thing that rumbled down over Donegan and the rest as they began to work their way east behind the van of led horses immediately followed by the cordon of Andrews's I.

It was only a matter of moments before the horse-holders encountered their first resistance as a sizable stream of warriors flooded past Vroom's company and succeeded in reaching the ground just east of the head of the ravine, where they started to direct some of their gunfire at the cavalry mounts and their horse-holders. As the bullets sang in and around them, the big animals bucked and reared, fighting their handlers. Men shouted, orders were flung up and down the side of the Kollmar drainage, while a few old soldiers who refused to listen to anyone else simply knelt calmly to aim at the enemy, fired, then ejected the empty casing from their Springfield, reloading and firing cartridge after cartridge. A few muttered under their breath, some more vocal than others, as they tore out pocket knives or yanked free the long-bladed skinning knives they carried at their belts, using anything with a point to it to pry the shiny brass cartridges stuck in a carbine breech grown hot with rapid, repeated use.

Suddenly Captain Guy V. Henry was bolting past the spot where Donegan knelt feeding cartridges down the loading tube of the repeater.

Five yards away the nervous captain brought his big dun mare to a halt, hollering at Royall above the din of battle, "Request permission to go to Vroom's aid, Colonel!"

Royall sawed the reins about, his eyes darting up the slope where L Company was slowly backing in a smaller and smaller ring, the warriors converging on them from all sides now. Many of the horsemen worked in close enough to swing at any stragglers with war clubs and knife-studded battle-axes. One of the patrol's soldiers dropped to a knee, no longer fighting the onrushing swarm of red ants, but struggling instead to force open the trapdoor breech on his Springfield.

He never heard it coming.

As Seamus watched, the soldier's head exploded in a crimson spray. A warrior swept past on horseback, screeching out in victory for the coup.

And now the white man's body lay exposed on the field, the rest slowly retreating with Vroom into an ever-shrinking circle.

Another young soldier rose clumsily from a crouch with his useless carbine as he was rushed, looking every bit as if he were courteously handing over the Springfield to the oncoming warrior in his frightening war paint, who savagely knocked the white man's rifle aside with a huge battle-axe, then swiftly whirled it overhead to bring the blade down on the trooper's head, cleaving it to the man's chin.

In the next breath it seemed the dirty blue of their uniforms disappeared behind a wall of Sioux horsemen, boots and hooves kicking up a veil of dust, a pall of gunsmoke swirling like the gauzy fingers of some curtain draped over the crest of the hill as the clamor grew and men cried out in terror and pain and the coming of certain death.

But as suddenly the warriors fell back slightly, and Seamus could again dimly make out the murky blue of the soldiers through the dust.

Somehow, only in God's own name, L Company had repulsed that first concerted charge.

Yet it changed nothing. On that crest Vroom's men stood all but back to back—those who remained of the doomed patrol now that one of every four were lost. The warriors swept along all sides of Vroom's men, probing here and there, feinting, screeching—preparing to make another rush.

"If you're going to save those men, Royall," Seamus

growled, a sour ball choking his throat, "you better see Henry gets his outfit moving now!"

Royall whirled about and flung his arm up the hill toward Vroom as he bellowed, "Permission granted, Colonel!"

Seamus was off like a shot behind Henry as the cavalry officer spurred his mount into motion, sprinting back to the most exposed part of what remained of Royall's battalion. By the time Henry reached his men and began to shout his terse orders, Donegan turned to see Vroom's men disappear behind a second concerted charge by the Sioux horsemen.

At the same moment, more horsemen poured past Vroom, down into the head of Kollmar intent on cutting off Royall's retreat, flooding through the confused and harried horse-holders. Bedlam ensued as the dark-skinned riders atop their small ponies darted among the rearing, bucking big American horses, flapping blankets and strips of rawhide.

"Form up!" Henry shouted. "Form up for a charge!"

A soldier rushed up to ask, "We going to the relief of those men on top, Colonel?"

"Damn right we are!" Henry cheered them.

"Lookee there!" an old soldier shouted near Donegan.

Another asked, "Is that Crook's Injuns?"

Seamus recognized them as the allies. "That's Crook's Crows all right. God bless 'em!"

Now a dozen, then thirty and more, darted on foot across the top of the Kollmar, where they halted and began to lay down some enfilading fire into those warriors harassing the horse-holders.

"Gloree! Some of them foot-sloggers coming too!" bawled one of the old horse soldiers nearby. "Lookit them double-timing it!"

" 'Bout time they did!" grumbled another trooper.

"Move out!" Henry growled, above them all on his horse, waving his arm and pointing up the slope toward Vroom's men beset by a third deadly charge that all but made the solitary company disappear in a maddening swirl of smoke and dust and racing ponies. Behind the captain rode his orderly atop a skittish, side-stepping mount, frightened at the clamor and gunfire.

"Move out, goddamn ye!" a raspy voice shouted among Henry's men.

An equally angry voice bellowed in reply, "Awright, Sergeant. I'm moving fast I can!"

Up and down the throbbing line of blue hurrying toward the crest, voices rang out.

"Damn right, boys—I'd rather die on that hillside yonder than down in that goddamn ravine with Royall!"

"Royall's had us fighting since breakfast, goddammit!"

"There's never gonna be no let-up—"

"You'll fight till the job's done or I'll have you drummed, bucked, and gagged when we get back to Fetterman!"

"Said I was hurrying, Sarge!"

Humping it up the hill, Donegan was nothing short of amazed that any of Vroom's men were left standing when the warriors withdrew after their third charge on his detached company. Three times they had held against the red horsemen, dragging all but one of their eight dead and wounded with them as their little circle shrank smaller and smaller still.

Three hundred yards for Donegan, and the rest yet to go.

And the warriors began to wheel, spotting Henry's relief detail coming.

Then two hundred yards remained of that open slope.

Wheeling about, screeching, those hundreds of copper-skinned horsemen were suddenly intent on the soldiers coming to the relief of that tiny, ragged circle of defenders gathered around Vroom, who stood at their center, bellowing his orders, slamming cartridges into the cylinder of his service pistol.

Only a hundred yards remained between Guy Henry's company and Vroom's butchered rear guard.

The maddened hordes came boiling down the slope, now intent on those who had come in hopes of rescuing their fellow soldiers. They tore down on Henry's men, racing their mounts along both sides of D Company's column. Into the ranks of blue, the warriors fired their guns and hurled iron-tipped arrows, some of the horsemen reaching out as they whisked past to swing clubs and tomahawks through the dust and maddening noise with a deadly hiss.

"We gonna make it?" some man shrieked up ahead of the Irishman.

"It's only a matter of cartridges," Donegan bellowed into the clamor and deafening noise as he levered the Henry repeater. "A fight ain't never done while you got cartridges."

Swiping the beads of sweat from his eyes with a bare forearm, Seamus fought to see, the sweat stinging, blurring his vision as much as the clouds of dust.

Bullets were whining overhead from all directions now, all but out of the east, where the infantry hesitated to lay in some fire. Up there to the northeast, however, the Crow and some Shoshone were inching along the ridgetop, advancing west slowly, aiming and firing, then crawling forward a little more as they tried to take some of the heat from Royall's retreat.

From what Donegan could see behind him, the colonel had evidently ordered the rest of his men to mount up rather than follow the led horses any longer. The men of Andrews's I and Lieutenant Reynolds's F Company were mixing among the horses, mounting on their own without order in all the confusion. A few were already galloping southeast down the narrowing Kollmar toward the creekbottom. It was turning into a rout. If not a massacre.

All around Seamus the air filled with the snarl of angry, scared men, the whine of bullets careening off the rocks, smacking into the ground, or slapping horseflesh. How the cavalry's animals did cry out, almost human, even infantlike, as they went down in a tumbling heap along the side of the Kollmar.

The eerie whistles, the keening of the war songs, grew louder and louder, like banshees tearing, tumbling, spilling out of the dark, bloody maw of hell itself into the land of the living.

Then before Seamus knew it, he was among those first gallant rescuers to reach the top of the crest with Guy V. Henry on that dun mare of his.

They had broken through to join what was left of Vroom's L Troop.

And found themselves surrounded by the minions of hell.

With nowhere left to run.

Chapter 35

Moon of Fat Horses

My heart is on the mountaintop.
My heart rides the sky.
My spirit sings with the eagles.
My spirit soars on the winds.
This is the day the ghosts of our grandfathers
Will arise.

Again and again Wooden Leg sang his personal medicine song as he raced round and round the small circle of soldiers shrinking ever smaller.

There were so many of the warriors now, their ponies snorting and heaving, lungs pounding against rib cages, all around him in the ever-tightening ring they rode on the fringe of that soldier circle. The noise was deafening: the incessant thunder of more than a thousand hooves; the crackle of gunfire from the Indian repeaters; the deep boom of the soldier carbines; the haunting, deadly, high-pitched wail of the eagle wing-bone whistles; the heart-thumping of the drums; the growl of voices both white and red; the cries of the wounded; and the deafening, noisy silence of the dead.

Beside him rode Limpy, a warrior six winters older than Wooden Leg. At birth the Shahiyena had suffered a deformity that made one leg longer than the other. While he struggled to run, was clumsy even in walking, Limpy was without equal once he mounted a pony. To some he was even more than equal with other young warriors. He was one born to be a horseman.

As soon as the small group of soldiers marched toward the top of the hill, Wooden Leg had joined White Shield, Goose Feather, and Limpy to be among the first charging in pursuit. The first time they and the Lakota charged, the soldiers had been spread out. Their soldier chief shouted his orders and the white men turned, pointed their rifles, and fired at the approaching horsemen. Most of the Lakota turned aside, dropping behind their ponies. Some, however, joined the Shahiyena in continuing to ride daringly near. As little as one arrow flight.

This was as close to calling death to seek out his heart as Wooden Leg had ever been. One arrow flight to the muzzles of the soldier guns. But now the white men were gathering. Drawing ever nearer to their soldier chief.

Then, with a sudden yell of courage, the Lakota surged forward to make a second massed charge with the Shahiyena. Tighter and tighter the circle of soldiers shrank. Yet still they held, and the Lakota broke again for the rocks and hillocks, where they would find safety while they regrouped.

As they withdrew, Wooden Leg saw the lone soldier left in the open by the others. White Shield had already seen him.

With blood oozing from his head, the white man was crawling about in a confused circle of his own, groping on hands and knees, blinded by the crimson shining on his brow.

White Shield and Goose Feather kicked their ponies into a gallop, daring the other soldiers to fire as they rushed down on the one left behind by the rest. Swinging his stone club at the end of his arm in passing over the lone soldier, White Shield made the kill as bullets whined around them.

It was so brave an act that the Lakota and other Shahiyena raised a mighty voice and rushed forward once more, making their third charge. Immediately wheeling about, White Shield brought his pony back to the white man sprawled on the ground, his legs still quivering slightly as the warrior dropped to the grass and pulled his knife.

With a swift stroke he slashed the enemy's throat, then took the scalp, which he stuffed under his belt while the rest renewed their pressure on the shrinking circle of white men.

"White Shield!" Wooden Leg hollered out as he raced toward the scene. He had been watching the larger band of soldiers down the hill. "The others—they are coming now!"

Goose Feather joined in giving warning. "Hurry, White Shield!"

Instead of instantly fleeing, White Shield calmly unbuckled the soldier's gunbelt and wrapped it around his own waist.

"Where is his gun?" White Shield asked angrily as Wooden Leg came sprinting up. He stuffed his hand down the empty holster.

"Mount your pony and ride—forget the white man's gun, or it will cost you your life!" Wooden Leg pointed down the slope. "The others are coming like a bad wind!"

As he swung atop his pony, White Shield replied, "It's all right: I have his gunbelt, and there are many bullets in it for my guns."

"You will find another soon!" Goose Feather was with them, appearing out of the dust of the swirling wheel that encircled the white men.

"See the others!" a nearby voice yelled. "I want their blood too!"

Once more their attack on the small circle was diffused. Three times they had charged on the soldiers, and three times the white men had turned them back. And now the others were coming. It made Wooden Leg's heart shrink to see them all turning to flee—

"Hoka hey! It is a good day to die!"

In astonishment Wooden Leg wheeled, recognizing the voice, yet amazed to hear the war chief speak in the Shahiyena tongue.

Crazy Horse called out again to the Lakota in their

language, to the Shahiyena in theirs. "Hold on, my friends! Do not forget your children! Be strong in our fight! Remember the helpless ones at home!"

"Hopo!" cried the one Wooden Leg knew as He Dog. He had remained at the side of Crazy Horse all morning long.

More and more of the Lakota turned about now as other war chiefs followed the greatest of them all, he who wore nothing more ornamental than the small buffalo calfskin cape about his shoulders. It billowed and snapped on the breeze as Crazy Horse led them toward the soldiers coming to rescue those trapped atop the crest of the hill.

"Remember the helpless ones in our village!"

"And kill the white men!"

"It is a good day to die!"

And another, angrier voice—"It is a good day for the white man to die!"

Back they swirled toward the rescuers coming in a massed column. Down both sides of the soldier lines the horsemen raced, swinging clubs and axes if they dared ride close enough. Others held back, arcing arrows into the summer blue of the sky so that they dropped down on the backs of the soldiers, as they had fired arrows down on the backs of the horses milling down in the head of the ravine.

It did not take an old warrior to see the fear in the eyes of those soldiers as they ran toward the top of the hill to save the lives of the others. They were all fighting for their lives now, these white men come to the Rosebud. And the red men who made this hunting ground their home.

And the fear from the bodies of those soldiers made a rank smell in Wooden Leg's nostrils.

Feathered Sun's pony went down in a tumble, but as Wooden Leg looked behind him, the young warrior rolled onto his feet and continued in the maddening race at the fringes of the soldier columns hurrying toward the top of the slope, this time on foot. More of the ponies went down in heaps, but on and on the warriors pursued their quarry.

As Wooden Leg circled the head of the ravine ahead of the soldiers, he saw Limpy go down in a tangle of legs and dust ahead of him, his pony dead. Dazed, the crippled warrior scrambled unevenly to his feet, shaking his head, blinking and swiping his eyes clear of dust—looking for rescue as some of the soldiers began to concentrate their fire on the one they had unhorsed.

Out of the red-and-yellow haze stained with the murky gray of gunsmoke dashed Young Two Moon, son of the Shahiyena chief. Lying low along his pony's neck, he pointed the animal's nose for the crippled warrior standing helpless in the open as if he were a waiting-to-die, staked to the ground.

Reaching Limpy, Young Two Moon held out an arm. They clasped, but as Limpy tried to leap onto the rear flanks of the pony, he found he could not because of his deformity.

It was too great a leap.

Wooden Leg raced in, yelling and pointing. "The rocks, Limpy! Go to the rocks!"

As quickly as he could hobble toward one of the low sandstone formations, Limpy scrambled atop the boulders and awaited his rescuer. This time Young Two Moon ran back toward the soldiers who marched along on foot. And this time Limpy was able to throw himself onto the back of his friend's horse.

Together with Goose Feather, White Shield, and Wooden Leg, Young Two Moon hurried back toward the crest with Limpy rescued.

From the corner of his eye, Wooden Leg spotted the lone soldier on his horse courageously at the center of the white men who were reaching the top of the hill. Something about him caught and held the young warrior's attention, almost mystically—so that as he watched, Wooden Leg saw blood splatter from the soldier chief's lower face, saw the white man swoon and sway from side to side with his terrible wound.

In the next instant Wooden Leg was gone into the dust. Swallowed in the tumult.

Thinking how great a prize it would be to take that soldier chief's shirt with all its pretty yellow markings and braid.

• • •

Across the wide coulee Plenty Coups watched the soldier chief stiffen as he began to fall, catching himself atop his horse, and straighten, his back gone rigid, both hands fumbling at the front of his army saddle for something to cling to. Slowly, slowly weaving backward a bit, the soldier chief rocked forward as blood gushed from his mouth.

He was trying to speak, his jaw moving up and down. But in this noise, any sound the soldier chief might have made was lost, swallowed by the battle raging across the coulee.

This one, he is a brave man, Plenty Coups thought as he aimed at another of the hundreds swarming down on all sides of the soldiers surrounded on the far slope of the coulee. A strong spirit he has: to stay on his horse when he is losing so much blood. His life pouring away.

As soon as the soldier chief was hit and began to swoon, another soldier nearby rushed to his side, only to be shot as well. But as the second white man lay unmoving on the ground, there began a general panic. At the same moment, the Sioux renewed their pressure on three sides around the trapped soldiers. The white men began falling back, moving east in a blind herd toward what horses were still held in the bottom of the coulee where the holders fought to maintain control over the maddened, frightened beasts rearing and kicking, heads high and nostrils flaring, dragging their handlers through the grass and brush.

In the pit of his belly Plenty Coups knew if those Lakota were not stopped now, they could roll right through the soldiers scrambling across the far side of the coulee, through the soldier horses and straight on to the creek bottom below. Uncontested, the enemy would have Lone Star and his soldiers surrounded along the ridgetop.

Slowly, like the flow of autumn water in the drying streambeds, the soldier chief slipped from his horse, one arm hanging a final heartbeat to his saddle as he struck the ground. When his horse bolted, the officer rolled onto his back and lay still, sprawled in the dust and trampled grass, all but alone.

Ahead to his right Plenty Coups saw little Humpy leading a handful of the Crow up from their positions, sprinting down the side of the coulee, into the bottom where they joined some of the Snakes, maybe more than two-times-ten, all of them rushing toward the fallen pair. Beyond the soldiers on the far slope the enemy massed in great black streams fingering toward the fallen men as well, each one of the Lakota wanting to be the first to count coup: to touch the body, take the gunbelt, or claim the dusty, braided shirt of that brave soldier chief.

In that moment Plenty Coups's heart went out to the brave little warrior called Humpy, so-named because of the curved spine and the misshapen lump on his shoulder. Although he was smaller than all the rest who followed, the little warrior's heart was as big as any man's this day.

For Humpy was the one out front of all the rest—sprinting to save the life of the fallen soldier chief.

"Face them, men! Goddammit—face them!"

At the commanding sound of the voice, Donegan whirled, finding one of the older sergeants, John Henry Shingle of Company I, in among troops, moving back and forth along his piece of that 325-yard front where less than a hundred soldiers struggled against more than seven hundred brown-skinned foes.

"Thought you was back there in charge of the horses, Shingle!" Donegan growled as he shoved some of his last cartridges down the receiver and repositioned the loading tube beneath the muzzle.

"I was, Irishman," Shingle replied with a grim smile, the dust on his face cut with rivulets of sweat.

"But an old soldier like you just can't stay away from the fighting, eh?"

He nodded, pulling the Springfield from his cheek after firing into the onrushing mass. "Give that livery job to a private, don't you know! And come here to the top of the hill to join in the dance. I didn't sign on back to '63 to take care of the goddamned horses. I joined to fight!"

"Good man, Shingle!" Seamus roared as he knelt and peered along the blued barrel of the Henry, the worn cheekpiece snugged below his cheekbone.

"Don't give up, men!" Shingle repeated as the line around them wavered and some of those nearby began to fall back a yard, then another. "Stand and look 'em in the eye!"

"Give 'em hell!" bawled another old soldier, nearly alone and standing his ground while others retreated first a foot, then gave more and more along that long skirmish line.

Off to the right side of Guy V. Henry's front the warriors pressed, trying to put their strength here, then there, to break through one flank or another while Vroom and the other officers with the gallant Henry tried desperately to hold their skirmish line together.

"Great God, men! Don't go back on the old Third now!" one of those officers hollered.

It sounded like Henry himself. Seemed he was everywhere in the dust and gunsmoke, still mounted, refusing to get down off that dun mare of his in the midst of all that gunfire. Closer and closer the warriors pressed them, daring to approach the lines like never before all morning. The captain rallied them for the moment. The soldiers no longer inched backward. Some came back to drop to their knees beside the old files, reloading and firing into the swirling dust and blurred mass of horsemen.

"That's it, boys! Stand firm!" Donegan himself shouted now.

"We're gonna be overrun!" someone shrieked nearby, his voice drenched in panic.

"Stand and give it back to them," Donegan bellowed, "or you will be overrun!"

The fight near the southernmost end of the ridge under Guy Henry's direct command grew fierce, desperate. Again and again Seamus swore but these stalwart men had to be blackening the hair on the muzzles of those ponies the warriors dared ride so close to the Springfields, rattling and booming with the coming of each new wave.

One warrior, then another, and finally a third fell less than fifty yards from Donegan, that last horseman tumbling over and over, then sliding another ten yards closer to the blue line before his body skidded to a rest on the dusty grass. Of a sudden it was yanked into motion, tumbling over at the end of a long rawhide tether lashed about the pony's neck and secured to the warrior's waist. The body spun wildly, over and over again, spewing up a cascade as the frightened war pony dragged its inert master away from the fight, away from the white man's thundering guns.

Behind them arose the sharp yips and war cries. Wheeling instinctively, Seamus knew they were being descended upon by more Sioux and Cheyenne who had made it to the ravine and had them surrounded. What he saw through the murk and haze was instead some of those dirty red arm bands Quartermaster Furey had given out to the allies two days before. The Crow and some Shoshone were coming now, falling on the thick cordon of horsemen who had Guy Henry's men all but swallowed. All but doomed.

His heart hammering in his ears, Seamus understood these soldiers needed to know the allies were coming—if for no other reason than Donegan knew that more than one of these frightened cavalrymen would shoot without thinking at anything that remotely looked like an Indian. The Crow and Shoshone were coming—daring to throw themselves into the fray, daring to take the chance of being mistaken for the enemy.

"Colonel Henry!" Donegan shouted as he rose to a half crouch, twisting about to peer through the dust and gunsmoke gloom, locating the mounted officer.

In turning to face the Irishman at that very moment, the captain might well have saved his life.

As Seamus watched, Henry's face was driven violently to the right as an enemy bullet smashed below his left eye, coursing through the hard upper palate below the nose before it blew flesh and bone and blood out below the right eye.

"Mither of God!" Donegan gasped as he lurched forward, just like the soldier was doing on the far side of Henry.

Like a child's toy on a string, the trooper was yanked off his feet, hurled backward. He lay still near the hooves of Henry's frightened mount as it sidled first this way, then sidestepped the other, getting no firm commands from its rider as the enemy pressed in—an enemy it could surely see and smell and hear as the warriors saw those two soldiers hit. Donegan knew the Sioux had to sense victory more at this moment than they had all morning. That uncanny fighting man's sixth sense told them when an enemy's leader had fallen.

In horror he rushed for the officer, seeing Henry's face become an ashen mask above the ghastly wound, blood shiny, soaking, darkening, blotting out everything below the stark pasty gray as the captain slowly keeled to the side in the vertigo of wound sickness, finally tumbling from the saddle and for but a moment clutching the front of his McClellan with one hand.

Donegan's legs pumped, his big boots clomping across the trampled, dusty grass as he muttered, "A damned good horse sojur, this one. This Henry."

A cavalry officer stayed with his mount. No matter what . . . until the captain's horse bolted, tearing itself from Henry's futile death-grip. In the dust kicked up by the animal's hooves, the captain collapsed to the ground, rolled onto his back, head lolling. And lay still.

Knowing the officer had to be dead, as dead as the soldier who had been shot while going to Henry's aid, Donegan lunged across the slope of the ravine, watching a tangled string of warriors racing for the bodies from the opposite direction. He leveled his repeater, not sure how many rounds he had left, but certain only of making each one count if he needed.

Simply that—because from the looks of things, the Indians were going to reach the bodies before him.

Dropping to one knee as he brought the Henry to his cheek, Seamus felt with his right thumb to be sure the hammer was cocked and sighted down the blued barrel on the chest of the first Indian racing for the fallen captain. His long black hair streamed out behind him, the breechclout that reached his knees like a swirl of dirty spring runoff at his legs. Donegan began to squeeze the trigger . . . and in that instant he saw the red arm band. A dusty, obscure strip of red cloth the white men had issued the allies at Goose Creek.

His lungs still burning from the run through the dusty haze, his heart hammering with a fierce pride, Seamus knew as all old plainsmen understood—these Shoshone scouts were no different from the Sioux or Cheyenne—warriors always exhibited their greatest courage and most reckless daring in rescuing the bodies of their own dead and wounded.

Bolting again to his feet at a dead run, Seamus reached the captain a heartbeat after that first Shoshone, where without a word exchanged between them, they both whirled about to stand over the two bodies, ready to meet the oncoming charge.

Four hundred yards was all they had left to go, less than a quarter of a mile to reach the end of Crook's line, where the infantry with their long rifles were coming on the run behind the allies to stem the red tide. Yet Donegan knew those foot soldiers could do nothing. Not really.

For to fire at Sioux and Cheyenne streaming toward Donegan and the lone Shoshone would mean firing at the backs of Henry's men. Rescue waited four hundred yards across that wide ravine. It might as well have been a hundred miles.

The infantry couldn't help now. Rescue was no more, no less, than these dismounted horse soldiers standing firm and saving their own hash on this bloody hillside.

Together they stood, back to back, the Shoshone and the Irishman, prepared to meet the enemy's rush, their ears battered by blood oaths and grunts of pain as the Sioux and Cheyenne lunged forward toward the two who stood over the bodies. Running with a fury into the fire, the rest of the allies poured into their enemies across the narrowing distance along the slope.

First came three of the Lakota, who made it through the dusty haze to reach the bodies before they fell to the bullets that could not miss. Then the rush of a handful as the Irishman and Shoshone levered cartridges through their overheated weapons again and again and again. And finally more than ten appeared like apparitions out of the dust, vaulting over the bodies of their fallen to rush the lonely pair.

Weapons empty now—both defenders swung their rifles savagely. Like two long and slender scythes reaping those stalks of wheat rushing before the giant blades.

Those rifles whistled and sang as they cut through the dust and gunsmoke, chopping viciously through the curses and war songs and shrieks of pain and grunts of terror as bones were broken and skulls cracked and bullets struck bare flesh and sinew.

And brave men went down in blood, thinking of loved ones back home.

As brave men always will.

Chapter 36

17 June 1876

He could almost feel their breath, smell their breakfast.

Seamus was closer at this moment to the screeching, painted, dust-furred faces than he had been in years.

Close enough that when he swung the Henry rifle, he gripped with two hands at the muzzle.

Face to face as he snagged a warrior by the throat and held on for his life, sensing, maybe even hearing, the windpipe snap and crunch beneath his grip as the enemy went bug-eyed before him, collapsing, limp and gasping at his feet, rolling away in the sheer agony that accompanied his last breath.

Swinging, lunging, slashing at them with the broken, splintered stock of the rifle.

The terror seemed to last longer than anything he could remember. Though it was over in a matter of minutes.

The Sioux and Cheyenne were gradually falling back, pulling away a few yards at a time—threatening a new charge. Then scurrying off in a more wholesale retreat as other sounds grew behind him.

Over his shoulder Seamus caught glimpses of the blue line returning from the sides of the ravine, more of Royall's battalion struggling back out of the bowels of the Kollmar. Henry's men rallied—coming back to reclaim the ground so gallantly held by less than two dozen of the Indian allies, having returned to help these horse soldiers redeem the honor of the Third Cavalry, willing to throw their bodies into the breech, to effect the rescue of the soldier chief, so that his body would not fall into the hands of the enemy.

The Crow and Shoshone, Donegan thought. Such brave, brave men . . .

Seamus whirled again to take a look, a good look now, at the tall Shoshone near him, the one who had been swinging the Springfield carbine by its muzzle at Donegan's back. In the warrior's eyes at that moment was a flicker of something like a smile, though it never did crease the paint and furred dust and grimly contorted features on that copper-skinned face.

Something that shouted of victory. Bellowed deafeningly of a shared victory.

And Donegan realized they had indeed shared something men of different races rarely share: a common enemy and a common fight, the same hand-to-hand bone-and-muscle struggle for their own lives and the bodies of the fallen two still lying at their feet. He and the Shoshone had shared that singular and unspoken camaraderie experienced by few in the heat of pitched battle. Theirs, a bonding of strong, unwavering, and unbroken spirits.

In a blur of brown and blue, saffron light and red dust, two horses were there, wide-eyed and prancing with fright as the Sioux continued to retreat up the ridge. Before he realized it, three cavalrymen were with him and the Shoshone, picking up the wounded orderly and their dying captain. Hauling the bodies across the McClellan saddles, the soldiers turned and sprinted away, yanking the horses behind them, retreating down the slope toward the bottom of the Kollmar.

Seamus and the Indian scout found themselves alone again. And together began to make their retreat.

From his pockets Seamus desperately dug out a handful of the brass .44-caliber cartridges as he backed up, his eyes scanning the surging, throbbing movements of the enemy above him at the head of the ridge. When Seamus went to twist the receiver tube, he found it would not budge. Again and again he tried turning it, growing a bit more frantic with each attempt, struggling to open the muzzle's under-barrel receiver.

Only then did he fully realize what he had done to the stock. From the wrist on back, the cheekpiece hung by but a few stout splinters of pale wood, flecked with drying blood. For the moment he couldn't be sure it wasn't his.

And in swinging the empty repeater like a club, he had damaged its reloading tube. Nearly a decade was gone since purchasing a pair of these guns with old Sam Marr from that sutler at Fort Laramie before they had pushed north along the Bozeman Road to reach the gold diggings of Montana. A decade gone this very summer since he had first put the Henry repeater to a severe test at the Crazy Woman CROSSING.* Ten long years—and Seamus had yet to reunite with Sam Marr.

Then for a heartbeat he stopped, taking his eyes off the Sioux and Cheyenne to lever open the action and stare into the breech. One cartridge remained. One only, as he set off again, catching up with the Shoshone scout who was yelling something at him, waving him on and pointing up the hill. As Seamus turned, he saw a half dozen or more of the Shoshone sprinting on angle in his direction, chased by a renewed assault from the Sioux. What seemed to anger the enemy most was that two of the allies shook and waved long-haired and bloody scalps behind them to taunt at the Sioux, flinging blood and gore in their pagan triumph merely to anger ancient foes, boasting of conquest in the face of enemies of old. Two fresh scalps—trophies taken from two of the dead who had fallen near Henry's body, close enough to the edge of the ravine in that dirty hand-to-hand struggle.

Without a weapon that could fire more than one shot —the one bullet a plainsman always saved for himself—Donegan wheeled and set off on a dead run as the Sioux raised an even louder and bloodier cry. He had to find a rifle, a carbine, something—for the enemy was coming, countercharging again as they saw the survivors of Royall's

---

* THE PLAINSMEN Series, vol. 1, *Sioux Dawn*

battalion bolting, fleeing for their lives into the ravine now that the bodies were rescued.

Already reduced to little more than a hundred, perhaps a hundred twenty at the most—what with the absence of the horse-holders in the ravine and accounting for those who had already fled, in addition to the dead and wounded lost during the opening salvos of that frantic retreat from that third position—those who remained in Royall's command turned to begin their wild break to rejoin Crook's infantry the moment they saw the Sioux temporarily driven back by the allies' furious countercharge. In confusion and disorder the lost battalion spilled down the slope of the ravine toward the frightened horses, a few of which already lay dead across the slope, more milling about wounded and soon to die.

Now fully in possession of the ridge recently vacated by the soldiers, the Sioux and Cheyenne proceeded to rake the coulee below them with a concentrated if not inaccurate rifle fire. If nothing else, it served to wound and frighten the horses even worse, to scare the retreating cavalry all the more.

Some six hundred yards across the ravine and northeast up the ridge, the infantry of Burt and Burrowes were brought to their feet and set in motion again, this time working south on the double in a foragers' charge to relieve what had all the appearances of a massacre in the making. The two captains suddenly called a halt, ordering their men to kneel and begin pouring fire at will into the enemy, just about the time the first of Royall's troops reached their frightened horses.

Not far down the near side of the coulee stood many of the Crow and Shoshone scouts, firing over the heads of the retreating soldiers running pell-mell toward the allies, those arms with the red arm bands waving the troopers on as the white men stumbled and spilled across the rocky, uneven ground, picking themselves up out of the dust and grass, continuing to careen down the slope toward the long line of allies who steadfastly held their line, staunchly holding back the great onrushing tide of Sioux and Cheyenne.

F Company, led by Lieutenant Bainbridge Reynolds and the last troop down off the slope, bore the brunt of the renewed attack on the rear guard of this, Royall's last retreat.

In a matter of seconds after the rout began, enemy horsemen had a platoon of troopers under Sergeant David Marshall separated from the rest and fully encircled, sweeping in with clubs and knives, lances and tomahawks. Yet the soldiers returned blow for blow, swinging their trapdoor Springfields like stout hickory axe-handles. Wounded in the face, Marshall crumpled, going down as his men fell back and ever back from the body, knowing they were next.

Yet one returned.

Private Phineas Towne whirled about and lunged back into the melee and the dust. Kneeling to snag hold of his sergeant's gunbelt, he hefted Marshall over his shoulder and started back downhill. Five yards, ten, then twenty—when Towne must have sensed the burning across his belly as he was shot by a hostile marksman. Collapsing in a heap, he spilled his sergeant.

Farrier Richard O'Grady was there in but a moment, as well as another second rescuer from Reynolds's troop. As O'Grady began to drag Marshall's body away, Towne struggled to rise in the arms of Henry Kett, his comrade from F Company.

Through that line of Crow and Shoshone, who continued to steadily fire their weapons, holding their ancient enemies at bay, the soldiers plunged toward what remained of their horses. And when Seamus saw that the last of Royall's men were finally moving southeast down the Kollmar, he found himself amid the allies who had staunchly waited out the frantic retreat. Only when the last soldiers were on their way, hooves and boot heels thundering down the ravine, did the scouts turn to take up the tail of Royall's fleeing troopers, wheeling and halting every now and then to fight a rear-guard action.

Across three hundred more yards the last of those beleaguered, wounded, weary cavalrymen and their brown-skinned allies fought their way through the red gauntlet. Sioux and Cheyenne lined the slopes of the ravine, raining bullets and arrows down on the retreating horsemen. Then as quickly as they could cut and slash their way free from the ragged end of the enemy's gauntlet, the horse soldiers were reining sharply to the left in an uneven procession, climbing back to the northeast in their maddening flight, ascending the slope that took them toward the waiting infantry.

Near the southwestern end of Crook's ridge, William B. Royall halted as the rest of his battalion raced on past, Adjutant Lemly at his side. There the colonel waited until the last of his men had broken out of the ravine. Not until then did Royall again put spurs to his mount, bringing up the tail of that retreat, riding among the allies covering their escape. This valiant commander of cavalry, cut off and all but abandoned that morning, was now the last to leave that bloodiest ground across the whole of what was Crook's Rosebud battlefield.

It was just after one P.M., Chicago time, as Royall led what was left of his whittled battalion past the mule brigade of Burt and Burrowes, proceeding on east where the horse soldiers dismounted and took up their position just west of the gap, this time on the far-right flank of George Crook's ridge.

For more than five hours already, on that day of Indian Wars infamy, those men from the Third Cavalry had seen their fiercest fighting since the bloody days of the Civil War.

"If you don't hump it on in here, you'll likely find yourself wearing some Injun lead in some painful part where you like to sit!" Richard Closter hollered at the Irishman, waving Donegan on.

Seamus ran the last fifty yards across the open ground to reach the stacks of sandstone rocks and deadfall, some of which nature had piled up, others erected by Tom Moore's packers and those sixty-five Montana miners hunkered down on the north slope of the ridge, almost due east of the conical hill where the brown-skinned horsemen were beginning to congregate and concentrate their fire on the white civilians now that Royall's battalion had slipped out of their trap.

Sliding in among these rocks that formed a spur nearly a hundred yards in length and jutting from the north side of the bluff, Donegan sighed with relief. Here some four hundred yards from Crook's hill, the Irishman hurriedly made a place for himself beside the old white-haired packer and lay panting on his back.

"You was with that bunch just got out?" Tom Moore asked, flicking a nod toward Royall's battalion passing in a ragged stream below them, moving east.

"Yes."

Closter clucked his tongue. "My, my. You don't value your hide much—do you, boy?"

"Things getting hot here now for us too," Moore declared as the racket of Sioux rifles grew in volume, more and more lead slapping against the rocks, singing in ricochet, smacking the nearby ground and hissing overhead as each moment went by.

"Better get to using that Henry of your'n," Closter growled as he rolled back onto his belly behind his pile of sandstone and gazed across the open ground between the packers' rocks and the conical hill, where the warriors were beginning to work their way toward the white men.

"Can't."

"Why the hell can't you?" Moore demanded. "Out of ammunition?" He turned away a moment, not seeming to wait for an answer to peer over some of the nearby men who made their living working for the mule-train master as the Sioux appeared to gather for a renewed charge. "Stands to reason, I suppose—as much shooting as you boys did over there. But I'll bet someone here has some cartridges oughtta fit."

"Not out of cartridges, Tom," Seamus explained, holding up the busted rifle.

Moore turned back to look at the Irishman's repeater. "Damn, will you look at what you done to your gun."

"He can damn well see himself, Tom!" Closter snorted.

Moaning, Seamus said, "Even with the busted wrist, I could still use her to shoot—but I can't reload the son of a bitch."

"Got a breech jam?" Closter asked.

"Loading tube."

Moore wagged his head. "A stock is one thing, wrap it

up stronger than new with wet rawhide. But that loading tube ain't something a man can fix in the field, Seamus."

Donegan shrugged. "Least I got a couple of pistols to work with, if them Injins ride in here close enough."

"They will now that they don't have you boys to play with over yonder," Closter warned. "Don't doubt that."

"That's right," Moore agreed. "Now that they haven't got Royall to cut up, they'll go to work on us right here, 'cause we're the closest to 'em."

Closter spat a stream of tobacco juice in a pretty arc over the rocks and said, "Besides, we been the ones giving 'em the most hell today anyway."

"That's a fact," Moore replied. "Ain't a man here don't have him a good piece. Most of these fellas here are pretty good with their guns too."

"Say, now, Seamus—I got me a extra rifle you could use. If you're of a mind to," Closter said.

"With you?"

"Not far. Over yonder, with the mules. I'll fetch it up for you."

"I'll go for you, Uncle Dick," Donegan volunteered. "No sense in you—"

The aging packer started to rise, putting a hand firmly on the Irishman's shoulder to hold Donegan down. "You wouldn't know what the hell to look for anyway, you young jack-assed idjit."

"You tell me what it is, I'll find it among your baggage and truck."

"Ever seen my Sharps?"

"Can't say I have."

"Ever seen one at all?"

Donegan nodded. "Several of 'em. Down to the buffalo country south of Dodge, down to Adobe Walls."

"Then you know one when you see it," Closter said, settling back down beside the Irishman.

Moore said, "I heard Sharps was the guns what held off Quanah Parker's Comanche couple years back at the Walls."

"Them, and this Henry of mine."

"That gun of yours is a busted flush now," Closter said. "But you use mine, you care to. Even let you fetch it so I can just stay right here and jaw with Tom and the rest while we wait for Crazy Horse to decide what fancy notion he's gonna pull on us next."

"What about the Sharps? So I know it."

Closter grinned in that tobacco-stained white beard of his and replied, "Oh, you'll know it. A fifty-ninety, she be."

"I saw some fifty-seventies down to Texas."

"What they call the big fifties. Heard 'em called the 'Poison Slingers' too. But like a lot of fellas, I load my own cartridges," Closter explained. "So I've come to like a little smaller bullet—still fifty caliber, mind you—but I stuff a full hunnert and ten grains of powder behind it just so's I can push that lead out there faster."

"Sweet Mither of God—that's gotta be a long chunk of brass to be filling with black powder," Donegan replied. "Likely it makes a hell of a buffalo load, I'll bet."

"Likely? Why, it'll *likely* bring down her share of drabbed redskins too, you idjit Irishman!" Closter growled. But the old packer grinned big as he said, "She does pack one hell of a punch. Ain't many like her. That's a big load to punch through a Sharps, or any gun. Look to my pannier, you'll find two belts of ammunition rolled up. A hunnert rounds. Best bring 'em both with you—"

" 'Cause it looks like Crazy Horse has opened the ball again!" Tom Moore interrupted.

Warriors furiously drove their little ponies across the open ground, firing and chanting as they charged the civilians ensconced behind their ramparts. Seamus began crabbing away toward the nearby mules, staying as low as possible, when the old packer hollered out above the growing clamor of gunfire and cursing mule-skinners.

"Don't make me no never mind who opens the godblame-ed ball, Tom," Closter growled, "long as I get to call the last dance!"

"A man would be hard pressed to convince me that I haven't this day met the entire Sioux nation, Major!" George Crook growled, watching the fray from his headquarters near the southern end of the top of the ridge.

Captain Andrew Burt had no reason to disagree as he peered at the unkempt general beneath the battered and dusty black hat. The confident, even at times mischievous, look was gone from George Crook's eye. No little wonder. All any man had to do was look across more than three miles of battlefield for it all to sink in.

Looking at the turnip watch he dragged out of his pocket, Burt saw it was past one-thirty P.M. They had been fighting now for more than five hours, without much of a lull on any part of the battlefield. To put this many warriors into the fight, to have them here and there and just about everywhere all at the same time—why, a man would have to be crazy not to think the exact same thing General Crook had decided.

They must surely have stumbled onto the fighting might of the entire Sioux nation.

A regular hornets' nest of hellish, buzzing fury they had unleashed. The slopes were spotted with the carcasses of their dead and dying horses lying here and there among some of the enemy's war ponies. Other animals, wounded and in pain, wandered aimlessly along the hillsides. Ammunition had to be running low on all fronts—what with the long hours and fevered intensity of this battle while these men had been fighting for their very lives. The wounded, and those of their dead who had been dragged away to prevent capture, were stacking up in the field hospital a few yards away from where Crook and Burt now stood. Hartsuff, Patszki, and Stevens had their hands full with those in agony who were forced to lie on the ground beneath the blazing one-eyed summer sun now ascended to its most ferocious height. At the same time, the Crow and Shoshone had erected small brush and blanket shelters over their own casualties, keeping out the sun and leaving one of their own to fan the torment of biting green-backed horseflies from the crusting wounds.

It was enough to give pause to that infantry captain, already himself a veteran of some ten years on the frontier. Enough to make Burt reconsider the confusing and paradoxical savagery of these copper-skinned people. Here on one hand he was witness to a certain civility, with a good measure of nobility, both of which dictated these stone-age people minister to their own with greater care than the soldiers could to their own comrades.

Yet—Burt mused—such a thing was really nothing more than a skill born of a culture where daily struggles of life and death were the rule, and not the exception. Besides, he had seen first-hand just what savage, brutal, obscenely cruel torturers these people could become when given the opportunity of propitiating some ancient blood debt on a captured enemy.

Especially hard to take was the sight of that man Henry, captain with the Third Cavalry. Nobody who got a look at the horse soldier's bloody, battered face could walk away not believing that Henry had received a mortal wound.

Burt knew with just as much certainty that, had it not been for the allies as well as most of the infantry who held off the Sioux long enough for Royall's cavalry to regroup and retreat, George Crook might well have gone down in history as the leader of a Wyoming column that was massacred by Crazy Horse's minions from hell. As things stood this late in the fight, Anson Mills seemed to be the only commander on this field who had been able to move off the defensive and take any initiative.

The rest of them—Burt brooded angrily here atop Crook's hill—had been fighting hours and hours of a holding action, nothing more than survival. It was hard to look over at the general with the braided beard now and not think George Crook had made some tactical mistakes.

Hard not to believe that, down inside, Crook himself knew it.

Yet, throughout much of the waning morning and into the early afternoon, the general had openly complained about others—more content to point his accusatory finger at subordinates who he felt had robbed him of the victory that was easily within his grasp and should have been his.

"If Royall had brought his battalion when I first summoned him," Crook had said time and again during the heat of the colonel's bloody retreats from the west, "I would not have been forced to recall Mills from charging the village."

It made Andrew Burt almost feel sorry for George Crook. After the humiliating and public debacle that was Reynolds's fight on the Powder River only three months before to the day, this proud, taciturn man had now to swallow more pride and eat more crow. And do everything he could to keep as many of his troops alive as he possibly could.

No longer was this an expedition to defeat the wild, free warriors of the northern plains, an expedition to drive the wandering nomads back to their reservations.

Instead, Burt worried, this had all the appearance of becoming General George Crook's Waterloo.

If the Sioux stayed the fight as long as the British . . .

If Crook's soldiers ran out of ammunition . . .

If Mills had been cut off and destroyed somewhere beyond the far hills, somewhere down the Rosebud—then this George Crook might well go down in the annals of military history as another tragic and unfortunate Napoleon.

Chapter 37

17 June 1876

"*You're sure you want to take the long way, Colonel* Mills?" Frank Grouard asked.

The officer turned to face south, asking, "The way we came—"

"The long way."

Mills was growing short. "Then by all means—we'll go over the hills."

There was no magical way out of the canyon and back to the battlefield. Either they took the long haul back, the way they got here by following the Rosebud, or they hurried just like Crook wanted them to—on the double—right up and over the hills to pop up behind the hostiles. So unlike the night-long march to the Powder River last winter, this summer afternoon the half-breed had no magic for Crook's soldiers.

Instead, nothing but a hard climb, and one hell of a ride.

On the west bank of the creek, Mills quickly formed up his troops, then gave Frank the order to lead them up the piney slopes.

He shook his head, slowly coming out of the saddle. "It's better if your men lead their horses."

Whirling angrily, Anson Mills peered south down the

creek the way they had come from the battlefield, as if reconsidering. As he did, the warm breezes brought the renewed boom and echo of distant gunfire. Things must surely be growing hot for those troops left behind to occupy the warriors.

"You hear the straits Royall is in?" Azor Nickerson asked, pressing his case.

"I can hear! I can hear!" Mills snapped, turning on his heel to study the steep hills to the west.

"If nothing else—that should convince you why Crook's recalled your battalions, Colonel," Nickerson said, using Mills's brevet rank earned during the Civil War.

Mills glared at Crook's aide. "I never had any intention of disobeying the general's order."

"Then we should be turning about—"

"No," Mills interrupted Crook's aide. "There"—and he pointed up the rugged slopes. "We'll take the route suggested by Grouard. Dismount!"

"Good God, Colonel!"

Shoving past Nickerson, Mills began shouting his orders to the rest of his company commanders. "My company will lead out. We'll proceed in a column of twos where practicable, by led horses."

"Up there?" Noyes asked.

"If Crook needs us back on the double—by the saints, he'll have us back on the double . . . by the shortest route possible." Mills glanced at the half-breed, then back to Noyes. "I'm trusting Grouard to get us there."

Noyes saluted and replied, "Yes, sir, Colonel!"

In that next moment they were all bellowing orders to their companies. Those troopers who had not tightened cinches hurriedly did so as Mills gave the command to his own M Company, pointing up the shady slope strewn with deadfall and boulders.

"Move us out, Mr. Grouard," the captain said, turning immediately to fling his voice back along the long column of dusty twos. "Move out—rout order! Rout order!"

Without another word, the half-breed tugged on the reins and got his horse moving behind him. The Crow trackers filled in the gap immediately behind him as Mills's troops moved away from the creekbank, defiling almost due west toward the distant, steady sound of the guns.

Frank had learned that was exactly the sort of talk a man could hear if he hung around the army long: soldiers always rode to the sound of the guns. And if Mills hurried his soldiers the way it appeared the captain would, then two fortuitous things just might happen for Lone Star Crook: when these eight companies of horse soldiers came riding to the sound of the guns, they should be able to lift the siege Nickerson said the general was suffering back at the ridge; and, as well, getting out of this valley should save the lives of these eight companies by escaping the ambush Grouard was dead certain lay among the narrowing, shadowy twists of the Rosebud, not all that far ahead.

After crossing the gently sloping bottomland that took him through the narrowing bottleneck of easy ground, Frank finally led his reluctant horse up the beginning of that craggy, uneven slope, pocked with all sorts of loose rock that tumbled backward so that those coming behind had to scramble out of the way. Back and forth he clawed his way up, picking the best path for those who followed, forced to lead his horse, so it seemed, over every fallen tree strewn on the river bluff. If that climb had actually been nothing more than a hundred feet straight up, Grouard and the soldiers who followed in his tracks had to travel three hundred feet or more, as if climbing in switchbacks to avoid the loosest of the rock fields, the thickest of the deadfall.

After a half hour of knee-wrenching, lung-searing work, Grouard reached the top of what proved to be a fairly level plateau. As he stood there catching his breath, wiping the sweat from his face with the greasy bandanna he wore around his neck, the half-breed realized why he was a horseman, instead of one of Lone Star's poor foot soldiers. Glancing back down the slope at the long, jagged line of troopers struggling up the hill, Frank knew why man was not meant to walk through country like this, knew why any man worth his grit here on the northern plains cared for his horse with as much attention as he gave to his weapons.

"Good Lord!" Mills exclaimed in an audible gush as he came to a stop near Grouard and removed his hat.

"Good climb, Colonel?"

"No—listen: the sound of the gunfire."

He did listen a moment. "Hear it real good from up here now, can't you?"

Mills nodded as he pulled the hat back on his damp brow. "Let's get these scouts of yours moving out in the advance, Grouard. I don't want any surprises as my men are formed up."

They both scanned the slopes of the nearby hills. Frank remained suspicious that they had been watched all along and were still under observation by the Lakota. If Crazy Horse had planned an ambush, then he would likely have his spies out watching the progress of the soldiers' march. As the half-breed signaled the Crow trackers to follow, pointing for a handful to go in one direction while the others were to take the opposite flank, Mills began to shout his orders to the officers and troops reaching the plateau behind him.

"Prepare to mount!"

On back the words echoed out of the canyon they had left below, each time augmented by another company commander as he brought his horse soldiers to the top of the ridge to join Mills's troops.

"Mount!"

When Mills gave the order, the hundreds went into the saddle, shifting the cumbersome carbines on slings, adjusting reins in their sweaty hands creased with red dirt, stuffing dusty boots into the hooded stirrups, and tugging hats back down on damp foreheads.

"Left front, by column of fours!"

As Grouard turned in the saddle to look back that last time as he led them down the slope, west toward the sound of the guns, he saw row upon row of horse soldiers re-forming beneath their swallowtail guidons, those little patches of multicolored fabric: red and white stripes along with that field of blue ablaze with its white stars, each with a company letter.

Then he heard the colonel's voice call out a last order across that plateau. "We'll be moving out at double-time!"

"You heard the colonel! Double-time!"

Going into a lope as they came off the top of the plateau, those horse soldiers did look pretty, the half-breed had to admit. All those eight companies, each troop riding horses of the same colors: Mills's on bays, the duns coming behind Noyes, Sutorious's men on the grays, Wells leading the band-box troop, Noyes's chestnuts, and on and on. They were something to behold, coming along now at a lope, their column of fours heaving down that gentle slope as Frank led them in a circuit from the north across the ground more suitable to cavalry moving out at the gallop.

Mills had them hurrying now—the lope increased into an easy gallop behind the tiny, swallowtail American flags flapping and snapping in the breeze as those dusty, tired horse soldiers came to the sound of the guns.

Crossing the last two miles to reach the ridge where George Crook's men were holding on.

Running desperately low on ammunition, but holding on.

When the first alarm was raised, Crazy Horse and the other war chiefs were noisily forming the horsemen for still another charge on the walk-a-heap soldiers and those white men huddled down among the rocks.

"Hopo! Look to the north!"

As more and more of the milling horsemen turned, the excitement growing, Wooden Leg found he had to rise to his knees on the bare-backed spine of his pony just to see over the crowd. At first all he saw was the faint cloud of dust along the skyline. Then, as he waited, concentrating on the distance, the young warrior saw what the distant scouts had spotted.

A wide, dark line snaking out of the northeast.

Someone panicked and shouted, "They're attacking us from the rear!"

Others immediately took up the cry.

Those first few who chose to flee reined their ponies away toward the hillsides at the northwestern edge of the valley, where the women cared for the wounded and prepared the dead for burial, a few busy in constructing travois. Most important, Wooden Leg understood, now some of the warriors would have to flee with the wounded while the rest held off this surprise attack from the north. It was so like soldiers to sneak around and jump their backs in just this way.

Why should it come as a surprise, Wooden Leg chided himself—these are the same sort of white men who attack sleeping villages of women and children, the old and the sick. Of course these soldiers would prefer to attack from behind rather than having to face a superior enemy.

There was no honor in that.

As if drawn magically, Wooden Leg turned, sensing something of the great war chief who sat atop his painted pony on the side of the slope, studying the approaching column. Crazy Horse was completely immobile, as if transfixed, more so a prisoner—locked there between the soldiers and white men they had been charging and attacking, and those horse soldiers riding quickly out of the north. The war chief wore nothing but his breechclout and moccasins, his only ornament the small stone behind his ear and that calf-skin lashed over his shoulders, as if forced to consider the souring of his medicine after so long a fight.

A cruel twist of events it must be for the Hunkpatila war chief—for here, just as they were preparing to charge in to crush the soldiers and white riflemen on the ridgetop, knowing the white men had to be running low on bullets, knowing his horsemen had been successful in dividing the soldiers into smaller groups, effectively attacking, robbing the white man of their warrior spirit, their will to fight . . . to discover that his fight might now be over.

As Wooden Leg watched, other Lakota and many of the Shahiyena chiefs rode up to join Crazy Horse, to argue over just what to do. But in less time than takes for a man to light his pipe, the chiefs were dispersing, waving, shouting their news throughout the hundreds upon hundreds of horsemen and those who had been forced to fight on foot.

"There has been enough fighting for one day!"

"Yes!" another war chief shouted. "The white man is beaten: he will not dare attack our villages now!"

"Let us carry our wounded back to our camps," a third

commanded. "We must bring our dead to bury and mourn over, for these have fought their greatest battle!"

And like the powerful and swift whirlwind that sweeps across the open ground in warming days of early summer, twirling and twisting with such magnificent speed and force, the copper-skinned horsemen turned their war ponies away from the north crest of Crook's hill, away from the muzzles of the white man's guns, showing the enemy their backsides.

Joining the others who loped past the conical hill, Wooden Leg looked back at the white men over his shoulder from time to time. Those pony soldiers coming out of the northeast would have no one to fight now. Come too late. It made him want to laugh. If not sing.

Maybe another day these soldiers would get their fight, he thought as he turned back to face the northwest where the women had the wounded and dead laid out on the travois they were leading away toward the camp circles raised in the foothills of the Wolf Mountains.

After all, he suddenly remembered—there was still this matter of Sitting Bull's vision: the soldiers falling into camp.

So . . . maybe there would come another day, another good day like this.

A day when these soldiers would come again to fight.

"Damn! But I don't believe these ol' eyes of mine!" the old packer exclaimed.

Seamus Donegan had to agree with Uncle Dick Closter. It was simply too good to believe—that sight of all those legions of warriors turning away, filing out from behind the rocks and trees, up from the ravines and coulees, streaming toward the northwest behind their war chiefs in a long and loping procession as that column of fours appeared along the distant northern skyline.

No sooner had the first Montana miner seen the narrow blue snake than he bellowed his news to all among those rocks forming the spur atop the northernmost part of Crook's ridge. And as the packers and miners all watched, the distant column of fours split left and right, going into a wide front once they reached more open, gently rolling ground as they raced after the fleeing brown-skinned horsemen.

"They'll never catch 'em, will they, Irishman?" asked Tom Moore.

He shrugged. "No telling. Likely depends how tired those mounts are."

"Don't matter. I'll lay money on the Injuns," Closter said.

"Now, don't be so quick now to lose your pay," Donegan advised. "Them Injun ponies may be wiry and strong and grass fed, but they been run hard all day."

With a grin the old man replied, "That's just my point, you stupid young'un. Them Injun ponies got their second wind already, and they'll leave them soldiers to eat nothing but hoof dust."

Seamus snorted and replied, "Uncle Dick does make sense once in a while, you know, Tom?"

"That mean you won't bet me, Donegan?" Closter growled with disappointment.

"That's right, old man. But I still aim to buy you a drink or two we get back to Fetterman."

"*If* we get back to Fetterman," Moore declared.

Seamus turned on him. "What do you mean, *if* we get back to Fetterman?"

"I don't have an idea one what makes you say you think we're going back to Fetterman," Moore began to explain. "This is George Crook's outfit, Donegan. And as long as I been working for that man—I'll be the first to tell you George Crook ain't the sort about to turn around and head back in to Fetterman."

"He did last winter!"

"That was the goddamned winter, Irishman!"

Donegan felt the frustration coming. "But this army's nearly run out of ammunition!"

"Got more back at the wagon train," Moore declared.

"Tom's right. General said he come to fight this time out," Closter agreed with his boss. "That's for certain."

In the space of mere moments, Seamus had allowed himself to go from feeling the desperation of men surrounded and with death staring them in the face, to sensing some rekindled glow of relief as the warriors withdrew and began their massed retreat, thinking that now he might return to Fetterman, from there back to Sam waiting with child down at Fort Laramie.

But suddenly, that glow was as surely snuffed as if Moore and Closter had rolled down the wick on Donegan's lamp—leaving him nothing more than fleeting hope and a lonely burned cinder of regret.

A rattle of gunfire interrupted his reverie, quickly dispelling that vision of Samantha he had cherished there atop the ridge. Behind their rocks, on the south and west sides of the bluff, the gunfire grew. Along with several others, Donegan trotted over with the big, heavy Sharps at the end of his arm, finding some of the infantry firing on a last party of warriors who were sweeping east along the creek bottom below the slope.

"Lookit those gamecocks," Closter grumbled.

"I'll be damned—riding right around us like it was a Sunday-go-to-meeting picnic," Moore said.

"A final, and most fitting, farewell tribute, don't you think?" Donegan replied sourly, kicking at a clump of grass with disgust. "So you boys still think Crook won this fight, eh?"

Closter turned on the Irishman. "And you don't think he did, is that it, Seamus? Just bercause some Injun horsemen ride off in retreat down there along the creek, showing us their red backsides?"

"No," Donegan answered the old packer. "Because even though the Sioux are retreating—they just showed you what they thought of the general's army, showing you that even in pulling back, they was still able to ride completely around Crook's army before they took off back to their village."

"Goddamn you, Donegan," Closter said, wagging his head. "Maybe you're due being right every now and again too."

"Yeah," Moore said, sounding his agreement. "Maybe Crook was fought to a standstill."

"No, Tom. Not fought to a standstill," Seamus said quietly as he watched nearly a hundred of the enemy horsemen ride out of sight, disappearing to the east around the big bend of the Rosebud where they galloped north, away to their village to celebrate their six-hour battle with Three Stars.

"Maybe, fellas," Donegan continued, "maybe—we was all pretty lucky we didn't lose our scalps here this day."

Chapter 38

17 June 1876

Just past two-thirty P.M. *Anson Mills leapt to the ground,* dismounting before his horse had come to a complete halt, hitting the ground at a sprint that took him across the last few yards of ridgetop and right up to George Crook.

"General—I want you to tell me why you recalled me."

Crook turned slowly, bringing his right hand to the brim of his crumpled black hat, eyes squinting. "Colonel Mills?"

The volatile captain quickly saluted, pressing on. "I had the village almost in my grasp—and I could have held it."

Looking away as if he could not bear to hold Mills's appraising gaze, Crook instead peered to the north. To not only the captain, but to many of those around him, the general appeared more sullen than they had ever seen him.

Quietly, Crook replied, "Colonel—we got ourselves into a more serious engagement than I thought. We have lost about fifty killed and wounded, and the surgeons refused to remain with the wounded unless I left the infantry and one of the cavalry squadrons with them."

"But you dispatched me with your promise of support if I attacked—"

Crooked wheeled on Mills, his voice sharp, metallic as new-rolled brass. "Dammit—if I left the infantry and some of my cavalry here, I knew I could not keep my promise to support you with what remained of my force."

Mills sighed. "And your plans now, General?"

Crook shook his head. "I have several ideas at the moment."

"The village?" Mills asked.

"Perhaps, Colonel. This has been a most dissatisfactory encounter. We've been stymied by an enemy who has clearly accomplished what he set out to do: hold us at bay while he effects the safe retreat of his village. So, yes—if I can, I still have every intention of marching on the enemy's camp."

The captain was weary of it all, the useless exercise of all the coming and the going. The wasting of time, and the infernal waiting. The final straw had been that fruitless charge after the retreating hostiles. It hadn't taken very long, nor all that many miles, before Anson Mills decided his men and stock had their fill of chasing the backsides of Indian ponies. After a pursuit of five miles, he had called a halt, turned his eight companies around, and led them back to Crook's battlefield, empty-handed.

With a sigh of fatigue and impatience, Mills inquired, "While you are considering what path to take next, I request permission to visit my wounded, General. Trumpeter Snow."

"Of course, Colonel. By all means."

Mills saluted and turned away, glad to be gone and hurrying down the slope to the field hospital nearby, where most of the dead and all of the wounded had been gathered during the six-hour battle. He moved among the men, recognizing those of the Third Cavalry who had served with Royall and had fallen in the disastrous retreat. Kneeling beside each trooper, Mills gently laid his hand on theirs if a man could not shake, sure to thank them for their heroic service, asking if their fellows could bring anything at all to make them more comfortable, trying to spread what cheer he could—remembering as he did the horrors suffered by all those wounded during the Civil War. Bad enough that a man earned himself a piece of enemy lead in support of his country. Perhaps the worst of all ignominy was his country failing to recognize the precious price of that man's sacrifice.

Such simple gestures these might appear—kind words and the touch of a hand, the expression of a superior's appreciation for the courage, sacrifice, and selflessness evidenced by only a bloody wound—yet these acts of kindness, courtesy, and respect were nonetheless lost on far too many commanding officers in the frontier army.

There among the wounded on that hillside above the Rosebud, Anson Mills vowed he would not forget those who had sacrificed so much to redeem the honor of the gallant Third.

He had knelt beside Anton Newkirken, who served with Vroom's L Company gone to the top of the crest to support Royall's third retreat. Nearby he found John Kreemer and Trumpeter William Edwards. Not far away the other five from L Company, army blankets as their only funeral shrouds.

As he was crouched beside William Edwards, Vroom's trumpeter, Mills heard his name called weakly.

"Colonel . . . Colonel Mills, is it you?"

"I'll be back in a moment," he promised the private. Mills rose and moved over to the soldier who had called him, expecting to find yet another of the troopers, perhaps one of the many who had served with Captain Andrews in Royall's battalion—one of the men who had recognized his voice and called out.

For a moment he stood staring down at the wounded soldier who was surrounded by three attendants and John Finerty, the correspondent from Chicago. Blood from the ghastly facial wounds had drenched the front of the trooper's tunic, turning the dark-blue wool instead a murky black in drying. As much as the surgeons and their stewards had tried to clean up the oozy wounds, both sides of the man's face were clotted with new blood, darkly shiny in the midafternoon light. Both eyes were swollen shut, tissues already grown purplish. His mustache and beard were clotted beneath a bruised and battered nose. From all the years he had been practicing war, it didn't take long for Mills to realize this hapless soldier would not likely make it through the night.

It wasn't until he knelt at the man's side that Mills noticed the bloody shoulder-board. This . . . was a captain.

"Colonel Mills—are you there?" the wounded officer asked as his head turned, his voice failing, coming in no more than a whisper, parched as sandpaper drawn across cast-iron.

"Guy? Guy Henry?"

Henry sighed through his cracked lips. "Anson."

"Lord!" Mills exclaimed, his belly knotting, going cold in finding a friend nearing death's door. He brought one of Henry's hands between his two. "I had no idea. Are . . . are you . . . is there anything I can do to make you comfortable?"

"My friend—I asked the doctors for the truth, and they told me that I must die," Henry answered stoically. "But I told them they're mistaken."

"Bully for you, Guy. Damned bully for you."

As brave as it sounded, the others kneeling there around their captain did not bear such confident countenances. A man with Mills's experience in the ways of war and wounds and sudden death knew in his gut that Henry had chances of something less than one in ten.

"The man's strong," said Julius Patzki as he came up behind Mills.

The captain looked back at the assistant surgeon. "He'll make it. If anyone can ride through hell and come back whole, it's Guy Henry."

Surgeon Patzki nodded. "That may well be what made Colonel Henry order me to patch him up so he could go back to the fight when they first brought him here to me."

John Finerty said, "I've done everything I could to cheer him up, Colonel Mills. All my best jokes, and we've talked about the finest of watering holes to visit in Chicago."

"A good job of cheering me you did too," Henry responded.

"I asked the Colonel how bad he hurt, and he told me it was nothing," Finerty explained. "Said that's what fighting men like him were here for."

A ball of sentiment stuck in Anson's throat. "I heard your battalion was hit hard."

"We were surrounded several times, Anson."

John Finerty looked up at Mills and said, "I told Colonel Henry here that I rode with you toward the enemy village, and he said I should have stayed and gone with him."

Henry whispered through his dry, cracked lips, "Told Finerty he would have a much better story to write for his readers back east, Anson. He could write about Indian fighting, instead of Indian chasing."

My, how the man clung to life tenaciously, even trying to laugh at his own joke.

"That's about all it seems I've done this day—chase Indians," Mills admitted gravely. "Is there anything I can do for you, Guy? Anything I can bring you?"

"Maybe you can help me talk Finerty here into signing up."

"Can you believe that, Colonel?" Finerty snorted, wagging his head in disbelief. "Henry here said I should join the goddamned army!"

"That's my army, mind you, Finerty," Henry growled in a whisper that, while being hushed, was nonetheless valiant.

"Colonel Mills?"

He turned to find John Bourke approaching. "Yes, Lieutenant?"

"The general's compliments. Wants to inform you he's decided on making another march on the village."

Mills peered into the summer sky, finding the sun less than halfway between midsky and the western horizon. "Perhaps we will have time to make that march after all, Lieutenant. I'll be only a moment here."

Then Anson turned back to Henry, squeezing the hand again. "I'll come back when we return, Guy. If we strike the village, it might not be for another day or more."

"It doesn't matter. When . . . when you get back."

"Yes. We'll talk some more." Mills arose.

Henry was able to follow Anson's rising as the captain blocked the sun from striking his face. He did his best to keep his sightless, swollen eyes fixed on the sound of Mills's voice. "I'd like that, Colonel. Do come see me as soon as you can. When our job's been done here on the Rosebud. And see to Crazy Horse personally for me, will you?"

"That I promise you, Guy. Everything in my power."

For the past ten days Samantha Donegan had been worrying herself out of eating and right into sleeplessness.

None of the women who had initially learned of the report wanted her to get wind of it. But she had overheard them whispering of the rumor back on that fateful Thursday, the eighth of June.

"An Indian courier just came in from the north country," one of the officers' wives said in a hurried whisper.

From that single tiny window in her room upstairs, Sam had seen the woman coming at a hurry across the parade, skirts and petticoats aswirl around her ankles as she waved over three more wives who were standing outside sutler Collins's store, chatting. A woman knew from all the signs that the anxious one had something important to share. Perhaps a bit of post gossip. Maybe a new copy of an eastern magazine brought in the week's post. Perhaps even a new pattern they could pass around among themselves. That is, if a woman had the desire to make herself a new dress.

All Sam wanted was to have a dress that she didn't have to keep letting out and out even more until she was left with nothing else to do but sew in a panel over her ever-expanding belly.

So in seeing the woman coming, and being as curious a creature as she was, Sam had begun to make her way slowly down the narrow staircase there at married officers' quarters, so slowly, step by step, that the others had not heard her coming—so intent were they on the news brought them that Thursday afternoon from the faraway north country.

Where George Crook had gone to do battle with Sitting Bull and Crazy Horse.

"Oh, dear!" one of them had gasped.

"Hush!" another chided.

Likely, she had even rolled her eyes heavenward, if for no other reason than to indicate they were being careful not to alarm the pregnant one upstairs. The wife of one of those who went north with the army.

A different voice asked, "You hear this from someone reputable?"

"This isn't another one of those rumors, is it?"

"No," answered the first with indignation in her voice as Sam drew down the last flight. "The news comes from Fred. I overheard several of them talking as I was on my way into the office to take him some lunch. Well, let me tell you—they shut right up when they saw me. So it must be true."

"Must be true," another agreed. "If they shut up when Maggie showed her face."

"Go on, Maggie. What's the whole of it?"

"The news given them by this Indian courier said there was a great concentration of hostiles near the mouth of the . . . oh, dear! I wanted so to get this right!"

"The mouth of a river?"

"Yes. Help me remember!"

"The Powder, the Tongue—"

"The Tongue! That's it—the hostiles have concentrated near the Tongue."

"Go on now. Hurry!" the voice grew whispery as gauze.

"Listen to this, ladies. The enemy village is said to consist of twelve hundred seventy-three lodges."

"I don't believe you remembered that exact number and you couldn't remember the name of the river!"

"Please, Hannah—I was always better at arithmetic than I was at geography. And the best tidbit of all is what the courier said there at the last."

"What was it—tell us!"

"The Indian reported that the big village was on its way to crush George Crook on the Powder River!"

"Dear merciful God!" Samantha shrieked at the doorway to the tiny drawing room.

Spinning about, surprised to find Samantha there listening to them, the others saw her keel, lunged out to catch her, carried her to the tiny love seat where they brought her a cool drink and a cold towel for her face.

Ever since, Sam had thought of little else. With not one shred of other news come out of that north country where

Seamus had gone traipsing along with that damned George Crook—

What was that? she thought, immediately lifting the hand that had been resting on her growing belly.

There it was again!

Now she was frightened, mystified, above all curious.

So she laid both hands gently over the apron she wore all the time to cover up the panel sewn into her dress, a panel that was far from matching the dress itself.

"Oh!" she exclaimed as her belly moved, as if it were rolling from one side to the other, left to right slowly.

Sam sensed the roll both from within, and with her hands felt the movement outside her belly. There was something almost hard there beneath her flesh, beneath the apron and dress panel and chemise and the slips. Something almost hard.

Gently, ever so gently, she began to push with the heel of her right hand against the hard object, finding that it moved a little at first, then withdrew, disappearing from her touch beneath the taut skin of her swelling belly.

As suddenly it exploded against the palm of her hand. As if it had kicked her from within. Protesting her pushing it. With a little . . . dear God! With a kick!

Rolling up on one elbow with a struggle, she tore off the apron, heaving it to the floor unceremoniously and began to frantically tear the shell buttons out of their holes, opening up her dress all the way down through the added panel. Next came the tiny buttons on the chemise so that she could bare her chest. Her chest—was it really her chest anymore? Sam hardly recognized her body anymore, all the changes that had come over it month by month, and week by week, changes almost by the day now. Skin so taut she was certain she'd awaken one night and find herself split in two like the rind of an overripe Texas melon.

But her hands went on down from those swelling breasts and tender nipples, down to push the buttons out of their holes on her two slips, shoving them aside so that she could finally look at the taut flesh for herself there in the afternoon light streaming like a shaft of golden benediction through the window.

She had always thought summer light the most flattering—

Sweet heaven!

Sam saw it.

It? Her baby wasn't an *it!* He was moving around in her belly now, tumbling almost. There it was again—a big knot poking out from her already-tight skin, as if he were pushing to get out of her already, free himself with that foot or a fist or an elbow.

It was the very first time she had felt him.

Him.

She stopped, running her palm gently over that bony, pointed knot of flesh where the life within her was shoving to get out.

"Not yet, little man," she said to him in a whisper, the tears coming to her eyes, starting her nose to dribble a little.

It sounded so right to call this little life a *he,* a *him.* So sure, as only mothers could be, she supposed. Sure that she was carrying Seamus's *son.*

Tumbling, active, kicking . . . it must be a boy. Without a doubt, Sam knew it was a boy. So active, and strong, and vital. So much like his father.

Dear God in heaven, please bring his father home. Pray you bring Seamus back to us both.

"When the Crows would not go another inch down that canyon," John Bourke explained to Donegan and Richard Closter, "that's when I think the general was finally convinced to give up on reaching the village."

"The Crows?" Uncle Dick asked.

"When we got to the same place where Mills turned around earlier today, the Crow refused to go on," the lieutenant replied.

"They act scared?" Donegan asked.

"Scared—yeah. Like scared of ghosts. Them, and Grouard too. He told Crook same thing he told Mills before: the Sioux had an ambush laid up ahead. It was suicide to go on."

"Damn the general's hide anyways," Closter grumbled. "Him and his idea of using Injuns to fight Injuns. Ever since they joined up, if them Crow ain't been skittish, they're outright skairt."

"I don't think I could ever call the Crow scared, Uncle Dick," Bourke said. "Not after the courage and steadfastness they showed us today—holding back the Sioux until we were ready to go on the attack. And what about that attack they and the Shoshone made on the conical hill over there?"

The Irishman asked, "The Crow say anything about not budging another step down the canyon?"

"Big Bat translated a story they told, talk of a few summers back when a lot of their village had been killed by the Sioux who were coming into this country for the hunt. Bat said they called the place down the Rosebud something like the 'Valley of Death.' I wouldn't really give it any credence, fellas—because one of the Crow named White Face even told Crook that the warriors we had been fighting were only a small war party!"

"Small war party! Shit!" Closter exclaimed, wiping some tobacco spittle from his lower lip. "Cain't be—many as jumped us this morning!"

"Damned superstitious of 'em, I'd say," Bourke continued. "According to White Face, the Sioux who are camped on down the Rosebud are as many as the grass. That's just the way Bat translated: as many as the grass. The scout warned Crook all his men would be killed if they attacked that camp. Said the spirits had vowed that all the white men would be killed if they attacked a village. Then White Face rubbed his two palms together, out flat like this—and stomped off. Leaving Bat to explain his surly impudence and all the rest to Crook."

"So that's when Crook decided to head back here?" Donegan asked.

"Not quite then. While we were dismounted there in the canyon and he was talking over the matter with the scouts, Crook sent me and Nickerson to all the company commanders to inquire as to their ammunition supply."

Donegan said, "That wasn't good news at all."

"But being desperately short on cartridges wasn't the only thing that made up the general's mind for him," Bourke continued. "The last straw came when Grouard said he wasn't marching any farther. That killed Crook's march right then and there."

"He believes Grouard about an ambush, eh?"

"I'd say he trusts that half-breed like he's never trusted any other scout," Bourke answered. "Without Grouard, without those Crow willing to go one more furlong—Crook had no choice but to turn around and come on back here where he left the infantry to guard the surgeons."

"Got a mite lonely here without you, Johnny boy," Closter said with a gentle grin radiant within that tobacco-stained white beard. "Just us civilians and infantry left to protect all the wounded."

It was just past four P.M. when a dejected Crook returned to the battlefield littered with the carcasses of horses and warrior ponies. As the cavalry troops broke up into messes and began to build their fires, the general ordered Major Chambers to have his infantry post rotating pickets on the high ground of the conical hill where sentries remained until seven P.M., when twilight began to sink over the northern plains.

Bourke sighed, saying, "As much as Crook wanted to snatch a victory right out of the jaws of the standstill we fought to against Crazy Horse this afternoon, I think he's still got plans to make a full-scale night march against them."

"Tonight?" Donegan asked.

"Yes. Crook's called an officers' meeting for sunset," the lieutenant declared. "Going to discuss with his company commanders this matter of marching his cavalry north under the cover of darkness . . . so he can strike the enemy camp at dawn."

Chapter 39

17 June 1876

As twilight eased down on the valley of the Rosebud, it reminded Seamus Donegan of another summer evening ten years gone. Another twilight, with darkness coming on, having fought for much of that long day against Sioux horsemen at the Crazy Woman Crossing of the Bozeman Road into Montana Territory.

As the air started to cool, the mosquitoes came out in thin vapors that drifted over the camp Crook's troops made along the creek bottom and across the gentle slopes. From the hospital the surgeons had established for themselves down among a copse of trees standing beside the sluggish Rosebud, Donegan occasionally heard a muffled shriek of pain or yelp of agonized torture as a probe was eased into a bullet wound, or the knife worked over sundered flesh. Or, worse yet—the raw-toothed saw began its grisly labors separating bone from bone, limb from limb. What was still alive from what was destined to die.

But with the advent of night came one blessing: at least the huge, droning flies disappeared after tormenting man and beast throughout the long day, meaning some small measure of relief for the wounded, including Guy V. Henry.

For most of the afternoon the Third Cavalry captain

had not been without constant care. Because the surgeons unanimously believed he could not last the night, they made certain that Henry was given what comfort they could provide for this lone officer among the day's casualties. Stewards and enlisted men were called to rotate shifts in keeping the flies fanned away from the blood still crusting on the frightful wounds, from the oozy eyes swollen shut. Meanwhile, clouds of the big green-bottle horseflies and their smaller, darker cousins had descended to crawl and bite at the rest of the wounded.

Henry's spirits remained remarkably high throughout the afternoon and into the evening as one after another of his men and fellow officers came to pay their respects, talk about the battle, speak of home and give what cheer they could. That long afternoon's summer heat, compounded by the severe bleeding from his wounds, intensified the captain's craving for fluids. For more than an hour Lieutenant William Rawolle sat at Henry's head, gently spoon-feeding his friend some red-currant jelly made soluble in water so that it could be easily swallowed.

With the return of Crook's second march down the Rosebud, bivouac had been ordered on the same ground where the soldiers had been enjoying their morning rest at the moment they were attacked, so the wounded would not have to be moved. Besides, water was at hand. With the creek as the southern border, the various cavalry and infantry units formed the four sides of a camp square, with their horses and mules left to graze in the center.

By the time Crook called his officers' assembly that evening, there was an official count completed on the battle. While the soldiers themselves had used up more that twenty-five thousand rounds of ammunition, the Crow and Shoshone had shot up ten thousand rounds on their own, which left the expedition with no more than ten cartridges per man.

Captain George Randall also reported that his Indian scouts had collected the scalps from thirteen Sioux and Cheyenne warriors abandoned on the field by their people unable to claim those bodies fallen so close to the soldier lines. Captain Andrew Burt stated that he had counted 150 dead horses and ponies scattered for nearly three miles along the ridges, as well as a few old blankets, war bonnets, and other plunder left behind in the fury of the fray, if not by the enemy's precipitous retreat.

While there was no reasonable way to tally the Sioux and Cheyenne casualties, medical director Albert Hartsuff gave his preliminary report of nine soldiers killed, all of whom had fought under Colonel Royall on the left flank of the battle. Besides Captain Guy V. Henry, the one officer wounded, there were another twenty wounded enough to require medical attention. The civilian packers and Montana miners had suffered no losses.

As for the general's allies, Baptiste Pourier told the assembly of the one death—a Shoshone boy caught and killed near the creek bottom during the battle—with another seven scouts seriously wounded. Bat said that the war chief Old Crow had been shot through the kneecap in the early fighting and had stoically refused to allow the surgeons near his leg with their knives and sawblades.

Lieutenant Rawolle reported that some of his men had gone out late that afternoon with the expressed purpose of exploring those positions the enemy had used so effectively against them. What they found at several locations were piles of empty cartridges. In one place they counted more than five hundred cases, representing at least four different calibers. At another position they found a dump of sorts, cluttered with empty ammunition boxes. The message was clear: let none of George Crook's officers fool themselves into thinking the enemy was not well armed.

When the preliminary oral reports were out of the way and he had asked that the various company commanders submit their written reports in three days, the general finally got to the heart of things for that weary assembly.

"Gentlemen, our wounded need proper attention. Better than what we can give them here. Though I have considered the option of transporting our casualties on travois or by mule litter as we hurry in pursuit of the enemy, I've come to the decision that to do so would be a most unthinkable act of barbarity against those very men who have borne the high cost of this battle."

"Then are you considering sending the wounded back

to the wagon camp on Goose Creek under an escort, General?" asked William B. Royall.

"No, Colonel. I would need to provide such a mission with an escort of sufficient strength that would only serve to dilute my already weakened force. No. Besides, gentlemen—this strike force of ours was originally rationed for no more than four days. If we had struck the enemy village —a village which I am dead certain has now flown, scattering to all parts of the compass—and gone ahead to defeat that camp in battle, we could have marched on north to rendezvous with either Gibbon or Terry on the Yellowstone. But now, with that village fleeing and likely dispersing in all directions, I can't make a reasonable argument for continuing our chase without rations."

"I don't think anyone will take issue with me, General," Anson Mills declared, "when I say we've lost all hope of surprising the village now—which was at the heart of our original plan."

"What we need besides rations and ammunition," Crook went on, "is reinforcements. Perhaps we can pull up some of the units General Sheridan transferred from the south to prevent more of the agency Indians from bolting the reservations and joining the hostiles here in the north country. I won't know what additional manpower I can expect until I can communicate with division headquarters."

"I agree that we might well need reinforcement," Royall stated. "If we expect to storm the hostile camps of Sitting Bull and Crazy Horse instead of being surprised by them."

"That brings something up I wanted to discuss, General," Major Alexander Chambers said. "What good was it having the Crow and Shoshone with us as our guides, trackers, scouts . . . if we were so completely and utterly surprised?"

"I take exception to your characterization of our scouts," John Bourke said as he leaned forward from the group encircling Crook. "No man here could have expected any more from our scouts. Not only were they courageous, but gallant as well."

"They likely saved our hash," Captain Peter Vroom

stated. "Not only at the start of the battle, but in my fight at the top of the hill."

"Gentlemen," Crook said, holding both hands up to quiet his murmuring officer corps. "You can save just this sort of discussion for your camp fires and after-dinner conversation. I, for one, have no complaints of any kind with our allies. So, if there are no further matters requiring discussion, this meeting is adjourned. We will move out for our base camp at dawn."

After supper with Closter and a handful of Tom Moore's packers, Seamus ambled up the slope until he reached the sandstone rocks where the civilians had held off a series of enemy charges that day. There he sat and loaded his pipe, smoking it as he stared off to the north while the deep hues of twilight bled to black and the first stars winked into sight just beyond his reach. When the high prairie night grew chilled, the Irishman turned away from the darkness to the north and faced about, moving back down the slope through the many twinkling watch-fires around which the cavalry and infantry units were gathering in muted, brooding conversations.

"I, for one, think the lives of this outfit were saved by the battle taking place right here, taking place *when* it did this morning," John Finerty declared that evening at a small fire where many of the correspondents had gathered with a few of Tom Moore's packers to talk of the fight.

"Hell," Reuben Davenport grumbled as Donegan came up to the group. "No matter where or when, we were caught flat-footed, and we're lucky we came out of it as cheap as we did."

"Listen, Davenport—had the Crow not discovered the enemy, and had they not jumped us right here," Finerty protested, "why, if we had carried out the general's original plan without being molested on our march down the river—our whole force of eleven hundred men would have been in the hostile village at noon."

Seamus asked, "And what do you suppose would have happened then, Finerty?"

Scratching his two days of chin growth, Finerty replied, "In light of the events of this day, it is not improbable that all of us would have settled there permanently."

"An early grave, for sure," said T. B. MacMillan.

"I've got to agree with you on that," Bob Strahorn of the Rocky Mountain *News* said. "Five thousand able-bodied warriors, well armed, and under the capable leadership of that red Satan, Crazy Horse himself, would have given Crook all the trouble the general was looking for when he pitched into that village."

"If we'd made the village at all," grumbled T. B. MacMillan, like Finerty, from Chicago. "Sounds to me like they were already in the process of luring us down the river toward their trap when our scouts fortunately ran into some of the warriors who were going to swoop in around on our rear and jump our backs when the moment of ambush arrived."

"If that had happened, right now we all would be sharing a lot in common with Potts, that poor soldier I saw them bringing in this afternoon," Finerty groaned. "Growing black and swollen from lying out in the sun, more than a dozen arrows bristling from his anatomy."

Davenport asked, "Is it true Grouard told Crook that he recognized Crazy Horse among the war chiefs during the fight?"

John Bourke nodded. "That's what the half-breed said. Grouard knew Crazy Horse from the way he always dressed going into battle, knew the red bastard's war pony too."

Donegan said, "Maybe that was the son of a bitch you and Randall said you kept seeing, striding around out in the open before you made your charge on that conical hill."

"A damned good chance of it," Bourke said. "Seemed to be orchestrating the warriors in their charges on us, so the major had his Crow scouts direct some fire in that bastard's direction. Can't believe it—but for all the lead we flung his way, not a single shot hit him as he pranced back and forth, back and forth as if immune to our bullets."

"No matter—we had to hurt them, and hurt them good," Davenport boasted. "Much more than they hurt this outfit of Crook's. How many of the red infidels do you think did we kill today? Maybe a hundred?"

"Maybe," Bourke replied, staring at the low flames.

"Well," Davenport continued, "I'll tell you that I have

no doubt in my mind, and have emphatically stated so in my first dispatch from this battlefield, that we here encountered all the Sioux warriors there are on the northern plains. Besides showing them we won't shrink from a fight, we proved we can cripple their kind."

Davenport's bravado was not shared up the slope at Crook's headquarters. While no one could find argument with the fact that the casualties were very light compared to the amount of rounds fired through those six long hours of constant fighting, nonetheless, a palpable sense of gloom had descended over that entire camp as the sun slid from the sky. Perhaps it was nothing more than weariness. Battle fatigue. Maybe nothing more than the coming of night and darkness, that long-held realm of the dead. If nothing more, it was a time each man had alone with his thoughts.

It was much as Anson Mills gave voice later as the officers gathered here and there in knots and began to recite the wrongs committed during the day's action.

"Every last officer I've talked with this afternoon realizes just as I do that we were lucky not to have been entirely vanquished," the captain declared. "In fact, we have been humiliatingly defeated."

That evening Donegan knew of only two men—George Crook and John Bourke—who maintained a paper-thin, shaky facade, a temporary masquerade in which they simply refused to acknowledge the suddenness of the attack, the completeness of the surprise, or the total lack of readiness in the troops allowed to lollygag along the creekbank.

At the same time, the rest of the officer corps and the line troops had grown thoughtful, if not outright wary, had perhaps even reluctantly come to hold some profound respect for the abilities of the enemy met that day in battle, as well as for that enemy's capable cavalry leader.

In walking down to the brushy swamp in the creek bottom to relieve himself, Seamus caught sight of Grouard moving through camp, heading through the maze of fires and soldiers, his horse behind him. Buttoning his canvas britches and slapping the suspenders back over his shoulders, the Irishman hurried to catch up.

"You just get back, Frank?"

The half-breed stopped and turned, waiting until

Seamus came close. Then he shook his head. "No. Leaving now."

"Where you going this time of night?"

"The general figures someone ought to find out for sure about that ambush Crazy Horse planned for us downriver."

"There really a deep canyon down there?"

With a shrug Grouard answered, "Lot of brush and deadfall. Boulders. Maybe no canyon. Maybe better to say a good place for a trap."

"Everybody's already calling it the 'canyon of death,' Frank. If it ain't a narrow place for a trap—then why doesn't Crook march right after the village?"

Grouard gazed back up the slope over the Irishman's shoulder. "All I know, Donegan—is that them Crow know the Lakota as good as I know 'em. The way a man knows his enemy. If Crazy Horse wanted to chew up a bunch of soldiers for lunch today, that'd been the place to do it."

Seamus watched the sullen half-breed turn away without another word, walking his mount on east past the last of the watch-fires, where Grouard climbed into the saddle and disappeared toward the dark hills. As the Irishman stood there gazing into the night sky, the mournful, solitary notes of a single trumpet floated over the encampment beside the Rosebud. *Tattoo.* Known to the nonarmy as "Taps."

Going to satisfy his curiosity, Donegan found many of the soldiers from the various cavalry and infantry units gathered in a great assembly on the grassy creekbank. Many held torches, which cast an eerie, dancing otherworldly light over the solemn crowd as one after another of the officers spoke a few words of praise over the long mass grave where the bodies of their dead had been wrapped in blankets before being lowered into the ground. The remains of one soldier, Private Richard Bennett of Vroom's L Troop of the Third Cavalry, had been completely dismembered by the enemy. His friends had accomplished the grisly task of replacing what remained of the butchered soldier in a grain sack begged off one of Moore's packers. That sack served as Bennett's only shroud as it too was lowered into the creekside grave with the other corpses.

After Colonel Royall led them all in singing "Shall We Gather at the River," some of the other officers continued in an impromptu serenade of heartfelt hymns and favorites like "The Old Hundredth," "Sweet Annie Laurie," and "The Girl I Left Behind Me," sung while soldiers worked in relays to fill in the mass grave. That completed, a fire was kindled along the trench, the better, they hoped to disguise the site from plundering wolves or marauding Sioux and Cheyenne.

Later that night beneath the stars and a pale sliver of moonrind, Seamus found himself unable to sleep, wondering on Samantha and the child they had given life in her belly. Thinking on Frank Grouard gone to scout the "dead canyon." Tossing fretfully in his blankets despite the cold of these summer nights come to the high plains.

In all the known civilized world there could be nothing more somber than a funeral for soldiers fallen far from home, far from the bosom of loved ones . . . laid here to eternal rest in the yawning, lonely wilderness where Seamus had come to wonder if God could even hear his prayers at all.

Chapter 40

Moon of Fat Horses

"*Kse-e se-wo-is-tan-i-we i-tat-an-e.*"

That night following the long day's battle, Wooden Leg's people were already calling the fight by name:

"Where the Young Girl Saved Her Brother."

In their winter counts the Shahiyena would long refer to the attack they made on Three Stars's soldiers as the rescue of Chief Comes in Sight by his sister, Buffalo Calf Road Woman.

With much, much joy the great encampment began celebrating their victory that very night at sundown as the first warriors returned north from the battlefield to their camp on Sundance Creek* with news of the victory. As the warriors fought that day, the women had moved the camp circles farther west down the creek, erecting their lodges a little closer to the Greasy Grass.†

Here they planned to remain for two nights before moving on to the mouth of the creek, where the Sundance itself flowed into the Greasy Grass. There the chiefs said they would stay for five or six sleeps while the young men

* Present-day Ash Creek

† Present-day Little Bighorn River

hunted the antelope herds reported in the nearby country. Although this was unknown territory to the Lakota, the Shahiyena had been returning to this very ground to hunt for the past ten summers.

For some in the village, it was not a happy return. Some of their own would never again charge the white man or his soldiers. Some would never again sit a pony, never again feel the wind caressing their hair as they darted through a buffalo herd on the run.

Although the count of the dead was already high, close to four-times-ten, Wooden Leg knew more of the wounded would not live long. There was not much even the medicine men could do once a bullet went through a man's chest and he found it harder and harder to breathe. Or when a bullet penetrated a man's belly and all he could expect was to die slowly, painfully, as his friends watched and prayed, beat their drums and shook their rattles, mumbling their prayers or speaking of the dying man's many brave feats in battle.

Custom dictated that the celebration of victory was to come only after a proper period of mourning. But in this singular case of battling an overwhelming force of soldiers and their Indian scouts to a virtual standstill, the Lakota and Shahiyena found much to honor in their warriors who had ridden forth to protect the great village. Throughout that first night and on into the rising of the daybreak star, the horsemen streamed back to their camps, where friends and family sang of their bravery and cheered their return. Like Wooden Leg, those who were last to return were warriors who had elected to tie the many travois to their ponies, bringing back both the dead and wounded as two of the old chiefs from each tribal circle led in the procession of weary ponies from the south.

While the women brought new life to their fires and put kettles on to boil so the hungry warriors could be fed, the old shaman Charcoal Bear brought out the sacred Buffalo Hat and hung it from a tall tripod in the center of the Shahiyena camp circle. To it that evening was tied the scalp of the young Snake warrior they had killed among the ponies herded down by the creek in the first minutes of the battle. Around and around that most ancient and powerful relic the women danced: mothers of young fighters, wives of older warriors, young and eligible maidens seeking to take a courageous husband who had proven himself in a great battle against the soldiers. So it was that the women danced with great vitality while most of the men watched, weary from their all-night ride south, as well as their all-day fight.

While there were some women of loss who keened and cut their hair, cried out in grief and cut themselves in mourning, there was much more joy, even laughter behind the hands when they learned how Jack Red Cloud had flown from the battlefield early that morning, fleeing south and east in great shame, straight back to the white man's reservation where his father ruled the land of white flour and pig-meat.

Here, among the mountains and high plains, the free and wild Indian ruled.

"He will return to his father without his father's bonnet!" Wooden Leg reminded his friends around that great, roaring bonfire.

"Without his father's special rifle!" added Lame Sioux.

"No matter. Perhaps now the soldiers will stay away!" Crooked Nose cheered at one of the many leaping bonfires fed throughout that first night after the battle. "Now that they know we will never again wait until they attack our camps of little ones and women."

"They should know we will attack them!" echoed Yellow Eagle.

"But—what of the great mystic's vision?" asked White Elk.

"Yes," agreed Young Black Bird. "What of Sitting Bull's talk with the Everywhere Spirit?"

"The soldiers will not return," Little Shield said as sour as gall.

Contrary Belly added, "They would not dare. There can be no soldiers falling into our camps now."

"But the vision was so strong, in such detail," Wooden Leg protested. "I hear from White Cow Bull that Sitting Bull has told the Lakota to expect another fight."

"Let us savor this victory first, young one," Brass Cartridge chided Wooden Leg.

"Yes," agreed Spotted Wolf as he chuckled. "It will be a long, long time before we have to worry about any soldiers marching on us now."

"They have learned their lesson well," Crooked Nose stated. "The Everywhere Spirit has taught them a painful truth: never again come to attack a village of women and children. Like our southern cousin—chief Medicine Arrow—vowed seven winters ago in his prophecy to Hiestzi, the Yellow Hair called Custer. If the soldiers come, then they will all be destroyed."

"Exactly as the shaman Sitting Bull has seen in his vision," Wooden Leg reprimanded them for forgetting. "Soon, he says—the soldiers will fall headfirst like grasshoppers into our camp."

With the coming of the sun the next morning, a very weary Wooden Leg reluctantly gave up the celebration and finally curled within his buffalo robe he laid beneath the blanket stretched over some willow branches to form a crude wickiup. Most young warriors too old to live with their parents but not yet married themselves used just such temporary shelters as the villages moved from campsite to campsite.

Inside, he felt the stirrings of his own true warriorhood at long last. It had been as Crazy Horse promised them when he led the hundreds south to meet Three Stars. This was indeed a new kind of fighting for the Shahiyena and Lakota.

Perhaps gone forever was the old way of doing battle: each man fighting on his own for coups and scalps and ponies; each man riding out ahead of the others to perform daring, risky, and often foolish deeds in the face of the enemy.

Perhaps from now on they would fight any soldier army come against the villages in this new way: riding knee to knee in massed bunches, swarming together over the white man as the bee flies in swarms that blackened the sky, charging into the soldier lines in numbers that could not help but roll over the helpless enemy.

While the Lakota and Shahiyena had attacked soldier

posts from the country along the New Cherry River* to the Buffalo Dung River,† even killed the Hundred in the Hand near the Piney Woods Fort nine winters before, nonetheless this long day's fight with Three Stars was perhaps the greatest of all battles simply because that soldier chief was as smart as a fox of an enemy.

But even still, as great as was the Fight Where the Young Girl Saved Her Brother, Wooden Leg drifted off to sleep that morning dreaming on greater things. Behind his eyes swam that vision they all still shared with the Hunkpapa shaman, Sitting Bull.

As the sun came up in the east. Wooden Leg dreamed of many, many soldiers falling into camp.

Seamus doubted how any of them could have slept last night, what with the way those Shoshone caterwauled until just before dawn when they finally buried the dead pony boy who was killed and scalped to the nape of the neck during the battle. All the while the warriors wailed and keened, thumping on their drums as they stomped and pranced around the grave, over which they ultimately built a fire to burn away all scent from savvy predator noses.

Such celebration of the dark arts was enough to turn a somber camp downright gloomy.

As weary as the troops were, Crook had the buglers blow reveille to roll his men out of their blankets at three A.M. while the east was only beginning to become a thin gray line on the horizon. A thick frost coated Donegan's wool blanket, grown shiny with the coming of first light. It rattled icily as he sat up, grinding knuckles into his gritty eyes. To his surprise he found the old packer already stoking life into a small cookfire.

"Morning, Irishman!" Richard Closter cried cheerfully.

"There any coffee ready?"

"Not yet."

Putting his nose into the breeze and gazing this way

---

* South Platte River: attack on Fort Sedgwick and the burning of Julesburg, Colorado—1864

† North Platte River: Battle of Platte Bridge—1865

and that along the slope where other fires and men were coming to life, Seamus asked, "You need water?"

"Yes. If you want coffee—we sure as hell need water."

"I'll get it," the Irishman replied, kicking free of his frost-stiffened blanket and sweeping up the bail to the blackened coffeepot as he rose. "Got to head down to the bushes anyway."

As the expedition finished a breakfast of their dwindling rations of hardtack and fried bacon, washing it down with steaming coffee, the sun made its appearance in a clear, cloudless sky. It promised to be a beautiful day for man as well as beast. The horses and mules appeared well recuperated after both the march and battle of the last two days.

Fortunate, Donegan thought as he saddled his gelding, that we had such good bottomland to graze the animals.

"Seamus!" Reuben Davenport called out as he walked by with his horse in tow, having taken the animal down to water at the creek. "Keep yours eyes peeled, as the old plainsmen always say. It may be we're still surrounded and the red bastards might give us another try while we're strung out on the trail."

"What makes you so sure this outfit is surrounded?"

Davenport stopped to reply. "Last night I commissioned one of Moore's civilians to carry my first dispatch down to Fetterman for me. Would have paid him good too—had I been first to get out word of the fight."

"But the fella didn't make it, did he?"

"Oh, he was gone about two hours or more," the correspondent explained. "Then showed back up after midnight, saying he was pursued back to our lines by some of the hostiles. Got so close to their village that he even heard the squaws wailing for their dead."

"He sure he headed south? That's where Fetterman is, while we all know the enemy camp is north of us, Davenport."

With a shrug Davenport said, "I suppose so, unless he headed out to make a wide circuit."

"So it sounds like you won't be the first one to get out any news of the battle after all, will you?"

The newsman wagged his head. "Couldn't talk that man into trying again, no matter what price I offered."

Over among the mule brigade the infantry were readying the travois Chambers's walk-a-heaps had constructed yesterday and into the long summer evening, using cottonwood limbs interwoven with willow branches, lashed together with rawhide strips and rope. On these crude litters the five surgeons placed their wards. For each one of the wounded, six volunteers were assigned to travel beside the litter, attending to the smallest of needs by those who were destined to suffer through every excruciating yard of the coming march. Experienced in such things, Sergeant John Warfield, F Company of the Third Cavalry, a veteran of much service with Crook's Apache campaigns down in Arizona, had been placed in charge of constructing the litters, as well as being designated superintendent overseeing the welfare of the wounded during their retreat to Goose Creek.

When the order came to mount up and move out, Crook put most of the Third Cavalry out in the van while two battalions of the Third covered both flanks. The remainder of his horse soldiers in the Second Cavalry were to bring up the rear and watch the backtrail against any surprises. Between the van and rearguard were stationed the litters bearing the wounded, followed by the mule brigade and civilians.

The general himself led out the procession so that every horse and mule passed over the mass grave of the fallen soldiers. With a fire kept burning over the trench throughout the night, and now the hooves of more than twelve hundred animals crossing that spot, Donegan was positive the site would be all but obliterated from discovery by the time he passed over it at the tail end of the column.

Now as he looked back at that unmarked plot of trampled ground, his attention was rudely snagged by the sudden whooping and joyful cries from some of the Crow scouts on the slope off to the west. They were gathering along the side of the nearby hill, dismounting. Several shots rang out, then more laughter. Finally Donegan caught the glint of early sunlight flashing from several tomahawks the scouts swung into the air about the time John Finerty galloped up to the scene.

A while later Seamus gave his mount the heel and loped ahead to find Baptiste Pourier.

"Found one of the Lakota, up in the rocks," Big Bat explained when the Irishman asked what all the joyous activity was about.

"A live one?"

Pourier nodded. "Probably crawled that far last night. He looked blind. Maybe shot in the face. One of our scouts already scalped him yesterday. Head was stripped clean—from brow to the back of his neck, covered with flies."

"And you said he was still alive?" Seamus felt the quiver course through his belly.

"Made it through the night anyway. Still alive when I got up to that band of Crow making sport with him. His skull was even cracked a bit, some of the brain coming out where the bone was caved in from a stone club." Now Pourier chuckled, almost regretful. "Likely the poor bastard heard our horses and figured us for Lakota because he started calling out for water in the wrong tongue: '*Mini! Mini!*' "

With the sound of hammering hooves, Seamus turned to watch a gleeful warrior gallop past, racing along the right flank of the slower-moving column. Behind him he dragged an object bouncing at the end of a long rawhide rope. The shapeless thing only faintly resembled the bloodied torso of a copper-skinned man. Two other young horsemen came traipsing along behind the first, each of them dragging a trophy through the dirt and rocks and hoof-cut grass: the hapless Sioux's legs.

With an involuntary shudder, the Irishman looked away, remembering what fiendish glee and butchery this same tribe had committed on a Sioux warrior they had captured back in the early spring of '67 when Donegan was exiled to Fort C. F. Smith, the northernmost post along the Bozeman Road.*

"Them Crow ain't the only ones, Irishman," Pourier

* THE PLAINSMEN Series, vol. 2, *Red Cloud's Revenge*

went on to explain. "Snakes were worked up in burying that pony boy, so some of 'em went out from camp last night. Ran across a couple more Lakota bodies they didn't find before."

"Cut 'em up pretty good, I'd wager."

"A real pretty thing, how these Injuns work with a knife," Bat replied.

"Maybe they're due, just to even things up," Seamus admitted. "Seeing how the hostiles cut that poor soldier into pieces so he was buried in a feed sack."

"Look there." Pourier had turned in the saddle, pointing back to one of the grassy crests north of the Rosebud.

"Figure they're Lakota?" Donegan asked.

"I suppose. Maybe Shahiyena."

"They ain't acting like they're scouts for a bunch come to devil our backtrail, Bat."

"Nope," Pourier replied. "Maybe they just come to look over the battlefield."

"See if they could rescue any more of their dead they couldn't drag off yesterday."

"There's fourteen they didn't get away with," the half-breed replied. "Look now. They're getting down off their ponies. You was right—ain't no scouting party."

"Just curious about things, I suppose," Donegan said as he watched the dozen or more distant horsemen slide to the ground. "A ghosty, superstitious people, they are."

Off to the extreme east near the gap, another small party of horsemen appeared along the skyline. Then a third, and larger, group dappled the morning blue near the crest of Crook's hill. Strangely eerie it felt to the Irishman now, watching those horsemen sitting bareback there, others choosing to stand motionless beside their war ponies as they watched the soldier column march away up the South Fork of the Rosebud.

Suddenly one of the Crow scouts came galloping past, chattering wildly, dangling something from one hand as he passed by Pourier, a great smile on his yellow-painted face.

"What'd he have to say?" Donegan asked.

With a wag of his head, Pourier replied, "Just bragging."

"Bragging about what?"

"About how all the Sioux squaws was going to be so sad now when they hear about that buck getting killed in the fight."

"Why the squaws?"

"He said the squaws gonna miss that buck something terrible."

"Why him? He some big chief?"

"No, Irishman. Because what the Crow warrior had hanging from his hand was that Lakota's cock and balls."

Seamus Donegan was as happy as any of them to be getting out of the valley of the Rosebud. Each step a little closer to Samantha, and the shelter of her arms.

Sane was how he felt when he was with her. No matter where it was, he felt sane with her—able to shut out the cruelty, the barbarity, the outright insanity of this war between an unstoppable force set in motion against an immovable enemy.

Oh, Sam—how I want to come home.

Chapter 41

18 June 1876

In leading Crook's army away from the big bend of the Rosebud on that Sunday morning, Grouard, Pourier, and Reshaw had taken the same trail they used in bringing the soldiers there. While the north fork of the creek continued west from the battle site itself, the Bighorn and Yellowstone Expedition instead turned south, hauling their wounded and backtracking up the South Fork of the Rosebud.

As the morning wore on, it grew more and more apparent that the route followed by their inbound march of the seventeenth was becoming steeper, less than ideal for the wounded on the litters and travois. The command followed the rugged terrain, climbing ever upward with those tiny tributaries flowing east to feed the Tongue River. Just after midmorning Crook asked the half-breed scouts to select a better route in consideration of his wounded, a different trail that might not prove so hard on those who stoically bore their discomfort and pain.

Grouard turned the command west by south toward the Wolf Mountains. But Crook's best intentions bore bitter fruit.

Time and again through the waning hours of the morning and into the afternoon their march was slowed, or even stopped altogether, as the six-man squads detailed to assist each wounded soldier had to hoist the travois poles to keep the wounded men level as they struggled down the slope of a ravine or scrambled up the loosened side of a coulee. It wasn't long before Crook found out he had made a crucial mistake taking them through this new piece of country.

Across the hours of jostling and bumping over the uneven ground, some of the rawhide and rope lashes tying Guy Henry's litter between the fore and aft mules loosened enough that on starting the descent of a steep-sided ravine some twenty feet deep, the end of one pole struck a boulder and was knocked completely loose. The wounded officer spilled, tumbling past the churning, sliding hooves of the front mule, down the loose dirt and grass of the slope, right onto the boulders and rocks at the bottom.

The captain's steward scurried down the slope, yelling for help, as the column came to an immediate halt, everything in an instant uproar. Nearby at the bottom of the coulee, the two hapless mules clattered to a halt, dragging the flopping litter pole.

First to the captain's side was Assistant Surgeon Julius Patzki, who quickly yanked his bandanna out to wipe dirt and fresh blood from the officer's crusted wounds, asking, "How—how do you feel?"

"Bully!" answered the redoubtable horse soldier in a hoarse whisper, spitting dirt from his swollen lips and blinking the dust from the slits that were his eyes. "N-never felt better in my life."

"Get me some water!" Patzki hollered at the stewards.

With a brave, gritty smile Henry continued, "Every . . . everyone is so kind."

Then he turned painfully to peer over at the pair of mules with the one eye left him after his horrid wounding. "Don't know what's better conduct from those beasts—throwing me off my litter or kicking me in the face."

"Kicked you in the face?" asked Patzki as a canteen was presented him. He pulled the stopper and slipped an arm under the officer's head before gently pouring a dribble of water into the waiting lips.

"Two or three ravines back," Henry explained after the

drink and licking his dusty mouth. "Climbing up. A long slope. The beast in front gave me quite a good kick in the head."

"Good God!" exclaimed William Royall, who came up.

"Nay, Colonel," the courageous Henry said, trying out a grin as he blinked into the bright sunlight. "If Crazy Horse can't do me in with his best . . . don't worry yourself over what these mules will try."

Some time in the early afternoon the column finally reached a piece of country where the terrain no longer heaved and broke itself apart. At last the landscape rolled gently, pocked with smooth-topped knolls. To the west and north stood the heights of the Wolf Mountains.

Almost due west of here stands Fort C. F. Smith, Seamus thought. More than likely the *ruins* of the post, put to the torch and plundered after the army abandoned the place in 1868 and the Sioux came in to revel in their victory.

With the first rattle of shots from the rear of their march, Donegan turned with a start, yanked out of his reverie. Gunfire had erupted from some of the five companies of the Second Cavalry closing the column that was strung out for more than a mile across the rolling grassland. It was sporadic but unchecked gunfire that continued unabated, the rattling working itself up the ranks, coming closer and closer as more and more horse soldiers got in their shots.

Then the Irishman spotted the target.

A single antelope had been spooked from its brushy cover near the tail of the march, bounding directly along the length of the column. Nearly half of the soldiers, more than five hundred, tried a shot at the skittish, but charmed, animal. Nimbly darting back and forth, the fleet antelope successfully ran the noisy gauntlet for practically the entire length of Crook's command, until it finally took refuge among some willow and alder along a narrow stream the column was then about to cross.

"More ammunition wasted," Richard Closter growled in that grumpy bullfrog tone of his.

"Don't go on like that," Donegan tried to cheer. "I figure from all the bullets these soldiers fired yesterday, and what with so few Indians killed—Crook's men can use all the target practice that antelope can give them!"

Just past midafternoon the column approached the summit of the gentle divide separating the Rosebud from an affluent of the Little Bighorn, which the Crow tribe called the Rotten Grass.* As the day had worn on, the six-man squads assigned to care for the wounded were having to lag farther and farther behind with the slow going of their travois or mule litters as the terrain grew rougher. It was here west of the Rosebud Gap that Crook ordered the head of the march to halt while those rear echelons caught up.

Rather than stretching out in the grass under the warm sun like so many of the others, Donegan picketed his horse, then climbed the slope of a solitary butte at the base of which the command was taking its rest. From the wide plateau at the top he could see miles in all directions, a magnificent panorama laid out at his feet.

"The Crow fought a battle here summers ago."

Seamus turned to find Baptiste Pourier approaching. He offered Donegan his canteen.

After taking a drink, Seamus asked, "Who they fight?"

"Blackfoot," Bat replied. "Not the Blackfoot Lakota. The big tribe. Ones come out of Canada, what the Injuns call the land of the Grandmother. Three tribes in the Blackfoot: called Piegans, some called Bloods. The rest are known as Gros Ventres. French for Big Bellies."

"S'pose they wandered into this country from up north to hunt buffalo, eh? Feed their big bellies?"

Pourier grinned, gazing into the glorious sinking of the summer sun, the fiery globe descending toward the northernmost reaches of the Big Horn Mountains off to the west. "No, they came for Crow scalps, most like. Crow and Blackfoot been bitter enemies for longer'n any man now alive can remember."

Seamus turned at the sound of many feet, the snorts of horses and the rattle of equipage scratching up the sides of the butte, finding more than a hundred of the Crow scouts

* Present-day Owl Creek

arriving. They passed on by the Irishman and half-breed to begin picketing their ponies.

"Ho, Left Hand!" hailed Bull Snake, the warrior who was shot in the leg during the early minutes of the battle but nonetheless dragged himself to a nearby tree, where he kept up a constant verbal assault on the Sioux, cheering his brother warriors on.

The day before, his fellow scouts had splinted his leg with limbs and strips of green horsehide. Once they had hoisted him onto the back of his pony that morning, others had lashed the busted leg to the neck of his pony so that Bull Snake's splint was kept as level as possible during the day's rugged overland journey.

A half dozen came over to the pony now, untied the leg's sling, and helped the wounded warrior hobble to the ground. In addition, there were nine more warriors nursing one sort of wound or another.

The rest spread blankets on the ground in a great circle across the plateau that stretched some fifty feet in diameter. At the center settled some of the older warriors, who promptly began to invoke the power of the heavens, beating their hand-drums or shaking their rattles. Out came the ten scalps taken from the bodies of their Lakota enemies, ten Apsaalooke warriors holding them aloft at the end of long willow wands where the long black hair danced on the breeze over the heads of the others. Most began immediately to yelp, keen, or wail, chanting their war songs and dancing around the drummers and singers sitting at the center.

Donegan finally asked, "You was going to tell me what happened here."

"Crow drove the Blackfoot here to this butte where you're standing now. And wiped every last one of 'em out."

Then Bat pointed to the west into the valley below them cut with sandstone ledges, grassy bluffs, and hills dotted with stands of scrub pine. "This is a piece of country the Crow been fighting over for a long, long time. Off yonder is the Rotten Grass, where the Crow met the Lakota a few winters ago when the Sioux first started coming into this country, making a strong show of it. It was a time the Apsaalooke say the icy creek ran red with Lakota blood."

"Crow may be a small tribe," Donegan agreed. "But sounds to me like they stand strong against any who come to take this land from them."

"That's why they put the faith of their hearts into Lone Star . . . into Crook," Bat explained. "They counted on this army of his to drive their enemies out of this prime hunting ground for good, for all time."

"But instead," Donegan replied sadly, "the Crow are forced to watch Lone Star's soldiers retreat."

Once the wounded and the Second Cavalry at the rear guard caught up an hour later, the general remounted his column and resumed the trail south.

That evening, after having endured a torturous march of some twenty-two miles across rugged terrain, Crook's command finally received the order to halt and bivouac for the night in a narrow valley. The soldiers and civilians set up their camp beside the headwaters of the Little Tongue River, spooking deer and elk, as well as a small herd of buffalo from the bountiful pasturage. Pickets were thrown out, and the horses and mules were turned out to graze in the tall, luxuriant grasses.

That evening, after holding their scalp dance, the warriors of Old Crow, Plenty Coups, and Medicine Crow took their leave of Crook's expedition.

They asked Big Bat to give Lone Star their regrets in leaving so abruptly but wanted the half-breed scout to explain to the soldier chief the reason why, as well as tell Crook of their promise.

By the time the warriors were on their way out of camp after sunset Pourier was at headquarters explaining to Crook that during the preparations to march that very morning one of the Crow warriors had come across a pony on the battlefield, an animal apparently left behind by the fleeing Sioux. The import of this discovery was that the abandoned animal just happened to belong to one of the Crow war chiefs—but was a pony he had left behind in the village when the warriors followed Pourier, Grouard, and Reshaw back to join up with the soldiers.

The Crow were hurrying home now, Big Bat declared,

anxious and convinced that the Lakota and Shahiyena had attacked and pillaged their village with their overwhelming strength witnessed firsthand only the day before. So concerned were they for their women and families, and the old chiefs they had left behind to protect the village, that Old Crow's young warriors planned to travel right on through the night until they reached the Big Horn River, where they would be able once more to protect their people and defend their homes from their ancient enemies. To soften their departure, the chiefs vowed to return in fifteen suns, promising to rejoin Lone Star at Goose Creek or somewhere on the upper Tongue if the general went in pursuit of Crazy Horse.

It was a vow the fleeing Crow never intended to keep.

Frank Grouard slept better that Sunday night than he had the first night after the battle. At least until around one A.M. when some of the pickets posted on the perimeter of the camp square opened fire with their carbines.

Shooting at sounds and shadows, seeing ghosts, spooked by something out there in the darkness.

Crook quickly ordered a reconnaissance from the Second Cavalry, but they returned after more than an hour, having discovered no sign of intruders or enemy scouts, no evidence of anything or anybody skulking around their encampment.

While the half-breed quickly fell back to sleep in his blanket, many of the soldiers and civilians were not so lucky. More than half of the expedition had been so frightened, grown so anxious at the threat of a night attack, that they were unable to close their eyes in peace. They stayed awake for the rest of the night: restoking fires, making coffee, smoking their pipes, and talking again of the battle. Brooding on the Crazy Horse warriors still out there.

First light was welcomed by the red-eyed and frightened among them.

The column was back on the trail, moving east, at dawn. An uneventful march on the nineteenth of no more than five miles that morning brought George Crook's expedition back to the forks of Goose Creek, where they found Quartermaster John Furey's wagon corral undisturbed, its inhabitants eager for any and all news of the fight, ready to do whatever they could to make the returning warriors comfortable, to welcome back those who had pushed north to fight the bellicose Sioux. Out to wave and whoop and holler with the rest of the teamsters was George Crook's prisoner—Calamity Jane herself—perhaps more excited than most to see old faces and hear the new stories of Injun fighting.

Those who had remained behind with the wagon train had not been without something to do in the three days Crook's cavalry and mule brigade had been gone. While their location in the grassy streambed had provided the men with an ample supply of water on all sides in the event they were put under siege, their first morning Captain Furey had them string ropes and braking chains from wheel to wheel between wagons so that no horsemen could easily charge through their corral. As well the men had sweated digging rifle trenches, throwing the earth up into breastworks around some logs and deadfall they had dragged into place.

Grouard approved of such preparations. If a wandering band of Crazy Horse's Lakota had stumbled onto the wagon corral, it looked as if these men would have made a hot time of it for the enemy, sharpshooting from behind their barricades.

Still, Furey had not worked his men nonstop. With a force consisting of no less than 80 mule-packers as well as 110 teamsters, the major assigned rotating details to go out daily in the hunt for fresh meat. The butchered carcasses of six buffalo and three elk on the nearby banks attested to the industry of those who had stayed behind with the wagon master.

Crook now chose to push his entire command on an additional two miles to a new campsite he selected where the stock would have sufficient pasturage. Pickets were dispatched to the bluffs overlooking the encampment, and the stock was unsaddled and put out to graze. At the same time some of the soldiers dispersed to scare up firewood or bring water up from the nearby stream.

A detail was assigned the task of erecting the hospital tents where Surgeon Hartsuff's wounded were soon made comfortable. A half-dozen officers who had lemons left in their haversacks gladly turned them over to Assistant Surgeon Patzki, who prepared a small kettle of lemonade that was quickly finished off by the grateful wounded who now rested upon thin mattresses, out of the sun and under canvas at last. That afternoon the surgeons' thermometer rose to 103 degrees.

Especially relieved was Guy Henry. The mules carrying his litter had again conspired against the captain, slipping and nearly going over so that the unlucky officer was swamped by the icy water and nearly washed off his crude cot as the command crossed to the east bank of the Tongue earlier that morning. Simply to be rid of his two favorite animals and allowed some real rest proved to be the greatest luxury to the horse soldier.

In the heat of late afternoon, Frank Grouard went in search of some shade along the creekbank with Baptiste Pourier. He stopped suddenly, parting some of the willows when he spotted the Irishman.

"I'd heard you white men aren't supposed to like water!" Frank roared, grinning as Big Bat came to a halt beside him. They both squatted on their heels there beside Goose Creek.

Seamus Donegan sat in a quiet pool where the sluggish waters eddied about him up to his armpits. "Feels good. You two ought to think about it. Way I see it, you both're beginning to smell no better than those mules out yonder."

The half-breeds lounged quietly for a long time watching the Irishman loll about in the creek, turning and splashing, taking a few strokes in this direction, then turning his white rump about to swim a few strokes heading upstream. Bat passed Grouard a dark plug of tobacco. From it Frank carved a long sliver, which he broke up between his thumb and fingers, dropping the fragrant leaf into the bowl of his pipe. When Pourier produced a lucifer, Frank set fire to the tobacco, then without much ceremony blew the first six short puffs to the four winds, to father sky and mother earth.

Old habits were hard to break, even had a man wanted to.

"Way me and Bat see it," Grouard began without preliminaries, lifting his chin to blow a stream of smoke into the leafy branches right over his head, "the general needs to find out what's going on north of here."

"See what the village is doing?" Donegan asked, slowly padding closer to the bank now, his interest piqued. He swept the long, wet hair back over his shoulder.

"Maybeso, yes. And see what the other soldier columns up to," Pourier answered.

"I don't think Crook would mind at all knowing what Terry or Gibbon are doing wandering around up on the Yellowstone," Donegan replied. "But I imagine it's going to be some dangerous work."

Tapping the chewed stem of his pipe against his lower teeth, Grouard grew thoughtful a moment before he spoke again. "One man—maybe two—could slip through that country, Irishman."

Donegan almost choked, spitting water as he growled, "Through that goddamned bunch of hostiles with Crazy Horse? Are you serious?"

Grouard grinned slightly. "That mean you're wanting to stay here with Reshaw?"

The Irishman's eyes flicked back and forth between the two half-breeds. "You boys have it all figured out, do you?"

Grouard only nodded, drawing again on his pipe.

Pourier spit a stream of tobacco juice into the creek, making a pretty, graceful arc in the steamy summer air. "Frank's going—ain't no talking him out of it."

"You still got something to settle with that Crazy Horse bunch, don't you, Grouard?" Donegan asked.

His only reply was a slight shrug with one shoulder.

"So if Frank goes," Bat said, "we all know Crook won't let me go with him."

The Irishman asked, "Why not?"

"Because the general don't wanna be left behind with Reshaw as his only guide."

"Why won't Crook take Reshaw?"

Now Grouard savagely yanked the pipe from his lips and grumbled, sour as green meat, "Because the general don't really trust the little black-hearted bastard."

The Irishman wagged his head. "You fellas come down here to talk me into going with you, Grouard?"

Frank stared off across the stream. "You wanna go—you're welcome to come. Up to you. I ain't begging. It's gonna be one of the most dangerous rides you ever took in your life, white man."

"Well, now—I've had me some pretty exciting rides in my lifetime—"

"Nothing like what's waiting out there," Grouard interrupted, jabbing at the afternoon air with the stem of his pipe. "A hundred miles and more of nothing but Lakota and Shahiyena warriors wanting nothing like they want my scalp on their lodgepole."

" 'Cause you went and led Crook's soldiers down on 'em twice now," the Irishman added.

Grouard leaned forward, elbows on his knees. "You decide to go with me, you better be damned sure it's what you wanna do."

"You got that right," Donegan grumbled, cupping his hand in the cool water and bringing it to his lips.

"So if you don't go, Frank goes on his own," Pourier declared. "But Crook needs to know who's going—needs to know tonight."

Back and forth between them the Irishman looked, first at one, then at the other, back and forth as if considering something. Hefting the weightiness of it. Then for a long, long moment Donegan stared off to the south, as if gazing far, far away. When he finally brought his eyes back to Grouard, he had a sad smile on his face.

"Tell me when you're figuring on us slipping out of camp, Frank."

"Tonight."

Epilogue

19 June 1876
Camp at the Forks of
Goose Creek
Wyo. Terr.

My dearest Samantha,

Woman of my heart and mind, of my very soul.

How many times I've taken your lace kerchief from my shirt pocket, pulled back the waxed paper, now much wrinkled. We were both so hopeful that by wrapping this keepsake in just this way I could carry with me the smell of you. With sad regret I find your fragrance fading from this scrap of cloth.

Yet my love for you has never been stronger.

Never doubt in that. I will continue to carry the kerchief in my breast pocket, there—over my heart, where you are always with me. Even into the throes of battle, you rode with me, my love. Never once did you leave my side.

Oh, how I am blessed by your love. Blessed by

your steadfastness. Never have I had such fidelity. Never before have I wanted to pledge my fidelity to another.

Hear again my vow, Samantha. Feel it course through you as it truly courses through me now as I sit down to take this pencil in my hand, poise it over these sheets of paper I have begged off one of the newspaper correspondents come on this trip north to Indian country. Another unredeemed Irishman, I'm afraid. Like that Bob Strahorn you heard me speak of so often after our return from the Powder River in March. This one, by the name of John Finerty, I would never trust near you, Sam.

He's far too much the rascal, and a handsome rounder to boot. I'm dead certain he could cause any lady's heart to swoon—even yours, my dear. So I am most relieved that for the time being he is here with George Crook's army and not at your unescorted elbow there at Fort Laramie.

I truly don't know what to ask you, to properly inquire of your condition. Not being accustomed to genteel company, I am not sure what is proper etiquette when one addresses a mother-to-be, asking about the changes she is undergoing as that new life grows within her. You see, I've never been a father before. How would I know what to ask?

Before I left for Fetterman, you were so worried, tears wetting your eyes, anxious that I would not recognize you when I returned. So afraid, you finally admitted to me, that I would not find you attractive—would not desire you—when you became "as big as a cow."

Do you remember what I told you then?

"Samantha—you will never be as big as a cow. Maybe a horse. But never a cow!"

What a thrashing you gave me, dear heart! What a joyful thrashing! One I admit I knew I would deserve even before the words had fallen from my lips.

Just as I took you in my arms when you had finished thrashing me, and held you while we laughed until we cried. Then I realized you really were crying. How I've always hated to see tears cloud those eyes of yours. But especially then—to find tears of sadness, regret, of longing already there as I raised your chin so that I could look into your sweet, sweet face.

Oh, how I wish I had you here now in my arms. So empty are they. So empty they ache. A cold, real ache.

To look now into your face, to see if there are the smallest of changes wrought of your condition. But all I have is this tiny chromo we had done of you in Denver City early last autumn. I trust you will hold as tightly to the one you wanted done of me. This image of my true love in no way does you justice, yet it must do until I finally embrace you in my hands. Touch your cheeks and wipe the tears from them. To feel your skin beneath my touch as I hold you close through the long, long nights.

It's then that I find this longing for you the hardest to bear. Like tonight, just now as the sun is falling behind the Bighorn Mountains. Where I sit is but a matter of miles north of Fort Phil Kearny, where I spent what one might call my coming of age here on the frontier. Ten years gone beneath my wandering boots, like the flowing of one of these mountain streams.

I suppose I was brought to you, nudged in your direction in one way or another in just that way, Sam.

If I hadn't found you, if you hadn't saved me—there's no telling what might have become of my life.

How I always tempted the fates. How I still tempt Dame Fortune, a fickle strumpet that she is, not much given to casting a favored eye on me.

But you—you, Sam have been my good fortune, my blessing above all others. How I do cherish you, and that new life we together have created.

By now you will have received some word from me, the barest of messages we are allowed to have sent on to you from Fetterman. Most of the officers who have wives stationed at Russell or Laramie will send their loved ones these brief notices that they have survived the fight we had with the Sioux and Cheyenne two days ago. I have no idea how long it will take you to get my message that I am safe. I can only hope that you get that news at the same time Fort Laramie is receiving the news of Crook's battle on the Rosebud.

If you don't, I pray you will not suffer with anxiety for me. I pray that you will not suffer because my message is late in arriving. Army business always takes priority. Next are the messages sent out by officers to their families. Only then will they allow anything from a civilian.

So I'm asking a fellow packer who tells me tonight that he will be going south tomorrow with some dispatches and telegrams from General Crook to his commanders, likely bound for the desk of none other than General Phil Sheridan himself. I fought for Little Phil in the Shenandoah, Sam. Had some Confederate steel laid across my back for Phil Sheridan and U.S. Grant and Uncle Billy Sherman and the rest too. Took that steel and the acid the surgeons poured in that slash across the great muscles of my back, vowing that I would never shirk doing whatever I could to preserve our Union.

Me—a poor Irish boy locked on a stinking ship and bound for a foreign land called Amerikay. Me, ready time and again to lay down my life for this Union I have come to love.

The way I came to love you. Ready to lay down my life for you, should I ever be asked.

If this land is to be settled, it is here I wish to put down our roots, Sam. Here to send out our branches—those children we will raise together.

The lives of those we will create together, more than anything I do alone in this great wilderness, will be my lasting legacy. Those children and grandchildren you will gather round my knee each night to hear my stories—they will be one of the greatest blessings God has ever given an unworthy man.

Johnny Bourke tells me tonight that Crook plans on waiting right here for the reinforcements he has asked Sheridan to send up to him from Kansas and Nebraska. The general has also requested complete resupply. Although we have an ample supply of ammunition among the wagons here at our base camp, enough to withstand any full-scale assault by the warrior bands, we still do not have enough when the time comes that General Crook desires to lead us back into the bosom of the red man's stronghold.

It is there that dangers await—enough danger to quicken the heart of even the most jaded adventurer.

I think Crook desires to link up with one of the two outfits said to be north of us on the Yellowstone. Even my old friend, Custer, is up there. You've not heard me tell of him before—but I am sure you will hear his name mentioned on this frontier, from Fort Abraham Lincoln down to Fort Laramie. We both fought for Phil Sheridan in the Shenandoah Valley. It was there that Custer stripped me of my sergeant's stripes. I never got them back until I had a fateful reunion with the man who wore them after me. Another old friend who was killed later with William Fetterman.

Yes, now Crook can't help but want to link up with another outfit and together go in search of the hostile village. Now that we've seen their strength, sensed the measure of their will and resolve, felt the caliber of their warrior spirit. Crook is not so anxious now—not near as anxious as he once was—to strike the enemy alone. I sense that he feels need of finding out about the other units on the Yellowstone. Communicating with them. But, alas—between us and them lies the disputed land of these noble savages.

Oh, as night comes down on this camp, I think all the more on you and my heart grows heavy in the distance between us.

Nearby some man is playing a mouth-harp, the mournful wail of some sad, sad song. And someone down in the teamsters' camp does a merry tune on his squeeze-box. Times like this I wish I were more talented and could bring others joy by making music. Times like this, I wish you were here to dance and whirl and kick up your heels with me—spinning, spinning around and around as I lead you in our merry reel beneath the stars, your skirts flaring at your ankles, a flush come to your cheeks, a smile on your lips and in your eyes.

How I so want to dance with you!

It grows late and I must go see a friend about purchasing from him a new rifle. The one I have carried for these ten long years has suffered some damage that makes it irreparable in the field. Since I am to stay here with Crook's army, I will be in great need of another powerful weapon. And this old packer I mentioned let me use one of his rifles during the last hours of the battle against the Sioux and Cheyenne horsemen who repeatedly charged us, although to no good purpose. So I'll go soon and try striking a deal with the old packer for his buffalo gun. A supremely serviceable weapon that should stand the test of time just like that Henry repeater of mine.

Then I will try sleeping. Last night the nervous pickets blasted away at shadows, and I wasn't able to fall back asleep because there were so many men in my own camp who were afraid to go back to sleep that they sat up the rest of the night talking and drinking coffee. It made it impossible for a man of my constitution and light sleeping habits to get any rest. Tonight will be the first rest I have had in the last three days.

As soon as I can I will send more word to you by the couriers who will regularly ply the road between this supply depot and Fort Fetterman. The moment I know when I will be coming back to you will be but the span of a heartbeat before I sit down to send you word of my return.

Until then, do not fear for me. Keep up your strength, and your nightly prayers. I so need them here in this wilderness, Sam. I send you my prayers, and beg the angels stay close to both of you while I cannot.

Pray the angels hover at your shoulder, to watch over my family until I can return home to your arms.

Your loving husband,
Seamus

Afterword

For all intent and purpose, Crook's Battle of the Rosebud lies in historical obscurity.

Few of those who have more than a speaking acquaintance with the Indian wars of the west really know much about this epic conflict.

Why? my readers might ask at this point, having finished *Reap the Whirlwind*. I would hope that they, like me, now have reason to cry out against this historical injustice that has pitted the Rosebud fight with the Battle of the Little Bighorn.

The dubious politics of the "modern" era have caused one battle to suffer in the shadows for more than a hundred years, while the other has reveled in every aspect of our national culture and thereby enjoys worldwide acclaim.

Yet this battle beside the Rosebud has every bit as much of the continuing intrigue and controversy as does that more famous battle against the Sioux which took place eight days later and some thirty miles northwest on what the white man calls the Little Bighorn River. More than a third of a century ago, J. W. Vaughn, the first author to write the in-depth story of Crook's battle on the Rosebud, aptly stated the case for a more popular—and long overdue

—examination of the duel with Crazy Horse: "One could spend a lifetime in the study of the Rosebud battle and still not cover all of the various angles and details."

So this first of the great fights against the "hostiles," the free-roaming warrior bands, taking place in this epic, watershed year during which Sherman and Sheridan's frontier army waged its "Great Sioux War of 1876," suffers only from lack of press, perhaps lack of public relations.

There's no better way to put this: the Battle of the Little Bighorn has enjoyed its place among America's popular culture, alone as one of the most enduring myths that rest in our national psyche, continuing year after year because of one reason and one reason only: George Armstrong Custer died on that hot, dusty hillside.

Otherwise, the fight the Seventh U.S. Cavalry had with the Sioux and Cheyenne beside the Greasy Grass was itself an inconsequential skirmish that proved nothing for either side, even though it was the *last* time the various warrior bands fought together in such massed strength.

But do not forget! The Battle of the Rosebud was the *first* time those warrior bands fought together—a remarkable event in the era of the Indian Wars.

Little Bighorn aficionados and Custerphiles point out that what you must take into account is that tremendous four-mile distance between Reno's attack on the Hunkpapa camp and where Custer's last held out briefly on "Massacre Hill." But, I caution, you must remember that there were only two concentrations of fighting north of the Reno/Benteen siege: Calhoun Hill and Massacre Hill, less than a half mile apart.

I can put it no more simply than to state that in the Custer battle there was *no* fighting over a wide territory despite that four-mile separation from Reno's position to the monument of present day.

At the Battle of the Rosebud, on the other hand, not only did the Sioux and Cheyenne hurl themselves at Crook's cavalry, infantry, and civilians along a four-mile front, but that battlefield was, in addition, more than two miles wide! All one has to do is walk some of that rugged, vaulting terrain, and he or she will get a clear picture of what the soldiers had to contend with that day, and begin to grasp just how Crazy Horse so masterfully drove his wedges between the various units, dividing the army into detail (with Crook's unwitting help), decoying, feinting, sweeping down to overwhelm in massed attacks.

Something the horseback warrior of the high plains had never before done!

While our nation was enjoying its Centennial year, celebrating by showing the latest in technology at the Centennial Exposition that summer in Philadelphia—a Stone Age people were gathering in heretofore-unheard-of numbers, making no pretense that they were preparing to mount their greatest defense of an ancient way of life. After all, total war had been declared on them.

With the opening salvos of that war, you can't help but be struck with the ignorance with which the military set about its task. One of the most common yet remarkable assets of the frontier army was the reluctance of its officers to recognize they had a tiger by the tail. Time and again in their ten years already on the Plains they had attacked the hostile villages, only to see the warriors fight just long enough for the women and children to flee before they would disappear.

Yet in this "Summer of Seventy-Six" both the hapless Crook and a week later the unfortunate Custer would discover the exception that is said to prove every rule. Both believed that the warriors would stay in character and flee if given the chance. The biggest problem for the army was getting the enemy to stand and fight. It simply wasn't in the nature of the warrior to initiate a major encounter with a large force of warriors.

But from the first charge Crazy Horse's warriors made into the valley of the Rosebud, there wasn't a man serving with George Crook who could say the enemy acted cowardly. The most important factor distinguishing this battle from all the previous fights was that never before had the Indians been so willing to ride into the soldiers' guns, so willing to stand and fight it out, to give blow for blow, while fighting *in concert.*

Because of the military's long-held mind-set, Crazy Horse gave the pony soldiers a rude shock that summer morning, pulling some tricks from his sleeves—yet he really did nothing more magical than use some savvy battlefield tactics: these "savages" displayed discipline before the enemy, decoying, drawing the soldiers beyond the point where they could be supported; and when the various companies that had gone in pursuit of the Indians finally turned around to retreat back to their support, they were time and again overwhelmed with not just numbers, but with the sheer ferocity of the hostiles' disciplined attack.

Again, because of the remarkable nature of the fight, the question is asked: Why is this battle fought on the one hundredth anniversary of the Battle of Bunker Hill so little known to the general public?

The more you learn, the more the injustice of how this battle has been ignored begins to nag at you for attention.

So the Battle of the Rosebud was a surprise. Remember—it is one of the supreme duties of a field commander to guard against surprise. Crook was surprised by Jubal Early in the Shenandoah Valley. And more than a decade later he was surprised again. You only have to give yourself a moment to consider just how George Crook was feeling that night after the long battle, as twilight came down on the Rosebud country. Perhaps he had learned his lesson. Perhaps he no longer held the horseback warriors with disdain, no longer underestimating their abilities.

But we won't really know that until we ride with Three Stars through the rest of that "Summer of the Sioux," and on into the autumn as the army, wincing in pain and licking its wounds after the Custer Battle, regroups and starts to fight back. We won't know if Crook, or the army for that matter, learned anything until the year is done.

Another one of the most important factors to make Crook's fight so remarkable is that the campaign was covered by so many newspaper correspondents. This ran counter to the expressed wishes of General William T. Sherman, who, some will remember, made it clear to Custer that he was not to take any of the press along with him when he marched out of Fort Abraham Lincoln. Yet the lieutenant colonel welcomed Bismarck's own Mark Kellogg, who was thrilled to have the chance to march with

Custer and the Seventh Cavalry, to ride in for the kill. Kellogg died on Massacre Hill.

Had the newsman survived, Custer might well have suffered some less-than-glowing reports in the national media, just the sort of negative press Crook was to suffer following the disaster of June 17. But more on that to come with Volume 10.

Besides the five newspaper correspondents, representing a total of twelve dailies, there were in fact two artists who that early summer sent their drawings in for publication in some of the nation's largest magazines. One of those soldiers, who was himself nearly a casualty of Royall's fight on the left, was Lieutenant James Foster. He kept a journal that was later serially reproduced by the Chicago *Tribune.* In addition, Foster's detailed, lively sketches of camp life at Goose Creek, as well as scenes from the campaign trail, enjoyed a wide audience when published late that summer in *Harper's Weekly.*

These artists were not the only ones to bring texture and life to the nonofficial side of the campaign. A remarkable number of officers maintained detailed and illuminating diaries that have proven beneficial to historians studying Crook's Bighorn and Yellowstone Expedition, as well as the battle itself. Much of those diaries later made it into print not only as individual stories of the fight, but as first-person articles adding incendiary fuel to a growing and continuing debate, grist written for the military magazines of the day, such as the *Army and Navy Journal.*

By now most of my readers should be well aware that John Bourke's records of the winter and summer campaigns provided the initial framework for the most widely quoted of books dealing with his boss, *On the Border with Crook.* While not as extensive, every bit as important is the work of Captain William Stanton, the campaign's official itinerist, who, along with infantry officers like Captain Gerhard Luhn and Lieutenant Thaddeus H. Capron, all maintained daily diaries, as well as holding on to their personal correspondence, which contained some very rich and more anecdotal accounts of the march to hostile territory.

All of you who want to learn more about the Battle of

the Rosebud in particular, as well as some of its key players, in addition to immersing yourself in this most Romantic Era, should enjoy reading the following titles I used in writing *Reap the Whirlwind.* I recommend them all.

The Battle of the Rosebud Plus Three by John M. Carroll, editor

Battle of the Rosebud, Prelude to the Little Bighorn by Neil C. Mangum

Before the Little Big Horn by Fred H. Werner

Black Elk Speaks by John G. Neihardt

Boots & Saddles at the Little Bighorn—Weapons, Dress, Equipment, Horses, and Flags of General Custer's Seventh U.S. Cavalry in 1876 by James S. Hutchins

Calamity Jane and the Lady Wildcats by Duncan Aikman

Centennial Campaign, the Sioux War of 1876 by John S. Gray

Confederate Cavalry West of the River by Stephen B. Oates

Crazy Horse and Custer, the Parallel Lives of Two American Warriors by Stephen E. Ambrose

Crazy Horse, the Strange Man of the Oglalas by Mari Sandoz

Custer's Luck by Edgar I. Stewart

The Fighting Cheyenne by George Bird Grinnell

Fighting Indian Warriors, True Tales of the Wild Frontiers by E. A. Brininstool

First Scalp for Custer by Paul L. Hedren

Fort Laramie and the Pageant of the West, 1834–1890 by LeRoy R. Hafen and Francis Marion Young

Frank Grouard, Army Scout by Margaret Brock Hanson

From the Heart of the Crow Country—The Crow Indians' Own Stories by Joseph Medicine Crow

Frontier Regulars: The United States Army and the Indian, 1866–1891 by Robert M. Utley

General George Crook, His Autobiography, edited by Martin F. Schmitt

The Gentle Tamers, Women of the Old Wild West by Dee Brown

The Great Sioux War, 1876–77, edited by Paul L. Hedren

Great Western Indian Fights by the Potomac Corral of The Westerners

Indian Fights: New Facts on Seven Encounters by J. W. Vaughn

Indian Fighting Army by Fairfax Downey

Indian Fights and Fighters by Cyrus Townsend Brady

Indians, Infants and Infantry: Andrew and Elizabeth Burt on the Frontier by Merrill J. Mattes

The Indian Wars of the West by Paul I. Wellman

Life and Adventures of Frank Grouard by Joe DeBarthe

On the Border with Crook by John G. Bourke

On Time for Disaster: The Rescue of the Custer's Command by Edward J. McClernand, Lieutenant, Second Cavalry, U.S.A.

Paper Medicine Man: John Gregory Bourke and His American West by Joseph C. Porter

The Plainsmen of the Yellowstone by Mark H. Brown

Plenty-Coups, Chief of the Crows by Frank B. Linderman

The Pitman Notes on U.S. Martial Small Arms and Ammunition, 1776–1933, Volume Three: U.S. Breech-load-

ing Rifles and Carbines, Cal. .45 by Brigadier General John Pitman

Sharps Firearms by Frank Sellers

Soldiers West: Biographies from the Military Frontier, edited by Andrew Hutton

Son of the Morning Star by Evan S. Connell

Warpath: The True Story of the Fighting Sioux Told in a Biography by Chief White Bull by Stanley Vestal

War-Path and Bivouac: The Big Horn and Yellowstone Expedition by John F. Finerty

Washakie by Grace Raymond Hebard

With Crook at the Rosebud by J. W. Vaughn

Wooden Leg, A Warrior Who Fought Custer, interpreted by Thomas B. Marquis

The World of the Crow Indians—As Driftwood Lodges by Rodney Frey

When we start talking numbers about the Battle of the Rosebud, we immediately run into discrepancy, if not downright controversy, in two primary areas. Our first concern becomes the number of Indians involved in the fight.

After the better part of a year marked by incessant fighting, Crazy Horse finally came in and surrendered in 1877, at which time, so the story goes, the Hunkpatila war chief told George Crook that he had brought sixty-five hundred warriors to the battlefield the day he dueled with Three Stars. Mind you, this figure is made through an interpreter, translating a very specific number supposedly rendered from an Oglalla war chief, a member of a culture that makes little distinction between very large numbers. To them there was no difference between one hundred and one thousand!

On the face of it, this sixty-five hundred figure is so big

as to be ludicrous. Yet the number becomes all the more fantastic when you consider what the scholars have subsequently stated was the total warrior strength in the encampment at the time of the Rosebud fight: anywhere between nine hundred and four thousand (depending, at times, on whether a scholar is talking of veteran warriors or all men of fighting age—from fourteen to forty).

Just as important, one must remember that Crook fought the Lakota before some of the best and most populous warrior bands came to join the large encampment, notably the great war chief Gall (whose leadership would destroy the Calhoun and Keogh resistance on Massacre Ridge eight days later).

But there is one historian/scholar all of us can trust to separate myth from reality: author John S. Gray, whose excruciatingly minute time studies are a marvel to read in his reenactments of Custer's final hours. Using the same dispassionate and scientific approach, Gray analyzes the agent's records from the various reservations in question and tribal rolls, as well as intelligence reports from army scouts, half-breeds, and those bands hanging around the forts, etc., to come up with a week-by-week accounting that tracks the growing size of that great village as it migrated from valley to valley, gathering its real strength on the Rosebud.

With the finest of data in hand, scholar Gray takes exception not only to the outlandish Crazy Horse myth, but more so to contemporary historians who continue to state there were fifteen hundred to twenty-five hundred warriors in the fight.

Gray unequivocally affirms a logical and most plausible argument for a much, much lower figure: seven hundred fifty.

Half of the lowest estimate made by every other historian!

Gray's number seems ridiculously low until one researches and studies the number of warriors who did not come in to the village until some time during the week following the Crook fight. When one consults the evidence, one can't help but believe that less than a thousand were in those various war parties able to make the trip south from the camp on Sundance Creek. Remember, the chiefs and headmen were still worried about other threats, so they left enough warriors in the village to protect against possible attack from not only the soldiers being watched daily along the Yellowstone, but also from any attack by Shoshone or Crow war parties.

Seven hundred fifty to fight for Crazy Horse. And Crook commanded almost twice that many when the duel began.

It becomes all the more remarkable when, having now completed the story, you sit back and ponder just what those seven hundred fifty warriors accomplished. Holding the greater numbers at bay, continually thwarting the attempts of the soldiers to hold them back, dividing the several soldier outfits into detail and continually flaunting the fact that they were surrounding the soldiers. For about five hours!

Seven hundred fifty. A truly heroic battle when one considers the reality of the odds against the Sioux and Cheyenne.

Then we come to the second matter of numbers—that of the total dead and wounded.

As we mentioned, after his surrender in 1877, Crazy Horse gave Crook information on their fight at the Rosebud. The war chief testified that thirty-nine warriors had been killed, and another sixty-three wounded. One of those wounded who was dragged away on the travois would later die, as did many who suffered death-dealing wounds. His family left the warrior's body behind in the Wolf Mountains along the path Custer's cavalry was following that Sunday morning the regiment descended to the banks of the Greasy Grass and rode into destiny.

These figures appear to be substantiated by Cheyenne historian John Stands in Timber, but as such, will readily seem high to any student of the Indian Wars era. Why? Because the Plains warrior had never before shown any desire to stay very long in a fight where he was being killed and wounded in such numbers. Heretofore, when a skirmish was going badly (i.e., a few warriors were suffering wounds), a war party would break off the fight and ride away, content to fight another day.

But at the Rosebud, Crazy Horse forced them to remain disciplined—following the commands of their war chiefs, flinging themselves again and again at the soldiers and allies. It was a new era in Indian fighting.

On the other side of the equation, the figures seem remarkable if for no other reason than for all the bullets the army and allies fired at the horsemen, they hit no more than a hundred warriors! Knowing what we do today of the nature of the army's green recruits, of the lack of shooting practice, of the inability of the line soldier to keep his weapon clean under field conditions—maybe the low numbers are not remarkable at all.

When you take into account all the costs of Crook's expedition to and from the fight, those few bullets that wounded or killed Indians became very expensive indeed. The government paid something on the order of one million dollars for every warrior killed at the Battle of the Rosebud!

In addition, there remains a little controversy in regard to the number of soldiers killed and wounded. While the character list provided in the front material shows the official military record, we have an entirely different set of figures offered by Frank Grouard—a character who much of the time has been found to give reliable testimony, but who might still embellish things on occasions. Because of that, all but one Indian Wars scholar has totally discounted Grouard's assertions, simply because his figures more than double the army's numbers.

In his autobiography, The Grabber stated twenty-eight soldiers were killed, and fifty-six had been wounded. Was he telling the truth and the army/Crook was not (downplaying the human cost of the ruinous expedition)?

One of the finest Indian Wars and military historians, Bob Utley, tends to agree with my assertion, writing: ". . . Grouard's statement . . . is closer to the truth than Crook's officially reported ten [killed] and twenty-one [wounded]."

Perhaps there's no way we'll ever know for sure since every other historian has repeatedly relied on the military's figures, pulled from archival sources. Still, there are those of us who remember the daily body counts issued by those "official government" or military sources during the Vietnam war, and how we did not know we were lied to until years later. The deceptive veil stretches across more than a century.

So in case you haven't caught my drift: I have my sneaking suspicions that the number of soldiers killed and wounded was really greater than it appears at first blush in the military record.

Take a look for yourself to bring home the point of just how brutal the fighting was during Royall's bloody retreats. You only have to comb the rosters to see that every last one of the dead came from that doomed battalion on the left. Although the Third Cavalry had less than half of its troopers engaged in the fighting, their total casualty loss was approaching four-fifths of the total loss—principally troops in Vroom's, Henry's, Van Vliet's, and Andrews's companies.

As for Captain Vroom's L Company, which suffered five men killed and three others wounded as they went into rear guard to protect the retreat of the rest, those eight men account for almost *a third* of the total casualties for the entire engagement!

No matter where you come down on this controversy of how many killed and wounded, the fact remains that—considering the total number of men involved on both sides, knowing how long the combatants fought, and keeping in mind the total number of bullets fired in that "daylong" battle, I find it totally incredible that there weren't heavier losses inflicted on both sides. Utterly amazing.

There is another hopeless conflict that will forever remain troubling to us who study the Indian Wars and seek to commemorate the hallowed ground where both white and red fell. Exactly where did Crook bury his dead?

Between the soldiers who left diaries or wrote letters home to wives, and those five newspapermen, things quickly got pretty muddled in this regard. Some reported that each company buried its men separately. Others stated that there was a mass, or common, grave for the dead.

Then there arises the matter of where. The young warrior Black Elk stated that he was with a group of Lakota who returned to the battlefield on the eighteenth and found the graves of soldiers at the site of the white man's encampment (on the night of the seventeenth). So while some Indians, soldiers, and civilians report that the grave(s) was (were) on the battlefield itself, other sources among Crook's men say "buried beside the Rosebud," and still more state that the soldiers were interred "in the streambed of the creek." This might be confusing to those who do not know much about northern plains geography and how creeks carve out their banks and channels in the early spring, what with mountain runoff and torrential rains. While I have no guess on the subject, it is probable that the grave was in the streambed. Right where fires were burned all night to destroy scent, where the next morning Crook had his soldiers and stock pass over as they retreated from the valley.

To this day not one of those graves has been located, although various superintendents (and Neil Mangum, former Chief Historian) of the Custer Battlefield National Cemetery have made several official and unofficial attempts, hopeful that these battle dead could be disinterred and given a fitting burial with full military honors with their fallen comrades less than thirty miles away.

An interesting and quite intriguing aside to this tale is the story about the body of a white man being found on the battlefield after the Indians had withdrawn. In fact, the July 22, 1876, issue of the *Army and Navy Journal* even went so far as to state, "It is said the body of a white man was found who had been fighting with the Sioux."

No mention of where he was found. Nor what he was wearing.

An old "squaw man" perhaps?

It becomes all the more interesting, and mystifying, in light of the reports given by several soldiers who were among Reno's brigade nine days later who clearly heard good barracks swearing, in clear and understandable English, being yelled at them from beyond their lines in those terrible hours they were held under siege.

Not so hard, then, is it, to believe that the camps of Sioux and Cheyenne might have included at least one old trapper or hide hunter, having married into the tribe, who willingly joined in any battle fought by his adopted people.

History cracks open a few of these doors for us, but . . . nothing more than a tantalizing crack.

In mentioning the numbers of men involved in the battle on both sides, I would be remiss if I did not give you cause to think a bit more on the "odds" in the fight. Namely, the weapons used by both sides. While the troops, packers, and civilians, as well as their allies, were all well armed with breech-loading rifles, in actuality the warriors possessed few "modern" weapons. True, there were a few repeaters of Henry or Winchester manufacture—but the amateur historians who have combed the battlefield with metal detectors over the years have all come to the conclusion that not only did Crook have Crazy Horse outmanned, the army had the Indians outgunned as well.

It's also curious to note that both J. W. Vaughn and Fred Werner (who combed the ground with their metal detectors more than twenty years apart) have repeatedly found errors in the maps of the battlefield drawn by the officers to accompany the articles they wrote for the military magazines of the day. On those old maps locations were highlighted showing where significant action took place. Problem was, neither of these historians were able to find cartridges on many of those positions.

Simply put, they were forced to look at the battle in a new and somewhat different light that took exception with how it was presented by the contemporary accounts. As Vaughn states: "I soon learned there was no action at a place unless shells could be found with the metal detector."

On the matter of animals, man's means of waging war against his fellowman at that time in the nineteenth century, I have to say that the advantage again goes to the soldiers. Their horses and mules had not been marched far that morning after resting the night before, and had been watered and were grazing at the time the first shots were fired.

The war ponies, on the other hand, had been given little if any rest since the evening of the sixteenth when the warriors set out from their villages on their march south. Crazy Horse had pushed their stock all night long before pausing to await word from those four scouts who bumped into the Crow trackers. All rest for the ponies was gone as the warriors immediately made their last mad dash on the heels of the fleeing Crow who raced back to the soldier lines.

As far as this author sees things, I can give the warriors the decided advantage in only one of the factors making for this most interesting battle. By and large the troops Crook marched north from Fort Fetterman that June were not much seasoned to Indian warfare. True, some had skirmished with the hostiles even before the Reynolds's Powder River fight. But the majority of those troopers and foot soldiers were green to this sort of conflict.

Meanwhile, the seven hundred and fifty warriors Crazy Horse led south from the great encampment either had participated in many years of internecine warfare against other tribes or had experience fighting the white man and soldiers. Or, at the least, they were eager young men whose blood ran hot to have a chance to kill soldiers and gain war honors. They made up for their lack of experience with an abundance of zeal.

Seems to me that the odds were clearly in favor of the warriors, despite the numbers arrayed against them, and the weapons they would have to face. All in all, it remains a most remarkable victory for Crazy Horse and his fighters. So remarkable a victory that I'm given cause to speculate on what might have happened on that one hundredth anniversary of the Battle of Bunker Hill if the Lakota would have thrown two thousand or twenty-five hundred warriors into the fight (the number, as you will recall, some historians have asserted were battling the soldiers!). Even with only fifteen hundred warriors, the outcome would likely have been far different (seeing how even that low estimate would have *doubled* what Crazy Horse did have in the battle against Three Stars).

Or had they possessed better weapons—the sort of weaponry they acquired eight days later after the Reno fight in the valley and the slaughter of Custer's five entire companies. All that ammunition and those Colt's revolvers and Springfield carbines!

Or had the Crows not bumped into the scouts and had Crazy Horse elected to wait in ambush a little north of where he caught the soldiers, where his warriors were resting ten or eleven miles north of Crook's soldiers—there to wait out the better part of that Saturday, June 17, while allowing the soldiers to march that much closer toward the encampment—which would have allowed Crazy Horse to surprise and attack Crook's troops at the break of dawn on June 18, with fresh ponies and Sitting Bull's Hunkpapa!

Remember, my reader—the Hunkpapa had not yet joined up at the moment Crazy Horse attacked those thirteen hundred men under Crook. The Hunkpatila war chief likely had something on the order of five hundred warriors to throw against more than twice as many soldiers, allies, and civilians. And Crazy Horse nearly seized the day before Sitting Bull even showed up!

Interesting to speculate on the possibility of a *far bigger,* and more earth-shattering, massacre than the massacre that did take place eight days later, and thirty miles to the north.

Make no mistake, the Crow and Shoshone saved the lives of the soldiers not only at the beginning of the battle while they held the warriors at bay, but during Royall's retreat from the left as well. None of the military reports of the battle fully explain just how serious those first minutes of the fighting really were. It remained for Cheyenne historian John Stands in Timber as well as Crow chief Plenty Coups to corroborate one another when both stated that Crook's soldiers were driven back to the banks of the Rosebud itself at the early stages of the battle. Grouard confirms this as well, saying: "I believe if it had not been for the Crows, the Sioux would have killed half of our command before the soldiers were in a position to meet the attack."

Hours later the Crow and Shoshone again threw themselves into the breech and saved Royall's men in frantic retreat. They, and the infantry of Burt and Burrowes. In the days to follow, Guy Henry himself gave the highest of praise to the infantry for saving his battalion. Some of Royall's men even stated that there was little chance they would have made it out alive, had the infantry not rescued them from massacre.

What did those horse soldiers of the Third Cavalry who had laughed long and hard at Chambers's "mule-brigade" have to say now?

An interesting footnote to the Battle of the Rosebud is this whole matter of the "dead canyon," the "canyon of death," or the "gorge of the Rosebud." Nothing but myth. But it goes to show how strongly held myth can color clear judgment under the stress of battlefield conditions.

Truth of the matter is there is no "canyon," nor a "gorge." Any person who travels the road north of the battlefield to or from Busby and the Northern Cheyenne Reservation will drive on a state highway that follows the Rosebud. The hills on either side of the valley are no more than four hundred feet above the valley floor. No deep canyon or gorge here.

And while the valley itself does narrow at one point to a little more than half a mile wide, you have only to stand at that point and look around to see just how ridiculous the notion is that Crazy Horse's warriors could have ambushed eight companies of mounted cavalry at that point, slaughtering them to a man.

"A veritable cul-de-sac," is one contemporary description. "Vertical walls hemming in the sides," wrote another. "A narrow defile," and "sides a thousand feet high." Not to mention the canyon being a "narrow gash overhung by continuous walls of rock." Such grossly exaggerated descriptions written at that time by the participants have totally painted a false picture of the terrain for no other reason (I can determine) but to substantiate their unmitigated fears of ambush. Nothing more. They had to justify their inability to prod the Crow scouts and, more specifically, Frank Grouard himself, down that trail. Hence, the birth of the ambush or "death-trap" theory.

The only warriors Crazy Horse had who could have ambushed Captain Anson Mills's battalion was that handful Sutorious scooted off the crest of the hill as Mills began his march toward the east bend of the Rosebud. No more Indians were spotted that day until the soldiers came busting back out of the north, in a dead gallop to rescue Royall's besieged command.

But the damage had already been done to Crook's ability to fight the sort of battle he had wanted at the outset. With half of his cavalry out of the fight on a wild-goose chase to find some phantom village, the expedition had doomed itself to defeat. Crazy Horse needed to send no warriors to lay an ambush in that "canyon."

The fertile and frightened imaginations of those scouts, guides, and soldiers did the rest. So by the time Mills's battalion got back to the battlefield—the day was lost. And Crook's men were lucky to get out alive.

Five of those who played one sort of role or another in our story need a brief bit of additional mention.

John Shingle, the sergeant who voluntarily left his post among Royall's horse-holders in the Kollmar ravine and returned to the Vroom/Henry skirmish at the crest to rally the troops who were buckling and ready to bolt in unmitigated retreat, stands as a singular hero in the conflict—yelling, so the history texts relate the testimony of witnesses, "Face them, men! Face them!"

It is just that sort of heroism that brings a lump to my throat and tears to my eyes no matter how many times I read over this tale of courage while around him knees are buckling. If ever there was a man who deserved his due reward, the sergeant was one, likely due the credit for keeping those green soldiers alive, stirring them to fight back. For his heroism, his "decisive action in the face of the enemy," John Shingle was awarded the Medal of Honor for bravery at the Battle of Rosebud Creek.

Another sort of deeply moral courage was evinced by Guy V. Henry.

But to begin, there remains some controversy over just who rescued the captain. Of course there was no Seamus Donegan on that battlefield that day beside the Rosebud. But who did stand over his body and fight off the Sioux and Cheyenne? Frank Grouard states that it was the Shoshone called Yute John. Trenholm and Carley's book, *The Shoshones,* credits a Shoshone called Tigee. Then we find that they were likely one and the same person.

Reporter Reuben Davenport, with Royall on the left, states that two soldiers stood over the captain's body and held off the enemy.

Henry R. Lemly, Royall's adjutant, says that Henry was rescued from the battlefield by two Crow scouts.

I suppose it really doesn't matter, does it? Because the

heroism that saved Henry was but the beginning of Henry's own heroic story.

After the two painful mishaps in returning the captain to the Goose Creek base camp that I've already recounted for you, Henry was fortunate to survive a grueling two-hundred-mile wagon ride to Fort Fetterman. Day after day his escort was able to shoot some small birds along the trail. Boiled, the broth from these was the only thing his attendants could pour past the shattered jaws and down the captain's throat to maintain some of the officer's strength. Now and again he records that he was rewarded for his stoicism with a teaspoonful of brandy.

Then, mind you—having survived the Crazy Horse attack and Royall's retreat, being kicked in the head by a mule and spilling from the mule litter, not to mention the horrid state of his wounds—Henry's escort comes within sight of Fetterman itself and reaches the north bank of the North Platte . . . just as the ferryboat cable snaps and unfurls into the turbid river.

Henry calls this a "disappointment."

Now only yards away from beds and roof, almost in reach of the fort's hospital where he can receive succor, he is again confronted with having to stay another night in the open.

Minutes later an officer from the fort crosses the river in a wobbly, leaky skiff and tells Henry that he will take the captain over to the fort if Henry is willing to take the chance of capsizing.

Now, realize the Third Cavalry officer has already been dunked in crossing the Tongue. He has been bleeding slowly for the better part of a week with suppurating wounds. He's totally blind in one eye and the other is swollen shut, filled with foul matter. If that skiff capsizes—the man is sure to drown.

So what does Guy Henry say to the offer?

You bet—"Let's give it a try."

With that officer cradling the wounded captain in his arms and two enlisted men paddling the ungainly craft, they pushed out into the current of the North Platte, hoping to cross the thousand feet of roiling water.

And made it across, thank God.

Still, they could really do little more for him at Fetterman than Surgeon Hartsuff was able to do in the field. He needed to get back to "civilization." And that was another *three hundred miles yet to go!* The next morning his litter was placed in the back of an army ambulance (wonderful conveyances—no springs!) where he was jolted and rumbled south all the way to the Medicine Bow Station. There he could at last be put on the Union Pacific for a ride east.

But, wait. Not that day—because it is the Fourth of July!

There's gunfire and fireworks, lemonade and whiskey, as well as plenty of raucous celebration for the nation's centennial. At twilight a stray bullet whizzed through Henry's tent near the station platform where he tried in vain to sleep.

You can imagine the captain lying there, blind and weak, wondering if he survived the very worst the Sioux could throw at him, only to die here at the hand of some drunk railroad worker reveling in the nation's one hundredth birthday.

Upon reaching Fort D. A. Russell near Cheyenne City, army surgeons began work on the man, probing his wounds, reopening them, and forcing sulfur and medicines into the cavities.

But even they could not kill the indomitable Guy Henry!

By the middle of August, he regained the limited use of one eye and was given a leave of absence, whereupon he journeyed to southern California to recuperate. By the next spring the captain was back, learning to live with the only eye left him, nonetheless assigned to active duty at Fort Laramie, Wyoming Territory, as the "Great Sioux War" raged on.

Guy Henry stayed in active service until the end of the Indian Wars, earning himself another "brevet rank." And during the Spanish-American War the redoubtable captain served as a cavalry general in Puerto Rico, where he contracted malaria and finally succumbed to the grim reaper—still on active duty. A horse soldier to the end.

One gets the impression that the man was much like an

owl—hard to kill because they are half head, and the rest is nothing but feather and bone! Indeed, Colonel Guy V. Henry of the Third Cavalry is the sort of man who, like Sergeant John Shingle, will long live in my memory.

Truth is many times more stirring than the fiction myth-makers manufacture.

The rescue of Chief Comes in Sight by his sister, Buffalo Calf Road Woman, lives to this day in Cheyenne oral legends. The Battle of the Rosebud was not the woman's first, nor was it to be her last, fight against the white man. Eight days after she rescued her brother, Buffalo Calf Road Woman fought alongside her husband, Black Coyote, when the Northern Cheyenne surrounded Custer's last holdouts at the northern crest of Massacre Hill.

Appealing to note that John Finerty, that whiskey-loving, woman-humping rounder of a newspaperman, later haunted the halls of the U.S. Congress as a representative from the State of Illinois. Ah, the checkered pasts of our elected officials!

Frederick Schwatka, lieutenant in Anson Mills's M Company of the Third Cavalry, was, like Finerty, a native of Illinois. He continually studied. In fact, a year before the Rosebud fight he had been admitted to the Nebraska bar, and a year after the battle obtained a medical degree from the prestigious Bellevue Hospital Medical College in New York City. Yet he was soon bitten by the bug to explore, and where better but the Arctic?

In the summer of 1878, Schwatka led a party of explorers that would take two years in crossing more than thirty-two hundred miles of frozen wilderness—showing the scientific world that man could live in arctic conditions for extended periods of time. He lived a fruitful, productive life until 1892, when he accidentally poisoned himself with an overdose of some remedy meant to relieve a painful stomach disorder.

Until the end of the Indian Wars, the Second and Third Cavalries, as well as the Fourth and Ninth Infantries, continued to serve among the outposts on the western frontier. Such duty was marked by long periods of excruciating boredom interspersed with brief interludes of terror. With so much time on their hands, it's not hard for me to see why the Battle of the Rosebud was fought again and again between the principal officers as well as the soldiers themselves. Petty differences became major causes.

Perhaps the worst of those conflicts was that waged between George Crook and William Royall, a long-standing fight that began the very afternoon of the battle itself.

Crook, and Bourke as well, blamed the colonel for not following orders to rejoin the infantry's left, that failure preventing the reuniting of the general's forces for (at the least) a counterattack on Crazy Horse's warriors, or (at the most) a full-scale march down the Rosebud on the enemy village. Privately, to Bourke at least, the general confided his views that Royall was "an ingrate, treacherous, and cowardly to boot."

Even Captain Henry waded into the melee when he subsequently stated that Royall hid during those repeated charges by the Sioux and Cheyenne. That was nothing less than heresy for a Third Cavalry officer to speak so openly in criticizing his commanding officer.

Bad feelings became raw poison as the regiment began to split down the middle over the affair. Anson Mills himself told Crook he thought the general should have shot some of the officers for their "mutinous language" the day of the battle.

A few of the officers who had served with Royall's battalion on the left accused Crook in turn of poor judgment, that the general's orders to rejoin him prevented them from dislodging the warriors from the bluffs on the western end of the battlefield. In substance, many saw Crook's criticisms as nothing more than one more slur on the honor and good name of the Third Cavalry, nothing less than the continuation of the general's attacks on their esprit d'corps that had begun with the court-martial of Joseph Reynolds.

It took a full decade for this very personal matter between Crook and Royall to come to a boil. For ten years Crook refused to publicly acknowledge the defeat while it continued to rankle the general, who insisted that, had the battle been fought according to his plan, that day the resistance of the Sioux would have been broken, the Custer fight would not have taken place, and the need for the remainder of the Sioux Campaign of 1876–77 would have disappeared as the hostile bands made their way back to the reservations.

In the summer of 1886 Colonel Royall finally ended his silence and gave an interview with two Omaha papers while he was in town (headquarters of Crook's Department of the Platte) on military business. The resulting articles became the source of the final explosion between the two men when on the night of 7 August at the home of General Crook several officers were gathered on the front steps of the house when Royall arrived for a dinner party. Among others, Captain Guy Henry was in attendance at the shouting match and argument that ensued.

Crook: "For ten years I have suffered silently the obloquy of having made a bad fight at Rosebud when the fault was in yourself and Nickerson. There was a good chance to make a charge but it couldn't be done because of the condition of the cavalry. I sent word to you to 'come in' and waited two hours—nearer three before you obeyed. I sent Nickerson three times at least. I had the choice of assuming responsibility myself for the failure of my plans or of court-martialing you and Nickerson. I chose to bear the responsibility myself. The failure of my plan was due to your conduct."

Royall: "I have never had any reason to think my conduct at the Rosebud was bad. Nickerson came to me but once and then I moved as soon as I received the order. Did I not move as soon as I could after Nickerson came, Colonel Henry?"

Henry: "Yes, I believe you did."

Royall: "I was the leading battalion with Colonel Henry. It was the leading battalion—I went with it where the enemy was the thickest. I was not responsible for the scattered condition of the cavalry."

What say you, reader?

Who won the Battle of the Rosebud? Who lost? Or do you think it was a draw?

I sympathize with George Crook for all those years left him following the fight at the Rosebud—because I can clearly feel the man having to grapple with the fact that he alone was the reason he lost that summer day to Crazy Horse.

Just days after the battle, on 30 June 1876, the Helena, Montana, *Daily Independent* published an article from one of the five unnamed correspondents, a person then writing of the battle from Fort Laramie:

> The officers [at Fort Fetterman] speak in terms of unmeasured condemnation of General Crook's behavior, and denounce his retreat in the face of the savage enemy as *cowardly.*
>
> . . . It is also reported that the Crows refused to stay with Crook any longer, and have gone off in a body to Gibbon on the Yellowstone. They call Crook the 'Squaw Chief' and say he's afraid to fight.
>
> The news of the battle brought consternation to the military here, and as the details of the affair become known, it is looked upon as humiliating and disgraceful to the last degree.
>
> The idea of two regiments of American cavalry being stampeded by savages and having to *rally behind* friendly Indians is regarded as incredibly revolting to the pride and honor of the army.

Remember—this was being said in light of what the world was yet to learn of Custer's defeat. They still did not know of the Seventh's fate.

By the next week, the same Helena paper printed an editorial placing the blame as many of those on the frontier saw it: "It is now clearly evident that General Crook was not the man to be intrusted with the conduct of the military expeditions in the Powder River country. His disastrous defeat . . . left the general impression upon the country that a want of proper management was at the bottom of the result."

Despite some of those statements the officers at Fort Laramie nonetheless passed a resolution in which they expressed their approval of Crook's strategy in the battle. He was, after all, their boss.

But to this amateur historian and student of the Indian Wars—there was no strategy. Or what strategy there was, was found wanting when confronted with the surprising discipline and unwavering resolve of Crazy Horse's warriors.

The Sioux and the Cheyenne clearly won that day.

For years Crook continued to state that he had won a victory because his army held the field at the end of the day. Nowhere is his steadfast refusal to recognize the fight as the defeat it was more apparent than in his annual report of September 25, 1876, which was devoted, as scholar John S. Gray states, to the "grand illusion." Gray's corrections to Crook's "record" are inserted in the text and italicized:

> The number of our troops was less than one thousand [*by a dozen, but reinforced by over three hundred Indian allies and civilian volunteers*], and within eight days after that the same Indians [*but in triple strength*] met and defeated a column of troops nearly the same size as ours [*actually only half as strong*], including the gallant commander, General Custer himself. I invite attention to the fact that in this engagement my troops beat these Indians on a field of their own choosing, and drove them in utter rout from it as far as the proper care of my wounded and prudence would justify.

Historian Gray goes on to say:

> Crook's thirteen hundred effectives had certainly not "beaten" and "utterly routed" the attacking seven hundred and fifty. The latter disengaged by choice and in perfect order, as was their wont after a good day's work. Crook's camping on the battlefield is a white man's empty symbol; the mobile hostiles celebrated in their comfortable lodges that night, while the chastened

> troops shivered on the bare ground under a single blanket.
>
> . . . The essential facts are undeniable. The fight itself was a tactical draw, although Crook commanded superior numbers. But the fight was also a clear strategic defeat for Crook. The Indians fully achieved their objective—to halt Crook's punitive campaign far from their village. Crook utterly failed to achieve his objective—to whip the hostile force into submission.

Some among the army were beginning to look at things a little differently than did the leader of the expedition. Maybe they had reached a turning point in the history of the Indian Wars.

While General Sherman still believed Crook to be the best field commander he had to fight the Indians in the west, Crook's immediate commander, Philip Sheridan, said in commenting on the battle, "The victory was barren of results. General Crook was unable to pursue the enemy . . . considering himself too weak to make any movement until additional troops reached him."

But the battle was all too quickly forgotten by all except its aging participants. Custer's defeat far overshadowed the bigger fight. Crook's fight, having taken place eight days before the Little Bighorn fight, was usually mentioned only in passing, as a footnote to the tragedy that occurred on the Greasy Grass. Only the two published accounts by Finerty and Bourke kept the story of the Rosebud from a total death.

For almost fifty years the battlefield lay in obscurity, unmarked and abandoned—while thirty miles away the Custer Battlefield became a national symbol of the Indian Wars. In the meantime, the white man settled the region and raised his cattle.

Not until 1920 did anyone do anything about the battlefield. Walter M. Camp, a scholar of the period, finally identified the site and was instrumental in placing nine marble markers on the field to pay homage to the soldiers who died there in 1876.

Despite the efforts of a small and dedicated group of

locals, the seasons continued to ebb and flow across that high land until fourteen years later, in 1934, the Billings, Montana, Chapter of the Shining Mountains Chapter of the Daughters of the American Revolution unveiled a stone monument on the knoll at the east end of the Rosebud where fourteen years earlier Camp had placed his nine. What was different was that this time more than a thousand people braved the rutted ranch roads to reach the site.

What was even more important—this time the ceremony was attended by four wrinkled Cheyenne veterans of the fight: Louis Dog, Limpy, Weasel Bear, and Bear Heart.

Still, it wasn't until the early fifties that anyone made a scholarly study of the fight. Colorado attorney J. W. Vaughn ran across the Finerty and Bourke references to the day-long fight and began to make regular pilgrimages to the battlefield, bringing with him his metal detector. It was in southeastern Montana that Vaughn met the rancher who owned the land where Crook and Crazy Horse had dueled.

Like the general and the war chief who met here that summer day long ago, these two men would change one another's lives.

Born in 1892 in the Cherokee Strip of what is now the state of Oklahoma, Slim Kobold left home at barely seventeen and began making the rounds, as cowboys still do, working ranches and haying across Oklahoma, Texas, and Kansas. By some good fortune for us who have a passion for history, that gritty cowhand made his way north to Montana in 1915 to file a homestead claim beside the beautiful Rosebud Creek. It wasn't until many years later that Slim discovered he owned a sizable chunk of what had been a battlefield.

Once he found out just how little was known, what little had ever been printed about the battle, Kobold made contact with the folks at the nearby Northern Cheyenne Reservation. Having gone in search of help, Slim became friends with the tribal historian, John Stands in Timber, who acted as interpreter when three of the old battle veterans made their first of several visits to the site. As Kobold moved slowly over the hills and down the ravines with Limpy, Louis Dog, and Bear Heart, they pointed out where the soldiers were positioned, how the various companies moved about, where the Crazy Horse charges originated—in exacting, anecdotal detail just how the battle was fought.

Kobold later said he was moved to tears, moved to realize that he just wasn't standing on some cattle land. He was standing on an important piece of history.

So when Jesse W. Vaughn showed up from Colorado with his metal detector in hand, land owner Slim Kobold proved to be an eager amateur historian, accompanying Vaughn as the two prowled the hills across that massive site, sharing stories and identifying both soldier and Indian positions as they dug up concentrations of cartridges. After years of extensive work by the pair, Vaughn was able to reconstruct the battle's major events, and in 1956 he finally published the first comprehensive work on the fight, *With Crook at the Rosebud.*

Because of that little-known volume, a few more people made the rare trek to the battlefield across the next five years. Still, it remained for someone to preserve the battlefield itself, just as the Custer site had been set aside, preserved, visited by growing legions of scholars, writers, and the just plain curious.

Slim Kobold went on raising cattle, remaining the battlefield's more ardent supporter. Then in 1961 he joined with a Miles City, Montana, archaeologist, and together they placed small concrete pyramids at key locations on the battlefield.

A decade later the battlefield was again "under attack." Big and small coal companies were operating just south of Kobold's land, digging out the rich veins of the black gold. Time and again developers came to the Kobold ranch house, offering increasing sums of money for his land. He could have sold. But he didn't.

That's how Slim Kobold became the hero of what I'd like to refer to as the "Second Battle of the Rosebud."

Through letters and phone calls, by buttonholing state legislators, and keeping his unrelenting pressure on the bureaucrats—besides turning away every one of those seductive offers from the coal companies—Kobold's efforts finally hit paydirt. Nineteen seventy-two saw the battlefield finally placed on the National Register of Historic Places.

Still, the offers to buy the ground kept on coming, with

the dollars offered continuing to escalate—but Slim held out, offering only to sell the battlefield to the State of Montana for a fraction of what he could have sold it to one of the private firms. It took four more years for Kobold's dream to come true: Montana finally agreed to buy the land and set it aside for future generations.

By that time Fred Werner, a man I'm proud to call my friend, had joined the cause. A western historian from Greeley, Colorado, Werner began to visit the site himself in 1975, metal detector in tow and with Vaughn's book in hand, plotting sites on his own. Eight years later in 1983 he self-published his own study of the Crook fight, shedding more light on this little-known battle.

The years marched on and on, taking their toll on the Rosebud Battlefield's greatest champion. While Slim Kobold had won his hard-fought battle to preserve a small piece of western history for the people of Montana and this nation, he was losing his very personal battle against an enemy no one had ever defeated: cancer.

Lying in a hospital bed in Billings in late 1978, Slim Kobold finally signed the papers that made the Rosebud Battlefield a state monument.

A year later, in 1979, the new chief historian at the Custer Battlefield National Monument made his first visit to the Rosebud site. It wasn't long before Neil Mangum learned that in addition to being an Indian Wars' treasure, the land is rich in archaeological terms. A four-thousand-year-old buffalo jump has been excavated nearby, showing how ancient man, the predecessors to the Indians who fought Crook, drove buffalo off cliffs before they had acquired the horse, spear, and later the gun.

The more he visited the battle site, the more Mangum was moved to tell the story of this little-heralded battle. While his own Custer Battlefield saw untold numbers of visitors every year, the Rosebud site rested in pristine beauty, undisturbed by but a few hardy visitors. In 1983 Neil completed a trail guide brochure for the Montana Fish, Wildlife, and Parks Department to explain the battle in simple terms, and to outline locations held during important events during the fight. The next year, Mangum compiled a "Rosebud Battlefield Historic Base Data Study" for the Montana state government.

But it wasn't until two years ago that this nationally recognized historian published his own monumental work on the Rosebud Battle. Taking up where Vaughn left off, clarifying the gray areas, focusing in on the oft-confusing events to make them easily understood to the common layman, Neil Mangum carved out his own place among the heros of this "Second Battle of the Rosebud."

Vaughn. Kobold. Werner. And Mangum. Men as stalwart and brave, tenacious and daring, as any of those who fought here over a century ago, red or white.

Anyone who visits the site today will see that there is an ongoing development in process. Huge metal plates have been erected which will withstand the vagaries of Montana weather, here to interpret the battle for any of the too-few visitors who wander this far off the beaten track, trekking back into some of the most beautiful country God ever crafted on this planet—among the pines and the hills, here along a stretch of a historic stream.

There is, thankfully, little development anywhere near the site. A ranch house here. Another quite some distance away over the hills. One around the bend if you look hard enough. It's very easy for the visitor to see how this ground where I now sit, indeed this astoundingly beautiful countryside for miles around me in all directions, looked on that summer day in 1876. Indeed, this astoundingly beautiful countryside for miles around me in every direction remains all but just as it was then. Save for a ranch building here and there, but for a narrow, rutted ranch road that runs along the bottomland where Crook's forces once unsaddled and began to boil coffee, playing cards and lounging in the sun. With no idea what fury was about to descend upon them.

There are simply far too few battlefields like the Rosebud—for here, like nowhere else, the visitor can truly experience the site, walk the ground as it existed those many years ago. Everywhere else the sites are developed, interpreted, paved and trailed, monumented and markered to death. But here, beneath the Big Sky, the Rosebud Battlefield lies waiting for the visitor to explore, to walk where

Sioux and Cheyenne ponies once charged on thundering hooves. Where the course of Indian Wars history was altered.

Here, like few other sites in the west, you can sit quietly, undisturbed by even a rare plane leaving a contrail overhead. Here you can listen to the wind. And the whispers in the grass.

After his duel with Crazy Horse, George Crook would himself visit the Rosebud Battlefield only one more time—but not until more than seven weeks had passed. One wonders what he thought about as he walked this hallowed ground that late summer evening.

That August he had twenty-five hundred men with him. That August he vowed he would not be surprised.

But the Indians did not attack. They had long ago scattered—only two days after winning their most stunning victory in the history of warfare on the northern plains.

The village circles disbanded. It was enough to have fought Three Stars to a standstill. Enough, eight days later, to have seen the glorious coming of Sitting Bull's greatest vision.

Now fleeing to the four winds, the warrior bands would be harried by converging armies that would eventually harass the Sioux and Cheyenne, starve them, whip the warriors into submission, driving the nomadic buffalo cultures back to the reservations.

But . . . that is another story. Many, many more stories yet for us to share. For me to tell another time.

So, for now, I'm not in a hurry. This afternoon I sit here at the top of the conical hill, where Crazy Horse himself once sat bare-legged atop his war pony and gazed down at the soldiers he dueled. Above me the fluffy clouds pass lazily across an incredibly blue sky. Clouds moved on the same wind that whispers through the buffalo grass all around me as I write these words.

Here on this hallowed ground. Where the ghosts of the past linger, and whisper their stories to me.

TERRY C. JOHNSTON
Rosebud Battlefield
Montana Territory
June 17, 1993

About the Author

Terry C. Johnston was born in 1947 on the plains of Kansas, and has lived all his life in the American West. His first novel, *Carry the Wind,* won the Medicine Pipe Bearer's Award from the Western Writers of America, and his subsequent books have appeared on bestseller lists throughout the country. He lives and writes in Big Sky country near Billings, Montana.